GHOST MUSIC

The dead can't seek justice – can they?

Gideon Lake, a successful composer, is immediately smitten by Kate Solway, who lives below him. They begin a passionate affair, and Kate invites him to Europe so that they can be together without her husband finding out. But when Gideon witnesses all kinds of strange and terrifying events, he soon realizes that nothing in Kate's world is what it seems. Gideon must work out who, and what, Kate really is, and what she wants from him...

Graham Masterton titles available from
Severn House Large Print

Chaos Theory

GHOST MUSIC

Graham Masterton

Severn House Large Print
London & New York

This first large print edition published 2010
in Great Britain and the USA by
SEVERN HOUSE PUBLISHERS LTD of
9-15 High Street, Sutton, Surrey, SM1 1DF.
First world regular print edition published 2008 by
Severn House Publishers Ltd., London and New York.

British Library Cataloguing in Publication Data

Masterton, Graham.
   Ghost music.
   1. Composers--New York (State)--New York--Fiction.
   2. Adultery--Fiction. 3. Supernatural--Sweden--
   Stockholm--Fiction. 4. Manhattan (New York, N.Y.)--
   Fiction. 5. Stockholm (Sweden)--Fiction. 6. Suspense
   fiction. 7. Large type books.
   I. Title
   823.9'14-dc22

ISBN-13: 978-0-7278-7839-7

Printed and bound in Great Britain by
MPG Books Ltd, Bodmin, Cornwall.

In affectionate memory of Fred Rickwood

'Is there anybody there?' said the Traveller
Knocking on the moonlit door;
But only a host of phantom listeners
That dwelt in the lone house then
Stood listening in the quiet of the moonlight
To that voice from the world of men.

The Listeners – Walter de la Mare

One

As she followed her husband down the front steps, she turned her head and looked up at me, and I was so taken by her smile that I totally failed to notice what was so unusual about her. Nearly three months would pass before I realized what it was, but when I did, it would make me feel like my whole world had collapsed, like some shoddily built stage set.

She was slight and thin-wristed, with ash-blonde hair that was cut in a very straight bob. She was wearing a short-sleeved blouse, in the palest of yellows, and high-waisted gray slacks. But it was that mischievous smile that got me – and the way her eyes narrowed a little, as if we already shared a secret.

'Hey, Lalo, where does this thing go?' called Margot, from the kitchenette.

'What thing?' I asked her, still watching the woman as she crossed the street.

'This thing that looks like a fire extinguisher.'

'That's no fire extinguisher. That's my batter dispenser.'

Margot came through to the living room, holding up the shiny metal gadget in disbelief. 'Your *batter dispenser*?'

'Sure. I couldn't live without it. It makes sure

7

that every pancake is perfectly circular. They still taste like latex, but they're perfectly circular.'

'Lalo, you stun me sometimes. You really stun me.'

It was a warm afternoon in the first week of September, on St Luke's Place, opposite James J. Walker Park in Greenwich Village – a row of fine Italianate brownstones, with ironwork railings and pillared doorways, and even gas lamps outside. I was leaning out of my window on the second floor, with a cold bottle of Michelob Amber, taking a five-minute chill from putting up shelves.

I had moved into this apartment three days ago, but even with Margot to help me I was seriously beginning to believe that I would never get the place straight. The hallway was blocked with three tea chests full of books and music scores and pictures and orange enamel saucepans. The bedroom was wedged with suitcases bulging with clothes and cardboard boxes full of towels and CDs. I had never realized that I owned so much *stuff*. As my dad used to say, 'You can't have everything, son. Where would you put it?'

Margot twisted open a bottle of beer and came to the window to join me. She was short, dark and pretty in a heart-shaped Betty Boop way, with flicked-up hair and enormous brown eyes. She was wearing oversized Oshkosh dungarees and a tight pink-striped T-shirt, and fluorescent pink Crocs. She made me feel more like her big brother than ever, although she was at least six months older than I was, and in some ways, she was a whole lot wiser.

Margot and I had been friends ever since our first day at the Brooklyn Academy of Music. We had simply liked each other the moment we had bumped into each other by the noticeboard, and I had asked Margot if I could borrow her pencil. In the spring of 2005 there had been several weekends when our affection for each other had grown so strong that we had been only a heart-beat away from becoming lovers, but by the time I had managed to disentangle myself from Cindy the PMT Pianist (as Margot used to call her), Margot had started dating a nostril-flaring Cuban dancer called Esteban, and so we had never managed to get much more intimate than sprawling on a couch, drinking red wine and listening to Beethoven piano concertos and old Dire Straits albums. Now we knew each other so well that going to bed together would have felt like incest.

'I just saw the people downstairs,' I told her.

'Oh, yes? What are they like?'

'Mid-thirties, I'd say. Smart-conservative. Well-heeled.'

'Well, you have to be very well-heeled to live here. You have to have diamonds on the soles of your shoes. Unlike East Thirteenth Street.'

'Your loft is wonderful. It's like Narnia.'

'Sure it is. Teeming with intelligent rodents.'

I said, 'How about I take you to the Cafe Cluny tonight, as a thank you for everything you've done?'

Margot looked around the apartment, with its

9

high white ceilings and its shining oak floors. 'You know, Lalo, what this place badly needs is a woman. In fact, what *you* badly need is a woman. Man cannot live by composing TV scores alone, even if he does have perfectly circular pancakes.'

I looked across at her. The trees outside made leaf patterns dance on her cheek. 'I have *you*, don't I?'

'Of course you do. But you need passion. You need *danger.* You need somebody who washes dishes in the nude.'

Two

I met her for the first time two days later, when I was climbing the stairs with a sackful of groceries from Sushila's. She was standing on the landing outside my apartment door with a fluffy white Persian cat in her arms. The expression on her face was curiously dreamy, but as I came up the stairs toward her she turned to me and smiled, almost as if she had been expecting me. I caught a hint of her perfume, very light and flowery, but I didn't recognize what it was.

'Hi, there,' I said. 'Were you looking for me?'

'I was looking for Malkin, as a matter of fact. She gets very inquisitive whenever somebody new moves in. She wants to know *all* about them.'

10

Close up, she looked younger than she had when I had first seen her on the steps outside. Twenty-nine maybe, just touching thirty. She had a delicate, finely drawn face, as if she had elvish blood on one side of her family. Her eyes were as gray as rain clouds, and slightly hooded. The muted sunlight on the landing made her ash-blonde hair gleam silver. See? I had known her for less than thirty seconds and already I was waxing poetic.

'Gideon,' I said, shifting my grocery bag to my left arm, and holding out my hand. 'Gideon Lake, but most of my friends call me Lalo.'

'Oh, yes?'

'It's after Lalo Schifrin, who wrote the music for *Jaws* and *Mission Impossible*. That's what I do. Write music for movies and TV and stuff like that. Well, commercials, too. *"Come on home, come on ho-o-ome, to your family and your friends ... just one taste of Thom's will take you home again."* You know ... Thom's Tomato Soup.'

The woman didn't stop smiling, but she shook her head.

'You never heard it?' I said. 'You must be the only person on the planet who hasn't. My mom says she's going to strangle me for writing it, she can't get it out of her head.'

Just as I had shifted my grocery bag from one arm to the other, the woman shifted her cat, and held out her hand. 'Katherine – Katherine Solway – but do call me Kate. Pleased to know you, Gideon. I hope you're going to be very happy here.'

11

I unlocked my front door. 'Would you like to come in for a drink? I haven't finished sorting the place out yet, but I'm getting there.'

'I'd love to,' said Kate. 'Thank you. You don't mind if Malkin comes in, too? You're not allergic?'

'Of course not. I'm only allergic to John Williams' compositions, and wasps.'

My living room was already beginning to look West Village-elegant, thanks to Margot's talent for interior decoration. She had arranged my two pale-blue antique sofas so that they were facing each other, and two spoon-back chairs at angles to the main window. In the center of the floor there was an oval blue rug, and a low table of lime-washed oak with a statuette of Pan on it, skipping through the reeds by the river.

On one wall there was a large gilt-framed mirror; and on the opposite wall hung a magical-realist oil painting of two women in pink bathing suits standing in a blue desert, signed 'Jared French'.

Kate set Malkin down on the floor. The cat shook herself and started to pad around the apartment, sniffing at the furniture.

'Have you lived here for long?' I asked.

Kate went to the window and looked out over the park. I could just make out her transparent reflection in the glass. 'It depends what you mean by "long". Longer than I should have done, I suppose.'

'I see,' I said, although I didn't. 'What would you like to drink? I have iced tea, or Zinfandel, or beer. I even have Dr Pepper.'

12

'Zinfandel would be nice. Did you know that Jared French used to live here once?'

'The realtor told me. That's why I bought a Jared French painting. I almost lost consciousness, though, when I found out how much they were asking for it.'

'All of the houses in this row have their ghosts,' she said, raising her voice so that I could hear her. 'Theodore Dreiser lived next door at number sixteen – that's where he started to write *An American Tragedy*. Sherwood Anderson lived at number twelve. Jared French shared this house with Paul Cadmus. He was another artist. Both gay, of course. Paul Cadmus was always painting sailors in ridiculously tight pants.'

I came back from the kitchenette with two large glasses of chilled white wine. 'Hey – I *like* places with ghosts. It makes you feel like you're part of history, you know? So long as I don't get goosed by some ice-cold finger when I'm taking a shower.'

'Oh, you don't have to worry about that. The ghosts in these houses are all at peace. Most of them, anyhow.'

'Glad to hear it. You haven't ever *seen* one, have you?'

'When we first moved here, I was sure that I heard somebody weeping, in one of the rooms up in the attic. A woman, it sounded like. But when I went up there and knocked on the door, nobody answered.'

'Spooky!'

'It was probably the wind, that was all. This house can be very drafty, in the winter.'

13

We sat for a moment in silence. I had an odd feeling that Kate wanted to tell me something, but didn't know how to say it. She kept glancing at me, but when I looked back at her, she gave that secretive little smile and sipped her wine.

'You don't have children?' I asked her. 'I haven't *heard* any children, anyhow. No skateboards in the hallway.'

'We did once. A little boy. But we lost him.'

'I'm so sorry. I didn't realize.' I felt terrible. Talk about opening my mouth and putting both feet in it, Nikes and all.

But she said, 'No, please, don't feel bad about it. It was a long time ago now, and you weren't to know.' She paused, and then she said, 'I wanted to try again, but Victor was too angry about it.'

'Angry?'

'I don't know. Angry with God. Angry with the doctors. Just angry.'

I nodded, although I didn't entirely understand what she meant. You feel grief-stricken when your child dies. But *angry*?

'I would have loved to have a little girl,' Kate told me.

'Really?'

'Oh, yes. I would have named her Melinda. I could have dressed her up in frilly frocks, and fussed with her braids, and taught her how to bake chocolate-chip cookies.'

'Wow. It's not too late, though, surely? Maybe you could twist Victor's arm.'

'Victor's arm is untwistable. Besides – it's *always* too late.'

14

I didn't really understand what she meant by that either, but she didn't seem interested in discussing the subject any further, and so I left my next question unspoken.

'How about you?' she asked me, after a while. 'Do you like to travel?'

'Travel? Are you kidding me? I *hate* to travel. I have to go to LA every month, to work at Capitol Studios. I can't wait for them to invent a *Star Trek* transporter. You know – step into one cabinet in New York, step out of another cabinet ten seconds later in LA. Mind you – knowing my luck, I'd have a fly in there with me.'

'I didn't mean *that* kind of travel. I meant Europe. You know – Rome, and Vienna, and Prague.'

'Oh, like *culture*? Well – I was in London once, for a week, but that was for work, too. I saw the inside of a post-production studio in Soho, and that was about it. I didn't even get to see Buckingham Palace.'

'You *should* travel,' she said. 'It's good for you – good for the soul. And you can learn so much. The further away you go, the more you discover about what you've left behind.'

I waited for her to explain what *she* had discovered, but she didn't say any more. I distinctly felt that we were talking at cross-purposes – either that, or she expected me to understand something about her that should have been obvious, but which I couldn't fathom at all. Everything she said made perfect sense, but somehow it didn't make any sense at all. It was like she was carrying on a different conversation

15

altogether, or else she was speaking in riddles. It was strangely provocative, as if she were flirting with me, but it was frustrating at the same time. Maybe she didn't want Malkin the cat to know what she was telling me. Maybe Malkin would report back to Victor – he of the untwistable arm.

'More wine?' I asked her, although she had taken only three or four sips. 'How about some potato chips? I have sea salt or jalapeño or something herby.'

Again she shook her head. 'Tell me something you've written,' she said.

'Well ... the theme music for *Magician*. Did you ever see *Magician*? That's the cop who used to be a stage magician, and he solves all of his crimes with conjuring tricks.'

'Yes, I think I saw *Magician* once. I can't say that I remember the theme music.'

I leaned over and picked up my Spanish guitar, which was leaning against the end of the sofa. I gave it a strum, and then played her that soft, eerie, complicated melody, which rose higher and higher with every bar.

'That was very good,' Kate nodded, when I had given her a final flourish. 'That was almost beautiful.'

'*Almost* beautiful?'

'Debussy is beautiful. Delius is beautiful. That, on the other hand, was a little too commercial for its own good.'

'Hey, be fair. Debussy and Delius didn't have to pitch their music to Jerry Bruckheimer.'

Kate laughed, and even when she had finished

16

laughing her eyes were filled with that same shared intimacy that I had seen on the steps outside. She didn't look away, she didn't blink. Instead, she stared at me as if she wanted to remember for ever how I looked this afternoon.

'Do you mind if I ask how old are you?'

'Thirty-one,' I told her. 'I know I look older. My hair started going gray when I was twenty-six. It's hereditary.'

'I like it. It makes you look as if I can trust you.'

'You think so? I guess that kind of depends.'

She didn't ask me what I meant. I think both of us knew that she didn't really have to. She continued looking at me for another long moment, and then she turned toward the painted wall clock next to the mirror, with its frantically swinging pendulum, and she glanced at her wristwatch, too. 'I have to be going, I'm afraid.'

'You're cooking dinner?'

'Oh, no. It's too late for that, too.'

'You could always get take-out. They do a great *arroz con pollo* at Little Havana. The chef will give you free *tostones* if you flutter your eyelashes at him.'

Either she wasn't listening or else she didn't like Cuban food or maybe she was a vegetarian, because she stood up without saying a word.

'Do you work?' I asked her. 'Or are you usually free during the day?'

'I'm a magazine designer. I do fashion layouts for Harper's. Well, I used to. Not any more.'

'So – at the moment – you're free?'

'It depends on your definition of "free".'

17

'Well ... if I said to you, come up again tomorrow around twelve, and I'll make you some lunch, and play you some more of my almost-beautiful music, there wouldn't be anything to stop you?'

Kate said nothing, but continued to stare at me. Her stare was so penetrating that I began to feel light-headed, as if I had drunk too many tequila slammers. But Malkin started to scrabble at the tassels that hung from one of the spoon-back chairs, and I turned and called, 'Hey, kitty! Cut it out, will you!' and that broke the spell.

Malkin trotted across to Kate like a scolded kid, and Kate knelt down to pick her up.

I said, 'Listen ... I understand you're married and everything. All I'm asking you to do is come up and eat some salad. Working on my own all day ... it almost turns me into a gibbering loony sometimes.'

'OK,' she said. She held up her hand so that I could help her back up on to her feet. Once she was standing, though, she didn't let go. 'You shouldn't worry about Victor. Victor is a very strong character who believes that he owns the world. He wouldn't imagine for a single moment that I would betray him.'

I was very tempted to ask, *would* you betray him? More to the point, would you betray him with *me*? But it was a little too soon to be asking questions like that. I definitely felt that Kate found me interesting; but maybe she was bored, and she was teasing me for her own amusement. Every minute that went by, I noticed things about her that were increasingly attractive: the tilt of her nose, the way the sunlight shone on the upward curve of her lips, the faint blue veins in her wrists. But she had a guarded side to her, a prickly defensiveness, and I suspected that she was capable of putting down any man she didn't like – in public, too.

'Right,' I said, releasing her hand. 'If you don't think that I should worry about Victor, I won't worry about Victor. How do you like tuna, with Chinese cabbage salad?'

'Sounds delicious. I'm sure that Malkin would adore it, too. I'd better not bring her, in case she's a nuisance.'

I saw her to the door. Before she left, she turned and reached up, touching my hair just behind my ear, like a conjuror pretending to find a nickel. Then she kissed me very lightly on the cheek.

I watched her go back downstairs. Once she had gone, I quietly closed the door and went back into the living room.

I stared at myself in the gilt-framed mirror, trying to see what *she* was seeing, when she looked at me. I always thought that I looked more like a second-rank tennis player than a musical composer. Six-foot-one, rangy, with kind of disconnected arms and legs, and the long, angular face of my Finnish grandfather Luukas, and the same ice-blue eyes. Same gray hair, too, when it came to that. But I like to think that I'm reasonably good-looking, in a Nordic Kris Kristofferson kind of a way, although Margot used to accuse me of looking morose for no reason.

I picked up my guitar again, and started to play the theme music to *Magician*, but I stopped in mid-chord, halfway through.

'Kate Solway,' I whispered, just to feel her name come out of my lips.

Three

Shortly before eleven o'clock that evening, I was working on the incidental music for *The Billy Wagner Show* when I heard car doors slamming in the street outside, and laughter.

I hesitated, with my fingers poised over the keyboard of my Roland electronic piano. I heard more laughter, a woman, and a man's voice saying, 'You're crazy. You know that? You're totally crazy.'

I knew I was being nosy, but I stood up and walked barefoot through the living room, and looked out of the open window. I saw a red-haired woman in a green satin dress climbing the front steps, unsteadily, as if she had been drinking. Close behind her came Victor Solway, in a white dress shirt with his bow tie dangling loose, and a maroon tuxedo slung over his arm. *Maroon*, yet.

He was deeply tanned, Victor Solway, with a white wing on each side of his jet-black hair. He looked like George Hamilton's shorter and bulkier brother. He made a playful grab for the

20

woman's bottom as she reached the top of the steps, and she screamed and flapped her pocket-book at him.

'My friend Daisy warned me about you! She told me you couldn't be trusted to keep your hands to yourself!'

'You're blaming *me*? It's all your fault, you temptress! You shouldn't go waggling your tush like that! What do you think I'm made of? Granite?'

At this, the red-haired woman collapsed with laughter, her hand held over her eyes and her white breasts wobbling. Victor Solway took out his key and opened the front door, and the two of them staggered inside.

I heard the front door slam, and then Victor Solway's door. After a while, I heard the muffled sound of Tony Bennett singing *Cold, Cold Heart*.

Shit and double shit. I could tolerate almost any composer in the world except John Williams. I mean, *Star Wars*, do me a favor. And I could tolerate almost any singer except Tony Bennett.

I went back to my keyboard. I had been scoring a link for Billy Wagner to accompany his interview with an eccentric family in Bakers-field who insisted on dressing in turn-of-the-century costumes, 365 days of the year. The mother and her two daughters even wore whale-bone corsets. But I had totally lost the mood now. How could I write tinkly 1890s' piano music with Tony Bennett droning through my floorboards?

'Another love before my time made your heart sad and blue—'

Jesus. Couldn't they play something halfway cheerful? Apart from that, what the hell was going on down there? I heard more hysterical laughter, and banging around. I couldn't believe that Kate was joining in. She had seemed far too aloof for a threesome with Victor and a tipsy redhead in a bulging green satin frock.

I played a few bars of *Magician*, and then I switched the keyboard off. I went through to the kitchenette, opened the fridge and poured myself a large glass of Zinfandel. Grow up, I told myself. Stop being such a stuffed shirt. Kate could do whatever she wanted, couldn't she? It's none of your business. If she wants to have a drunken orgy, that's entirely her affair. She can take the whole cast of *Spamalot* to bed with her if she wants to.

But this afternoon she had seemed so distracted, and so fey. I simply couldn't imagine her rolling around in bed, screaming and laughing. And – rightly or wrongly – I had felt that she had been asking for my help, or my protection, or somebody to confide in, at the very least.

I went to the front door, and opened it a little way. Tony Bennett was singing, *'Why do you run and hide from life? To try it just ain't smart.'*

I was still listening when Malkin, Kate's fluffy white cat, came up the stairs. She sat on the opposite side of the landing, giving me a baleful stare.

'Hey, puss,' I coaxed her. 'What's your mistress up to? Come on! Just for once, stop pretending that you don't know how to talk. All cats can talk, don't try to deny it.'

Malkin continued to glower at me, saying nothing, but purring like a clapped-out air-conditioning unit.

'You want to come in? How about a saucer of milk? I'm sorry, I don't have any Wild Kitty in the fridge, but I might be able to stretch to a can of anchovy fillets.'

I opened the door a little wider, and stepped back. 'Come on, puss. What is it, you don't like milk? You'd rather have a shot of El Tesoro? That can be arranged.'

My phone started to play *Hang On, Sloopy!* and I briefly turned around. When I turned back, however, Malkin had disappeared, like one of *Magician*'s conjuring tricks. Vanished, evaporated, without even the sound of her paws pattering down the stairs.

I closed the door and went to answer the phone. It was Margot. She sounded as if she were calling me from somebody's party. A girl in the background was calling out, 'Margot! Margot! Come here, will you? Michael has something *so-o-o* wild to show you!'

'Are you OK?' I asked her.

'Sure, I'm terrific. I'm at Lydia's birthday party. I just wanted to know if *you* were OK.'

'Of course I'm OK. I've been working, that's all. At least I *was* working, until they started having an orgy downstairs.'

'An orgy? Your well-heeled neighbors? How about that! Maybe you moved into the right apartment after all!'

'Well, I don't know about that. They're playing Tony Bennett records.'

'Oh, God. Better than Barry Manilow, I suppose.'

'Listen ... did you call me for any special reason? I really need to get some sleep now, so long as all this orgasmic screaming doesn't keep me awake.'

'I did, yes. I was worried about you. I just wanted to make sure that you were OK.'

'Of course I'm OK. Why shouldn't I be?'

'We did this fortune-telling tonight, with real Tibetan beads. They're so accurate, it's scary. They even knew that my sister was sick.'

'OK ... but why are you calling me?'

'Because I asked the fortune-teller if you would be happy in your new home. And he kept coming up with two beads, which means "raven", and that means bad luck. He said you would suffer pain, and broken bones, and burning in a fire. Most of all, he said you had to stay well away from a woman who had nobody walking beside her.'

'So what the hell does that mean?'

'I don't know. I asked him myself, but he kept on saying the same thing, again and again. And the other thing he said was, "a white memory is watching you ... so keep your door locked".'

' "A white memory"? What's "a white memory" when it's at home?'

'I have no idea, Lalo. Don't shoot the messenger. I simply thought you ought to know how your divination turned out, so that you can take the necessary precautions. As it is, I'm glad you're OK.'

'Thank you, Margot,' I said, tiredly.

'That's all right. I love you, Lalo, and I don't want you coming to a sticky end. Ever.'

I put down the phone. Downstairs, the Tony Bennett song had ended, although I could still hear voices and bumping sounds. What the hell where they doing – rearranging the goddamned furniture? I felt like putting on my hiking boots and doing a thunderous Cossack dance all around the living room. But then I thought – no, that would be childish. I was going to have to live with the Solways for the next few years, I would just have to get used to their little soirées. They wouldn't have an orgy every night. At least I hoped not.

I took a long hot shower, until the plumbing began to rumble, and then I toweled myself off and went to bed in my NY Mets boxer shorts. I could see a three-quarters moon through the bedroom window, until it disappeared behind the Franks Building. The night was much quieter now, except for the echo of sirens and the rumbling of traffic. At least Tony Bennett had put a sock in it.

I wondered what was going on downstairs – whether the three of them were lying in an octopus-like tangle on their bed, passing a joint from one to the other.

To my annoyance, I found myself murmuring, under my breath, *'Another love before my time made your heart sad and blue...'*

25

Four

I was coming down the stairs the next morning when the front door to the Solway's apartment opened and Victor Solway stepped out. He was wearing a dark brown linen sport coat, almost the same color as his deeply-tanned face, and tasseled brown loafers.

'Hey, the new neighbor,' he said. He smelled very strongly of Armani aftershave, and there were dark circles under his eyes. 'Victor Solway. Welcome to the madhouse.'

'Gideon Lake. Hi. Doesn't seem too mad so far.'

'Oh-ho. You obviously haven't met Pearl.'

'No. I haven't had the pleasure.'

Victor Solway put his arm around my shoulders as if he had known me for years, and said, in a confidential tone, 'Jonathan Lugard used to live upstairs from you. Jonathan Lugard the artist? Pearl was his model.'

'I never heard of Jonathan Lugard, sorry.'

'Well, to tell you the truth, I hadn't either, before we moved here. But apparently they revered him in art circles. He died about five years ago, and when he died Pearl inherited everything. The third-floor apartment, and all of his paintings. She's worth *millions*. The trouble

26

is, she's going doolally, and she keeps forgetting that Lugard has shuffled off to Buffalo. She wanders around wearing nothing but this old pink bathrobe, expecting him to come back at any moment and ask her to pose for him.'

'Wow,' I said, for want of anything better to say. Victor's breath smelled of hexachlorophene mouthwash, but there was an underlying odor of stale Shiraz, and I prayed that he would take his arm off my shoulders and give me some personal space.

But Victor gripped me even tighter, and glanced behind him as if he were making sure that nobody else could hear what he was saying. 'I'm giving you a friendly warning, that's all. If Pearl sees you coming up the stairs, she's very likely to think that it's her long-lost Lugard, and she'll drop that bathrobe before you have time to scream.'

He laughed, three sharp barks like a German Shepherd, right in my face, but then he let me go. I tugged at my shirtsleeves to straighten them, and tried to smile.

'But honestly, you'll love living here,' Victor told me. 'And from the investment point of view, you couldn't have made a better choice. I should know. Victor Solway International Realty, Inc. – that's me. Top class property, all over the world. You keep this apartment for five years, you'll get at least two-point-five when you sell it. Maybe three. In fact, I'll sell it for you, myself, personally, with cut-price commission. Two-point-five million, plus, and I kid you not.'

'Wow,' I repeated. I wished that I would stop saying 'wow'.

Victor said, 'I hear that you write music for the movies. Well, I was told that you were a musician, and I made a point of checking, before you moved in. I didn't want a heavy metal band living upstairs. *Ha!*'

'No, no,' I assured him. 'I've scored some movies, yes. But I mainly write TV commercials, that kind of thing.'

'Obviously you're *very* successful at it. Written anything I should know?'

'I doubt it.' I wasn't going to sing the Thom's Tomato Soup song, not again, especially if Victor had never heard it either.

'Well, *muchacho* ... I guess we'll be bumping into each other, from time to time. Come on down for a drink, why don't you? How about Saturday morning, around eleven thirty?'

'Sure. Sounds good. Thank you.'

Victor leaned very close to me again, and I found myself tilting backward.

'By the way,' he said. 'I invite some of my friends back, now and again. If it ever gets a little too boisterous for you, don't hesitate to knock on the floor. One knock for keep it down, two knocks for shut the fuck up.'

He let out three more barks, and slapped my shoulder.

'Thanks,' I said. 'I'm sure I won't have to. Knock, I mean.'

I was just about to tell Victor that I had met Kate yesterday afternoon, and that she was supposed to be having lunch with me today, but for some reason I decided not to. I didn't exactly know why, but I thought that maybe I should wait until I knew a little more about Victor and Kate's relationship.

Victor opened the front door, and the morning sunlight flooded in. 'I'll see you Saturday, OK, if I don't see you before?'

He bounded down the steps and hailed a passing cab. I stood in the porch for a few moments, watching his cab until it reached the end of St Luke's Place and turned right into Hudson Street. When it had disappeared, I felt strangely relieved.

I looked across the street toward the park. Behind the high wire fencing, three small children were running around and around, their arms outspread, trying to make themselves giddy. Two men were perched on the back of a bench, with their feet on the seat, talking and smoking. And there, half hidden behind one of the trees, stood a young woman with a baby stroller. It was Kate.

I shaded my eyes with my hand. Maybe it was somebody who just *looked* like Kate. But, no – it was definitely her, wearing a charcoal-gray coat and a light gray woolly hat. In the bright sunlight, her face looked very pale, almost blurred. The baby in the stroller looked about five or six months old. I guessed he was a boy: he was wearing a blue knitted bonnet with ear flaps, and a little dark-blue duffel-coat. He was twisting around to catch Kate's attention, but she seemed to be ignoring him.

I half raised my hand and gave Kate a wave,

but she didn't wave back. I didn't even know if she had seen me. I thought about going across to her, but she seemed so lost in thought, and after the rumpus I had heard last night I wasn't sure what I was going to say to her. 'Have a good evening, did you – you and Victor and whatever-her-name-was?' I waited for a moment longer, and then I went down the steps and started to walk east, toward Seventh Avenue. I was heading for The Two Brothers seafood market on Carmine Street for fresh tuna. Before I went around the bend in St Luke's Place, however, I turned back, to see if Kate were still there, standing by the tree, but she had gone.

A ragged cloud passed over the sun, and the day suddenly turned chilly.

Five

I opened the front door just as my wall clock chimed 10:30. I went through to the kitchenette and unwrapped the two inch-thick steaks of yellowfin tuna. I rinsed them under the faucet, patted them dry, and then laid them in a shallow white dish.

I hummed a new theme I was writing for *Eagle's Pass*, a new TV series about a pioneering family in Oregon. Part adventure, part comedy and part mushy-sentimental *Waltons*-type weepie.

From another shopping bag, I took out a Chinese cabbage, two bunches of scallions, a knobbly piece of ginger and a clear cellophane envelope filled with *hijiki* seaweed. I emptied the seaweed into a bowl, and covered it with warm water to soak.

I was grating the ginger when I heard the most timorous of knocks at my door. Wiping my hands on a tea towel, I went to answer it. Standing on the landing was an elderly woman with wild white hair, wrapped in a soiled pink satin bathrobe.

'I'm very sorry if I'm being a nuisance,' she said, almost in a whisper. 'But I was wondering if Jonathan was with you.'

I shook my head. 'He's not, no.'

The woman craned her head to one side, trying to see past me, into my living room. 'You're quite sure? He was only going to Blick's to buy some new brushes. He said he'd be back in twenty minutes.'

'No, I'm sorry. There's nobody here but me.'

She stared at me, her mouth pursed like an Egyptian mummy. I could see that, decades ago, she must have been beautiful. Her bone structure was perfect. Wide forehead, high cheekbones, finely delineated jaw. But now her skin had withered, and her green eyes had faded. She was barefoot, underneath her bathrobe, and her feet were like claws.

'*You're* not Jonathan, are you?'

'No, I'm not Jonathan. But if I see him, I'll tell him that you were looking for him.'

'Thank you,' she said. Then she frowned at me

31

again, and said, 'I *do* live here, don't I? I'm not just visiting? This isn't a hotel?'

'No ... you live here. Do you want me to take you back up to your apartment?'

'Yes, that would be very noble of you. Whatever happened to nobility? I used to know Claude Rains, you know. I knew him very well. Now *he* was nobility.'

'Claude Rains? Didn't he play The Invisible Man?'

'That's right. The Invisible Man. But they used a double, most of the time, when he was wearing his bandages. It was only the *real* him in the inn scene.'

I stepped out of my apartment and took hold of the woman's elbow. 'Come on, let me show you back upstairs. You must be Pearl. Mr Solway downstairs, he was telling me all about you.'

'Mr Solway? Never heard of him. The people who live downstairs, their name is Huxtable. George and Doris Huxtable. They have an awful dog, but don't tell them I said so, will you? Never stops barking. I heard it this morning. Yap, yap, yap!'

I steered Pearl toward the stairs, and helped her up to the next landing. The door to her apartment was wide open, and I could smell age, and airlessness, and cauliflower that was long past its sell-by date. But as I guided her inside, I smelled something else, too. The pungent aroma of fresh oil paint. Unmistakable.

Her apartment was chaotic. Although it was such a sunny morning, the living room was in semi-darkness, because the drapes were drawn –

heavy brown velvet curtains that were thick with dust. An ottoman stood in one corner of the room, its green brocade covering burst open, so that its horsehair stuffing bulged out. In the opposite corner, there was an armchair, upholstered in cracked brown leather, and a folding Turkish stool. Against the walls, dozens of canvasses were stacked, as well as portfolios filled with drawings, and sketchbooks, and unframed watercolors.

In the center of the room, however, stood an artist's easel, with a large canvas on it, and as I assisted Pearl toward the armchair, I could see that it was still wet, and gleaming.

'You're such a good fellow,' said Pearl. 'Have I ever met you before? You're not Walter Montmorency, by any chance?'

'Gideon Lake,' I told her. 'I just moved in downstairs.'

But at the same time I was staring at the half-finished oil painting on the easel. It was a life study of Pearl, sitting on the end of the ottoman. She was smoking a cigarette in an elegant, almost arrogant pose, her chin tilted upward. So far the artist had painted only her basic flesh tones, but I could see that it was going to be a strikingly strong portrait.

'Gideon Lake,' Pearl repeated. She thought for a while, muttering to herself, and then she said, 'You're not related to the New Rochelle Lakes, by any chance? What a sad lot they were, if you don't mind my saying so. Especially that Matilda Lake. My goodness. What a mess *she* was.'

'Who's painting this?' I asked her.

'Who's painting what, dear?'

'This picture of you. Who's painting it?'

Pearl frowned at me as if I had asked her a question in Chinese. 'Who do you think, dear?'

'I really don't know. I'm a musician. I'm not very knowledgeable when it comes to artists.'

'Well, it's my beloved Jonathan, of course. Who else would it be?'

I said nothing. Some old friend of hers must be using her as a model, and she was simply confused. I had to admit, though, that even in her old age she had a very passable figure. Slim hips, long legs, tiny breasts with faint pink nipples.

'I have to get back downstairs now,' I told her. 'I have a lunch guest.'

'If you see Jonathan, you will tell him to hurry up, won't you?'

'Of course.'

'And do be warned,' she said, lowering her voice back down to a whisper. 'The people in this house ... *they're not always what they seem to be.*'

'Excuse me?'

Pearl raised her hand to her face and stroked her cheek, as if she were making sure that she were still there.

'They tell you one thing, but they do another. That's their trouble. And they watch you, all the time. They covet your possessions, that's why. They want everything that's yours, and not theirs. They covet every breath that you take. They even covet the sunlight that shines into your eyes. *They wants it*, like Gollum wanted the ring.'

'Well ... I'll be careful,' I assured her.

Pearl stood up. I thought for one alarming moment that she was going to drop her bathrobe, but she simply came up to me and took hold of my left hand.

'One door opens and another door closes,' she told me. 'But don't forget that doors never open and close by themselves. There are people walking through them, even if there aren't always people to be seen.'

With that, she closed her eyes and lifted her face toward me, as if she expected me to kiss her. I hesitated for a moment, and then I gave her the lightest kiss on her forehead.

'You're such a good fellow, Gideon Lake,' she said. 'I think I might be able to remember you.'

Six

Kate came up about twenty minutes later, while I was chopping up the Chinese cabbage. I had left the door on the latch, so that she could walk straight in.

'So sorry I'm late,' she smiled. She was wearing narrow black jeans and a yellow scoop-neck T-shirt, and she was holding up a bottle of Cuvée Napa sparkling wine. She kissed me as if she had known me for years.

'Hey, no problem. Glad you could make it.'

'Something strange happened to a friend of mine this morning, and I had to go see her.'

'Something strange?'

'Somebody broke into her apartment and broke all of her flower vases. They didn't steal anything, just broke all of her vases, and threw her flowers all around the room. She's very distressed about it.'

'Does she have any idea who did it?'

Kate shook her head.

'Does she have any idea *why* they did it?'

'No. But there are so many psychos around these days.'

I took the wine bottle from her. It was intensely cold, and beaded with dew, as if she had just taken it out of the fridge. 'I don't have any champagne glasses,' I admitted. 'You don't mind slumming it with a regular wine glass, do you?'

'Of course not. I've drunk it straight out of the bottle before now.'

I took two glasses out of the cupboard, and opened the Cuvée Napa with a sharp, suppressed hiss.

'That's good,' said Kate. *'Le pet d'un ange.'*

'Excuse me?'

'An angel's fart. That's the way you're supposed to open champagne. Not like Victor. Every time he opens a bottle of champagne you'd think he just won the Indy 500. It sprays everywhere.'

'I met Victor this morning.'

Kate looked away, and said nothing.

36

'He was telling me about Pearl, upstairs,' I persisted.

'Pearl? Yes, she's something else, isn't she? She didn't drop her robe?'

'No. She was very ladylike. Kind of forgetful. I mean, her mind wanders, doesn't it? She asked me a couple of times if *I* was Jonathan Lugard.'

Kate smiled, although she still didn't turn around to look at me. 'Her mind's unraveling, yes. But she isn't stupid. She can see things that nobody else can see.'

'Like what, for instance?'

But Kate didn't answer me. Instead, she leaned over the dish with the tuna steaks in it, and sniffed them. 'Are these what we're having for lunch? They smell wonderfully fresh. It's a good thing I didn't bring Malkin.'

'I bought them this morning, from The Two Brothers on Carmine Street. I saw you in the park.'

Again, she didn't answer, but walked into the living room, and started to look through my CD collection. I followed her, with my glass of Cuvée Napa in my hand, and watched her. I loved her profile, the tilt of her nose, and her very long eyelashes.

'You like Van Morrison?' she asked me. *'Days Like This*, that's a really great song.'

'I like just about everybody, almost. Classical, rock, you name it. All except for Tony Bennett.'

She turned to me. 'Why did you say that?'

'Because I don't like Tony Bennett, that's all. He brings me out in hives.'

'Victor hero-worships Tony Bennett. Some-

37

times I used to think that Victor would like to *be* Tony Bennett. He's always singing along.'

I said nothing for nearly a minute, still watching Kate sort through my music. But then she held up a copy of Beethoven's Piano Concerto No. 5 and said, 'I used to have this. I love it.'

'What's going on?' I asked her.

'What do you mean, what's going on?'

'I mean, why are you here?'

Kate looked bewildered. 'Because you invited me for lunch. Did you think that I wasn't going to come? Did you not *want* me to come?'

'Of course I wanted you to come. It's just that – I'm sorry.'

'Sorry for what?'

'Last night. I couldn't help hearing what was going on downstairs.'

'Oh. *That.* You don't have to worry about that.'

'I'm not. I mean, whatever you want to get up to, that's your business. Here – let me make us some lunch.'

She came up to me, very close. 'You *do* like me?' she asked.

'Of course I like you. I like you very much. I mean, I hardly know you, but somehow—'

'Do you think that matters? That you hardly know me? I could come up here for lunch every day for a year, and the chances are that you still wouldn't know me very much better. Victor and I, we got married in April, two thousand two. He still doesn't know what music I like, or what perfume I wear, or how much I love sunflowers.'

I looked closely into her eyes. It was like looking out of a window on an overcast day.

38

'Sunflowers,' I repeated, and I laid my hand on her shoulder and kissed her. I had kissed women like that before, just because I felt like it, but I felt that Kate had been *expecting* me to do it. We kept our lips pressed together only for a moment, and neither of us closed our eyes, but when I stood up straight again, Kate was smiling at me with obvious pleasure.

'Tuna,' I told her.

'My God, Gideon Lake. You say the most romantic things.'

'Don't I just? But I have to sear the tuna. Otherwise lunch won't be ready till supper time.'

She followed me into the kitchenette and stood close beside me as I took down my cast-iron skillet and put it on to the gas to heat up.

'Sing me something else you've written,' she urged me.

'I'll play you some more of my TV themes after lunch. You ever watch *Laurel Canyon*? I wrote the theme for *Laurel Canyon*. And *Foznick & Son* ... you know that comedy with Sean MacReady? "Are you *ready* for this, Mister Foznick, *s-i-rr*?"'

'Yes, but I want to hear you sing.'

I licked the tip of my finger and dabbed it into the skillet, to test how hot it was. 'Ouch. Almost ready.'

Kate raised her eyebrows, to show me that she was still waiting.

'OK,' I relented, lifting both hands in surrender. I cleared my throat, and then I sang, to a *Sound of Music*-style melody, '"When it's spring *across the meadows ... when the wild flowers smell so sweet ... when the air is fine like sparkling wine ... then you know you've chosen Zweet.*"'

Kate stared at me. 'Zweet? *Zweet*? That's one of those things you hang in the toilet bowl, isn't it?'

I shrugged. 'What did I tell you? I write music for anything.'

She laughed. 'You're incredible. It's such a romantic melody. And it's for Zweet!'

'I've written music for frankfurters, too. And for adult-sized diapers.'

The skillet was good and hot now, so I sizzled the tuna steaks for two minutes on each side, and then tossed the salad with lemon-juice dressing. The kitchenette filled up with tuna smoke.

We sat at the small antique table in the corner of the living room. Kate said, 'This is really good. The last time I had seared tuna it was like shoe leather.'

'Thanks,' I said. 'The secret is, cook it hot but don't cook it long.' I watched her while she ate. Then I said, 'How did you and Victor first meet?'

'Oh ... I was working for *Perfect Home* magazine, and we were doing a layout on remodeled apartments in TriBeCa. Victor owned one of the apartments, and that's how we met. We finished late one evening, and he invited me out for dinner. I was hungry, and it was the end of the month, so I didn't have any money. So I said yes.'

I didn't say anything, but waited until she had

40

finished her next mouthful of fish.

'Victor...' she said. 'I know he doesn't seem like my type. He's self-made, he's brash, but he used to be very funny sometimes, and he never took no for an answer. Up until then, all of my boyfriends were very serious and academic, and when something upset them all they did was clear their throat. So Victor came into my life like a hurricane.'

She paused, and sipped a little wine. 'Five weeks after we met, he asked me to marry him. I couldn't think of any reason why not. He made me happy. He made me laugh. He had plenty of money. So I did.'

'So how long have you been living in St Luke's Place?'

'Sometimes it seems like forever. Other times, it seems like the blink of an eye.'

For some reason, she didn't want to give me a straight answer. But I didn't press her. I didn't really care, to tell you the truth, although I should have. If I had only known *then* what it took me seven more months to find out.

'How about you?' she asked me. 'Anybody special in your life?'

'Nope, not at the moment. There was, up until recently. But, you know. She wanted more attention than I could give her, what with work and everything.'

'Was she pretty?'

I looked at her narrowly. Why did she want to know that?

'Yes, she was pretty. She was *very* pretty. She was half Czech, as a matter of fact. Her name

41

was Milka. It means "hard-working" in Czech, but she was one of the laziest girls I ever dated. It was "peek up my nail polish for me, Tobee, I kent quite reach eet".'

Kate laughed. 'I can't see you putting up with that. You're too—' She circled her hand around, trying to think of the right word.

'Too chauvinistic? Too self-important? Too goddamned stubborn?'

'I don't know. Too sure of yourself. Quiet, yes. But sure of yourself. I guess you have to be, to write music. I mean, you're revealing yourself, aren't you, when you write music? You're exposing your emotions. Even in a Zweet commercial.'

'You're very perceptive,' I told her.

'Really?'

'I wrote that music just after Milka and I broke up. I have to admit I still miss her, in a way. She was lazy, for sure, but she was lots of fun.'

'It's a lovely song. I know it's for toilet freshener, but you could always change the words, couldn't you?'

'I guess so. Let's try it.'

I sang it again, soft and off-key. *'When it's lunchtime in Manhattan ... and there's tuna on your plate ... when the sparkling wine makes you feel just fine ... then you know you've chosen Kate.'*

She put down her fork, reached across the table and laid her hand on top of mine.

'What's this?' I asked her. The moment was charged with such erotic electricity that I felt as if my hair were standing on end.

42

'You know what it is,' she said, and her eyelids were very heavy, almost as if she were falling asleep. 'It doesn't happen very often. But when it does, you *always* know. I turned around, and I saw you looking out of your window, and I knew right away that you were the one. And *you* knew it, too, didn't you?'

I thought: *no, I didn't*. But then I remembered that secretive smile that she had given me, and I thought: *yes, I did*.

Seven

I hadn't even made the bed, not properly, just thrown the red-and-gold tapestry cover over it, so that underneath the sheets were still twisted like the Indian rope-trick and the pillows were all bashed in, but Kate didn't seem to care.

She crossed her arms and took off her yellow top. Then she sat back on the bed and pulled off her jeans. Meanwhile I was struggling to get out of my polo shirt and unbuckle my pants.

But after that brief moment of frantic comedy, it was beautiful. I fell back on to the bed and Kate climbed on top of me. She was skinnier than any other woman I had ever known, all collarbone and ribs and hips, and her skin was almost translucent. Yet she was so passionate, so greedy. She took my face in both hands and kissed me, thrusting her tongue deep into my

43

mouth. Then she trailed her fingernails all the way down my sides, so that I jerked in nervous reaction when she touched my hips.

'I never thought ... nobody ever told me,' she panted.

'Nobody ever told you what?'

'Nobody ever told me this was possible.'

There she was again, speaking in riddles. But right at that moment I wasn't looking for logic. The afternoon sun was reflected from an upper window in the Franks Building, like somebody shining a searchlight on her. It lit up her hair, and shone on her shoulders, and gave her an almost unnatural radiance. I felt as if I were making love to a fairy queen, rather than a human being.

I couldn't help watching as I entered her, the way the glistening folds of her skin opened up, like dew-soaked lily petals.

She rode up and down on me, her back arched, her head thrown back, and both hands raised. It was like no love-making I had ever experienced. I felt as if our nervous systems were wired together, and that everything that she could feel, I could feel too. I could almost imagine tiny sparks coursing out of her body and into mine, and making me tingle everywhere.

She began to gasp, higher and higher. I took hold of her hips, and pulled her down on me, harder and harder. I was very close to climaxing, and I couldn't stop myself from letting out a loud *haugh!*

She quaked, and trembled, and then she screamed. At least I think she screamed. It was almost beyond the range of human hearing. The glass of water on the nightstand shattered, and the mirror on the wall cracked diagonally from one side to the other.

I lifted my head and looked at the broken glass, and the water running off the edge of the nightstand. 'My God. I thought only opera singers could do that.'

She half covered her face with her hand, but her eyes were smiling. 'I'm so sorry. That's never happened to me before. Ever. I *always* scream – but—'

'Hey, it doesn't matter. It's only a glass.'

'But your mirror.'

'It's only a mirror. Forget it. You were wonderful.'

She carefully climbed off me and lay very close beside me, with her head resting on my chest. I put my arm around her thin, bony shoulder blades and I felt as if I could have lain there for the rest of the day, and the following evening, too. She traced patterns on my stomach with her fingertip.

'Do you believe in fate?' she asked me.

'You mean, do I believe that whatever's going to happen to us, it's going to happen to us, whatever we do? I don't know. Don't you think we have choices?'

She propped herself up on one elbow and stared at me, a little too close for me to be able to focus properly. 'But it was fate that brought you here, don't you think? Some old woman could have moved into this apartment. Or two gays, like Paul Cadmus and Jared French.'

'Well, I guess. If *Magician* hadn't been so suc-

45

cessful, I never could have afforded it.'

She touched the tip of my nose, and smiled. 'You and I were destined to meet. I just know it. I've been waiting for you for so long.'

'What about Victor?'

'What *about* Victor?'

'I don't know. Are you unhappy with Victor, or shouldn't I ask?'

'It depends what you mean by unhappy.'

She climbed off the bed and went to stand, naked, by the window. The sun was lower now, and the room was mostly in shadow. I lay there and watched her and I didn't know what to say to her next. I didn't even know how I was supposed to feel about her; or how she felt about me.

'Look at the time,' she said, without turning around. 'I'd better go.'

'Don't you want to hear some more of my almost-beautiful music? I started to write a piano concerto once. It's called *The One-Hand-ed Clock*. I could play it for you.'

'Maybe another time.'

'And that means what? That there isn't going to *be* another time?'

She came back over to the bed, and knelt next to me, and kissed me. 'Of course there will be. Don't you understand? You and me, we've only just started.'

I kissed her back. 'In that case, I'd better stock up on drinking glasses, and mirrors.'

We dressed. Somehow, once we had put our clothes back on, we felt quite awkward and formal. 'Do you want me to help you with the dishes?' she asked me.

'Don't worry about it. But you could send Malkin up, to finish off those bits of tuna.'

'I might just do that.'

We kissed again, at the open doorway. She turned to go, and it was then that I asked her the question that I should have asked her as soon as she walked in.

'In the park. Whose baby was that?'

She didn't turn back. She had one hand resting on the newel post at the top of the stairs, and her face was hidden by the curve of her hair.

'His name was Michael,' she said. She hesitated a little longer, as if she were waiting for me to ask her another question, but something told me not to press her any further – not yet, anyhow.

'OK,' I said. 'I'll see you whenever.'

She left, without another word. I heard her go down the stairs, but strangely I didn't hear her open the door to her apartment, and I didn't hear her open the front door, either. I listened and listened, but it was almost as if she had gone down the stairs and vanished.

A few seconds later, however, Malkin came running up the stairs, purring, so Kate must have opened her apartment door to let her out.

'Come on, puss,' I coaxed her. 'It's tuna time!'

Malkin trotted after me into the kitchenette. I scraped the remains of our tuna steaks on to one plate and set it down on the floor. Malkin immediately started to wolf it down.

I stood and watched her, feeling unexpectedly bereft. If there was one thing I had already learned about life, it was that the happiest moments are always over, and in the end we are always left alone again, with nothing but the plates to clear away, and the sun sinking down behind the trees.

Eight

Margot thought it was brilliant.

'It's *brilliant*! A wonderful new apartment, in a street with a bend in it! An adulterous affair with the wife of an international realtor with halitosis! How come you *always* fall on your feet, Lalo?'

'Don't forget the demented nude model upstairs.'

'Even *more* brilliant! It's like *Through The Looking Glass*!'

We were sitting on a bench in James A. Walker park, enjoying the sunshine. It was warm enough to go out without a coat, but it wasn't as balmy as it had been the previous week, and around the corner I could feel the first cold drafts of winter, coming from the north-west. Margot was wearing a chunky red sweater with green apples embroidered on it.

Not far away from us, an old man in a raincoat tied up with string was slowly pacing around the grass, bending over now and again to pick up something. Cigarette ends? I couldn't really tell.

'So what are you going to do, Lalo? Are you going to see her again? You *have* to see her again!'

'I think so. I'm not entirely sure. She said we had just got started, but half of the time I don't really understand what she's talking about.'

'What do you mean, you don't understand what she's talking about?'

'It's hard to describe. It's like if I said, "How do you like my haircut?" and you said, "Maybe next Wednesday." Like it *could* make sense. It's perfectly good English. But somehow, when you try to analyze it, it doesn't make any sense at all.'

'Does it matter, if she's good in bed? At least she doesn't make love in a way that you can't understand. My last boyfriend did, Patrick. You remember Patrick? I swear he learned the facts of life from a goatherd, in Uzbekistan or someplace like that. When I was trying to do one thing, he was always trying to do something else.'

After a while, the sun sank behind the buildings, and it began to grow chilly.

'Let's go inside,' I suggested. 'I'll make you some Russian tea, with honey.'

Before we left the park, though, I went across to the old man in the raincoat and I held out a ten-dollar bill. He looked at it suspiciously.

'What's that for?'

'Anything you like. Food, cigarettes, hooch. I'm not telling you how to spend it.'

He came up close to me. His chin was thick with white stubble, but he looked reasonably

49

clean. He reminded me of the late Rod Steiger, for some reason. He didn't take his eyes off me, not for a second, not even to look down at the ten-spot.

'You should be careful,' he said.

'Oh, yes? And why is that?'

'Because some people can seem like they care for you, if you know what I mean, but all the time they have an agenda. They're playing you.'

'I see. And you think that's happening to me?'

'Just warning you, that's all. I used to take people at face value, and look what happened to me.'

He eased the folded bill from between my fingers as if he were trying to take it without me being aware that he had done it.

'You're a good man,' he told me. 'You watch out for that young lady of yours.'

'Oh, we're just friends,' said Margot, taking hold of my arm.

'I know that,' the old man told her. 'I was talking about the other young lady. The one with the stroller.'

'You *know* her?' I asked him.

But all he did was crumple the ten-dollar bill into his cuff, and raise one finger as if he were testing which way the wind was blowing. Then he walked away without another word.

'Weird,' said Margot, as he made his way around the chain-link fence and disappeared behind the trees.

'You're right,' I told her. 'Mega-weird. Let's go inside and have that tea.'

As I unlocked the door to my apartment, Margot sniffed, and frowned, and sniffed again.

'What is it?' I asked her.

'Paint,' she said. 'It definitely smells like paint.'

'Oh, that's coming from Pearl's apartment. Somebody's painting a life study of her. She says it's Jonathan Lugard, but he's been dead for five years, according to Victor, so I don't think *that's* too likely.'

I went through to the kitchenette and Margot followed me. She said, 'It must be quite comforting, though, to be sure that somebody's alive, even when they're dead. I mean, if you really believe it, what difference does it make?'

'I don't know. None, I guess. Maybe that's what ghosts are.'

I boiled the kettle and made two glasses of Russian tea. Margot poured a large dollop of orange-blossom honey into hers, over the back of her spoon. Then she tugged off her ankle-length boots and stretched herself out on one of my sofas.

'You definitely seem *different*, Lalo.'

'You think so?'

'Yes. I get the feeling that you're expecting something to happen, but you're not sure what it is. Maybe you're expecting Kate's husband to come tearing up the stairs and punch you on the nose.'

'Well, maybe. But I don't think so, somehow. It seems to me Kate and Victor have a pretty relaxed kind of marriage, to say the least.'

'Maybe you're waiting for Kate to say that she

51

loves you.'

'Hey, come on. We've been to bed together once, that's all. I may not even see her again.'

'There's something about her, though, isn't there? Something that's stuck on your brain, like one of those jingles of yours.'

I tried to sip my tea. It was so hot that it scalded my lip. I didn't know what to say to Margot, but she was right. I kept thinking about the way that Kate had felt when she had rested her head on my chest; and the strange cloudy look in her eyes whenever she looked at me. I felt as if I needed to see her again, as soon as possible, just to touch her and make sure that she still wanted me.

'I'll tell you what,' said Margot. 'Me and Dorothea and Jimmy the Squib and Duncan Bradley, we're all going to Sal's Comedy Hole tomorrow night, to see Maynard Manning. Why don't you come along? Get yourself back in the real world, you know, where people talk baloney but at least it's *logical* baloney.'

'Yes, maybe I will.'

'Come on, promise me. You need to get out more.'

'*OK*, already! I'll come.'

For the next hour and a half, I played her some of the incidental music I had written for *The Billy Wagner Show*. I opened a bottle of Zinfandel and poured us a large glass each. Margot lay back on the sofa and sang along with me, making up the words as she went along.

'*Nobody ever told me ... I wish that they had*

52

said ... how much it hurts when a concrete block ... drops right on your head!'

She was funny, Margot, but she had a wonderful voice. She could sing anything from blues to light opera, but her specialty was zydeco songs, like *Would You Rather Be An Old Man's Darling Or A Young Man's Slave?* She was terrific, Margot.

Eventually my wall clock chimed seven. 'Lalo – I really have to go,' she told me. 'My fridge is empty and I need to do some heavy-duty shopping.'

'We could go out for pizza if you're hungry.'

'No, I'm so sick of pizza. I need actual food. I've even run out of tofu.'

I showed her downstairs to the front door. She gave me a warm, squashy-breasted hug and she smelled strongly of vanilla musk. She said, 'Tomorrow, remember. You need to get you back to reality.'

'I promised, didn't I?'

She went skipping down the steps and I closed the door behind her. As I started to climb back up the stairs, I saw an elderly man standing on the second-floor landing, half hidden in the shadows, looking down at me. White-haired, skeletal-faced, with bushy white eyebrows. He was wearing a pale gray smock with dozens of paintbrush marks all over it, like birds' footprints, and a floppy gray beret.

'How's it going?' I called out. But the elderly man didn't answer. Instead, he turned his back on me and disappeared up the next flight of stairs.

I reached the landing and looked up, but there was no sign of him. I didn't even hear a door close. I guessed he must have been Pearl's friend, the one who was painting her life study. Pretty darn unsociable, whoever he was.

I let myself into my apartment, switched on the flat-screen TV that stood in the corner, and poured myself another glass of wine. I hadn't called my parents since the weekend, so I picked up the phone and dialed their number in New Milford. All I heard was my mother's voice warbling *'This is the Lake residence! Randolph and Joyce are unable to come to the phone right now, but they would absolutely love to hear what you have to tell us, so please leave us a message. And make it heartfelt, won't you?'*

'Dis is da plumbah,' I said, in a thick Bronx accent. 'I'd love to come by and fiddle wit your cistern, sweetheart.' Well – it served her right for being so precious.

I eased myself back in one of my armchairs with my feet propped up on the coffee-table, and watched *My Name Is Earl* for a while. Earl, as usual, was talking about karma. I think I would, too, without question, if I lost a $100,000 lottery ticket and then found it again, the way that Earl had.

Actually, I was beginning to think that Kate was right about fate, and that karma was at work in my life, too. As every day passed, I was beginning to feel more and more like a bit-part player in some long-running TV drama, in which everybody knew the storyline except me. How can you make choices when nobody explains to you what the choices are? Just stand here, Gideon, and say these lines. Don't worry what they mean.

There was a quick, soft knocking at my door. I went to open it, and it was Kate. There was karma for you. She was wearing a black roll-neck sweater and jeans, and her hair was tied back with a black velvet ribbon. She looked pale, and she was chafing her hands together as if she felt cold.

'Hey,' I greeted her. 'I didn't expect to see you again so soon.'

'Can I come in?'

'Sure, of course you can. You just missed Margot. How about a glass of wine?'

'Yes, thanks.' She sat down on the end of one of the sofas, clutching herself tightly.

'Are you feeling the cold?' I asked her. 'I can turn up the heat.'

'No, no. I'm fine. I was wondering if you were free for the next two weeks.'

'Free? When? To do what?'

'To come away with me.'

I brought her a glass of wine and then I sat down next to her. 'You want me to come away with you? You mean on vacation?'

'Well, kind of. I'd like you to meet some people I know. You don't have to worry about the cost – I'll pay for everything.'

'What's Victor going to say?'

'Victor won't know.'

'Oh, come on, Kate. You and I will both disappear for two weeks, and Victor won't even get suspicious?'

'Gideon, you'll *love* it! When you see this family's apartment, you won't believe your eyes! It's truly spectacular. Marble bathrooms, antique furniture. Views out over the harbor.'

'I'm really not sure.'

'Why? I've told you I'll cover all of your expenses.'

'Well ... I have to admit to you, Kate, I'm not the most sociable guy in the world. I can't sit down at the breakfast table in the morning and have meaningful conversations over the Cheerios, especially with people I've never met before. As it is, I don't usually utter a sound until noon, and then it's a strangled growl.'

'Don't worry about it. We'll have our own private suite, with a four-poster bed and our own bathroom and our own living room. If we want to keep ourselves to ourselves, I promise you, nobody will mind at all.'

I had to admit that the offer did seem attractive. I hadn't had a real vacation in over three and a half years, and I hadn't had a woman in my bed since Milka – apart from one-night stands with a red-haired flight attendant called Genna and a backing vocalist for P Diddy called Lateesh. Nobody as poised and as magical as Kate. Even if she *was* another man's wife.

'So, ah – where are we talking about?' I asked her.

'I'll give you a clue. You'll need your coat, and your gloves, and a scarf, maybe.'

'Oh. Someplace chilly. Someplace chilly with a view of the harbor. Seattle, maybe?'

'Further east,' she smiled. 'Much further east.

Stockholm.'

'Stockholm, South Dakota? No, there's no harbor there. You mean Stockholm, *Sweden*?'

'You got it. In the old town, close to the Royal Palace, looking right out over the harbor. You won't believe how beautiful it is, especially at this time of the year.'

'Sounds amazing. I mean it. Sounds *really* amazing. But who are these people you want me to meet?'

Kate sipped her wine. 'They're a family of four. He's a doctor, the mother works as a physiotherapist. They have two daughters.'

'And can I ask why you want me to meet them?'

'I can't explain, but it's important. And you have to admit that Stockholm in late September – it's different. Different from Palm Springs, anyway.'

'Do you think I *need* a doctor?'

'Of course not,' she smiled. 'In any case, he's a gynaecologist.'

'I'm baffled. We only just met, we went to bed together just once, and now you want me to come away with you for two weeks to meet a Swedish gynaecologist and his family. Do you want their approval? Am I being vetted or something?'

'No, Gideon. It's nothing like that, I promise you. I just want you to come to Stockholm and see things differently.'

I didn't know what to think, but I stood up again, and went over to my desk. I leafed through my diary and said, 'Yes ... well, I guess

I could manage it. I have to finish one more link for *Billy Wagner*, but I should have that all wrapped up by tomorrow. So long as I'm back by the fourteenth. I have a meeting with DDB about a Diet Pepsi commercial.'

'Oh, yes. You'll be back by then, I promise you.'

Just after nine o'clock, Kate finished her glass of wine and said she ought to think about leaving.

'Do you have to?' I asked her. It was much warmer now, because I had lit tall white church candles all around the living room, and the walls were alive with shadows, like dancing witches. 'Have one more drink before you go.'

'All right. You've persuaded me.'

'Is Victor home tonight?' I asked her, as ten o'clock struck.

'He might be, later. But Thursday night is his squash night, and sometimes he stays at his club.'

'Doesn't he miss you, when you stay out all night? Doesn't he ask you where you've been?'

'Victor never misses me.'

'Well, I have a confession to make. *I* missed you today. I really felt like I wanted to hold you.'

Kate turned her eyes toward me, her chin resting in the palm of her hand, and for some reason she looked wistful. Sad, even. 'Ah well,' she said. 'We can't always have everything we want, can we? At least, I can't.'

'You don't think so? I don't agree with you. If you want something badly enough, what's to stop you? Victor?'

Again, there was one of those long pauses, during which it became increasingly obvious that she wasn't going to explain herself.

At last, I said, 'I don't understand you and Victor. I mean, I've met swingers before. I've met couples who have open marriages, and sleep with anybody who takes their fancy. But what's going on with you two? It's almost like you're not really married at all.'

She gave an almost-imperceptible shrug. I guessed that meant she didn't want to talk about it. I got up and changed the CD, from Brian Wilson's *Pet Sounds* to plinky-plonky piano studies by Debussy. The music sounded as wistful as Kate.

I sat down close to her. 'I can't help the way I feel about you. It's just you. Your face, your voice, the way you kiss me. I feel like I knew you even before I ever met you.'

She pressed her forehead against my cheek, as if she were trying to tell me telepathically that she felt the same way, but didn't want to commit herself by saying it out loud.

I stroked her hair for a while, and then I said, 'This family we're going to be staying with in Stockholm? What are they like?'

'The Westerlunds. You'll like them. Dr Axel Westerlund and his wife Tilda, and their two daughters Elsa and Felicia. I'll write their address down for you.'

'Why do you need to do that?'

'Because you and I won't be traveling to Sweden on the same flight. You'll have to find your own way there. You can do that, can't you?'

'Because of Victor? Is that it? You don't want Victor to find out that we've gone on vacation together? What does it matter, if he never misses you?'

'It's better if he doesn't find out about you, that's all. He has a very bad temper.'

'I'm not scared of him, Kate.'

'No? Then you should be. Victor ... well, Victor's not like ordinary men. He's not even like ordinary bad-tempered men.'

I lit candles in the bedroom, too, and we went to bed together, with Debussy playing in the background. Our love-making was slo-mo, almost balletic. I loved the transparency of her skin, and the pale shine of her lips, and the flowery smell of perfume in her hair.

As she came close to her climax, she closed her eyes and opened her mouth wide, as if she were silently singing. There was a bottle of Armani aftershave on the window sill, and it started to rattle. It rattled more and more furiously until her hips began to spasm, and she clung to me, and pressed her face against my shoulder, and then it abruptly stopped.

'Has that always happened?' I asked her, with a grin. 'Or is it just when you make love to me?'

With one fingertip, she traced the outline of my lips. 'It never used to happen at all. Not when I was making love. Not when I was singing. Never.'

'So what do you think it is? It's like one of those Memorex commercials, when they used to make a wine glass shatter.'

'I don't know. Maybe it's ecstasy.'

She kept on touching my lips, and it was then that I knew that I was going to Stockholm next week, for sure.

Nine

On Saturday morning it was raining hard, and my apartment was very dark. I rolled out of bed with my hair sticking up like a scarecrow and shuffled into the kitchenette to make myself some very strong coffee. I hadn't been drinking the night before, but for some reason I felt thick-headed, as if I had a hangover. Maybe it was the thought of winter approaching.

I went into the living room and drew back the drapes. St Luke's Place was slate-gray and glistening wet and almost deserted. As I walked back toward the kitchenette, I saw a white envelope peeking under my front door. I bent down and picked it up. It was addressed in blue ink to *Mr Gideon Lake, Apt 2*. I shook it, and I could feel some weighty objects inside it.

I tore it open. Inside, there was an SAS air ticket, flight 904 to Stockholm Arlanda on Tuesday, returning on Tuesday the following week. Business class, costing $2,882. There was also a sheet of heavy white writing paper, with the name Dr Axel Westerlund on it, and the address

Skeppsbron 44, 111 30 Stockholm.

I turned the envelope upside down and two decorative brass keys dropped out into the palm of my hand. Not only had Kate given me the Westerlunds' address, she had given me access to their apartment, too.

I made myself a strong cup of espresso and sat by the window drinking it, while the raindrops slowly shuddered down the glass. I juggled the two keys in the palm of my hand. If Kate and I weren't going to be flying together, and the Westerlunds were going to be out at work when I arrived, I guess it made sense that I should be able to let myself in. But it seemed unusually trusting to give me their keys. The Westerlunds didn't know me from Adam, after all. And apart from two or three oblique conversations, and going to bed with me twice, Kate didn't really know me, either – any better than I knew her.

I took a shower, and pulled on some loose-fit jeans and a blue-and-white striped shirt, and played around on my keyboard. I was scoring the moment when Billy Wagner climbs into a horse-drawn carriage and the Bakersfield family gather around him to say goodbye, tossing up their hats and waving their handkerchiefs. I based the melody on an old British Boer War song *Goodbye, Dolly Gray.*

'*Goodbye, Dolly, I must leave you ... though it breaks my heart to have to go...*'

I couldn't think why, but the music just flowed out of me, as easily as if I had written it already. Before I composed that score, it usually took me hours to write only half-a-dozen bars. Hours?

Days, sometimes, and still I wasn't satisfied. I was my own pickiest critic, to the point where I really annoyed myself. But this morning I felt inspired. Uplifted, even. In fact I was enjoying myself so much that I had almost finished the entire score when my wall clock struck twelve and I remembered that Victor Solway had invited me downstairs for a drink at half after eleven. Shit. I brushed my hair, smacked on some Hugo Boss aftershave, and stepped into my loafers.

When I opened my front door, I found Malkin sitting right outside, so close that I nearly tripped over her. She looked up at me and gave me that thick, rattling purr.

'What do you want, puss? Are you checking up on me?'

Malkin retreated to the far side of the landing, but she didn't take her eyes off me.

'Where's your mistress?' I asked her. 'Sorry, I'm right out of tuna. But next time I go to Carmine Street, I'll bring you back some nice stinky swordfish, how about that? Stinky-winky swordfish?' You have to talk to cats in a language they understand.

Malkin closed her eyes disdainfully. I left her there, on the landing, and went downstairs. I could hear voices and laughter coming from the Solways' apartment. Tony Bennett, too, singing *Are You Havin' Any Fun*. I think if I ever feel like hanging myself, that will be the track I put on the CD player before I step off the kitchen chair.

I hesitated, thinking, do I really want to do this? But then I thought: come on, you're always

63

too antisocial. You have to learn to get along with people. Even people who admire Tony Bennett. So I knocked.

Victor opened the door so quickly I could have believed that he was standing on the other side waiting for me. He was wearing a pink checkered shirt and red jeans that were much too tight for him, so that his penis looked like a picnic-size polony.

'Gideon! You made it! I thought you might have forgot the address!'

He barked with laughter, and ushered me in.

'Jack – Sadie – this is our new *opstairsikeh*! Gideon – meet Jack Friendly. And this is the lovely Sadie!'

Jack and Sadie were sitting in the living room. Jack got up and shook my hand. He might have been Friendly by name but he didn't look particularly friendly by nature. He was forty-ish, not as tall as I was, but underneath his black designer coat and his black turtleneck sweater I could tell that he was very fit and well muscled. The kind of guy who could hit you very hard, if he wanted to.

He had greased-back hair, and an almond-shaped face, as if he had Asian blood in him. His nose was pointed, but very flat, like a falcon's beak. He was wearing three or four silver chains around his neck, with various pendants hanging from them: a heavy silver cross, a bunch of four or five silver dollars, and a hunched-up creature that looked like a baboon, with red crystals for eyes.

'Victor says you write music,' Jack challenged

64

me. He had a hoarse, strained voice, with a distinctive accent which I couldn't quite place. Philadelphia, maybe. 'Anything I might have heard?'

'Thom's Tomato Soup?' I suggested. 'Mother MacReady's Self-Raising Muffin Mix?'

Jack stared at me and his eyes were like polished gray stones. 'What are those? Like, jingles?'

'That's right.'

'I know that Thom's Tomato Soup one!' said Sadie. '"*Come on home, come on ho-o-ome ... to your family and your friends!*"'

Jack turned around. Although he didn't actually say 'shut the fuck up' out loud, the expression on his face said it for him.

Sadie said, 'I think it's *beautiful*, that song! It always makes me feel like calling my mom!'

'What would be the point? Your mom's a vegetable.'

'So we have a one-sided conversation? It still makes me feel like calling her.'

Sadie must have been about my age, but she looked at least five years older. She had bleach-ed-blonde hair with dark brunette roots, pinned up with sparkly zircon barrettes. She was quite pretty, in a bruised, cheap way, with a fake tan and blotchy mascara and a bright scarlet pout.

She was wearing a low-cut sweater in strident blue, and jeans that were even tighter than Victor's. Her breasts were enormous, squashed together in her sweater like two orange party balloons, and spattered with dozens of tiny moles.

Victor said, 'What's your poison, Gideon? Hey – I have some Thai whiskey if you're interested. One of my customers gave me a whole case of it. I didn't know whether to be flattered or insulted. Hey – at least I can "Thai" one on – get it?'

'White wine will be fine, thanks,' I told him. I was tempted to retaliate by calling him 'Vic'.

He went over to an antique-style sideboard and opened one of the doors to reveal a minibar. The whole living room was furnished with reproductions, although some of them were very high-quality ones, and must have cost almost as much as the originals. There was a huge Empire-style daybed, on which Sadie was sitting cross-legged, and three hefty armchairs, and a carved oak chest which served as a table. Everything was upholstered in dark crimson brocade, and even the walls were dark red, with gilt-framed oil paintings of sailing boats and racehorses and early explorers in the West Virginia wilderness.

I tried to imagine Kate in here, but somehow I couldn't. She was so feminine, and yet this room had no woman's touches at all. The only flowers were dried red chrysanthemums, under a glass dome on the mantelpiece, and there was no smell of perfume in the air, or pot-pourri, or even room-freshener.

'You must make a pretty good living, then, writing these jingle things?' said Jack. 'Apartments like this, you don't get them for peanuts.'

'I struck it lucky, I guess.'

'Like Victor here? Victor struck it real lucky, didn't you, Victor?'

Victor was opening a bottle of Stag's Leap

Chardonnay with one of those carbon-dioxide gadgets. He stopped long enough to point his index finger at Jack, almost as if he were aiming a pistol at him, and the look on his face was so malevolent that I thought at first that he was joking.

But Jack let out a hoarse, unconvincing laugh, and changed the subject straight away. 'Do you play the horses?' he asked me. 'There's a great nag running at Belmont Park this afternoon. Move The Cat, in the three twenty, fifteen to one.'

I shook my head. 'I only bet on the horses three times in the whole of my life. The first one threw its jockey, the second one ran around the wrong way, and the third one broke its leg and had to be put down, right there on the track.'

'Move The Cat,' Jack repeated, as if he hadn't been listening.

Victor handed me a large cut-crystal wine goblet with too much wine in it. Then he took hold of my elbow and said, 'Come and take the tour. You should see what I've done in the bedroom.'

He ushered me out of the living room and along the corridor. On either side there were framed photographs of Victor with various singers and TV stars. Victor shaking hands with The Fonz. Victor with his arm around a stooped, gray-haired man in glasses who looked suspiciously like Perry Como. Victor standing next to Mickey Rooney, trying to look as if he was an old friend of his.

He opened the door to the main bedroom. It

had been decorated as ornately as the living room, with a massive four-poster bed with twisty pillars, and heavy drapes in chocolate-colored velvet, and a large oil painting of a fat nude woman inexplicably milking a goat.

'This is what I always wanted,' said Victor. 'Classic, you know? Ornate. I don't have any time for that minimalist stuff. I had enough of minimalist when I was a kid. One couch, one broken chair. Three of us boys in one bed.'

He sniffed loudly, and looked around. 'Opulence, you know? That's what I go for. *Luxury*. A feeling of *pomp*.'

'It's pompous,' I agreed. 'I have to give you that.'

Victor put his arm around my shoulders and gripped me tight. I was looking around for photographs of Kate, but I couldn't see a single one, which was strange, since there were so many photographs of Victor.

Victor said, 'When I started out in real estate, I used to visit all of these uptown apartments, you know, and some of them, they were so luxurious, you only had to walk inside and your suit felt cheap and your shoes felt cheap and *you* felt cheap. I remember standing in this entrance hall on the Upper East Side, waiting for my client to show. It had brown marble floors and brown marble pillars, and I remember looking at this marble table and thinking, my whole year's salary wouldn't buy me that table. That *one* fucking table. And here was this apartment, this entire apartment, with a view over Central Park, and it was *crammed* with tables. Not only tables,

68

but chairs, and couches, and bookcases, and beds, and paintings, and statues and Christ alone knew what else.'

'Well, I know the feeling,' I told him, wishing he would stop squeezing my upper arm to emphasize every item of furniture. 'I started out in a studio on East Sixteenth. It was so small I had to climb out on the fire escape to get dressed.'

Victor at last let me go. He walked over to the bedroom window and looked out into the gray, rainy yard. There were sunflowers planted in the window box outside, bright yellow and blurry, and the rain was making them nod their heads. I wondered if Kate had planted them.

'I made myself a vow,' said Victor. 'I swore to myself that *I* was going to live like that. I was going to have all of that antique stuff, and my address was going to be so goddamned prestigious that I would never have to explain to nobody that I had class, and substance. Know what I mean by *substance*, Gideon? Substance, that's not just money, that's like *depth*. Money gets you envy. But substance gets you respect.'

He paused for a moment, still staring out of the window. 'There's only one thing that's lacking in my life. Can you guess what that is?'

'A boat? Your own private jet?'

He turned away from the window. He didn't look at all amused. 'Family,' he said, prodding my chest with his forefinger. 'Family – that's what's lacking. A Solway dynasty. Like, what is the point of having all of this fucking substance, if you don't have nobody to pass it on to? A son

69

to send to Princeton, and be a lawyer maybe, or the CEO of some investment bank, and give me about a dozen grandchildren. First-generation substance, that's OK. But second- and third-generation substance, now you're not just talking respect, you're talking *reverence*.'

'Surely it's not too late for you to have kids.'

'Nah,' he said, shaking his head, as if it was out of the question. He didn't explain why, but I strongly felt that this was not the moment to bring up the subject of the baby boy that he and Kate had lost.

'How about you?' he asked me. 'You going steady, or anything like that?'

'Not right now. Too busy to have a woman in my life.'

'You must be pretty damned successful, buying one of these apartments, at your age. How old are you?'

'Thirty-one. It's the hair that makes me look older.'

'No, I would have guessed thirty-one. I'm good at telling people's ages. It's not the color of their hair, it's their confidence. Older people don't scare so easy. You – you're still a little wary. Know what I mean by wary? But you're not scared of me, are you, Gideon?'

'Should I be?'

He gave me a carnivorous grin. 'Depends if you're straight with me. If you're straight with me, you don't have nothing to worry about.'

'Why wouldn't I be straight with you?'

'Exactly. Successful young man like you. Thirty-one, and bought your own apartment on

St Luke's Place. That's something.'

'Well ... I still have a long way to go,' I admitted. 'I just hit paydirt with a couple of songs, and I was looking to move to someplace quiet, with a whole lot more space. A friend of mine at CBS told me this place was coming up. I liked it – who wouldn't? – and that was it.'

Victor slapped me on the shoulder. 'You're a pretty spontaneous guy, Gideon. You don't take life too serious. I like that. Me – I like to have my fun, don't make any mistake. But underneath, you take my word for it, I'm totally focused. Totally, *totally* focused. You – what did you have to do get rich? – *blinkle, blinkle, blinkle* on the ivories, that's all. Don't get me wrong, you got natural talent. But me, I had to fight for what I got, inch by bloody inch. Iwo Jima wasn't in it. But I raised the flag in the end, Gideon. Just don't any bastard try to take it down again.'

'Right,' I said, raising my eyebrows, and I remembered what Kate had told me about Victor's temper. He didn't exactly frighten me, but at the same time I decided that it would probably be wiser not to rub him up the wrong way. Like by telling him that his bedroom looked like a nineteenth-century whorehouse, or that I was flying to Sweden to spend two weeks with his wife.

Ten

As I carried my shoulder bag out of the main entrance of Arlanda Airport, it was snowing. Not heavy snow, but light, mischievous whirls, like ghosts; and the wind was freezing.

Nothing prepares you for the head-breaking coldness of the air in Sweden, especially after nine hours sitting in an airplane. You can feel it slamming directly down from the Arctic, making your eyes water and your nose run, and your ears tingle so much that they hurt.

Nothing prepares you for the gloom, either, even at two o'clock in the afternoon, but then Stockholm is even further north than Moscow, and by late September winter is already setting in.

I stood in line for a Volvo taxi and it drove me due south to the city center. It was so hot in the taxi that I had to unbutton my coat, and the taxi driver reeked of cigarettes. Outside, I could see nothing but snow-covered fields, and pine forests, with only an occasional light shining through the branches. You have to wonder to yourself: who would want to live out here, so far from civilization, in the gathering darkness of a Scandinavian winter?

At last, however, we reached the suburbs. A

few clusters of small cement-colored houses at first, and then brightly-lit apartment blocks and shopping malls. Then we arrived at the city center, with its busy overpasses and crowded squares and its streets of tall, narrow, eighteenth-century houses.

'This is Old Town,' the taxi driver told me, as we drove around a square with a bronze fountain in the center. He pointed across a dark stretch of glittering water, to a tall brick building with a lantern-like tower. 'That is City Hall. That is where they talk all elk shit.' He gave a cigarette-thickened laugh, and turned around to wink at me.

We drove along Skeppsbron, the wide street overlooking the harbor. I could see three-masted sailing ships moored beside the dock, as well as yachts and motor launches. In the near distance, beyond the harbor, there was another island, with lights twinkling. Only a faint reddish streak remained in the sky to remind me that it was still daytime. I don't think I had ever felt so far away from home.

The taxi driver did a U-turn and pulled up outside an ochre-colored five-story building with an arched doorway and a decorative bay window.

'Three hundred forty-five kroner,' he announced. 'You want sex club?'

I tugged four hundred-kroner bills out of my wallet and handed them over. 'It's OK, thanks.'

'Chat Noir club, Birger Jarlsgatan. Very good live genuine sex.'

'Really, no thanks.'

'You want gay club?'

'No thanks. Just keep the change, OK?'

'How about restaurant? Fem Små Hus, Nygatan. Very good reindeer with lingonberry sauce.'

I climbed out of the cab and approached the front door of No. 44. There were three worn-down steps and the door itself was solid ten-panelled oak, bleached by hundreds of years of sunshine and salt, with a black iron knocker in the shape of a grinning troll. There were five doorbells, with tarnished brass name plaques beside three of them, but the plaque for the second floor, where the Westerlunds lived, was engraved with the name *B. Olofsson*. Maybe the Westerlunds had never bothered to change it.

I pushed the button and waited. For some reason the taxi driver hadn't driven away, but was still sitting in his cab, with the engine running, watching me. I pushed the button again.

Now I knew why Kate had given me the keys. It may have been dark, but it was only 3:35 in the afternoon, and the Westerlunds must have all been at work, or at school. I took the two keys out of my coat pocket, chose the larger one, and let myself in.

Inside, the hallway was gloomy and cold, with a flagstone floor. I managed to find a light switch, and it illuminated a bright clear-glass lantern hanging from the ceiling. On one side of the hallway stood a side-table, with a vase of cream silk roses on it, and a brass letter rack. On the other side hung a gold-framed mirror, blotchy with age like the surface of a stagnant pond, with a reflection of me in it, looking pale and tired and unsure of myself.

There was a *smell*, too, quite unlike New York. A smell of very old building, and coffee, and something that might have been cheese.

At the far end of the hallway I could make out a shadowy spiral staircase, with stone steps, leading upward. I picked up my bag and was just about to climb up to the second floor when there was a sharp knocking at the front door. I put down my bag and opened it.

It was the taxi driver, and he was smoking.

'Yes?' I asked him.

Smoke streamed out of his nostrils. 'You stay in this house?'

'That's the idea, yes. And, listen, I don't want to know about sex clubs or gay clubs or restaurants or any other tourist attractions, thank you.'

'You know what happen in this house?'

'No, I don't know what happened in this house, and to tell you the truth I don't care. Now, please, I'm very tired and I just want to get my bag upstairs.'

'If you know what happen in this house, you stay in hotel. I know good hotel. Amaranten, on Kungsholmsgatan. I fix you best room, cheap.'

'Please, no thank you,' I told him. 'Now, go away, will you?'

The taxi driver was about to say something else, but then he shrugged, and walked back toward his cab. Halfway across the sidewalk, however, he stopped, and turned around. 'I give you warning, remember that!'

'OK, OK. You give me warning. Now, goodbye, already.'

He shook his head one more time, climbed into

75

his taxi and drove away. Jesus. And I used to think that New York taxi drivers were persistent.

I closed the front door, picked up my bag yet again, and climbed up the spiral staircase. Halfway up to the second floor, the timer on the lights clicked off, and I was left in total darkness. I shuffled my way up the next few steps, keeping my left shoulder against the wall, and even then I took one too many steps when I reached the top, and stumbled forward into the darkness, colliding with another side table, and knocking something metallic on to the floor. It sounded like a vase.

Putting down my bag, I groped around the walls until I found a light switch. Another lantern showed me that I was standing on a long landing, with a narrow mustard-colored rug running along it. I had knocked over a tall copper jug, so that dried stalks of honesty had scattered across the floor. I picked them all up and re-arranged them as artistically as I could. Any broken bits and pieces I brushed up into my hand and dropped inside the jug.

At the end of the landing there was a wide black-painted door. I approached it, and took out my second key. The door unlocked almost silently, and I pushed it open. Inside the hallway, there was a table lamp with a green-and-yellow glass shade, which had obviously been left on for my benefit.

I carried my bag inside. Kate had been right. This apartment was vast, and awe-inspiring. The hall alone was nearly half the size of my living room at St Luke's Place, with a window which

76

looked out over the harbor, and a huge faded tapestry hanging on the wall, with an ocean scene of galleons and sea monsters and scudding clouds.

To the right of the hallway, a long corridor led to a wide pair of double doors, glazed with small octagonal panels of yellowish glass, and then further, to seven or eight more doors.

The apartment was warm, but very stuffy, and silent. I took off my overcoat and hung it over the back of a carved wooden chair. Kate had promised that she would arrive not long after me, and she had told me that I should make myself at home, but all the same I couldn't help feeling as if I were trespassing. A silver clock chimed a quarter of four, with a very fussy, elaborate melody.

I opened the double doors and stepped into the living room. Three table lamps had been left on in here, too, and I began to feel a little more welcome. The living room was at least forty feet long, with a bay window and two side windows, and a huge fireplace with a stone surround. It was furnished with three large couches, in pale Scandinavian oak, all of them upholstered in blue and gold, as if they had once belonged to some minor Swedish royalty. Between two of the couches stood a walnut table with a checkered top and chess pieces on it, and it looked as if the players were coming close to the end of their game. I picked up the red bishop and, strangely, he had his hand held over his eyes, as if he were grieving, or didn't want to look at me.

I wandered around the apartment for a while,

unsure of what I should do, cautiously opening doors and peering inside. The first door opened into a cloakroom, with at least a dozen coats and padded jackets in it, including three long black furs, and dozens of different walking sticks, and two pairs of snowshoes. The next door led into a broom closet, smelling of furniture polish. Then I discovered a restroom, with a mahogany-seated toilet that truly deserved to be called a throne, and a sepia stained-glass window. The cistern was gurgling softly to itself, and the faucet was dripping.

Four doors along the corridor I found the kitchen, which was tiled floor-to-ceiling with blue-and-white ceramic tiles. Against the left-hand wall stood a stainless-steel range with a polished brass handrail, like a Central Pacific locomotive, and almost the same size. Scores of ladles and sieves and shiny brass saucepans hung from the ceiling, and on the massive oak hutch there was a gathering of antique kitchen gadgets whose purpose I couldn't even guess at.

I picked up one of the gadgets, which looked like a cafetière, except that it had a double-jointed brass handle attached to it. I tried pumping the handle up and down to see what it was supposed to do. It made a sharp squeaking noise, but I still couldn't work out what it was for. Slicing coleslaw? Churning yogurt? But as I pumped it faster and faster I thought I heard somebody crying. I stopped, and listened. Silence, for a moment, but then I heard it again. A child's voice. A young girl's, very high, very distressed.

I carefully put the gadget down, and went to the kitchen door. I could hear a child talking and sobbing at the same time, although I couldn't understand what she was saying. It sounded as if she were down at the far end of the corridor, where one of the doors was slightly ajar, and I could see a dim light flickering, like the light from a candle.

I thought: go easy now, dude. If there's a young girl in this apartment, you need to be extremely careful, especially if she's hysterical.

I walked along the corridor until I reached the room where the crying had been coming from. I knocked, and called out, 'Hallo? My name's Gideon! I was invited to spend the week with your parents! Is everything OK?'

I waited, but the crying had stopped now, and there was no answer. I knocked again. 'Is everything all right in there? I thought I heard somebody crying.'

Still no answer. The poor girl probably didn't understand a word I was saying, and was sitting there terrified. Very slowly, I pushed open the door, and said, 'It's OK ... I'm a friend of your parents. I won't hurt you, honestly.'

Inside the room there was an old-fashioned wooden bed with a high headboard and a multi-colored patchwork quilt. Beside it was a wooden chest with heaps of dolls sitting on top of it, most of them home-made rag dolls with mad grinning faces. A single candle was flickering in a glass bowl, almost down to the end of its wick.

A royal-blue dressing-gown had been thrown across the end of the bed, but there was no sign of its owner, nor anybody else. No crying girl. In fact, no girl at all.

I ducked down sideways and looked under the bed. Nobody. Then I went across to the painted wooden clothes closet. I hesitated for a moment or two, and then opened it. Nobody in there, either.

If there *had* been a crying girl in here, she must have climbed out of the window. I went to look out. The window was bolted top and bottom, from the inside, and the window ledge outside was only a couple of inches wide, and covered in rotten lead. Apart from that, it was a sheer drop down to a very narrow alleyway, with nothing at all that anybody could have clung on to. Thirty feet below I could see people jostling their way up and down the alleyway with woolly hats on, and scarves wound round their necks. It was dark out there, and growing colder all the time.

I blew out the candle before I left the bedroom. Then I went back to the living room. I might as well watch some TV before Kate showed up. Maybe I could catch up with some Swedish news, and even practice a few words of the language. I had bought a Swedish phrase book at Newark airport, and tried to familiarize myself with 'good morning' and 'good evening' and 'where can I get beaten with birch twigs?' but I had discovered from my first few minutes on Swedish soil that the Swedes don't pronounce their language anything like they spell it. I had said *'talar du engelska?'* to the female customs officer at Arlanda and she had said, coldly, 'Sorry, sir, I do not speak Greek.'

I went back to the kitchen to see if I could find myself a beer. I was sure that the Westerlunds wouldn't begrudge me one bottle of Pripps. There was a huge old-fashioned Electrolux fridge in the corner of the kitchen, but when I opened it, I found that it was completely empty. Not even a bottle of mineral water.

I checked my watch. Maybe I should venture out and find myself a bar. But then Kate should be here at any moment, and I didn't really relish the idea of drinking in an unfamiliar city on my own, like some lonely salesman.

It seemed strange, though, that the Westerlunds should have nothing in their refrigerator at all. Even if you eat in restaurants every single night of the week, you always have *something* in the refrigerator, even if it's nothing more than a few shriveled tomatoes and a triangle of moldy Kraft cheese.

I settled for a mug of water, from the kitchen faucet. It was very cold and very clear, and made my teeth ache. Then I went back into the living room.

As soon as I walked through the door, I stopped dead. Two young girls were sitting at the walnut table, playing chess together.

Eleven

Both girls were blonde, although one of them had slightly darker hair than the other. One was about eleven years old, I would have guessed, and the other was maybe nine. The older one wore jeans and a scarlet cable-knit sweater. The younger one was wearing a dark blue woolen dress, and dark blue knitted leggings.

'Hi, there,' I said. They didn't seem to hear me, so I walked across to them, and stood beside the table.

'Hi, there. My name's Gideon. I've come to stay for a few days.'

Still they didn't seem to hear me. They didn't even look up, so I began to think that maybe they couldn't see me, either.

Eventually, I said, 'Which one of you is Felicia?'

At last the younger one lifted her face and stared at me. She was very white, almost anemic, and her hair was cut in the straightest of pageboys. Her eyes were pale blue, but swollen and pink, so I guessed that she was the one who had been crying.

'Me – *I* am Felicia.'

'OK ... so this must be Elsa, right?'

Elsa looked up, too. Her caramel-colored hair

was elaborately braided, as if she were prepared to appear in some Scandinavian opera about trolls and gods and Vikings with horns on their helmets. She was pretty, too, with a high forehead and wide-apart eyes and a mouth that was wonderfully sulky. When Elsa grew a few years older, she would have men walking into lampposts.

'I did not know that anybody was coming here to stay,' she said. Her English was almost perfect, although her Swedish accent made her sound as if she were trying to talk and drink a smoothie at the same time.

'Nobody *told* you two guys?' I asked her.

'*Nej*,' they both echoed, shaking their heads.

'They should have. If you're anything like me, you don't like surprises. Especially strange men appearing in your home without any warning.'

'No, I do not like that, either,' Elsa agreed, with an odd, sideways look that for some reason reminded me of Kate.

'Do you like music?' I asked her, trying to change the subject.

'*I* like music,' Felicia chipped in. 'I won the singing prize at my school. I sang *Ack Värmeland Du Sköna* and I won ten CD tokens.'

'Yes,' said Elsa. 'And you traded them all for two Barbies and a Barbie house.'

'So what is so wrong about *that*?' Felicia retaliated.

'Barbie is a bad role model, that's what.'

I pulled a face. 'Bad role model, hunh? You're talking about all of those trashy clothes she wears? All of those gold miniskirts and silver high-heeled boots?'

'No, I mean that all Barbie cares about is material possession. Things like house, and car, and roller-boot. Barbie has no spirit.'

Kind of serious for an eleven-year-old, I thought, but then she *was* Swedish. 'I see where you're coming from,' I told her. 'But she's only a plastic doll, after all. She doesn't even have a brain.'

'Like Elsa,' laughed Felicia, pointing at her sister.

'Still, I'm glad you like music,' I said. 'That's what *I* do. That's my job, writing music. Maybe this evening I can play some music and you can sing for me. I can teach you a couple of new songs.'

'Do you know any songs about people who are lost and do not know how to find their way back?' asked Elsa.

I looked at her carefully, trying to work out exactly what it was she was asking me. 'I'm not sure. I guess I know *The Whiffenpoof Song* – "we are three little lambs who have lost our way – Baa! Baa! Baa".'

Felicia laughed again, but Elsa remained serious.

'I mean songs that they can sing, so that the people who remember them will hear them, and know that they have not gone for ever.'

'I'm sorry, Elsa. I don't think I know any songs like that.'

Elsa didn't answer, but looked down at the chessboard.

'Who's winning?' I asked her, gently. I could

tell that something had upset her.

'Nobody.'

'How come?'

'Because nobody ever wins. Because we never have time to finish it.'

Felicia said, 'You cheat, anyhow. Whenever I have to go to the bathroom she hides my prawns.'

'*Pawns*,' said Elsa, as if she were tired of telling her. ' "Prawns" is *räka*.'

I said nothing for a while. I was tempted to lay my hand on top of Elsa's, just to comfort her and show her that I cared about whatever it was that was bugging her. But of course it wouldn't have been a good idea.

'Did I hear Felicia crying a short while back?' I asked her.

Elsa shook her head. 'No. We never cry now.'

'Never? Why not? Sometimes it can do you good, to have a darn good cry. I do it all the time.'

'You do?' asked Felicia, in amazement.

'For sure. I was moving into a new apartment not long ago, and I dropped a packing case right on my foot. You should have heard me howl!'

Felicia giggled, but Elsa looked at me with the ghost of a smile and said, 'You are telling a lie.'

'Yes. But sometimes it doesn't matter, telling a lie. Sometimes telling a lie is the only way we can face up to the truth.'

'You think this?'

'Yes, I think this. And I'll tell you what I'm going to do, Elsa. I'm going to write a song especially for you, about people who are lost and can't find their way back. Whenever you sing this song, you can think of me. And whenever I hear it, I'll know that you're not too far away. Okey-dokey-chimney-smokey?'

At last I got her to laugh. She had a really cute way of doing it, pressing her fingertips against her lips, as if she were trying to push the laughter back in.

'Check,' said Felicia, moving her queen two squares.

'And you say that *I* cheat!' Elsa protested. 'Your queen wasn't there at all!'

'Of course she was! You weren't looking, that's all!'

The two of them were still squabbling when I heard the front door opening, and Kate calling out, 'Hello? Gideon? Are you there?'

'Hold on, girls,' I told them, and went out of the living room door into the hallway. Kate was there, wearing an ankle-length silver-fox coat, and a matching hat, with ear flaps. Her cheeks were pink from the cold.

'Look at you!' I said. 'You look like Lara out of *Doctor Zhivago*!'

'I'm sorry if we kept you waiting too long,' she smiled at me, and gave me a very chilly kiss. 'We had to go to Stortorget to buy some food ... otherwise we would have had nothing for supper tonight!'

She tugged off her black leather gloves, and turned, and as she did so I realized that there were more people coming along the landing, carrying grocery bags. A bearded man in a long black coat; a woman in a puffy red windbreaker

86

and black leggings; and two young girls, one wearing a blue windbreaker and the other a yellow one, both of them giggling.

The landing light was behind them, and so it was only when they crowded into the hallway that I realized who the giggling girls were. I had the same feeling as standing in an elevator which suddenly drops down fifteen floors without any warning. They were Elsa and Felicia. There was no question about it. Although they were both wearing white furry earmuffs, Elsa had the same Valkyrie braids, and Felicia had the same straight pageboy.

I stared at Kate, totally stunned, but she didn't seem to notice.

'Gideon – I want you to meet Dr Axel Westerlund, and his wife Tilda, and their two daughters Elsa and Felicia. Everybody ... this is my friend Gideon from New York!'

Dr Westerlund took off his glove and held out his hand to me. His beard was tinged with gray which made him look older than he actually was. He couldn't have been more than thirty-seven or thirty-eight, with a broad handsome face and brambly gray eyebrows and deep-set green eyes. It wasn't difficult to see who Elsa had inherited her looks from.

'*Hej*, Gideon!' he said, and gave me a muscular handshake. 'Kate was telling us so much about you.'

'Oh, yes?' I was so confused that I couldn't think what else to say.

'You are composer, yes? She says you write beautiful music.'

'*Almost* beautiful,' Kate corrected him. 'You can't compose truly beautiful music to advertise baked beans.'

I tried to turn around and take a look back into the living room, but Axel grasped my elbow and said, 'This is my wife Tilda. Tilda works at St Göran's Hospital, in the pain clinic.'

Tilda smiled and said, '*Hej*, Gideon! Welcome to Stockholm.' She was a very petite woman, blonde and pale, like Felicia, with strikingly unusual looks. Her nose was a little too long and pointed to be conventionally pretty, but her eyes were huge and mesmerizing, like two dark ponds you could drown in.

'The pain clinic, huh?' I asked her. 'That sounds pretty painful.'

'That is what I do,' said Tilda, with great seriousness. 'I ease people's pain. To me, easing people's pain is the most important of all things in the world.'

I mentally kicked myself for being flippant, but I was finding it difficult to think about anything else but Elsa and Felicia. I had just left them playing chess in the living room, only a few seconds ago, and yet here they were again, freshly arrived from shopping. I was so thrown by the whole illogicality of it that I couldn't decide if I was asleep or awake. Maybe I was still sitting on SAS flight 904, high up over the Arctic, snoring, with my head leaning on the shoulder of the passenger next to me.

But – 'This is Elsa,' said Tilda. 'And this is her younger sister Felicia.'

I took the girls' hands, one after the other, and

kissed the back of their wrists. 'Very pleased to meet two such delightful young ladies,' I told them. I could feel the warmth of their hands, where they had been buried in their thick padded mittens, and they certainly didn't *feel* like characters out of a dream.

Kate took off her coat and gave me another hug. 'It's so good to see you, Gideon. How was your flight?'

'Great. Very comfortable. They even fed us with caviar. When did *you* get in?'

Kate gave me another kiss. 'Tilda's going to cook her special meatballs for supper. I hope you're starving! Here – could you carry this shopping for me?'

I picked up her shopping bags and followed her along the corridor toward the kitchen. When I reached the living room doors, however, I sidestepped and looked inside. There was nobody in there. No Elsa. No Felicia. And the chess pieces were all arranged just as they had been when I first arrived.

'Come on,' said Kate. 'Is anything wrong? You look very serious.'

'I always look very serious. It's my default expression.'

Axel took everybody's coats and hung them up in the cloakroom, while Tilda and Kate went into the kitchen and started to unpack the groceries. Elsa and Felicia rushed to their bedrooms, and I could hear them laughing and chattering in Swedish. I wished that I could understand what they were saying to each other.

'You would like a drink?' Axel asked me,

coming into the kitchen.

'Absolutely. One of your Swedish beers would go down well.'

'I have only Finnish beer, I'm afraid. Lapin Kulta. We Swedes always prefer Finnish beer. Mind you, the Finns themselves prefer Norwegian beer while the Norwegians always buy their beer from Estonia. It is a kind of musical chairs of beer.'

Kate and Tilda were unwrapping ground beef and smoked fish and purple broccoli. I laid my hand on Kate's shoulder and gave her a kiss. It was great to see her, and I couldn't believe how much I had missed her. The only trouble was, her arrival here had given a sense of reality to an event that couldn't possibly have been real. Axel and Tilda had only two daughters, not four. So who had I been talking to in the living room?

'Kate told me what an incredible apartment you live in,' I told Axel, as he passed me a glass of beer. 'She was right. I've never seen any place like it.'

'Well, it was in the Westerlund family for over a hundred and thirty years,' said Axel. 'Passed down, from one generation of Westerlunds to the next. There are so many photographs of my grandparents and my great-grandparents, sitting on the window seats, looking out over Norrström harbor. And myself, too, when I was a child, in a little sailor suit.'

He led me into the living room. He lifted seven or eight hardwood logs out a large brass scuttle beside the fireplace, and stacked them into the grate. Then he took a copy of *Dagens Nyheter* from the magazine rack, crumpled it up, and pushed it underneath the fire basket.

'I understand that Felicia is good at music,' I told him. He was patting his pockets, looking for his matches.

'Felicia? Yes ... she won a school prize for her singing.'

I sipped my beer. I was going to have to be careful how I phrased this. The beer, incidentally, tasted like watered-down Bud. Or even watered-down water.

'Have you known Kate for long?' I asked him.

'Kate? Hm, for a little while.' He scratched a match into flame and lit two corners of the crumpled-up newspaper.

'I guess I was just wondering why she invited me here to meet you.'

There was a long silence. Axel stood up, staring down at the hearth, while the dancing flames were reflected in his eyes.

'You are a friend of hers, *ja*?'

'Yes. A new friend, admittedly. But a very *good* friend. At least I hope I am, anyhow.'

Axel sat down in a large armchair opposite me. The arms of the chair were carved like oak leaves, and he kept rubbing them, and fondling their curves. In the fireplace, the dry logs began to spit and crackle, and sparks flew up the chimney.

'Do you have a family?' Axel asked me. 'Do you have children of your own?'

'No. Never quite happened. But I guess I still have plenty of time.'

'Yes. But maybe, until you have children of

your own, you cannot understand what sacrifices you are prepared to make to keep them safe.'

I waited for him to explain himself, but he didn't. Instead, he said, 'You are enjoying your Lapin Kulta?'

I raised my glass. 'Terrific. Never quite tasted anything like it.'

'Be careful,' he cautioned me. 'It's strong. We don't want you falling over.'

The fire blazed more fiercely. One of the logs began to make a high, piping noise, like an asthmatic child fighting for breath.

'You still haven't told me why Kate invited me here,' I coaxed him.

He looked me in the eye for the first time since he had started to light the fire. 'You have to witness what happened for yourself. There is no other way around it. I cannot explain. I cannot accuse.'

'Accuse? I don't understand you. Accuse *who*? Of what?'

But before he could answer me, Kate and the girls came into the living room. The girls were dressed differently from before – Elsa in a scarlet sweater and a short denim skirt, Felicia in a skinny blue sweater and jeans. Felicia kept putting the neck of her sweater into her mouth and chewing it, the way kids do.

'It's all coming together in the kitchen,' said Kate, perching herself on the arm of my chair and running her fingers into the back of my hair. 'How are you two getting along?'

'Well, we're trying to find some common

92

ground,' I told her. 'Gynecology and song-writing – they're kind of opposite ends of the conversational spectrum. Unless you count, *Yes, Sir, She's My Baby*.'

I was trying to lighten the mood, but Axel didn't seem to get the joke. 'Elsa – Felicia—' he said. 'Please to set the table in the dining room.'

'Which place mats, Papa?'

'Any you can find.'

Once the girls had gone, Kate and Axel and I sat together in front of the fire. I tried to think of a way to explain that I had talked to Elsa and Felicia here in the living room, before they had actually come home. But Axel had talked so gravely about protecting his children that I thought he would probably find it unsettling, rather than amusing.

And who could say for sure if I had really seen them at all? Maybe I had experienced some kind of weird déjà-vu. After all, it might have been 4:00 p.m. in Stockholm, but it was still 10:00 a.m. in New York.

'So, Gideon!' said Axel, summoning up a smile. 'You must play us some of your music this evening, and sing us some of your songs.'

'Of course. I promised Elsa that I would make up a special song, just for her.'

Axel looked quizzical. 'You did? When did you do this?'

Oh, shit. 'I mean, when I heard you had two daughters, I promised myself that I would make up a special song for them.'

'That is very thoughtful of you, Gideon. We look forward to it.'

93

Kate took hold of my hand and squeezed it, and smiled at me. Maybe *she* knew what was going on here. I was double-damned if I did.

As far as our conversation was concerned, our meal that evening was like *A Dream Play*, by the Swedish playwright August Strindberg, which is all about a girl who comes from another world to find out if life is really as difficult as people make out. The characters change their identities, and merge, and say things like, 'Who lives in the tower?' 'I can't remember.' 'I think it's a prisoner and he wants me to set him free.'

In other words, one of those plays that you can't make heads nor tails of, and makes you wish you'd stayed at home and watched *The Simpsons* instead.

But the food was tasty, and the dining room was wonderfully gloomy and atmospheric. Although the ceiling was so high, Axel lit only two candelabra on the table, with five candles in each. The cutlery and the glassware sparkled, and the white linen shone, but we were surrounded on all sides by darkness, so that it was more like a séance than a supper.

'Tilda,' I said, forking up another mouthful of meatball. 'You are the best cook I ever met in my life. These meatballs are out of this world.'

'I miss to make them,' she said.

'Don't you make them very often? If I could make meatballs like this, I'd be cooking them for breakfast, lunch and dinner, every day.'

Tilda shrugged. 'They are a good family meal, when everybody is together.'

'Well, you have a great family. Two beautiful daughters.'

Elsa and Felicia giggled again, but Axel turned away, frowning, as if he thought he could see something in the shadows that he didn't like the look of.

Kate took hold of my hand. 'Glad you came?' she asked me.

'Of course I am. Sorry if I'm a little laggy. I don't know where you get all your energy from. Did you fly in yesterday?'

She leaned over and kissed me on the cheek. 'You're not going to be too tired to play for us, are you? I love *The One-Handed Clock*.'

'Sure, I can play that for you. And I promised Elsa that I'd make up a special song for her.'

Elsa smiled at me, her eyes bright in the candlelight. Tilda smiled, too. Axel, however, was still staring into the corner of the room, although all I could see in the darkness was a high-backed chair, and a painting of a light-house, beside a bleak gray ocean.

In the living room, between the two tall windows, stood a Malmsjö upright piano. I sat down, opened up the lid, and played a few scales. The piano was slightly off-tune, but it was overstrung and underdamped, and had a very sweet tone to it, just right for *The One-Handed Clock*, and a sentimental song about people who are lost and can never find their way back.

Kate sat next to me on the long piano stool, while Tilda and the girls arranged themselves on

95

one of the sofas. Axel stood alone by the darkened window, staring out at the harbor lights. He had hardly spoken a word since we had finished our supper, and he definitely seemed to be anxious about something.

Again, I felt inspired, and the music that came out of my fingers was so perfect and so poignant that I found it hard to believe that I had composed it myself. For Elsa's song, I plagiarized my own score for Mother Kretchmer's Frozen Scrapple. Apart from making you want to buy frozen scrapple, it was one of those melodies that make you feel warm and secure, and hopeful, too.

'I call this song *The Pointing Tree*,' I announced, and played a soft, slow introduction. 'I wrote it especially for a lovely young girl I met in Stockholm ... a girl I will always remember for her laugh and her smile ... and the way that her younger sister was always hiding her prawns.

' *"I don't know how it happened ... I didn't mean to roam ... but I was walking through the forest ... and I lost my way back home..."* '

'Oh, Gideon,' Kate teased me. 'This is so *sad*.'

'It's meant to be. But listen. *"I came into a clearing ... and there in front of me ... was a tree that pointed homeward ... and a skylark sang to me...*

' *"The Pointing Tree will guide you ... along the forest track ... your loved ones soon will weep with joy ... so pleased to have you back.*

' *"The forest may be tangled ... but every time you stray ... you can always find a Pointing Tree*

... to help you find your way.'''

I played a last gentle scattering of notes, and then sat back.

'What do you think?' I asked Elsa.

But it was Axel who answered me. 'There is no such tree. Once you are lost, there is no way back.'

'Hey ... it's only a song.'

'Yes. But songs put hope into people's hearts. Even when there *is* no hope.'

'I'm sorry, Axel. I didn't intend to upset you. Listen, if you know any really miserable Swedish songs about people who get lost and can *never* find their way home, I'd be happy to play them for you.'

'I *liked* my song,' Elsa protested. 'And I think there *is* a Pointing Tree.'

'It's absurd,' snapped Axel. 'And look at the time. You girls should have gone to bed an hour ago.'

'What difference does it make?' said Elsa.

'The difference is that I am your father and you have to do what I tell you.'

'Why? What can you do to me if I say no?'

'You know the answer to that,' Axel told her. I couldn't believe how agitated he had suddenly become. He was breathing hard and he kept jerking his head to one side as if he were suffering from some sort of spasm. 'It is the family ... it is your mother and your sister ... you want them to suffer for ever? Do *you* want to suffer for ever?'

Kate stood up and went over to Axel. She took hold of his arm and said, 'Axel ... don't get so upset. *Please*. Everything's going to work out fine, so long as you're patient.'

Axel lowered his head for a moment, although he was still breathing like a man who has run up three flights of stairs. 'You ask me to be patient? I do not believe that I have a second of patience left in me. Not a second.'

Tilda came up to him, too, and said something soothing in Swedish. *'Du må inte oro så mycket ... vi all älska du ... flikama och jag.'*

'I know,' Axel told her, patting her hand. 'But sometimes I cannot believe that this will ever end.'

Twelve

That night, well past eleven o'clock, we could hear Axel and Tilda having an argument, although the apartment walls were too thick to be able to make out anything but muffled shouting. After ten minutes or so, their bedroom door was noisily opened, and we heard Axel shouting, *'Vill du tro på vad hon saga? Jag inte!'* But then the door was slammed shut again.

'Do you know what he's saying?' I asked Kate.

She nodded. 'He's asking Tilda if she believes what I've been telling them. He says that *he* doesn't.'

'So what *have* you been telling them?'

98

'I've been telling them to keep the faith, that's all.'

'But why? What's bugging Axel so much? They seem like a perfectly happy family to me.'

'That's the trouble.'

I was sitting up in bed, watching Kate brush her hair in front of the dressing-table mirrors. I could see three Kates – four, if you counted the real one as well as the reflections. She was wearing a simple white nightdress with a scalloped lace collar, which made her look even younger and more enchanting than ever.

The bedroom suite that Axel and Tilda had given us was huge, and dimly lit. We had a massive four-poster bed, with green tapestry hangings, and a couch like a Viking longboat heaped with cushions. Next door, the bathroom was vast, more like a green-and-white-tiled cathedral than a bathroom. We had sat together in foaming pine-scented water, right up to our necks, and sung an echoing duet of *'love ... ageless and evergreen ... seldom seen by two...'*

But now that we were alone together, there were so many questions that I needed Kate to answer for me; and as tired as I was, I knew that I wasn't going to be able to get to sleep tonight until she did.

I climbed off the bed and stood close behind her, so that there were three of me as well as three of her, and I laid my hands on her shoulders. They were so bony, under her thin linen nightdress, and she smelled of flowers.

'I know what you're going to ask me,' she said. 'You're going to ask me the *real* reason why I invited you to come here and meet the Westerlunds.'

'That, and a few other things, yes.'

'Will you be angry if I ask you to wait and see?'

'Angry? I don't know about *angry*. Confused, yes. And more than a little spooked, if you want to know the truth.'

'Spooked? Why should you be spooked?'

'Well ... you're probably not going to believe this, but I met Elsa and Felicia in the living room, about five minutes before you guys got home from your shopping. You don't think *that's* spooky? Because I sure do.'

She turned around and looked up at me. 'Is that what happened?'

Now, if somebody had told *me* that, I would have said, 'Say again?' or 'You're *shitting* me,' or 'How many glasses of schnapps did you drink at supper?' But Kate seemed completely calm about it.

'I thought I might have been dreaming,' I told her. 'Or jet-lagged, maybe. Or God alone knows what. But I swear on my mother's life that when I first arrived here I walked into the living room and there were Elsa and Felicia, playing chess.'

'Did you talk to them?'

'Sure. Felicia told me that she had won a singing prize at school, and Elsa told me that she wanted me to write a song for her. Then the front door opened and you came in, with Axel and Tilda, and with Elsa and Felicia, too. I looked into the living room, but Elsa and Felicia weren't there any more – and the chessmen were right back where they had been before. Now is that spooky or is that spooky?'

Kate turned away for a moment, the same way that Axel had, at supper. Then she said, 'What's *your* explanation?'

'*My* explanation? I don't have an explanation. That's why I'm asking *you*.'

She looked back up at me. 'You didn't mention it to Axel or Tilda.'

'Are you putting me on? I didn't want them to think that I was out on license from Bellevue psychiatric wing.'

'Perhaps it *was* a dream. Or a kind of a dream.'

'Oh, yes? And maybe I can fly back to New York and get there before I leave.'

Kate stood up, and gently touched my face, as if she were blind, and she was trying to discover what I really looked like. God, I loved those eyes. They reminded me of gray days and walks along wintry seashores, and that time of day when it gradually grows too gloomy to read, and you don't switch on the light, but close the book instead.

'Do you trust me?' she said, and there was a little catch in her throat, which she had to cough to clear.

'Of course I trust you. Is there any reason why I shouldn't? It's just that this is all so goddamned *weird*. You giving me the Westerlunds' keys like that. Flying here separately. Elsa and Felicia. *Two* Elsas, for Christ's sake, and *two* Felicias. And I was talking to Axel, too, and he kept saying stuff about children, and how you had to make sacrifices to keep them safe. And then he

101

was staring into the corner, all through supper, didn't you notice that? It was like he could see a ghost standing there.'

I paused, and gestured toward the door. 'And then Axel and Tilda arguing like that. I mean, for Christ's sake, Kate, what's really going down here?'

'We're here to help,' she told me. 'That's all I can tell you.'

'We're here to help? How? If you ask me, this family needs therapy.'

'That's a good way of putting it, as a matter of fact. Therapy brings healing, doesn't it? Or closure. Or an acceptance that things aren't going to get any better, no matter what.'

'Meaning?'

'Meaning that I'm asking you to wait and see. Before you understand, you have to *know*.'

'But come on, Kate. How the hell can you expect me to *know*, unless you tell me?'

'Because you have eyes, Gideon, and you have ears, and unlike most people you're very aware of everything that goes on around you. But you have much more than that. You have a very rare gift.'

'Oh, really?' I asked her, suspiciously. 'What kind of a very rare gift?'

She kissed me, on my cheek, and then my lips.

'You have music in your whole being. You don't even realize how much. You don't just write music, you *live* music ... You *are* music. There are so few people like you. I'll tell you one very famous one: Mel Tormé. He could hear a plate dropping in a restaurant kitchen and tell

102

you precisely what key it was.'

'I still don't understand what you're saying.'

'Since you and I have been together, don't you think that you've been writing better?'

I nodded. 'Yes, I have. Yes. I mean, I don't like to boast, but eat your heart out, Mozart.'

'And can you think why?'

'I don't know. I put it down to being happier, I guess.'

She kissed me again. 'I'm pleased. But it's more than that. You can *feel* me. You can feel the emotions inside of me – my grief, and my affection, and my hope, in just the same way that you can hear music. Like Elsa and Felicia. You can feel *their* resonance, too. What they were, what they wanted to be. What they are now.

'When you see them, when you touch them, they come to life. They appear because you're here.'

I looked at her narrowly. I was gradually beginning to get some germ of what she was talking about. I was gradually beginning to realize that I could only understand what was happening to me if I understood myself, and what I was capable of. And according to Kate, I was capable of much more than I had ever dreamed.

'It's not just your music that's blossoming,' she added, with a smile. 'It's *you*.'

'Oh, yes? How, exactly?'

'Take me to bed, and I'll show you.'

I was woken by the sound of somebody running past our bedroom. Somebody with bare feet, running very fast. I sat up but it was so dark that

I couldn't see anything at all. Nothing, just total blackness.

I heard the runner again, and then another one. It sounded like children, both running in the same direction, from the bedrooms toward the hallway.

'Kate?' I whispered, and shook her shoulder. *'Kate!'*

But Kate continued to breathe deeply and steadily and didn't stir. I reached out toward my nightstand, trying to locate my wristwatch, but I knocked over my glass of water and I heard it pouring on to the carpet.

More running, and then bumping noises, too, as if the children were colliding with the sides of the corridor.

'Kate!' I said, and shook her again.

She stirred, and said, *'Wha...?* What is it?'

'Listen! It sounds like the girls are running all around the apartment!'

'What?'

I found the lamp beside my bed and switched it on. My wristwatch said it was 3:11 a.m. Kate was blinking at me as if she had never seen me before in her life.

'What's happening?' she said.

'It's the girls. They keep running up and down.'

'What?'

'Listen – there they go again. And they're bumping into the walls, too!'

I started to get out of bed but Kate took hold of my arm. 'Gideon – leave them. Whatever they're doing, it's no concern of ours.'

'Come on – what if something's wrong? Supposing there's a fire or something?'

'There isn't a fire. You don't smell smoke, do you?'

'So what are they doing? Sleepwalking? Or sleep *sprinting*, more like.'

We heard bare feet rushing up the corridor yet again, and this time one of the runners banged right into our door. There was a wail of pain, and then a high voice shrilled out, *'Inte röra jag! Låta jag gå!'*

This was followed by more running and more bumping.

I swung off the bed and went across the room to the door. 'Gideon—' said Kate, and reached out her hand toward me, but then lowered it again, as if she were accepting that I was going to take a look outside, no matter what. Which I was.

I opened the door. The corridor itself was in darkness, but the hallway at the far end of it was illuminated by cold white moonlight, shining in through the window that overlooked the harbor. There must have been clouds passing across the moon, and passing quite quickly, because the light faded and brightened every few seconds. One second brilliant and blurry, the next second nothing but shadows.

Standing in the hallway in a white nightdress, her arms outspread, was Elsa. Her hair was no longer braided, but waving loose. I thought at first that the window was open, because her hair kept rippling, as if the wind were blowing it. One moment I could see her staring at me, and the next her face was completely obscured. But her eyes when I could see them were like milky glass marbles, pale blue, rather than eyes, and her mouth was tightly closed, as if she were trying to prevent somebody from force-feeding her.

'Elsa?' I called out. 'Elsa – are you OK?'

I started to walk toward her. As I did so, she began to shake her head from side to side. She did it slowly at first, but as I approached her she shook it faster and faster.

'Elsa – listen – you're sleepwalking. You need to get yourself back to bed.'

I held out my hand to calm her. Abruptly, she stopped shaking her head, and stared at me with those colorless eyes, as if she couldn't understand who or even *what* I was. But now that I was really close to her I realized that she was just as tall as I was, if not taller. Not only that, she was much *bigger* than she had been before.

I began to feel distinctly unnerved. But I thought to myself, this is some kind of optical illusion, that's all. Perspective playing tricks on you. You know how small this girl is really. Maybe it's something to do with the window, or the sight lines in the corridor. Maybe *I'm* the one who's still asleep.

'Elsa?' I said.

She came closer, so that she was almost touching me, but she appeared to do it without actually taking a step. I saw then that she was soaking wet. There were drops of water clinging to her eyelashes, her hair was bedraggled, and her nightdress was drenched, so that it clung to her.

'Elsa, what's wrong? How did you get wet like that?'

She paused for a moment, and it seemed as if she were swaying slightly.

'*Hjälpa mig*,' she said, in a high, thick whisper.

'What? I'm sorry, I don't understand.'

'*Hjälpa mig! Jag kan icke andas! Jag er drunkna!*'

'You're drunk? Is that it? Listen, sweetheart, I need to wake up your parents. You just hold on here for a moment. Kate? Kate, are you there?'

I turned around to see if Kate was following me. As I did so, both Elsa and Felicia came running toward me along the corridor, both wearing nightdresses, both barefoot, both panic-stricken. They stumbled and collided with the walls, as if somebody were pushing them, and Felicia ran into a tall three-legged display-stand, so that the bronze statuette on top of it went flying across the floor.

They scrambled past me. I shouted, 'Stop, Felicia! Stop!' but she didn't seem to hear me. I snatched at her nightdress, but she spun around and twisted herself free. For a split second, though, I saw the look on her face, and she was wide-eyed and white with terror.

'*Låta jag gå! Låta jag gå! De nöd till mord oss!*'

She went running into the shadows and disappeared. Vanished, as if the darkness were an open door. But it was what happened to Elsa that stunned me the most. She ran headlong into the Elsa who was standing in the hallway, and it was like watching somebody run headlong into a

107

mirror. The two Elsas shattered into a thousand glittering fragments of light, and then they were gone.

I stayed where I was for a few seconds. I could actually hear my heart beating. Then I slowly hunkered down and ran my fingertips across the rug to feel for any broken pieces of glass. Nothing at all. The two Elsas may have looked like mirror images, but they had been nothing more than mirages. No glass, no silver backing. Only reflections.

I picked up the bronze statuette that had bounced across the floor, and replaced it on its stand. It was a slender woman in a flowing robe, with one breast bare, carrying a spear.

At that moment Kate came up to me. Her face was very serious. She reached up and adjusted the statuette to straighten it. 'Freya,' she said. 'Goddess of Love and Beauty. They named Friday after her.'

'What's happening, Kate?' I asked her. I thought that my voice sounded oddly muffled. 'Is this a dream? It's not a dream, is it?'

Kate took hold of my hand. 'You should come back to bed.'

'What the hell happened here, Kate? I saw *two* Elsas ... I saw Felicia disappear! She went straight into those shadows and she was gone. I'm not asleep, Kate! I'm not dreaming any of this – this is *real*!'

'Come back to bed, Gideon, please.'

The Westerlunds' bedroom door suddenly opened and Axel appeared in the corridor, wearing a black silk Japanese-style bathrobe. He tugged the belt tighter as he approached us. His calves were white and hairy, but very muscular, like a cyclist's.

'I heard noise! Is everything all right? What are you doing out here?'

'I'm sorry,' I said, 'but it was the girls.'

'The girls?' He looked around him in bewilderment.

'They were running along the corridor. They were frightened of something but I couldn't understand what they were saying.'

'*Running?*'

'Yes ... both of them. They knocked over this statue.'

Axel shook his head. 'No, Gideon. I think you will find that the girls are both asleep.'

Tilda came out, wearing pale green pajamas. 'Axel? Is anything wrong?'

'Gideon must have had a nightmare,' said Axel.

'I'm sorry,' I told him, 'but I saw what I saw. And Kate saw it, too.'

'Well...' said Kate. 'I have to admit that I really didn't see anything.'

'Oh, come on, Kate. Even if you didn't see them, you *heard* them.'

'I did hear *something*, yes. But I'm not really sure what it was.'

'Kate—'

'Let us clear up this matter, shall we?' said Axel. He went along the corridor to Elsa's bedroom and quietly opened the door. He looked inside, and then he beckoned. I hesitated, and then I followed him and looked inside, too. Elsa was in bed, fast asleep, wearing a cotton night-cap with pink ribbons around it.

Axel closed the door and went along to Felicia's room.

'OK,' I said. 'That really won't be necessary. It seems like I've made some kind of mistake, that's all.'

Tilda laid a gentle hand on my shoulder and said, *'Du drömde*, Gideon ... you were dream-ing.'

'En mardröm,' added Axel, quite angrily. I guessed *mardröm* meant 'nightmare'.

We all returned to our bedrooms. Kate leaned over me and kissed me on the ear and said, 'Are you OK?'

'No, I'm not. I just saw something totally impossible. I don't know why *you* didn't.'

'I did.'

'You did? You saw what I saw – Elsa and Felicia, running along the corridor? Why didn't you say so?'

'Because I didn't want to upset Axel and Tilda for no reason. For them, it didn't happen. Not in the way we saw it, anyhow.'

'Now I'm really baffled.'

'I know. But you're very tired. Let's talk about it in the morning.'

I dragged the comforter up to my neck. The central heating was on, but the air in the bedroom still felt chilly. If it hadn't been so dark, I was sure that I could have seen my breath smoking.

'These old apartments,' said Kate. 'They have

so many memories in them. So much reson-ance.'

'So I'm not going bananas? I *feel* like I'm going bananas.'

She snuggled up very close to me. 'Of course not. And anyhow, what if you are? I like bananas. Especially yours.'

I lay in the darkness for a while, stroking the nape of her neck. 'Do you know much Swedish?' I asked her.

'Only a little. Why?'

'Do you know what *drunkna* means?'

'Yes. It means "drown", or "drowning". Why? Where did you hear that?'

'Elsa said it, out in the corridor.'

Kate kissed me again. 'You really need to get some sleep. Do you want me to sing you a lullaby? I know a lovely one, called *The Pointing Tree*.'

'Don't make fun of me, Kate,' I told her. 'My head's going round like a goddamned Mix-master.' But she was right. I was totally bushed. I closed my eyes and fell asleep almost at once. I didn't dream, even if I had been dreaming before. Or – if I *did* have any dreams – I don't remember them.

The next thing I knew, Kate was dragging the drapes open, and the sun was sparkling over the harbor, so that the water looked like shattered glass.

Thirteen

Axel and Tilda had already left for work by the time I had showered and dressed. It was the Friday before *Alla Helgons Dag*, so the girls had a day off school, and they had gone out shopping with some of their friends. Kate and I had breakfast at the kitchen table, cold meats and St Olof cheese and slices of chilled melon. We tried watching television while we ate, but SVT doesn't have a whole lot to recommend it, unless you have a keen interest in pine forestry in Lapland, or how to make a hatstand out of elk antlers.

'Do you feel better now?' Kate asked me.

I poured myself some more black coffee. 'I still can't work out what happened last night.'

'Like I said, darling, you should wait and see.' *Darling*, she called me, as if we were married.

'Wait to see *what*? You're being so darned mysterious.'

'Don't you like mysterious women?'

'Of course I like mysterious women. It's mysterious children that worry me. Children who can appear in two places at once.'

Kate smiled, but didn't say anything more. Her floral cotton robe was open, and I could see her bare right breast, like the statuette of Freya in the

112

corridor. I had never known a woman so alluring – nor a woman who had inspired me so much. She had made me feel really strong, for the first time in my life, as if there was nothing that I couldn't do. The thought of her going back to New York and climbing into bed with Victor made me feel as if my skin was shrinking, like Saran wrap.

'Today I thought we could go to the Wasa Museum,' she suggested.

'Oh, yes? What's a Wasa when it's at home?'

'The Wasa was a fabulous Swedish galleon, which sank on its maiden voyage. They brought it up to the surface and restored it. It's really awesome. You'll love it.'

'I don't know. It looks pretty darn chilly out there. Maybe we could just stay in bed.'

'Oh, come on. We'll have plenty of time for that later. You can't come all the way to Stockholm and not see the sights.'

'I can see all the sights I want to see, just sitting here.'

Kate took hold of my hand. 'You mustn't be jealous, Gideon.'

'Why not? Every time I think of you and that husband of yours being together, I work out a new way of offing him. How about I wedge the door shut when he's taking a shower, and then tip a whole bucketful of fire ants into it? Maybe I should just strangle him with my bare hands. That would be easier.'

'You wouldn't do anything like that. It's not in your nature.'

'You want to bet?'

She leaned across the kitchen table and kissed me. Her nipple brushed the back of my hand. I can still feel it now, as if it happened only a few seconds ago.

It was a brilliant morning, sharp as a craft knife. The sky was intensely blue, with only a low bank of white cloud behind the city skyline, like a distant range of snow-covered mountains that can never be reached, no matter how far you travel.

We took a taxi to Djügarden Park, on the opposite side of the harbor from Axel and Tilda's apartment. The Wasa Museum was right on the waterfront – a huge box-like building with a tarnished copper roof and three stylized metal masts to represent the original masts of the galleon when she was fully rigged.

We shuffled inside, along with a party of chattering Swedish children and a contingent of bewildered Chinese nuns, and there was the galleon herself, lavishly carved and decorated with hundreds of sculptures – lions and cherubs and mermaids and Roman emperors.

Kate said, 'Do you know what I think of, when I look at this ship? I think of Victor. Vain, bombastic, overblown, and full of himself.'

'Can we forget about Victor?' I asked her. I was trying to read an information board which described how the Wasa had sunk. She had capsized on a calm spring day in 1628, without ever leaving Stockholm harbor, and she had rested on the seabed for over three hundred years before a salvage team had located her, and brought her back up. 'I thought this trip was just about you and me and the two of us spending some non-furtive time together.'

'I'm sorry. You're right. Look at these amazing sea monsters! And look at all of these cannons!'

'Wow,' I said.

We wandered around the exhibition hall for twenty minutes or so, but when it comes to history I have to admit that my span of attention is shamefully short. I always agreed with my dad. 'History? Why worry about history? History's over, by definition.'

We went outside and strolled along the waterfront, where four other historic ships were moored, including Sweden's first ice-breaker, *Sankt Erik*, and a lightship. The wind was so clean you felt you could have washed your face with it. On the other side of the harbor I could see Skeppsbron, and the Westerlunds' apartment, with the sun sending us heliograph messages from their living room window.

'How about some lunch?' asked Kate. 'I'm dying for some smoked salmon blinis.'

'Sure. And then we could have a siesta, yes? Before the Westerlunds get home.'

We turned around and walked back toward the taxi rank. But it was then that I that I heard somebody shout out, in heavily accented English, 'Here! Here! Get some help! There's somebody in the water!'

A small crowd of people had gathered on the jetty where the ice-breaker was moored. Two young men were climbing down a wooden ladder, while another bearded man was throwing a red-and-white lifebelt into the water.

'Hey, come on!' I told Kate. 'Maybe I can help.'

Together we hurried along the jetty. I pushed my way to the front of the crowd and looked down into the water. One of the young men had reached the bottom of the ladder, and was stretching out his hand to reach a body that was floating face down, close to one of the piers.

The body looked like a young girl, in a dark green sweater and a tan-colored corduroy skirt. Her hair was floating like yellowish seaweed. She was wearing long green socks and only one shoe.

'Do you need any help?' I shouted. 'I'm a good swimmer if you need me!'

But the young man had managed to catch hold of the girl's right ankle, and was pulling her in. In the distance, I could already hear the *whip-whip-whip* of an ambulance siren.

Together, the two young men lifted the girl out of the water and heaved her up the ladder. Her head lolled back and her arms swung loosely.

'She's dead, isn't she?' said Kate, with her hand held over her mouth.

An old man standing next to her turned and nodded. The water in Stockholm harbor was so cold that nobody could survive in it for very long, especially a young girl weighed down by a heavy-knit sweater and a corduroy skirt.

They brought the girl up to the top of the ladder and laid her on the jetty. Her face was gray and her hair half covered it like wet string. A gray-haired woman knelt down beside her and put her into the recovery position, and started to give her CPR. But although dirty water came gushing out of the young girl's mouth and nose, she showed no signs of life at all.

An elderly woman beside me crossed herself and said, '*Gud vila henne ung själ*,' and I didn't need a translator to tell me what *that* meant. *God rest her young soul.*

An ambulance arrived in the museum parking lot and two orange-jacketed paramedics came running out to the jetty. Then two police cars turned up, and four officers climbed out. They ushered all of us onlookers away from the water-front and back toward the museum gardens. Everybody was subdued. The only sound was the crunch of our feet on the shingle pathway, and the keening of seagulls overhead, like lost children looking for their parents.

'That poor young girl,' said Kate. 'I wonder how she fell into the water.'

'Maybe she jumped in. Sweden has a pretty high suicide rate, doesn't it?'

Kate put her arm around my waist and held me very tight. 'I don't feel like lunch anymore. Let's just go back to the Westerlunds', shall we?'

'Sure.'

As we made our way around the back of the museum, however, I caught sight of a man and a young girl, hurrying along one of the pathways toward the exit gate. What caught my attention was the way that the man was pulling the young girl along, in repeated jerks, as if she was dragging her feet. They were too far away for me to be able to hear him clearly, but every now and then he shouted something that sounded like *'skinder!'* and gave her another jerk.

I stopped and shaded my eyes with my hand so that I could see them better. They gave me a really disturbing feeling, those two. Even from such a distance, I could tell that something was badly wrong. If I had thought that it was possible, I would have said that the man was Victor's pal Jack, the falcon-nosed guy in black that I had met in Victor's apartment on Saturday morning, or at least Jack's twin brother. But the young girl unsettled me even more. I couldn't see her face at first, because she kept tossing her head from side to side. But as the man pulled her around the corner of the museum building, she twisted her head around and stared in my direction, as if she were making a last appeal for someone to help her break free.

And I swear to God it was Felicia.

'Jesus,' I said. 'Do you see who that was?'

'Who?'

'That young girl!' I started to run along the path after her.

'Gideon!' called Kate. 'Gideon, what is it?'

'Felicia! That guy has got hold of Felicia!'

Several tourists turned around and stared at me as I pelted along the path. I almost collided with three of the Chinese nuns, and had to double-skip over the flowerbed to avoid them.

I reached the corner of the museum, panting, but there was no sign of Felicia anywhere, nor the man who had looked like Jack. Only a coachload of Japanese tourists, gathered around their bus, and a line of schoolchildren in red and blue windbreakers, following a teacher who was holding up a red and blue umbrella.

I jogged toward the parking lot to see if the man had managed to pull the young girl into a doorway, or if they had been obscured from view by one of the signs saying *Wasamuseet*. But they had completely vanished, as if they had never existed.

'Gideon! Gideon – wait up!' Kate caught up with me and took hold of my hand. 'You're sure you didn't make a mistake?'

'No way. I'm *sure* it was Felicia. She was even wearing the same coat that Felicia was wearing when she came home yesterday. And the guy who was pulling her along – he looked so much like Victor's friend Jack.'

'*Jack*? You're serious?'

'For Christ's sake, Kate! I *saw* them!'

'OK, OK, you saw them,' said Kate, trying to calm me down. She looked around the parking lot. 'So where are they?'

'I don't know. Maybe the guy had a getaway car waiting for him. Maybe they went back inside the museum.'

She squeezed my hand tightly. 'It's all right, Gideon. I believe you.'

I looked at her. 'Is this the same kind of thing that happened last night? I mean, is this real, or isn't it?'

'If you saw it, my darling, then it *is* real. Or it was real, once.'

We walked slowly back across the parking lot, and as we did so I kept turning round and around

119

to see if the man and the young girl would reappear from behind a bus, or suddenly drive past us in the back of a taxi.

'They're *gone*,' Kate insisted. 'Why don't we leave it?'

I heard the deep, mournful hooting of a Viking Line car ferry, heading out to Helsinki. Then, from the waterfront, a small cortège came into view – the two paramedics and two of the police officers, carrying between them a stretcher with the body of the young drowned girl on it, covered in a blue blanket. As they passed, people bowed their heads or took off their hats, and the Chinese nuns all crossed themselves three times over.

The paramedics reached the ambulance just as Kate and I were passing close to it, and we stopped and waited while they opened the rear doors and lifted the stretcher inside. As they lifted it up, the blanket slid to one side and for the first time I was able to see the young girl's face clearly, without her wet hair straggled across it.

I stared at her in disbelief, and then I laid my hand on Kate's shoulders and said, '*Look*. Tell me that's not Elsa.'

Almost immediately, the ambulance doors were slammed shut, and the ambulance started up.

'Kate – didn't you see her? I swear that's Elsa!'

'I don't know, Gideon! I didn't get a good enough look at her!'

I approached one of the police officers, a

young man with bulging blue eyes and a blond moustache. I pointed to the ambulance and said, very slowly, 'Can you stop them from leaving, please? That girl who drowned, I believe I know who she is.'

The police officer frowned at me. 'You know her name?'

'We think it's Elsa Westerlund. She lives at 44 Skeppsbron. Her father's a doctor, Axel Westerlund. I think her younger sister's around here, too – Felicia. I'm sure I saw some guy dragging her around the back of the museum.'

One of the paramedics leaned out of the ambulance cab and said, *'Vad är skedde? Kanna vi gå nu?'*

'You saw some guy what?'

'Pulling her along with him. It looked like she didn't want to go.'

The second police officer came up to us. He was older, grayer, with weary-looking bags under his eyes, as if he used to smoke a hundred a day. 'What is wrong here?'

'These people think they can identify the dead girl. They want to look at the body.'

The older police officer said, *'Nej.* Impossible. Not here.'

'Hey, excuse me – I think that somebody might have pushed her into the water deliberately. I saw her younger sister Felicia only a few minutes ago – there, behind the museum – and it looked like this man was abducting her – trying to take her away. He might have been trying to do the same to her, but she wouldn't let him.'

'Gideon,' said Kate, 'you can't be certain that
121

it was Felicia.'

'It sure *looked* like Felicia.'

'But she's supposed to be shopping in the city center with her friends, isn't she? What would she be doing here?'

'I don't know. But I'm sure that's Elsa, in the ambulance, and if that's Elsa then the chances are that it *was* Felicia, wouldn't you say?'

The older police officer looked at me gravely. 'Where are they now – this girl and this man?'

'They just disappeared.'

'They disappeared? Where? In which direction?'

'I don't know. But they couldn't have got far. They could be inside the museum.'

'Can you describe them?'

At last, I thought. Somebody who believed me. I gave him a quick description of 'Jack' and 'Felicia', and he beckoned to the two police officers who were still standing on the jetty.

'You are looking for a man in a black coat with a nose like *en hök*. Also a young girl with blonde hair wearing a yellow windbreaker.'

The two police officers went back toward the museum, pushing their way briskly through the crowds of tourists.

'I saw them about *there*,' I told the older police officer, pointing to the gardens. 'I ran after them but they just vanished.'

The older police officer looked at me and his left eyelid twitched. 'If they are still here, sir, I assure you we will find them. Do you have any idea why anybody should want to take this girl?'

'None at all. Kate? You know the Westerlunds

122

pretty well.'

Kate shook her head. 'No idea. But then I didn't see her.'

I turned back to the older police officer. 'Please – if we can take a look at the girl in the ambulance—'

He thought for a moment, tugging at his nose as if it helped him to think. Then he said, 'Very well. Yes? But it is not normal protocol. What do you think would happen if we permitted everybody to stare at dead bodies, just because they said they knew who they were?'

He called out to the paramedics, and one of them climbed out of the ambulance and came around to open up the rear doors.

'Kate?' I said. But Kate said, 'No. You do it.'

I stepped up into the ambulance, along with the older police officer and the paramedic, and the paramedic folded down the blanket that covered the girl's face.

'Well?' asked the older police officer. 'You know her?'

The girl's face was bloated, and what really disturbed me was that her eyes were open. It was Elsa, no doubt about it, and she was giving me the same milky stare that she had given me in the hallway.

'It's her,' I said. It was airless inside the ambulance and I felt as if I could hardly breathe. 'Elsa Westerlund.'

'You're sure of this?'

'We're staying with her family. We had supper with them last night, and spent the whole evening with them. Of course I'm sure.'

The paramedic looked warily at the older police officer and said, 'This girl has been in the water at least three days.'

'That can't be possible,' I told him. 'I wrote a song for her yesterday evening, and sang it for her.'

The paramedic pulled down the blanket further. 'You see how swelled up her stomach is? The sea here is very cold, never more than five degrees, so people who drown do not decompose so quickly as they would in warmer water. But I can tell you for certain that she has been dead for more than seventy-two hours. The medical examiner will confirm it for sure.'

The older police officer looked at me with an expression that was partly regretful and partly pitying. 'I'm sorry, sir, it seems that you have made an error.'

'I don't understand it. It looks so much like her.'

'It is easy to do, especially when the victim has been dead for some time.'

I looked down at the drowned girl again. I couldn't believe that it wasn't Elsa, but I couldn't argue with cold forensic fact. Elsa had been alive last night. This girl had been floating in the harbor.

'I'm sorry,' the older police officer repeated.

We all climbed out of the ambulance. Kate was waiting for me with her hands thrust deep into her coat pockets.

'She can't be Elsa,' I told her. 'She looks exactly like her, but apparently she's been floating in the water for several days.'

Kate said nothing, but took hold of my arm, and drew me close to her.

'You're not going to stop looking for the other girl?' I asked the older police officer.

'Of course not. If you say that you saw a young girl being taken away against her will, then I have to take the matter seriously. But maybe your wife here is right, and you have mistaken her identity.'

I didn't correct him for calling Kate my wife. It would have been too complicated, and in any case I was quite flattered by it. But, 'I really don't think so,' I told him. 'Maybe that isn't Elsa, but I'm certain I saw Felicia.'

'Do you know which school she attends?'

'Adolf Fredriks Folkskola,' said Kate. 'But of course they have a free day today. Look – I have her mother's cell number. Why don't I call her? Then she can call Elsa and Felicia and make sure that they're both OK?'

The older police officer shrugged his assent. Kate took out of her cell and flipped it open. She waited for a few moments, listening. Then she said, 'Tilda? Sorry to disturb you at the clinic ... it's Kate.'

She paused, and then she said, 'Listen, Tilda, do you have Elsa's number? She asked me to buy something for Axel today, and I've forgotten what it was. Aftershave, as a matter of fact, but I can't remember the brand. OK, thanks. I'll see you later, OK?'

The older police officer said, 'Very diplomatic, madam. You would make a good police officer.'

Kate dialed the number that Tilda had sent her.

Again, she had to wait for a while, but eventually she said, 'Elsa? Elsa, can you hear me? It's Kate. Where are you, Elsa?'

She turned to the older police officer and said, 'Åhlens, in the cafe, with her friends.' Then, 'Is Felicia there? Yes? I can hear her laughing. Can I talk to her?'

Elsa must have passed her cell over, because Kate said, 'Felicia? It's Kate. No, nothing. We just wanted to know if you were having a good time.'

The older police officer held out his hand and Kate gave him her cell. He listened, without saying a word, and then he gave it back again.

'OK,' he said. 'Whoever you saw, sir, it obviously wasn't *this* particular girl.'

The ambulance gave a single whoop and drove away. A crosswind had sprung up from the north-east, and although it was still sunny, it was beginning to grow bitterly cold. As we stood talking, the two police officers came out of the museum entrance shaking their heads.

'No sign,' one of them said, as they approached us. 'Many children, but no men with noses like hawk-birds.'

'Well,' I said, 'It looks like I've made a mistake. But even if it wasn't Felicia I *did* see a man taking a young girl away, and he was taking her by force.'

The older police officer said, 'That is what you have told us, sir, and I assure you that our officers will continue to look for this man and this girl. But I have to tell you that the none of the museum staff saw anybody answering your description, and nobody else has reported seeing them, either.'

Kate said, 'We're sorry. We really seem to have wasted your time.'

'Nej. Don't worry, madam. If there is one thing I have learned in this job, it is that nothing is ever what it seems to be.'

Fourteen

Back in the old town, in one of the narrow cobbled streets, we went into an old-fashioned cafe called Den Gråtande Fisk and ordered a bottle of Zinfandel. The cafe was gloomy and paneled in dark oak, with even gloomier land-scapes hanging on the walls. The windows were glazed with amber glass, so that the endless stream of passers-by looked like characters in a shadow theater.

'You're very quiet,' said Kate.

'I'm totally confused, that's why. I was so darn sure that was Elsa.'

'I know. But the poor girl had been floating in the water for three days.'

'Kate, I can't get my head round any of this. But whatever it is, I've had enough of it.'

Kate took hold of my hands. 'I've explained to you, darling. You can see things that hardly any-body else can see – and *feel* them, too. You're a very creative guy and you're stressed out, that's all. Remember that this is the first vacation you've taken in three years. Give yourself a few days and I'm sure you'll feel better.'

'No ... I'm sorry. I'm going to cut this trip short. I don't understand what's going on and I don't *want* to understand it. I'm packing my bags tonight, Kate. I'm going home. Are you going to come with me?'

'You *can't* leave, Gideon. Not yet.'

'Oh, no? Give me one good reason why not.'

'Because I'm asking you. Isn't that enough? '

'But why? This thing with Elsa and Felicia ... it's too weird for words. And I don't think Axel has exactly warmed to me, do you?'

'Please, Gideon, I need you. The Westerlunds need you, too. You don't even know how much.'

'You keep telling me that, but you never explain what it all means.'

'Because I can't.'

'You can't, or you won't?'

She was silent for a while, although she didn't take her eyes off me. Eventually, she said, 'I promise you, Gideon, everything will fall into place. Not tomorrow, maybe. Not the day after. But soon. So please don't go. Not if you really do care for me.'

'I do care for you. As a matter of fact, I love you.'

I waited for her to say something, but all she did was lower her eyes and part her lips slightly, as if she were finding it difficult to breathe.

'Did you hear what I said?' I asked her. 'I love you. But you have to tell me what the hell's going on.'

She looked up again. 'Do you think we're good together?' she asked me. 'Not just in bed, but in every other way.'

I thought how much I had changed since Kate and I had been together. Not just my music, but everything about me. Up until the day she had first come around for that lunch, I had always acted just like my father: clever, yes, but cynical. Kate had shown me that I was someone else altogether. I wasn't exactly sure *who* – not yet, anyhow. But I was much more concerned about other people than I had ever been before, and much more sensitive to other people's feelings. That was why I wanted to leave Stockholm. The Westerlunds were trapped in some kind of surrealistic madness, but if I couldn't help them to escape from it, I didn't want to be there.

Kate leaned forward a little, and lowered her voice. 'Would you like it if we could spend much more time together?'

'You mean—?'

'You and me. It's not impossible.'

'What about Victor?'

She hesitated, and then she said, 'It's not impossible. Not if you decide to stay.'

I sat back. She had taken me by surprise. I had fallen in love with her much more quickly and much more inextricably than I had ever expected. It was like getting caught in a thorn thicket: the more I pushed my way forward, the more entangled I became. But I hadn't yet considered the possibility that our relationship could be anything more than a clandestine affair, whenever Victor was playing squash, or out of town on business, or sleeping off last night's orgy.

'OK,' I said, slowly. 'I'll stay. I hope I know what I'm letting myself in for.'

That night, Tilda served us smoked elk for supper – three thin slices each of dark, almost prune-colored meat, with sweet red lingonberry jelly, and potato salad.

She was exceptionally chatty, and told us about a patient of hers whose left foot had been amputated more than a year ago, but who insisted that it still gave him agonizing pain.

'He says it is proof that ghosts exist. If I can feel a left foot that isn't there, he says, why is it not possible to have a whole person who isn't there?'

'I don't believe in ghosts,' said Felicia.

'Neither do I,' said Elsa. 'If there were ghosts, where would they all live?'

'And what did you two do today?' Axel asked Kate.

'I took Gideon to the Wasa Museum.'

Axel said, 'Ah, *ja*,' and carefully buttered himself another piece of rye bread, but said nothing more.

Tilda said, 'You found it interesting, Gideon, the Wasa?'

'Very interesting, Tilda, yes. Especially all of the stuff they found in her, like barrels that were still filled up with beer, even after three hundred years.'

I looked across the table at Elsa. She was staring at me, unblinking, almost as if she were challenging me to tell her mother what we had

130

seen, when we visited the Wasa Museum. But she couldn't have known, because Kate and I had decided not to tell the Westerlunds what had happened, and there had been no mention of it on the SVT news that evening.

Kate said, 'Tomorrow we'll probably go to the royal palace at Drottningholm.'

'You will love Drottningholm,' Tilda assured me. 'The gardens are wonderful, with statues and fountains. The Swedish royal family still live there. Maybe you will meet one of them.'

Elsa was still staring at me, so intently that I began to feel uncomfortable. 'I am going swimming with my school tomorrow,' she told me.

'Oh, yes?' I replied. 'Be very careful, won't you?'

She didn't answer me, but kept on staring. I almost had the feeling that she was trying to tell me something telepathically. *You were right about that drowned girl, Gideon. That was me.* But of course it couldn't have been. I was just giving myself the willies.

We played charades that evening, until well past eleven o'clock. Axel mimed *The Devil's Eye*, by Ingmar Bergman, by closing one eye and holding his fingers up over his head like horns.

Felicia's mime was *High School Musical 2*, while Kate acted out *A Doll's House*.

For her charade, Elsa lay on her back on the floor, with both hands held up, and her head slightly raised, swaying very slightly from side to side. She gave us no other clues but the pose

131

was so distinctive that Kate guessed it immediately.

'Ophelia,' she said. 'Hamlet's lost love, drowning herself.'

Elsa looked up at me, from the floor. I still had the feeling that she was trying to tell me something, but I was damned if I could work out what it was.

All the same, I was much more relaxed by the time we went to bed. Three glasses of Merlot with my supper had helped to convince me that Kate was right, and that I had simply been suffering from stress. After my dad had died, I thought that I had seen him several times – once in Gristede's grocery on Third Avenue, down by the deli counter, and once on 42nd Street, staring out of the rain-beaded window of a cross-town bus. Maybe I was suffering the same kind of delusion with Elsa and Felicia.

Kate and I made love that night in a very slow, stylized way, as if *we* were swimming, too. Kate came close to an orgasm time and time again, without ever quite reaching it, and after nearly an hour she was slippery with perspiration. Eventually, though, she pushed me over on to my back, and sat astride me, guiding me inside her with both hands. Then she moved up and down in a complicated rhythm, her thigh muscles clamping me harder and harder.

As she climaxed, she took a deep breath, and I thought she was going to scream. But she bent her head forward and bit my shoulder, very hard, and her teeth stayed buried in me while she quaked and quaked and snuffled through her nose.

'*Ouch*,' I said, when she had finished. But believe me, 'ouch' was an understatement.

'Oh God, Gideon, I'm sorry.' She switched on the bedside lamp. I could clearly see the marks of her teeth in my shoulder. She pulled a tissue out of the box on the nightstand and folded it into a pad. 'I was scared that I was going to break a mirror or something.'

I winced and examined my wound. 'Next time, try biting the pillow instead.'

'I'm so sorry. I wouldn't hurt you for the world.'

I held her close and kissed her. 'Don't worry about it. You can make it up to me before we get up tomorrow.'

She put her hand down between my legs and squeezed me. 'That's a deal.'

I had only just fallen asleep, however, when I was woken up by the sound of Axel shouting and Tilda screaming, and their bedroom door slamming – not once, not twice, but three or four times.

I sat up in bed. 'God almighty! Those two seem so mild-mannered, don't they? But listen to them now!'

Kate said, blurrily, 'Typical Swedes. They bottle up all of their emotions, but then they explode.'

I lay back down. I don't know what Axel was raging about. I couldn't hear him very clearly and in any case he was yelling in Swedish. But

Tilda was simply screaming, on and on, like a demented soprano in a Verdi opera.

After more than five minutes of this, I sat up again. 'Do you think they're OK? Maybe we should knock on their door or something, see if we can calm them down.'

'Leave them,' said Kate. 'It's none of our business, is it?'

'But listen to Tilda! It sounds like he's murdering her!'

'Gideon, it's nothing to do with us! We'd only embarrass them!'

I lay down for another three or four minutes. Axel stopped shouting so loudly, but now I could hear Tilda sobbing. 'Jesus,' I said. 'What are we going to say to them tomorrow? "Have a restful night, did you?"'

At that moment their bedroom door opened again, and Axel shouted out, *'Du djävul! Du demonen! Lov henne ensam!'*

This was followed by a catastrophic crash, like a huge wardrobe falling over. Tilda screamed again, and kept on screaming.

'Come on,' I said, and vaulted out of bed. I opened our bedroom door wearing nothing but my blue stripy shorts. It was totally dark in the corridor, but Kate switched on one of our bedside lamps. Axel and Tilda's bedroom door was half open, so I crossed over and knocked on it, and called out, 'Tilda! Are you OK? What the hell are you guys doing in there?'

Axel gave a hoarse, desperate-sounding shout, and then Tilda came rushing out of the bedroom, screaming. She was wearing a long white night-

134

gown, but the collar had been half ripped loose, and her sleeves were flying in ribbon-like tatters. Axel tried to seize her arm and I tried to grab her, too, but she pulled herself away from both of us and went running barefoot along the corridor, still screaming.

'Axel!' I shouted at him. 'What the hell is going on?'

Axel didn't answer. All he did was stare at me wildly, as if he didn't even know who I was.

I went after Tilda. She had reached the hallway, and was flinging herself from one side to the other, colliding with the walls. It looked as if she was being thrown around by an invisible assailant, because she was hitting the walls so hard that she was bruising herself, and she crashed into one of the side tables, too, so that a lamp toppled on to the floor, and its glass shade smashed.

'Tilda!' I said, and managed to take hold of her wrists. 'Tilda, you have to calm down!'

'What?' she said. Her eyes were darting from side to side, as if she were terrified.

'Tilda, I don't know what the problem is, but you're really going to hurt yourself!'

She babbled something in Swedish, breathless and hysterical, like somebody begging for their life. Then she suddenly dropped on to her knees, pulling her arms down so that I lost my grip on her wrists.

'For Christ's sake, Tilda!'

But she ducked to the left, and then to the right, and then she half rolled and half scuttled away from me on all fours, like a wounded animal. She made it to the front door before I could catch her, opened it, and ran along the landing to the spiral staircase.

'Tilda!'

She threw herself down the stairs so violently that I really thought she was going to break her neck. I went jumping down the stairs after her, three steps at a time, but she still managed to make it down to the hallway before I could catch her.

She tried to open the door to the street, but it must have been double-locked. She hammered on it in frustration, but it still wouldn't open. Her eyes wild, her chest heaving, she turned around and faced me.

'Inte röra jag!' she shrilled. *'Vill du höra?'*

Then she clenched her fists and screamed louder and higher until my eardrums sang.

She screamed on and on, until suddenly the mirror on the wall beside me cracked all the way across, and then the glass lantern hanging from the ceiling above me burst like a bomb, and I was showered in sparkling fragments. I lowered my head and covered my eyes with my hand.

The screaming abruptly stopped. I took my hand away from my face and looked up. Tilda was gone. The door to the street was still closed, so she must have run back upstairs. I followed her, panting with effort. The apartment door was open, and I could see Kate standing in the hallway.

'Are you all right?' she asked me. She looked up, and said, 'Your hair is all glittery.'

'Glass,' I told her, picking some of it out.

'Tilda screamed and the lantern broke.'

'It's all right. Tilda's in her bedroom.'

'What?' I couldn't believe what she had just said to me.

'Tilda's in her bedroom, Gideon. Everything's fine.'

'But you must have seen her as well as I did. She came running down the corridor in her nightdress, and started to throw herself all over the place. Look – she knocked over that lamp.'

The lamp was back on top of the side table, although its shade was badly bent and it was missing several pieces of colored glass. But Kate said, 'It's been like that ever since we've been here.'

'Kate, I know what I saw. Tilda broke it only a couple of minutes ago.'

Kate said, 'I know she did. But she's in bed now. And we ought to get back to bed, too.'

She reached up and carefully picked some more pieces of glass from my shoulders. I looked into her eyes while she was doing it, and they had that smoky lack of focus, as if I were a window and she could see right through me.

'I need to see Axel and Tilda,' I told her.

'I don't think you should disturb them. They're quiet now.'

'Maybe they are. But I still want to make sure that Tilda's OK. She was throwing herself around like a rag doll. Then she broke the lantern, and the mirror, too.'

We walked along the corridor together, until we reached our bedroom door.

'I'm telling you, Kate. Lanterns and mirrors

137

don't shatter by themselves.'

'All right,' said Kate. She went across to the Westerlunds' bedroom door and softly knocked. There was no answer at first but then she knocked again and Axel opened the door. He blinked at us unhappily.

'Yes? What is it?'

'We wanted to make sure that you and Tilda were OK, that's all.'

'Of course we are. Are you going to keep us awake *every* night, while you're here?'

'We're sorry,' said Kate. 'Gideon's a little stressed, that's all. He's been working very hard and he just moved house.'

'Well, I have a very important conference tomorrow, and I would rather try to sleep, if that is OK with you two.'

'For sure,' I told him, although my voice was shaking. 'Sorry for disturbing you, OK?'

Axel closed his bedroom door, but before he did so I glimpsed Tilda sitting up on her pillow, staring at us. There was something strange about her face which really disturbed me. It was oddly out of focus, as if she had moved her head while having her photograph taken.

But there she was, no mistaking her. Somehow she had managed to run back up the spiral staircase into the apartment without Kate noticing her, and climb back into bed without Axel noticing her, either.

Kate switched the light off. We lay there in absolute blackness for a while, listening to the faint sounds of early-morning traffic, and the deep throbbing of a car ferry, crossing the harbor.

'That settles it,' I said. 'I'm leaving tomorrow. Are you going to come with me? I can't go through another night like this.'

Kate put her arm around me. 'We can't leave, Gideon. We're going to Drottningholm Palace tomorrow, and the day after we can go to Uppsala.'

I eased myself free from her. 'I'm sorry, Kate. I've had enough of the Westerlunds for one lifetime, thanks all the same. I want to go back home. There may be people in New York who are just as crazy as the Westerlunds, but at least they don't appear in two places at the same time.'

'Please, Gideon. I've told you how much I need you to stay.'

'Sorry, sweetheart. I'm leaving. I don't know who's real around here and who isn't, and that seriously scares me. I don't even know if *I'm* real any more. Am I real? Somebody chased Tilda down the staircase, even though Tilda never went down the staircase, and if it wasn't me who chased her when she didn't go, then who was it?'

Kate kissed me, six or seven times. 'You're tired. You're not making sense.'

'*Nothing* is making sense. And that's exactly why I'm leaving. Are you coming with me?'

There was a very long pause, during which I could feel Kate breathing steadily against my shoulder. Then she said, 'All right, then. We'll leave. But can I ask you one favor?'

'It depends what it is.'

'When you fly back to New York tomorrow, can you make one stopover on the way home?'

'A stopover? Where?'

'Only one night. Two at the most. I'll have to call and find out first.'

'*Where*, Kate?'

'London. I have some old friends who live in South Kensington. I'd really love you to meet them. And we can take in some of the sights you missed. Buckingham Palace, the Tower of London, the London Eye.'

'Hold up a moment. You said when *I* fly back to New York tomorrow. What about you?'

'My ticket's non-transferable. But it's OK. I'll meet up with you at my friends' house, when you get there.'

'Why don't you come with me on my flight? It won't cost much.'

'No. no. That's OK. In any case, I've arranged to see some more people here in Stockholm before I leave.'

'What people?'

She tapped the side of her nose. 'Don't be inquisitive. They're just business acquaintances, that's all, from *Bleck* magazine. And they're all women, so you don't have any reason to be jealous.'

'OK...' I said, reluctantly. Then, 'These friends of yours in London ... do they fight a lot?'

'No ... they're devoted.'

'Do they run and up down their apartment in the middle of the night?'

'Not that I know of.'

'All right, then. London it is.'

Kate kissed me again. 'You're an angel, do you know that?'

I stroked her hair. It was so dark that I couldn't see her at all, but I could feel her breathing. I thought about what my life had been like, before I met her. Could I really go back to it?

'I'm not an angel,' I told her. 'I'm just a musician. But I don't want this to end, that's all.'

Fifteen

The next morning I slept late again. I didn't open my eyes until a quarter after nine, and when I sat up I felt as if I had a hangover, with a hammering headache and a mouth that felt as if it had been carpeted. I climbed out of bed and drew back the drapes. There were low gray clouds hanging over the harbor, and the smaller sailboats were jumping up and down at their moorings as if they were trying to break free.

I pulled on my navy-blue chinos and my white roll-neck sweater and went through to the kitchen. There was nobody there, so I went along to the living room, calling out, 'Kate?' But there was nobody in the living room, either. No Kate, no Westerlunds. The whole apartment was deserted.

I went back into the kitchen and opened up the blue ceramic coffee jar to make myself a mug of coffee, but the jar was empty. I opened up the fridge, to see if there was any orange juice, but the fridge was empty, too – just as it had been when I first arrived. There was no food in any of the overhead cupboards, either. Not even a can of beans.

I stood there for a long time feeling as if I had woken up in a parallel universe. Maybe I needed to go back to bed, fall asleep and try waking up a second time.

A seagull landed on the ledge outside the kitchen window, and tapped on the glass with its beak, as if it were trying to warn me to leave. It stared at me beadily for a few seconds and then it flapped away.

I returned to the bedroom. It was then that I saw the pale-blue envelope lying on the floor. It must have dropped off the quilt when I climbed out of bed. I picked it up and tore it open. There were two Yale door keys inside, and a hand-written note on deckle-edged paper. *Darling Gideon – your flight AY5927 leaves Arlanda at 11:45 a.m. Collect your ticket at the Finnair desk. We are staying with David and Helena Philips, 37 Wetherby Gardens, London SW5. See you there later! Love, Your Kate.*

I sat down on the side of the bed. I leaned over and smelled the pillow that Kate had slept on, but it had retained none of her fragrance at all, as if she had never been there.

I always used to wonder if people who were going mad *knew* that they were going mad. But at that moment, I seriously felt that I was losing my sanity. I felt as if the carpet were sliding away from under me, and the whole room was shrinking like a dolls' house. What gave me the deepest sensation of dread was the knowledge that there was no turning back. If I was going to find out what was happening to me, and why I was seeing two Elsas and two Felicias, and a drowned girl dragged out of the harbor, and visions of Tilda hurtling down the stairs, I would have to follow Kate to London, and face whatever visions she wanted to show me.

Maybe 'David and Helena Philips' would scream at each other in the middle of the night, and run around their apartment breaking lamps when in reality they were still in bed? Maybe I would find *their* children floating in the Thames?

But I urgently needed to be reassured that I wasn't suffering from some kind of breakdown. Kate had told me I was capable of seeing things because I had 'resonance', but what did that really mean? Maybe it simply meant that I was mentally exhausted and out of my emotional depth, and that I needed a long rest, and a course of diazepam.

Most of all, though, I had to see Kate. I had to talk to her, and touch her, and hold her close to me. She had left no perfume on her pillow but she had left the memory of her perfume in my mind. Without her, this apartment seemed cold and completely empty; and outside the window, the city of Stockholm seemed as two-dimensional as a picture postcard. I had never felt such a physical need for another person's presence.

I looked at myself in the dressing-table mirror.

143

I looked tired, and foxy-eyed, and different. I thought: what if I didn't follow her? What if I simply flew non-stop back to New York? I wasn't sure that it would finish our affair, not immediately; but I would be letting her down in the meanest way possible; and I would either be showing her that I was lacking in nerve, or that I wasn't really interested in helping her friends, or both. I doubted that our relationship could survive for very much longer if I treated her like that.

I admit it, yes, I *was* lacking in nerve. Wouldn't you be? But I loved her too much to risk losing her, no matter what she asked me to do. How could I go on seeing her every day at St Luke's Place, if we broke up? How could I sleep at night, knowing that she was directly underneath me, in bed with the hairy orange-tanned Victor?

I packed my shirts and my sweaters, and left the Westerlunds' apartment, closing the shiny black door behind me. Outside, on Skeppsbron, it had started to rain, and it was so gloomy that it could have been evening, instead of morning. I managed to hail a taxi, and ask the driver for Arlanda airport.

Along route E4 the serrated pine forests looked even darker and lonelier than ever – forests where even your happiness could get lost – and as I sat in the back of the taxi and stared at them through the rain, I promised myself that I would never come back.

But if you make a promise you're making a prediction. And when you wake up in the morning, you can never tell for sure what the day is going to bring you, or even if you'll still be alive by nightfall.

It was raining heavily in London, too, as the black taxi inched its way over Hammersmith Flyover and into Earls Court, with tall Victorian apartment blocks on either side. But I was feeling less depressed. I had flown to England with a men's choir from Helsinki, who had sung boisterous Finnish folk songs all the way. I had jotted down two or three of the choruses for possible TV jingles, especially *Isontalon Antti – Big House Andy*.

'This is it, mate,' said the taxi driver. He pulled into the curb outside a massive tawny-brick house with white-painted pillars and a porch that looked only slightly smaller than Washington Square Arch. I paid him and probably tipped him too little because he stared down at the coins in his hand as if I had spat on them.

'Isn't that enough?' I asked him.

'No, mate, that'll do. Wouldn't like to see you go short, would I?'

I had never understood British humor (if that's what it was) so I said, 'No, I guess not,' and left it at that. I climbed the steps of No. 37 and peered at the doorbells. There were four of them: one for each apartment. Three of them carried neatly written name-cards, except for the first floor bell, which I assumed was the Philips'. I pressed it, and I could hear it ringing: but just like 44 Skeppsbron, there was no reply.

Taking out my two Yale keys, I opened the front door and let myself into a high-ceilinged entrance hall, with black-and-white tiles. On a gilded Regency-style side table, there was a fan-shaped vase containing a huge arrangement of orange gladioli. At the far end, a tall mirror showed a wet American jingle composer wearing a black raincoat.

The door to the Philips' apartment was on the left, just past the spray of gladioli. I let myself in, calling out, 'Hi! Hello? Anybody home?' as I did so. I knew that British people weren't legally allowed to be armed, but it was better to be circumspect than have your head blown off.

Inside, there was a smaller entrance hall, with doors leading off it on all sides. Two of the doors were open. Through one of them I could see a library, with rows of bookshelves and fox-hunting prints on the walls. Through the other, a large yellow-painted kitchen, with a long pine dining table, and French windows that looked out on to the garden, where two stone cherubs stood dripping under a leafless pergola.

I put down my case in the hallway and took off my raincoat. I opened the double doors right in front of me, and found myself in the living room, which was vast, bigger than my whole apartment in St Luke's Place. It was decorated in varying shades of brown, with thick beige carpets and chocolate velvet drapes.

It was almost silent inside this apartment, except for the faintest swish of traffic on the wet road outside, and the sound of somebody upstairs trying to play the violin, and constantly faltering and stopping after the first six or seven bars.

Despite the quietness, or maybe *because* of it, I felt a dark wave of unease pass over me. I can't describe it exactly, but it was almost as if somebody invisible had walked through the room, and even walked through *me*. I had an irrational urge to put my coat back on, pick up my suitcase and quickly leave.

When I had first entered the Westerlunds' apartment in Stockholm, I had felt like a trespasser – simply because there was nobody home. But here, the apartment itself made me feel unwelcome. A stern portrait of a woman in a brown dress was staring at me from over the fireplace, and the look on her face said, *Who are you? We don't want the likes of you here.*

I crossed the silent carpet to the window, where I could get a good signal on my cellphone, and I tried calling Margot. Right then, I badly needed to hear a friendly voice.

She answered almost at once. 'Lalo? Is that you? How's Stockholm?'

'I left Stockholm this morning. I'm in London now.'

'I thought you were going to stay in Sweden for at least two weeks! What the two-toned tonkert are you doing in London?'

'I'm not sure. Kate hasn't arrived here yet. But I had some really freaky experiences in Stockholm. That's why I left.'

'I've tried to call you a couple of times.'

'Really? At what sort of time? Remember that Stockholm is six hours ahead.'

'I know that. I called you once around four in the afternoon and once around nine in the

147

morning. But both times I got this terrible rustling noise like somebody crumpling up tissue paper. I could hear voices in the background but I couldn't hear what they were saying.'

'Must have been some kind of technical glitch. You can hear me OK now, can't you?'

'Pretty good. I can still hear some voices in the background, though. Are you in a bar or something?'

'No. I'm in somebody's apartment, and there's nobody else here.'

'Well, I can definitely hear somebody else. They sound like they're arguing, or crying. No – I can definitely hear somebody crying.'

'Like I say, I'm all on my own. You must be picking up interference.'

I was still talking to her when I caught sight of something out of the corner of my eye. A small white shape running across the kitchen, and then disappearing behind the half-open door.

'Margot, can you hold on for just a moment?' I asked her.

'You sound odd, Lalo. What's the matter?'

'I've seen something. I just want to check it out.'

'What have you seen?'

I went into the kitchen and looked under the table. At first I couldn't see anything at all, except chair legs. Then I saw the white shape sitting in the corner, motionless, and it was staring at me.

I circled around the table and approached it slowly.

'Here, kitty-cat. Don't be afraid.'

The cat remained where it was, still staring at me. I hunkered down close to it and I could see then that it was Malkin.

'Margot? Are you still there?'

'Yes ... but you're breaking up. I'm getting that rustling noise again, and I'm still hearing those voices.'

'Margot, Kate's cat is here.'

'What did you say?'

'Kate's cat! It's a white Persian. It's here, in the kitchen, in London.'

'I'm sorry, Lalo. I really can't hear you. I'll try calling you later, OK?'

'Margot! It's Kate's cat, Malkin! How in *hell* can it be here?'

'I'm sorry. I can't hear you at all.'

I closed my cellphone. Malkin kept on staring at me, but not moving.

'What are you doing here in London, Malkin? Come on, cat, I know you can speak if you want to.'

But Malkin only yawned, squeezing her eyes tight shut.

Eventually I stood up and went back into the living room. I stood close to the window and tried to get through to Margot again, but all I got was a recording of a snotty British woman saying, *'Sorr-ee! The number you have dialed is not recawgnized.'*

A large gilded clock on the mantelpiece struck five. There was still no sign of Kate, or of David and Helena Philips, so I decided to take myself out for a drink. I was feeling tired and lonely, a stranger in yet another strange land, and I needed better company than a cat who couldn't possibly be here.

Before I left, though, I looked into the kitchen, and Malkin was still there, still sitting in the same position, still staring at me. For some reason, I thought of what Margot had said to me when she had consulted that Tibetan fortune-teller. *'A white memory is watching you.'*

I walked out in the rain, along streets crowded with black taxis and red double-deck buses. A few minutes from Wetherby Gardens I found a triangular corner pub called The Duke of Clarence. Outside it looked more like a ship than a pub, but inside it was bright and airy, with a high ceiling and comfortable couches, and plenty of mirrors. All the same, there were only five people in there, including me, and one of them was asleep, with her head tilted back and her mouth wide open. I ordered a glass of wine and sat in the corner on my own. I looked so exhausted in the mirror next to me that I had to move, where I couldn't see myself.

I had drunk only half a glass of wine when two hands covered my eyes. Two female hands, with rings on – hands that smelled of a light, flowery perfume.

'Guess who-oo?' she teased me.

I lifted her hands away from my eyes and turned around. It was Kate, wearing a putty-colored trench coat and a black beret, which was sparkling with raindrops. Her eyes were wide with amusement.

I stood up, and hugged her close, and kissed
150

her. 'When did *you* get here? And how the heck did you know where to find me?'

'You weren't at David and Helena's, so I assumed that you'd gone looking for a drink. My God, I felt *so* sorry for you when I saw you sitting here, all on your own.'

I beckoned to the waitress. 'What do you want? This Chardonnay's a little on the warm side, but it's just about drinkable.'

She took off her raincoat and sat down close to me. 'David and Helena weren't at home, then, when you arrived?'

'No ... but I'll you who was. Malkin.'

She blinked her eyes in exaggerated disbelief. 'Malkin? You can't be serious! How could Malkin be here in London?'

'I was going to ask you the same question. But it's definitely Malkin. I'd know that disapproving stare of hers anyplace.'

'Well, Malkin must have a British twin. If I had wanted to bring Malkin here, I would have needed to have her vaccinated against rabies at least six months before she traveled.'

'OK ... so maybe I made another mistake. If I can see two Elsas and two Tildas, I don't suppose there's any reason why I can't see two Malkins. Maybe I need to stop drinking so much.'

Kate took hold of my hand. 'It's probably Helena's cat. She did tell me that she was thinking of buying one, to keep her company. The Philips lost their only son Giles about two years ago, and I don't think that Helena ever got over it.'

'That's sad. How old was he?'

'Thirteen. I think he wanted to be an architect when he left school.'

'So how did he die?'

'They never talk about it.'

The waitress brought Kate's wine. I ordered another glass for myself, and paid her. She looked down at the tip that I had given her in the same way that the taxi driver had looked at his.

'Something wrong?' I asked her.

'Oh, no, sir. Seven pence ... that's more than generous.'

'OK. Good. Thank you.'

'No, sir. Thank *you*.'

The waitress strutted off and I turned back to Kate. 'You look great, you know that? Very European, like Marlene Dietrich.'

'Why, thank you. You're looking pretty cosmopolitan yourself.'

'Just tell me one thing,' I asked her. 'Taking me to meet these friends of yours, the Westerlunds and the Philips ... you're trying to *show* me something, aren't you? Because that's the feeling you're giving me.'

'Ah,' she interrupted. 'First of all I have a question for you. Do you know how much seven pence is worth?'

'I have no idea.'

'That's pretty obvious. At today's exchange rate, seven pence is worth a little over fourteen cents. Talk about the last of the big tippers.'

We walked back to Wetherby Gardens arm in arm. It had stopped raining but the streets still reflected the red and white lights from the traffic, and there was a constant sizzle of tires on wet asphalt. London had a definite smell to it: wet, and exhaust fumes, and a warm, stale draft from restaurant ventilators.

'Look,' she said. We had reached No. 37 and the living-room drapes were drawn, although I could see two lamps shining through them. 'David and Helena must be home now.'

She led the way up the steps. I used my key to open the porch door but when we reached the Philips' front door, Kate knocked on it.

'David! Helena! It's Kate!'

We heard a chain rattling, and two bolts being drawn back. Then the door opened and we were greeted by a tall, fifty-ish man with polished chestnut hair and a reddened face.

'Kate, how good to see you!' he said, and kissed her on both cheeks. He turned to me and held out his hand. 'And you must be Gideon. I gather we can call you Lolly, if we want to.'

'Lalo, actually, sir. Good to meet you.'

David ushered us inside. He had the lean, long-nosed looks of an upper-class Englishman, with faded blue eyes, as if he had been abroad in the sun for much of his life. He wore a tattersall check shirt and brown corduroy pants and shiny brown Oxfords. Although he was so lanky, he had the paunch of a man who always ate well, and probably enjoyed a glass or two of port after dinner.

'Kate, my darling girl!' Helena came out of the kitchen to embrace her. 'It's been far too long, hasn't it?'

153

'Far too long,' David echoed, patting Kate on the shoulder as if she were his daughter, or a pet dog.

When she was younger, Helena must have been stunning – a real British dolly bird. Now her hair was backcombed and hairsprayed into a kind of blonde Greek helmet. She had a plump, doll-like face, with a tiny nose and sparkling eyes, although I guessed that the tightness of her eyelids owed something to cosmetic surgery. She was wearing a tailored black velvet suit which didn't do a whole lot to minimize her very large chest and her very ample hips.

She was warm, though, and garrulous, and funny. David poured us all drinks while she told us about the time she had mistaken the US Ambassador for a waiter and sent him off to find her a smoked salmon sandwich.

'Talking of smoked salmon,' I said, 'I met your cat when I first arrived.'

'Our *cat*?'

'She's a dead ringer for Kate's cat. In fact I thought she actually *was* Kate's cat.'

Helena gave me a quick little shake of her head. 'We don't own a cat, Gideon. She must have been a stray.'

'A stray? She was sitting in the kitchen like she owned the place.'

'No, never owned a cat,' David put in. 'Helena thought of it, but never did.' He tugged his nose, and sniffed. 'Allergic, don't you know?'

'Well, that's really strange. I mean, if she was a stray, how did she get in?'

'Kitchen window, I expect. Probably came

154

from upstairs.'

'Oh.'

We sat in silence for a while. Then Helena said, 'Kate tells me you're a composer, Gideon.'

'Advertising jingles, mostly. Soup, diapers, spaghetti shapes. You name it.'

'But they're very superior advertising jingles,' said Kate. 'He's written one for toilet-bowl freshener that almost made me cry.'

David poured us some more wine. 'What line of business are you in, David?' I asked him, as he filled up my glass.

'Banking,' he said. 'International loans, that kind of thing.'

'This credit crunch must be affecting you pretty badly.'

I waited, but he didn't answer. Instead he stared at me with his eyes unfocused, as if he were thinking about something else altogether. Then suddenly he said, 'Do excuse me,' and walked quickly out of the room.

I looked across at Kate, raising one eyebrow. Kate shrugged, to indicate that she didn't know what was going on, either. Helena was prattling on about the time she had accidentally spilled red wine all down the front of Princess Margaret's white silk evening gown. 'My dear, I was *mortified*! But she took it so well! She gave me this sweet, sweet smile and said *fuck*.'

With David temporarily absent, I took the opportunity to go to the bathroom. I splashed my face with cold water and combed my hair. I was beginning to feel much more relaxed. In spite of the freakiness of what had happened at the

155

Westerlunds' apartment in Stockholm, maybe this trip was going to be enjoyable after all.

As I came out of the bathroom, however, I heard a mewling noise coming from a room on the other side of the hallway, next to David and Helena's bedroom. I hesitated, and then I crossed over and listened at the door. The noise stopped for a while, but just as I was about to go back to the drawing room, it started again. The door was only an inch ajar, so I pushed it open a little further, and peered inside.

It was a small bedroom, with a single bed. There were three or four posters of Chelsea soccer team stuck to the walls, and a dozen plastic airplanes suspended from the ceiling. Definitely a boy's room.

I heard the mewling again, and I put my head around the door, expecting to see 'Malkin' sitting on the bed.

But I couldn't see the cat anywhere, whether it really *had* been Malkin or a lookalike stray from upstairs. What I did see was David standing by the window, with his back turned to me. It was David, making that mewling sound. His head was lowered and he was gripping the window sill as if he were trying to stop himself from sinking to his knees.

What the hell do you do when you find your host sobbing? Especially if you hardly know the guy. Do you go up to him and gave him a manly hug, or do you simply ask him if everything's OK?

Or do you do what I decided to do – close the door as quietly as you can and return to the living room, rubbing your hands together and smiling cheerily as if nothing was wrong?

Kate held out her hand to me. 'Are you hungry?' she asked me. 'Helena was thinking of ordering some Indian take-out.'

'I hope you like it really, really hot,' said Helena. 'I love chicken vindaloo, with extra green chillies, but David could never stand it, so we always used to end up with pasanda.'

'Fine by me,' I told her. 'Do you know what they call Indian food in India?'

'I don't have a clue.'

'Food.'

Sixteen

'David was crying,' I told her, as Kate crossed her arms and pulled off her tight-ribbed sweater.

'Was he?' she said. She didn't sound very surprised. 'When was that?'

I was sitting on the edge of the bed, taking off my socks. 'When we were first talking, in the living room. When I went to take a leak. I came out of the bathroom and he was standing by the window in one of the bedrooms, sobbing like a baby. He didn't see me.' I paused. 'It looked like their son's room. It had model airplanes hanging from the ceiling. Guess they keep it as kind of a shrine.'

Kate said, 'He was OK later, wasn't he, when

we had supper. He was even telling jokes.'

I stood up and unbuckled my belt. 'It's none of my business. But it was so sudden – the way he walked out of the room like that, and went to have a cry. I mean – what makes a man like David do something like that? He seems, like – so stiff-upper-lip.'

'Grief, probably. Something must have reminded him about losing his son. Grief can suddenly hit you like that, even after years.'

We climbed into bed, and Kate snuggled up close to me. The guest bedroom wasn't as grandiose as the suite we had shared in the Westerlunds' apartment, but all the same the walls were decorated with gold-patterned wallpaper, and the furniture was all genuine English antiques, with a bow-fronted mahogany bureau and a pair of Sheraton armchairs which must have cost upward of thirty thousand dollars.

'I remember when my grandmother died,' said Kate. 'My parents inherited her house – a really huge colonial, in Sherman, Connecticut. I used to roam around it when I was young and I was sure that I could hear my grandmother walking along the corridor upstairs, or hear her laughing, in another room.

'I used to get so frustrated and upset because no matter how fast I ran upstairs, or hurried into the room next door, I could never catch her. I always had the feeling that I had missed her by a fraction of a second. I could even smell the lavender perfume she used to wear. But I never saw her again, and sometimes I missed her so much that I couldn't stop myself from crying and crying like I was never going to stop.'

'Is that where you spent most of your childhood, Connecticut?'

Kate nodded. 'I was very happy, most of the time. My mom and dad were very argumentative, but they did love each other, in spite of all of the rows. I miss them, too, really badly.'

'They're both dead? They must have died pretty young.'

She turned her face away. 'Yes, well. Sometimes bad things happen to very good people.'

'I'm sorry.'

She turned back again, and kissed my shoulder. 'You don't have to be sorry. If anybody should be sorry, it's me. I just wish I'd visited them more often, after I moved to New York. I just wish I could have one more meal with them, around the kitchen table. I wouldn't even mind if they argued, which they *always* did.'

'Pity you didn't have any brothers or sisters. Somebody to share your memories with.'

'But *you* have a brother, don't you, and you're always telling me what a pain in the ass he is.'

'Toby, yes. But he and me, we couldn't be more different. He's a jock. He thinks that a diminishing chord is a piece of string that you keep cutting bits off.'

Kate laughed. 'I think we'd better get ourselves some sleep. I want to take you sightseeing tomorrow, Kensington Gardens. And on Thursday we can go to Buckingham Palace, and Trafalgar Square, and the Houses of Parli-ay-ment.'

Kate fell asleep first, curling herself up into the

159

fetal position, with her back to me. I put my arm around her waist and held her close. The Philips apartment was very hushed, but I could still hear the muffled roaring of London's traffic, like a distant stampede.

I don't know how much longer it took me to fall asleep, but I was right down in the bottom of a well when I heard a phone ringing. At first I thought I was dreaming it, but it went on and on. After it had been ringing for over a minute, I sat up.

Kate was still fast asleep, and breathing heavily. But the phone kept on ringing, with one of those shrill, demanding, old-fashioned rings, and it didn't seem as if anybody was going to answer it.

I eased myself out of bed. The drapes didn't quite meet in the middle so the room was suffused with enough orange street light for me to see where I was going. I made my way to the door and opened it. The phone was ringing in the library. I considered knocking on David's bedroom door and waking him up, but then I thought, no, if he's so comatose that he can't hear this persistent ringing, he needs his sleep more than I do.

I went limping into the library, went across to David's desk and picked up the receiver. Hoarsely, I said, 'Hallo? This is the Philips' residence.'

At first, I could hear nothing but a soft crackling noise.

'Hallo?' I repeated. 'Do you know what time it is? It's a quarter of two in the goddamned morning!'

160

More soft crackling. It must have been a wrong number, or a fault. I was about to hang up when I heard a desperate voice shout out, 'No! Please! No! That hurts too much! No! Please don't do that, please don't do that! No! Not my eyes! No no no that hurts!'

It sounded like a boy, maybe twelve or thirteen years old, his voice barely broken. 'Hallo?' I replied. 'Hallo, who is this? Can you hear me?'

'Please I can't stand it, please don't do it again! Please, I'm begging you!'

'Who is this?' I shouted. 'I can't help you if I don't know who you are!'

'No no no, please! *Aaaaaahhh!*' the boy screamed, and went on screaming.

It was horrifying, but he wouldn't answer me and tell me who he was, or else he couldn't. In the end I couldn't stand the screaming any longer and I clumsily hung up.

I stood there for a few moments, my heart thumping, wondering what to do. Then I picked the receiver up again and dialed the operator.

After a long wait, a disinterested West Indian voice said, 'Operator services. How can I help?'

'I've just had a phone call. A young boy was screaming. I don't know who he was but it sounded like somebody was hurting him.'

'I suggest you call the police, sir.'

'I wondered if you could tell me what number he was calling from, that's all.'

'Have you tried ring-back? You dial one-four-seven-one.'

'No, I haven't. Can't you do it for me?'

'Hold on, sir, and I'll try.'

161

I waited and waited, and eventually she came back to me. 'Your number has received no calls, sir, since August the twenty-second.'

'That can't be right. I just answered it, only a few minutes ago.'

'I'm sorry, sir, I have the records on my computer screen, right in front of me. The last incoming call was received on Thursday, August the twenty-second, at thirteen-oh-three.'

'But there's a banker living here ... and his wife. You can't tell me that nobody's called them in over a month.'

'I'm sorry, sir. That's what the records are telling me. There have been no outgoing calls, either.'

'OK.' I didn't know what else to say. I put down the phone and tried to think what to do next. I had heard a boy screaming, no doubt about it, but if there had been no phone call, how?

One thing I was sure of: there was no point in calling the police. I had never had any dealings with the British constabulary, but if they were anything like the New York cops who had investigated the break-in at my previous apartment, I would finish up feeling like I was some kind of crackpot, or worse.

'Heard a lad screaming, did you, sir? Even though nobody actually rang? Taking any medication, sir?'

I left the library and went back to bed. As I tried to make myself comfortable, Kate stirred and muttered something in her sleep, but didn't wake up. I lay awake for more than an hour, with my mind churning over and over. How come the Philips hadn't received any phone calls since August? Maybe they always used their cell-phones, instead of their landline. Maybe they always communicated with their friends and their business colleagues by email.

Outside, it began to rain again, and I could hear water gurgling down the guttering. I kept hearing that young boy's voice, too, screaming in pain.

'Please don't do that, please don't do that! No no no that hurts!'

When I woke up the next morning, it was still dark and it was still raining. David had already left for the office, but Helena made us a break-fast of boiled eggs and toast and Earl Grey tea. We sat at the kitchen table looking at the puddles on the patio.

Helena said, 'Look at it. Hard to think we had so many barbecues out there, isn't it? I love barbecues.'

'Helena makes the most wonderful lamb kebabs,' said Kate.

'So how did you and Kate first meet?' I asked Helena.

'Oh, we've known Kate for a long time, haven't we, Kate?'

Kate smiled, and nodded.

'You should take Gideon to the Courtauld Institute. They have some wonderful Impres-sionists – Renoir, Gauguin – Van Gogh with his bandaged ear.'

'Actually I was thinking of taking him to

Kensington Gardens, to see Peter Pan.'

'Oh,' said Helena. For some reason she didn't look too happy about that. She stood up and collected our plates and our egg cups. I had a strong feeling that something was wrong, but when I looked across at Kate, I couldn't catch her eye.

'Helena ... it's important. He needs to see it sometime.'

'I know. But that doesn't make it any easier.'

Kate stood up, and laid her hand on Helena's shoulder. 'It won't go on for ever, Helena, I promise you.'

Helena had her back to me, but she lifted her hand to her eyes, and I could tell that she was wiping away tears. 'You're a good girl, Kate. Don't worry about me. I'm just being ridiculous.'

Kate hugged her. 'No, you're not. Don't ever think that. After what you and David had to go through—'

Helena gave a sniff and turned around, smiling. 'Don't you take any notice of me, Gideon. I was always too emotional. Would you like some more toast? I have some lime and lemon marmalade if you fancy it.'

We walked to Kensington Gardens, arm in arm, under a large black umbrella.

As we walked, I told Kate all about the phone call, and the boy screaming.

'I called the operator, but he said that nobody had called the Philips' phone since August. They hadn't made any outward calls, either. I mean, that just doesn't make any sense, does it?'

'It will.'

'What do you mean, "it will"?'

Kate kissed me. 'Look,' she said. 'There's Prince Albert.'

'What do you mean, "it will"? Are you trying to tell me you don't believe me?'

'Of course I believe you. I don't sleep with liars.'

'What about Victor?'

'Victor is a whole lot of things, but he's not a liar.'

She led me up toward the tall Gothic spire of the Albert Memorial. It was surrounded by sculptured animals from all four corners of the Victorian Empire – a camel, a bull, a buffalo and an elephant. Under its elaborately decorated canopy sat a gilded statue of Prince Albert, looking seriously miserable.

'He doesn't seem too happy, does he?' said Kate.

'Of course not,' I told her. 'He's dead.'

'Being dead doesn't make people unhappy. It's *how* they die.'

'And you know that for sure, do you?'

Kate laughed, and pulled herself away from me, and went skipping off along the path. 'Come on, slowpoke! You keep boasting how fit you are!'

Seventeen

She ran out of breath after fifty yards, and I caught up with her, and held her tight, and kissed her. Her hair was wet, and when she looked up at me her eyes were as gray as the sky.

'Let's go see Peter Pan,' she said. 'He never died, but *he* was never happy, either.'

We walked along the criss-cross pathways, between the leafless trees. A group of nannies were sitting under a cluster of umbrellas, surrounded by prams and strollers. A small boy was throwing sticks for a golden retriever. Above our heads, completely obscured by the clouds, a passenger jet thundered on its way to Heathrow airport, almost drowning out our conversation.

'Here he is,' said Kate. 'The boy who never grew up.'

The bronze statue of Peter Pan blowing his pipes was much smaller than I had imagined. He was standing on top of a sculptured tree-stump, which was infested with fairies and mice and squirrels and rabbits.

Kate said, 'They put up this statue in the middle of the night, so that it would look as if it had appeared by magic.'

A boy who had appeared in the middle of the night, as if by magic. *Please don't hurt me.*

166

Please don't hurt me. Please I'm begging you.

'You're thinking about that phone call again.'

'I feel guilty about it now. Maybe I should have called the police.'

'Gideon – if there was no call, how could they have traced it? You said yourself there was no way of knowing who the boy was.'

'All the same, I still feel I should have done *something*.'

'Such as what?'

We left Peter Pan with raindrops dripping from the ends of his pan-pipes and we walked back toward the Albert Memorial.

'Maybe we should go to the theater tonight,' I suggested. 'One of those British farces where everybody winds up in everybody else's bedroom. I could use a little light relief.'

As we neared the Albert Memorial, I saw two men and a young teenage boy walking toward us on one of the intersecting pathways. The men were wearing heavy overcoats, one black and one dark gray. The boy, who was walking between them, wore a navy-blue duffel coat with the hood up.

I wouldn't normally have noticed them, but when they were less than seventy-five yards away, the boy appeared to stumble, and both men took hold of his arms to support him. Is he *drunk*? I thought. It was only eleven fifteen in the morning. A little early to be plastered.

The three of them came nearer and nearer. The man in the black coat was wearing a black cap and dark glasses so it was difficult for me to see his face, but all the same he had a hawklike nose

167

which reminded me of Victor's friend Jack. The other man had iron-gray hair greased straight back from his forehead, and one of those rough, broad, Slavic faces with sandblasted skin.

They crossed our path only a few feet in front of us. As they did so, the boy turned toward me and for a split second I saw his face inside his hood. Both of his eyes were scarlet, as if he had been hit in the face. One side of his mouth was swollen and his lips were split. Underneath his nose he wore a black moustache of dried blood.

I stopped. The men and the boy continued on their way, walking quite fast. I stood staring at them as they headed away from us.

'What's wrong?' said Kate.

'Didn't you see that boy's face? It looked like somebody had beat up on him.'

'Gideon...'

'I'm going to go after them ... just to make sure he's OK.'

'Don't, Gideon. Those two men seem to be taking good care of him.'

'Well, maybe they are and maybe they aren't. Maybe it was them who beat up on him. I'm only going to ask.'

The men and the boy were already a hundred yards away. When they reached the next intersecting path, they turned sharp right, and for a moment I lost sight of them behind the trees.

'Look – wait here,' I told Kate. 'I'll only be a minute.'

I jogged off along the path. It was starting to rain again, hard, and when I glanced back I saw that Kate had put up our umbrella.

I glimpsed the men and the boy up ahead of me, between the trees, and I couldn't believe how far they had managed to walk in such a short space of time. I ran faster, with my shoes splashing in the puddles and my raincoat making a loud jostling noise. A Japanese couple in plastic rain-hats turned around to stare at me.

When I reached the right-hand path, however, the men and the boy seemed to have disappeared, even though the path ran dead straight for over a quarter of a mile. There were two nannies, pushing strollers, and an old woman in a pink nylon raincoat, walking her poodle, but no sign of the men and the boy anyplace.

I thought that maybe they had left the path and made off between the trees. I ran a short way across the grass, so that I could catch sight of them again, but they had vanished.

As she passed me, the old woman in the pink nylon raincoat said, 'You should be careful, young man. You'll catch your death.'

I walked back to rejoin Kate. 'You're soaking,' she said. She handed me the umbrella to hold, and she took out an embroidered handkerchief and dabbed my face with it.

'I can't understand it,' I told her. 'They totally disappeared.'

'That's London for you. One minute somebody's there, the next they're not. So many twists and turns, not like New York. So many blind alleys.'

I shook my head. 'That still doesn't explain how they lost me so quick.'

169

'Come on,' said Kate. 'I'll buy you some good old British fish 'n' chips.'

That evening, back at the Philips' apartment, the atmosphere was noticeably strained, although I couldn't work out why. Helena made only a light supper of crackers and cheese because we had eaten so much at lunchtime. She seemed fidgety and nervous, and she kept getting up from the table and peering out into the back garden, as if she thought that there was somebody out there.

David didn't join us for supper, but stayed in his library with the door only a little way open. He was talking on the phone, but with very long pauses in between his sentences. As I passed on my way to the living room, I heard him say, 'Yes ... yes, I know what you want. But I can't. How can you expect me to agree to that?'

Around 8:30, Kate and I went out for a walk. It had stopped raining, and the wind had changed, so that it was much warmer, and the sidewalks were drying up. We walked all the way down to Chelsea Embankment, and along the Thames. The Albert Bridge was strung with colored lights, and their reflection danced in the darkness of the water.

Kate said, 'There's something about London ... I always think the people here are very secretive. I think the whole city is secretive. All kinds of things go on behind closed doors, but nobody talks about them.'

We leaned on the parapet overlooking the river. 'Is David in some kind of trouble?' I asked her.

'You heard him on the phone?'

'Yes ... it sounded like somebody was trying to put the squeeze on him.'

'He *is* a banker. He must be under a whole lot of pressure, most of the time.'

'I know. But it didn't sound like a business call to me.'

Kate said nothing. I watched her for a while, the way the evening wind stirred her hair. Then I said, 'Would you ever leave Victor? Divorce him?'

'For you, you mean?'

'No, for Brad Pitt. Of course I mean for me.'

She was silent for nearly half a minute. Then she said, 'It would be good, wouldn't it?'

'It's already good. If you left him, it could be terrific.'

'The trouble is, I can't. Not yet, anyhow.'

'Why not? The guy's an orang-utan. And he's a Tony Bennett fan, for God's sake.'

She smiled, and took hold of my hand. 'Let's go for a nightcap, shall we? There's a wine bar just up there.'

'So you're not going to answer my question?'

'I thought I already did. I *can't* leave him, Gideon, no matter how much I might want to.'

'What – he has some kind of secret hold over you? He knows that you cheated in your grade school spelling bee? You had "necessary" written in ballpoint pen on the palm of your hand? What?'

We went to a crowded wine bar called Corkers, sitting next to a couple who had obviously had the row to end all rows, because they spent

171

over a half-hour glowering at each other and not saying a word.

Kate said, 'I just want you to know that you are more important to me than anybody I have ever met. *Ever.* And for so many different reasons. And I do want to see much more of you.'

'But you still can't leave Victor?'

She gave me the smallest shake of her head. 'No, I can't. And if you understood why, you wouldn't want to see me again.'

'Kate – I'm a very open-minded guy. At least I like to think so. What can you have possibly done that would make me not want to see you again?'

'It wasn't my fault, Gideon. But it's the one thing you couldn't bear.'

'You used to be a man? You had a sex-change operation?'

Again she shook her head, although she gave me a smile, too.

'Please,' she said, 'can we just enjoy these moments together as much as we can, without worrying about the past?'

By the time we returned to the Philips' apartment, David and Helena had already gone to bed, although they had left a lamp on for us in the living room, and Helena had written us a note saying *Do help yourself to whatever you want. There is cold chicken in the fridge if you feel hungry. XXX H.*

However, we were both tired and neither of us wanted anything more to eat, so we showered and went to bed, too. We held each other very close for a while, but eventually Kate turned over one way and I turned over the other, and we fell asleep.

I had a dream that I was walking over the surface of a frozen lake. It was almost dark and I knew that I had to reach the other side of the lake before night fell. On my left I could see a dark pine forest, like the forests that lined the road to the airport in Sweden. Ahead of me, on the bank, there was a cluster of strange tents, of all different shapes and sizes, with a haze of smoke rising above them.

As I crossed the lake, every step made a sharp crackling noise, and I was worried that the ice was going to collapse under my feet. I hurried faster and faster, and the crackling grew louder. I could feel the ice giving way underneath me, and I was sure that I was going to fall into the water and drown.

I opened my eyes. I wasn't crossing a frozen lake at all, but lying in bed, with Kate sleeping next to me. Yet the crackling was still going on, as loud as it had been in my dream. Not only that, the light between the drapes was flickering, as if the street lamp outside the house was just about to sputter out.

I climbed out of bed and went to the window. When I parted the drapes, I could see the Philips' bedroom windows, at right angles to ours. Orange flames were leaping and dancing in the left-hand window, and it looked as if their bedroom was ablaze.

I shook Kate's shoulder and shouted, 'Kate!

173

Wake up! There's a fire!'

Kate sat up immediately. 'What? What did you say?'

'There's a fire in David and Helena's bedroom!'

I dragged the drapes right back, so that she could see it. But when I looked across again, I realized that the fire wasn't inside the Philips' bedroom at all. It was simply being reflected in the window from outside. In fact, I could see David standing close to the window, staring out. Although it was difficult to make out David's expression behind the flickering flames, I could see tears glistening on his cheeks, as if he were suffering excruciating physical pain.

What was totally weird, though, was that there *was* no fire outside. It should have been right in the middle of the brick-paved patio, between the two stone cherubs, but there was nothing there at all.

'Do you see that?' I asked Kate. 'There's a reflection of a fire in that window, right? But no fire.'

Kate came up behind me. 'That's not a fire. It's only the street.'

I looked again. I could hardly believe it, but she was right. There was a dancing orange reflection in the Philips' bedroom window, but it was nothing more than the light from a sodium lamp, on the other side of the street, shining through the branches of a leafless tree.

Without a word, I picked up my pants from the chair where I had hung them, and pulled on my sweater. 'Come on,' I said, and went along to the

174

Philips' bedroom and knocked.

There was no reply. I knocked again, and called out, 'David! It's Gideon! Is everything OK?'

I was just about to let myself into their bedroom when the door opened. David was standing there in red paisley-patterned pajamas, blinking at me.

'Yes?' he said. 'Was there something you wanted?'

'I saw you at the window,' I said. 'It looked like there was a fire.'

'A fire? Where? What do you mean, a fire? I've been asleep.'

'I saw you. I saw a fire reflected in the window and you were looking at it, and you were crying. Well, you had tears in your eyes, anyhow.'

'Really?' said David, 'I have to admit that I'm mystified. Perhaps what you saw was some kind of optical illusion. You know, like a mirage. We used to see them all the time, when I was in the Sudan. You could see what looked like whole cities sometimes, out in the desert, but they simply weren't there.'

I didn't know what else to say to him. I couldn't really accuse him of being a liar, not in his own home. But I was convinced that I had seen a fire reflected in his window, and I was sure that he had been staring at it, and weeping.

'OK,' I said. 'I'm sorry if we woke you up.'

'Oh, think nothing of it. I'm a very poor sleeper in any case. I usually wake up two or three times a night and have a little read, or have a crack at *The Daily Telegraph* crossword.'

He closed the door. Kate said, 'Let's get back

to bed. We have a really full day tomorrow.' At that moment, the clock in the living room chimed two. *'Today,* I mean,' she corrected her self.

But I said, 'Not just yet. I want to take a look outside, in the back yard. If that *was* an optical illusion, I want to see how it happened.'

I went through to the kitchen and shot the bolts on the French windows. Outside, the night was windy but not too cold. The wind was making the trees thrash around, and it carried the sound of a distant train rattling on its way to one of the London termini, one of the loneliest sounds in the world.

'You should put on your shoes,' Kate admonished me.

'I'm only going to take a quick look around.'

I circled around the back yard. I was trying to work out exactly where the fire must have been located for us to see it reflected in David's bedroom window. I had been pretty much right the first time: it must have been burning right *here*, between these two stone cherubs.

I hunkered down and pressed the flat of my hand against the bricks. They were quite cold, but when I examined them more closely I saw that some of them were cracked, as if they had been subjected to a fierce heat, and that there was a dark elliptical shape in the middle of them, which could have been a scorch mark.

'I believe that there *was* a fire here,' I told Kate. 'The only thing is, it wasn't tonight.'

I stood up. 'I definitely saw David crying, too, but David says that he wasn't. He says he was in bed asleep. But supposing what I saw was something that actually took place some other night, instead of tonight?'

We went back into the kitchen. 'Is this the same kind of experience I had in Stockholm? You know, when I saw Jack abducting Felicia? Can I see things that have happened in the past, as if they're happening all over again? Or things that are *going* to happen, but haven't happened yet? Or even things that *might* happen, but never actually do?'

Kate said, 'Only you can answer that.'

I shook my head and said, 'Don't ask me. I didn't pass seventh grade math, let alone advanced physics. But I've read about stuff like that. Some couple who lived near Gettysburg swore that on the last night in June, every year, they could hear horses and wagons and soldiers marching past their house, hundreds of them, heading for the battlefield.'

'Gideon, you realize you're talking about ghosts.'

'No, I'm not. Not actual ghostie ghosts, in bed sheets. But it's like time getting out of sequence. Like dropping a deck of cards and putting them back in all the wrong order. I'm sure that might be possible. Well – I've seen it for myself, so it *must* be possible.'

We went back to bed. I was beginning to feel that I was close to understanding what was happening to me – why some events and conversations seemed so oblique and out-of-sequence. Kate had told me that I had a rare gift, and maybe this was it – an ability to glimpse both the

177

past and the future as if they were happening *now*. Not just glimpse it, in fact, but live it, complete with sounds and smells and feelings.

Kierkegaard said that life can only be understood backward, but has to be lived forward. Maybe I was the exception to that rule.

The following day was sunny but much colder. Huge white cumulus clouds rolled across London like Elizabethan galleons in full sail. As she had promised, Kate took me to see Buckingham Palace and Trafalgar Square and the Houses of Parliament.

We behaved like typical American tourists, but Kate wouldn't let me take any photographs of her. 'I don't want to come across them in twenty years' time and be reminded of how young I was, and how happy I was. Life is sad enough as it is, don't you think? So why take pictures that are only going to make your future self cry?'

'Kate – I want to remember this day, that's all, and if it makes me cry, that'll be my tough luck.'

She kissed me. 'You'll remember it, I promise you.'

We had lunch at Rules in Maiden Lane, the oldest restaurant in London, sitting on a red plush banquette, surrounded by gilt-framed oil paintings. We ate native oysters and roast pheasant, with golden syrup sponge to finish with, and felt like two characters out of a Dickens' novel.

Afterwards, we took a walk in St James's Park. We stopped by the lake, where two park officials were feeding fish to a small but greedy cluster of pelicans. The wind rustled noisily in the horse-

178

chestnut trees, almost drowning the noise of the traffic. I felt as if we had found ourselves in one of those strange 1960s art movies, like *Blow-Up*, in which everything that happens is totally mundane, but inexplicably threatening, too.

Kate said, 'What would you like to do tomorrow? We haven't done any shopping yet. We could go to Harrods.'

I was about to answer her when – with a prickling of recognition – I saw the same two men that we had seen yesterday in Kensington Gardens, walking along the opposite side of the lake with the boy between them. As before, one of the men wore dark glasses and a black cap, while the other wore a gray overcoat – although today he also wore a gray scarf, which covered the lower part of his face. The boy was dressed in the same duffel coat, with the hood raised.

'Kate – look. Would you believe it? It's those same two guys, with that boy.'

Kate shaded her eyes and said, 'You're right, yes. That's a coincidence.'

Like yesterday, the boy seemed to be unsteady on his feet, and kept stumbling, and every now and then the men grasped his elbows to prevent him from falling to his knees.

We watched them for a while, as they made their way along the path, and then I said, 'Maybe I should call the police.'

'Do you think so?' said Kate. She looked around. 'Nobody else seems to be worried about them.'

'Maybe they're not. But look at the way that kid keeps staggering.'

179

'He looks as if he could be disabled. You don't want to embarrass him.'

'I don't know. It all looks pretty damn strange to me.'

Whatever misgivings I had about the two men and the boy, there wasn't very much I could do. Although there was a bridge across the lake, it was too far away, and even if I ran, they would have been long gone by the time I had crossed over to the other side. The boy may have been unsteady on his feet, but the three of them were walking deceptively quickly. Soon they were nearly opposite us, heading east toward the nearest road.

It was then that the boy turned his head and looked at me directly, and called out. He was too far away for me to be able to hear what he said, but he sounded as if he were distressed.

I said, 'That's it. I'm going to call the police.'

But Kate took hold of my arm and said, 'No, Gideon, don't.'

'You can see it for yourself,' I protested. 'The kid's in some kind of trouble.'

'Gideon, leave it. It's far too late for you to be able to help him now.'

I stared at her. 'What do you mean by that? How do you know?'

'I just do. You were right, what you said last night. This is the same kind of thing that happened in Stockholm.'

'You *know* that kid? You know who he is?'

'I can't tell you.'

I watched the two men and the boy as they walked to the main road, and crossed over, and were lost from sight amongst the traffic. They seemed to disappear in a matter of seconds.

'Kate,' I said, 'I can't go on like this. Whatever's happening, I need to know what it is.'

'You said that you trusted me. Please, Gideon – don't stop trusting me now.'

'I want to. But give me a *reason* to trust you. Just one.'

'I can't. I shouldn't have to. Trust is trust.'

'Well ... just tell me one thing. Is that kid in any danger? Have those guys been hurting him?'

Kate looked at me but I couldn't read her expression at all. It was like the statue of Peter Pan, elvish and secretive. Behind her, with a loud explosion of flapping wings, scores of waterbirds suddenly rose from the surface of the lake.

'He's not in any danger,' she said. 'I can promise you that.'

'But you can't tell me who he is? And you can't tell me how you know him, or where he and those two guys are going, and how they just happened to be in the same park as us two days running?'

'No.'

'No? Just like that – *no*?'

She started to walk away, toward The Mall, and for one stomach-churning moment I was tempted to let her go. I felt angry and frustrated and hurt, and more than anything else I felt that she was lying to me. How could she expect me to trust her if she couldn't trust me, in return?

I waited until she was almost a hundred yards away, and then I called out, *'Kate!'*

She didn't answer, didn't turn around, but

181

stopped, and waited for me.

I caught up with her. She still didn't look at me.

'Kate – you can't expect me to go along with this. Not any more.'

'I'm not forcing you, Gideon. If you really can't bring yourself to trust me, then go back to New York, and forget that we ever met. I won't pretend that everything isn't going to fall apart, if you decide to do that. But it's your decision entirely.'

A fire truck went past, with its siren warbling, so I missed what she said next, but I caught the word 'wasted'.

'Wasted? What would be wasted?'

She looked at me at last. 'All the time we've spent together. All the visions you've seen. If I explained everything to you, before you came to understand it for yourself, then we might just as well not have bothered. It's one of the rules.'

'What are you talking about? What rules?'

'The rules of life, Gideon. The rules of human existence, and what happens after it, when it's over.'

'I still don't get it.'

'Well – how about this for a rule? Unless you're terminally sick, or you've decided to kill yourself, you never know in advance what day you're going to die. But that day is determined at the very instant of your conception, and even if you could find out what it was, there would be nothing you could do to change it.'

'So who makes these rules? Are we talking about *God*?'

'We're talking about who we are and what we are, that's all. The limitations of being human.'

'You're twisting my brain into knots. I don't follow any of this.'

'Trust me. Please, Gideon. I know I'm probably asking too much of you, but I don't know anybody else I can turn to.'

I saw a flicker of lightning, over toward Hyde Park. This was followed a few seconds later by a threatening barrage of thunder. I looked around. I was still angry, still confused, but I didn't want to let Kate go.

'Come on,' I said. 'It's starting to rain.'

We walked together back to The Mall. As we reached it, a contingent of Royal Horse Guards came trotting past, in their shiny silver helmets and breastplates and bright red tunics, with their spurs jingling. We stood and watched them, and Kate said, 'There – you can't say I haven't shown you London.'

'What do they say? If you're tired of London you're tired of life.'

A black taxi approached us, with its amber FOR HIRE light on. Kate raised her hand and gave a piercing whistle that any New York doorman would have been proud of.

Eighteen

That evening, the atmosphere at the Philips' apartment was even more unsettling than it had been the evening before. David joined us in the kitchen for a supper of thick lentil soup, but every few minutes the phone would ring in the library and he would get up to answer it. Each time, when he returned, he looked increasingly anxious.

Helena kept glancing out into the back yard, and when Kate tried to talk to her she hardly listened.

'You two went on a Mediterranean cruise last winter, didn't you?' Kate asked her.

'What?'

'I just wondered if you enjoyed it.'

'Oh ... yes. We didn't care for the other passengers much ... kept ourselves to ourselves. But the food was very good. And so *much*.'

'What cities did you visit?'

Helena frowned, as if she hadn't understood the question at all. But then she said, 'Oh! Gibraltar, Barcelona, Ajaccio. Yes, we did enjoy it. But I don't think we'll ever do it again.'

David came out of the library and sat down at the table. He stirred his soup for a moment, and then he pushed his bowl away.

'Is everything all right?' I asked him.

'What? Yes, I suppose so. It's life, that's all. It's just one damned thing after another.'

'Maybe I can help.'

'Help?' he said, bitterly. 'God knows how anyone can help.'

We started to make love when we went to bed that night, but I was very tired and Kate seemed to have her mind on other things, so after a few minutes I fell back on to my pillow and said, 'Maybe in the morning.'

'OK,' she said, kissing my shoulder. I still had the purple teeth marks where she had bitten me, and they were still sore.

'When we go shopping tomorrow, I want to buy myself one of those Pringle sweaters that David wears. And one of those check shirts, and a pair of those sandy-colored corduroy pants.'

'You want to look like a middle-aged middle-class Brit?'

'Why not? I think he looks very superior.'

'Poor David.'

'Why do you say that?'

'I think there's something tragic about him, that's all. Like a doomed king in a Shakespeare play. No matter what he does, he can't change fate.'

'There you go again, making out that we don't have choices.'

'We don't. Like I told you, it's the rules.'

'You never saw that movie. What's it called, *The Butterfly Effect*? The guy keeps trying to change the past, to make his life work out better, but whatever he does it always turns out worse.'

She kissed me again. 'Well, there you are, then. That proves it.'

'That proves what, exactly?' I asked her, but she turned over and she wouldn't answer me. 'That proves what? I mean, *what*?'

I had the same dream that I was trying to cross a frozen lake, and the ice was crackling beneath my feet. This time, however, I felt a cold flood of panic. And I could hear thumping, too, like drums beating, and somebody shouting.

I sat up abruptly. The crackling was still going on, and so was the thumping, and an orange light was jumping and dancing outside the window.

'Kate!' I said. *'Kate* – it's happening again!'

I clambered across the bed and pulled back the drapes. This time, there *was* a fire outside, in between the stone cherubs. Again, it was reflected on the Philips' bedroom window, and again, David was standing close to the window, staring out. But he wasn't just crying, he was shouting and beating on the glass with his fists.

I looked back at the fire, and it was only then that I realized what it was. It was a woman, on her knees, with her arms upraised, and she was blazing fiercely. The flames were leaping up so high that at first I couldn't see her face, but then a breeze must have blown across the yard because they dipped down a little, and I could see that it was Helena.

Her hair was now charred, and crawling with orange sparks. Her face was blackened like a minstrel's, and she was screaming.

'*Kate!*' I shouted, and shook her shoulder, but she lolled from side to side and wouldn't wake up.

I didn't hesitate. I dragged the comforter off the bed and pulled it after me along the corridor into the kitchen. I tried to unlock the French doors, but the key was jammed solid. Outside, I could see Helena still ablaze, waving her arms as if she were drowning, rather than burning.

I gave the doors a kick, but they were bolted as well as locked, and they wouldn't budge. Helena's screaming was shriller than ever, and I knew I had only seconds to save her, if I could save her at all. There was a heavy black saucepan on the cooker hob, and I picked it up, so that I could smash the windows and get out into the yard.

Before I reached them, however, Helena let out a scream so high-pitched that it actually hurt my ears, and the windows shattered right in front of me. The glass showered on to the floor like a bucketful of crushed ice, and the next thing I knew I was crunching through it in my bare feet.

Kate appeared in the kitchen doorway, blinking, her hair sticking up on end. 'Gideon, what are you *doing*?'

I ducked down, trying to maneuver my way through one of the empty window frames. But before I was even halfway through, I realized that the flames were dying down.

I managed to climb through the window and tug the comforter after me, but when I stood up straight I saw that the fire had burned itself out, and the yard was lit only by street lamps.

187

Not only was there no fire, there was no smoke, and no sign of Helena either. Between the two cherubs there was nothing but a darkened mark on the paving bricks, and I didn't have to reach down to touch it to know that it was stone cold.

I turned around. The Philips' bedroom drapes were closed, and there was no sign of David staring out. Behind me, Kate was unlocking the French doors, and opening them up.

'Are you OK?' she asked me. 'Your feet aren't cut, are they?'

My left foot was bloody, but when I lifted it up to take a look, I could see that the cuts were all superficial. 'I'm fine. I just don't know what happened. I saw Helena, right out here in the yard, and she was on fire. It looked like somebody had poured gas all over her and set her alight. You know, like those Buddhist monks.'

Kate said, 'Come on, Gideon. Come back inside.'

I looked around. 'I saw her burning, God damn it. She was waving her arms around and she was screaming. But she's not even here, is she?'

Kate held her hand out to me. 'Come on, Gideon. You need to come back to bed.'

Reluctantly, I hobbled back into the kitchen, and Kate closed the doors.

'No point in locking them, really,' she said. 'But I'll call a glazier first thing, and arrange to have them repaired.'

I pulled out one of the kitchen chairs and sat down. My heart was still banging hard against my ribs. 'This is it, Kate. I don't care why I'm

seeing things, or what you're trying to show me.
I can't take any more of it. Tomorrow morning,
I really am going home.'

She went to the sink and came back with a
damp kitchen towel. 'Here, lift up your foot.
Let's clean up these cuts before you get tetanus
or something.'

'You're not going to beg me to stay?'

'No,' she said. 'I think you've probably seen
enough.'

'Then you believe that I saw Helena?'

'Yes.'

'Well, hallelujah. That's the first straight
answer you've given me. So how come I could
see her when she wasn't really there?'

'Because you *can*, my darling. That's why.'

We locked the kitchen door behind us, and then
went back to our bedroom. I don't know how
David and Helena had managed to sleep through
all of that noise, but we were both reluctant to
wake them up.

Kate found some Band-Aids in the bathroom
cabinet and stuck them criss-cross on the soles
of my feet.

'So I was right?' I asked her. 'I *can* see things
that have happened at different times? Like
yesterday, or even tomorrow?'

'In a way. Like I told you before, it's a very
rare gift, and only a very few special people
have it. The people who *do* have it are very often
musicians – or composers, like you.'

'Oh, yes? And why is that?'

'Because, my darling, everything that happens

189

in this world has its own resonance, like a tuning fork that goes on singing long after you've struck it. Hardly anybody can pick up that resonance, but you can. I knew that, the moment I first saw you looking out of your apartment window.'

'So – how did you know that, exactly?'

'I just did, that's all.'

'And so you took me to Stockholm and you brought me here to London, so that I could see things happening that nobody else could?'

'That's right.'

'But *why*? That's what I really need to know.'

Kate climbed into bed and pulled the comforter up to her chin. 'It's time you got some sleep, if you're going to fly back to New York tomorrow.'

'You're not coming with me?'

She shook her head. 'There's someplace else I have to go first – somebody I have to see. But I'll be back in the city by the weekend.'

I climbed into bed next to her. 'Helena – she's not really going to burn, is she?'

'Gideon – don't worry about it. Nobody's going to hurt her.'

'The way she was screaming – I can still hear it now. I was going to break the windows with a cooking pot, but her screaming broke them first. It was like what happens when *you* scream.'

She kissed my cheek, and then my eyelids. 'If that's the way you remember it. But get some sleep, OK?'

By the time I had showered and dressed the next

morning, David had already left, so I didn't have the chance to say goodbye to him. But Helena was still there, taking coffee in the living room with Kate. She was wearing a cream silk blouse and she looked unusually pale, almost faded, like a black-and-white photograph of herself.

'Kate told me about the French windows,' she said, as I came in. 'You're not to worry ... it could have happened to anyone.'

'Oh, yes?'

Kate said, 'I found an emergency glazier in the yellow pages. He's coming around after lunch.'

'That's good. You'll have to let me know how much it costs.'

'Oh ... don't even think about it,' said Helena. 'It was an accident, that's all. Would you like some coffee? I'll go and get another cup.'

She went into the kitchen. I sat down next to Kate and said, 'What did you tell them?'

'I told them that you woke up in the middle of the night and felt like a breath of fresh air. You went out into the back yard but you accidentally left the French windows open. A gust of wind caught them and they slammed shut and broke.'

'And they *believed* you?'

'There was no reason for them not to.'

'And Helena really had no idea that she did it herself, by screaming so loud?'

'She wasn't there, remember? So of course she had no idea.'

I was about to protest that I had seen her there, whether she was there or not, but I didn't really want to get into another argument about what Kate was hiding from me and what she wasn't, especially at that time of the morning. At that moment, anyhow, Helena came back into the living room.

'Would you like a biscuit, Gideon? Or one of these scones?'

I left for Heathrow Airport around eleven thirty. I gave Kate one last embrace on the front doorstep. My taxi was already waiting for me by the curb, and because it was London, it was raining.

'I'll meet you back at St Luke's Place, then?' I asked her.

'Of course you will.'

'I don't know. I have this very bad feeling that I'm never going to see you again.'

'You will – I promise you. This is only the beginning.'

'I love you,' I told her. 'Visions or no visions. Rules or no rules. And there's something I want to ask you.'

'I know,' said Kate. She touched my lips with her fingertips, as if to stop me from saying any more. 'But give me a little more time.'

'I'm that transparent?'

'I can see it in your face, my darling. I can feel it in your *resonance*.'

The taxi driver tooted his horn and pointed at his watch. 'Cutting it a bit fine, mate!'

I kissed Kate again, and then I went down the steps and across the sidewalk. As I opened the taxi door, I turned around to wave to her. She was already closing the front door – but in the living room window, staring at me, I saw Malkin, or the white cat that looked like Malkin.

192

I hesitated. I almost felt like going back. But then I thought, let's leave this mystery to unravel itself in its own time, and I climbed into the taxi and closed the door.

When I arrived back at St Luke's Place, just after seven that evening, there were more than a dozen letters in my mailbox, mostly bills, and as many messages on my phone, including an invitation from my mother to come up to Connecticut for lunch last Sunday. She had obviously forgotten that I was in Europe, which didn't surprise me at all. When I was a kid, she regularly forgot to pick me up from school, and she never remembered my birthday.

It was a still, foggy night and my apartment was as chilly as a meat locker, so I kept my coat and my scarf on and turned up the heating. Victor must have been at home, because through the floorboards I could faintly hear Tony Bennett singing *The Boulevard of Broken Dreams*.

I called Margot and told her that I was home.

'I'm so relieved,' she said. 'I had such a bad nightmare about you last night.'

'I've told you before about eating pizza just before you go to bed,' I told her, but even as I said it, I thought about Helena blazing and screaming in her back yard, and Elsa standing in the moonlight, glistening wet, and those nightmares had been real, as far as I was concerned.

'You were dead,' said Margot. 'I went into this cellar and you were sitting on a chair, and your face was white. In fact it was so white it was almost *blue*.'

'Margot, I'm alive, and I'm fine, and if you want to take a look for yourself, I'll take you to The Pinch tomorrow for a drink.'

'OK. I have to give a piano lesson at two o'clock, but after that. Did you have a good time in London?'

'I did and I didn't. I'll tell you all about it if you come over later.'

'Who are those people with you?'

'Nobody. Only Tony Bennett, God help me.'

'No ... I can hear that crackling noise and somebody whispering. Is it Kate?'

'Margot,' I told her, 'there's nobody here but me.'

'Maybe it's your cell. It's exactly like that whispering I heard when you called me from London.'

'I'm not using my cell. This is my regular phone.'

'Listen, Lalo, I'm not being nosy. If you have somebody there and you don't want to tell me about it, that's perfectly OK with me. It's not that young guy you met at the Dance Theater Workshop, is it?'

'*Margot*—'

'OK, OK. Don't get your panties in a twist.'

By the time I had finished unpacking my case and throwing my shirts and shorts into the washing-machine, my apartment was a whole lot warmer, and I could take off my coat and my scarf. I popped open a can of Dr Pepper, kicked off my Timberland loafers and sprawled out on one of the couches. The strange thing was that I didn't feel as if I had been away at all. If it hadn't been for the Wasa Museum Guidebook on the table, and the postcards of Peter Pan's statue in Kensington Gardens, I could easily have been convinced that the past few days had been nothing but a series of disconnected dreams.

It was still only 5 p.m. out on the coast, so I called up Dick Bortolotti at the DDB Agency and Jeanette Hirsch at Thunder Music and my old friend Randy Spelman, who was helping me to arrange the theme music for a new NBC comedy series called *Jack The Snipper*, set in a small-town barbershop someplace in the Midwest.

I was still talking to my LA agent Hazel McCall when I heard bumping and shouting below me in Victor's apartment. The Tony Bennett music abruptly stopped, and then there was a crash which sounded like a side table tipping over, maybe with a lamp on it.

'Sorry about this, Hazel,' I told her. 'I'm going to have to call you back. It sounds like my neighbor is starting World War Three.'

There was more shouting, and then I heard a woman screaming. I sat up straight. She screamed again, and then again, and this time I was sure of it. It was Kate.

I couldn't think how she had managed to get back to New York so quickly, but that wasn't really what worried me. It sounded like Victor was yelling at her and hitting her and throwing things at her, and she was trying to get away from him.

I pulled open my apartment door and hurried downstairs. Kate had stopped screaming but I could still hear Victor shouting. I thumped on his door and called out, 'Victor! Victor, it's Gideon, from upstairs! What the hell is going on, man?'

Inside the Solway apartment everything went quiet. I waited for a few seconds, and then I knocked again.

Victor opened the door. He had a cellphone in one hand and a glass of whiskey in the other. He was obviously still talking to somebody, because he said, 'Hold up a moment, Ken.' Then he smiled at me and said, 'Gideon! Back from your travels? What seems to be the problem?'

I tried to look past him into his apartment. 'I heard screaming. It sounded like you two were having a fight.'

'You heard *screaming*?'

'That's right. Screaming. And yelling. And furniture falling over.'

Victor opened the door wider, so that I could see into the living room. None of the chairs or tables had been disturbed. The red-haired woman was sitting on one of the couches, wearing a blue satin robe. She was watching some TV show about movie stars' homes. When she saw me, she gave me a little finger-wave and called out, 'Hi, there!'

'Maybe what you heard was the people next door,' Victor suggested.

'Well, yes, maybe. But it really sounded like it was coming from down here.'

'These old buildings ... it's the cavity walls, and the air vents. Funny how sound can carry.'

'I guess,' I conceded. 'Sorry I bothered you.'

'That's OK, Gideon. Glad to know you're so concerned. If you ever hear us fighting for real, make sure you come down quick, before Monica murders me.'

He gave me a toothy laugh and closed the door.

I went slowly back upstairs. I was convinced that I had heard Kate screaming, yet Victor must have been right. All that commotion must have come from the couple next door, although I had never heard them before. Apart from that, Kate had still been in London at eleven this morning, and when I left her she hadn't even started to pack.

When I reached the landing, I found Malkin waiting for me. She was sitting beside my front door, her paws neatly tucked together, and she was purring loudly.

'OK, puss,' I told her. 'Why don't you come inside for a can of anchovies, and tell me what in God's name is going on around here?'

Nineteen

Margot came around the following day and I took her to The Pinch on Sullivan Street for Guinness and shepherd's pie. The Pinch is a scruffy Irish-style pub: two narrow red-brick rooms, with a huge flat-screen TV and a well-worn dartboard. But the atmosphere is always cheery and boisterous, and that was just what I needed after my trip to Europe.

'Lalo – you've changed so much since you and Kate have been together,' said Margot. 'You're worried about something, aren't you?'

'Yes, frankly. But I don't know what it is.'

'I don't understand. How can you be worried about something and not know what it is?'

As soberly and as factually as I could, I told her about my experiences at the Westerlunds' apartment in Stockholm and the Philips' apartment in London. I told her about Elsa and Felicia being in two places at once and Helena Philips burning, and about Malkin, too. I wasn't sure why, but I was beginning to think that in some way, Malkin held some kind of key to all of this, like the missing piece of sky in a jigsaw.

'Maybe I *was* seeing things,' I told Margot. 'Like hallucinations, or optical illusions. But I know I'm not crazy. I don't *feel* crazy and everything else in my life is perfectly sane and logical.'

'But Kate knows what this weirdness is all about? Or you think she does?'

'She's pretty much admitted that she does. But no matter how often I ask her, she flat-out won't tell me. Or *can't*, for some reason.'

Margot forked up another mouthful of shepherd's pie. 'Maybe you need to give her an ultimatum. I mean, you have enough on your plate, don't you, without inexplicable hallucinations to contend with? Tell her that she *has* to explain what's going on, or else you're going to walk.'

'I've done that already. Twice.'

Margot narrowed her eyes. 'And she still wouldn't tell you? But you still didn't walk? You're madly in love with her, Lalo. Don't try to deny it.'

'OK, yes. She makes me feel that I can do anything. Some of the new scores I've written, since I've met her. They're so damn brilliant that even *I'm* blown away.'

'And does *she* love *you*?'

'I think so.'

'Enough to leave the vile and horrible Victor?'

I shrugged. 'I don't know. She says she can't, not yet, although I don't have any idea why. Not "won't". Not "doesn't want to". But *"can't"*. How about another one of those Pinch Bull cocktails?'

Margot shook her head. 'If I have another I won't be able to play *Chopsticks*, leave alone Chopin.'

We walked back to St Luke's Place together, arm in arm. It was a sharp, breezy day and dozens of sheets of newspaper scampered across James J. Walker Park and clung to the fencing.

'You want to come up for a coffee or something?' I asked her.

'No, thanks. I have another piano lesson at four thirty, a little Chinese boy who actually plays better than I do. But I could see you tomorrow.'

I gave her a hug and a kiss and climbed up the front steps. I opened the front door, and there, waiting for me, was Kate. She looked very pale, and her pallor was emphasized by the gray button-through dress she was wearing, and the gray silk scarf she wore on her head.

'Hallo, darling,' she said, and reached out both her hands to me.

'What's wrong?' I asked her, after I had let her in to my apartment. 'You look like you're sick.'

'I'm OK. A little tired, that's all. Do you have a glass of water?'

'Sure.' I went into the kitchenette, opened up the fridge and poured her a glass of Evian. I said, 'I saw Victor last night. I heard a whole lot of shouting and screaming and I thought it was coming from your apartment. As a matter of fact, I thought the woman who was doing the screaming was you.'

Kate looked up at me and gave me a wan smile. 'You worry about me far too much.'

'Well, obviously. When I went downstairs and knocked on the door, nobody was shouting and nobody was screaming and you weren't even there, although that redhead was. She had really made herself at home, too.'

'What do you want me to say?'

'Nothing. Whatever goes on between you and Victor, that's your business. That doesn't mean I don't get incandescently jealous.'

'You don't have any need to, Gideon, I promise you.'

Malkin came into the living room and jumped up on to the couch. She sat close to Kate and Kate stroked her and gently tugged her ears.

'Maybe we shouldn't see each other for a while,' she said.

'Why the hell not?'

'Because I can see that this is hurting you, and I don't want you to be hurt.'

'It's not hurting me, it's just frustrating me.'

'Gideon – I need you, but not if the price is too high for you to pay.'

I sat down next to her. 'I've already made up my mind,' I told her. 'If you want me to wait and see what this relationship is all about, and what all that weirdness with the Westerlunds and the Philips was all about, then OK, I'll wait and see. I can't say that I enjoy being kept in the dark, but if it means that you and I stay together, I'll sit here with the light off for as long as it takes.'

She kissed me. Her lips felt very cold. I was sure that she was going down with the flu. I took her hands in between mine and they were freezing, too.

She stayed until nearly six, which was when

201

Victor was due home. I had turned the heating up to 'ox-roast', and by the time she left she had some color back in her cheeks, even though she still looked feverish. Malkin loved it being so warm: she lay on her back on the rug with her legs spread wide apart.

'No modesty,' Kate smiled.

I kissed her at the top of the stairs. 'Go to bed,' I told her. 'Take a Tylenol and don't let that husband of yours anywhere near you.'

She started to go downstairs. Halfway down, she turned around and blew me a kiss and said, 'Go back inside. I'll be fine, I promise you. I probably won't be able to see you tomorrow, but maybe the day after. And look – you have a friend!'

I turned around and saw that Pearl was standing close behind me, in her stained pink bathrobe. She had one hand raised to her forehead and she was frowning.

'Pearl?'

'I think I've forgotten where I am,' she said. 'Is this a hotel?'

I took hold of her elbow and steered her back along the landing. 'No, Pearl. This is your home. This is where you live.'

'I was afraid of that. There are too many people here, aren't there?'

'What do you mean?'

'They come and they go. There are far too many of them. Always opening doors and closing them again. It never stops. Opening doors, and closing them again. You see them, don't you? You see them as clear as day.'

'I don't really understand what you're talking about, Pearl. Come on – let me help you get back upstairs.'

'There are far too many. And it never stops. Did you see my Jonathan downstairs? He went to Blick's to buy some new brushes.'

'No, I didn't see him. I'm sorry.'

We had reached the second-storey landing now. Pearl's front door was open and I could smell the familiar waft of fresh oil paint and stale cauliflower.

'He's been such a long time ... I get worried. It's all these people, you know. They covet everything you own, even the sunlight that shines into your eyes. *They wants it.*'

I helped her into her living room. She sat down and reached for a crumpled pack of Lucky Strikes. She took out a cigarette and lit it with a worn-out brass lighter, blowing smoke halfway across the room.

'How's the painting coming along?' I asked her.

The easel was turned away from me at an angle, and the light was shining off the oil paint, so I couldn't see her life study at first.

'Very good,' she said. 'But I think there are too many people in it now. It's far too crowded.'

'I thought it was just you.'

'It was, to begin with. But see for yourself.'

I walked around the easel. Whoever was painting Pearl's life study, he had made unbelievable progress since the last time I had looked at it. The nude portrait of Pearl was almost completely finished, and the artist had caught her expression completely: a coquettish old woman who knew that her naked body was still capable of attracting men's attention.

But around the ottoman on which she was sitting there were now seven other figures – two women, two men, two children, and a baby. The two women were both naked, but the two men were dressed in black three-piece suits, and the two children were wearing old-fashioned pinafore dresses, with narrow blue-and-white stripes. The baby was lying on the floor, in the bottom right-hand corner of the painting, wrapped in a dark-maroon blanket.

So far, the artist had painted only the children's faces in any detail: the adults' faces were still a muddy blur, as if he had painted them and then smeared them with a paint rag while they were still wet. The baby's face was blurry, too. But the children had both been rendered in meticulous glowing detail, like Pearl.

I didn't know what to say. I felt as if my hair was crawling with hundreds of lice. The two children in the painting were both girls. One was Elsa and the other was Felicia. And even though their faces were partially obliterated, it wasn't hard to guess who the adults were.

'You see what I mean?' asked Pearl, with twin tusks of smoke streaming out of her nostrils. 'Too many people by far.'

'But they didn't actually come here and sit for this painting, did they?'

'What are you talking about? They're always here. I told you. Opening doors and closing them. Coveting your very breath. They didn't

come here, Gideon Lake. They're *always* here.'
She paused, and then she flapped her hand at
me. 'You see? I remembered your name. I told
you I would, didn't I?'

I stood and stared at the painting for more than
a minute. I couldn't make any sense of this at all.
How could the Westerlund girls have come all
the way from Stockholm to pose for this
painting? How could Axel and Tilda have come
here, and the Philips, too, from London?

No – Pearl must be mistaken. These portraits
must have been painted from photographs. But –
even so – why these particular people? What
possible connection could Pearl have with
Kate's acquaintances in Europe? And why had
they been included in this painting?

And another mystery: who did the baby belong
to? It seemed to be wrapped in the same blanket
as the baby I had seen Kate pushing, in the park.

'When is your painter coming again?' I asked.

'You mean Jonathan? He went to Blick's to
buy some new brushes. He always goes to
Blick's, but it seems to take him for ever. I think
he stops for a drink on the way home. Not just
one drink, either. Either that, or he's seeing some
floozie. He always had an eye for floozies, the
floozier the better. He likes tiny little breasts.
That's why he fell for me. Tiny, teentsy little
breasts. His friend Gordon calls him the tiny
titter.'

'So you're not sure when he's coming back?
I'd like to talk to him, when he does.'

Pearl crushed out her cigarette. 'In that case,'
she coughed, 'I shall tell him to come downstairs

and see you. But I can't tell you for certain when that might be. I think he stops for a drink on the way home from Blick's. I'm sure of it. Either that, or he's seeing some floozie.'

Now she started coughing in earnest, coughing and coughing until she had to reach for a Kleenex. When she took the tissue away from her mouth, it was speckled with blood.

'Are you OK?' I asked her. 'Maybe I can get you some water.'

She shook her head. 'I'm all right. It's *you* that I'm worried about.'

'Me? Why should you be worried about me?'

She coughed again, pointing her finger at me. 'I saw you with that woman. You should be very careful with that woman. I know what she's up to.'

'Oh, yes? What?'

'She's getting you to do her dirty work. That's what she's up to.'

'Pearl,' I said, 'I really don't think so. She and I, we're just enjoying each other's company, that's all.'

'But to what end? That's what you have to ask yourself.'

'Pleasure. Affection. Friendship. Isn't that enough?'

'Not for *her*, Gideon Lake. I know what she's up to. She can't do it herself, so she's getting you to do it for her.'

'So what exactly is it, this thing that she can't do for herself?'

Pearl shrugged one shoulder, so that her bathrobe slipped off it, and exposed the deep hollow above her collarbone. 'How should I know? Everybody has a different agenda, don't they? Coming and going, opening doors, closing them again. You can't follow each and every one of them, to find out where they're going.'

'No,' I said, even though I had no idea what she was talking about. 'I guess you can't.'

I looked at the painting a little longer, while Pearl looked at me.

'Déjeuner sur l'herbe,' she said.

'What?'

'It's that famous painting by Manet. Ed-oo-uard Manet. Picnic on the grass. The men are both fully dressed but the woman is *completely* naked. It caused a tremendous scandal when it was first exhibited.'

The portraits of Elsa and Felicia were uncanny. They were so lifelike I felt as if they might suddenly speak to me from out of the canvas.

'Jonathan always says that women ought to be naked all the time, day and night,' said Pearl. 'Then we would see them for what they really are. One day you'll see that woman downstairs for what she really is. *Then* you'll need a shoulder to cry on, believe you me.'

She stood up. Without any warning she let her bathrobe drop to the carpet and stood in front of me naked. She was very bony, and the painter had generously given warmth to a skin tone that was almost transparent, but even in her mid-seventies she was still very feminine and even erotic, like an elderly nymph.

She lifted her chin proudly. 'Now you can see *me* for what I am, and you know that I am telling

207

you the truth.'

I picked up her robe and hung it gently around her shoulders. 'You're a great-looking girl, Pearl,' I told her. 'And I *do* believe that you're telling me the truth.'

That night, when the moon was shining into my bedroom, I heard it again. Tony Bennett singing *The Boulevard of Broken Dreams*, and then shouting and screaming and furniture toppling over.

I sat up and listened. The noise was coming from Victor and Kate's apartment, right below me, that was for sure. I could hear Victor shouting, 'What did you ever do? What did you ever do? Tell me! What the *fuck* did you ever do?'

I heard Kate then, but very muffled. Then another crash, which sounded like a picture being broken, or a mirror. A door was slammed, and then another door. After that, there was silence.

I lay back down again. I didn't know what the hell I was supposed to do now. My natural instinct was to tear downstairs, kick open the Solways' apartment door, and punch Victor very hard. On the other hand, Kate had made it clear to me that she wasn't going to leave Victor – not yet, anyhow – and I had a very strong feeling that no matter how catastrophic her marriage was, and no matter how badly Victor mistreated her, she wouldn't thank me for interfering.

Now that everything was quiet, I decided to do nothing until the next time I saw her. But I would have to make it clear to her that if I heard

Victor shouting at her or beating up on her, I wasn't going to let him get away with it. She was Victor's wife, but she was my lover, too, and I loved her, and I was determined to protect her.

I had an hour-long wrestling match with my sheets, but I couldn't sleep. I got up and went to my Roland keyboard, and played a few experimental riffs for *Jack The Snipper*, with my earplugs in so that I wouldn't disturb Pearl upstairs or Victor and Kate below me.

Then I played a slow, regretful melody, and made up some words for it.

'Kate ... she came into my life oh much too late ... and now, no matter what I do or say ... she always smiles and turns away ... and never tells me if the things I see ... are real or if they're just my fantasy...'

I didn't see Kate at all for the following three days. Twice, when I saw Victor leave the house, I went downstairs and knocked on her door, but there was no reply. I didn't see Malkin, either. I left out a plate of anchovies that I had picked off a take-out pizza from Joe's on Carmine Street, but on the second morning they began to smell so much that I had to scrape them into the InSinkErator.

I was beginning to wonder if Kate had decided to finish with me, or at least to cool things for a while. Maybe Victor had given her a black eye, and she didn't want me to see it, in case I tried to give *him* one, by way of retaliation.

The weather was strangely still and gray. It

was like living in a 1950s photograph. On Saturday evening, my chilled-out friend Johnny Stuber came to visit from Fort Lauderdale, where he usually divides his day between surfing and writing highly lucrative ballads. We went to Suzies for Chinese, and then to Bowl-mor Lanes on University Place for a couple of beers and a couple of hours of bowling. Johnny wore a bright blue windbreaker and yellow pants and he was so suntanned he made me look as if I only had ten days left to live.

'What's wrong, dude?' he asked me, as we sat at the bar, waiting for a lane to come free.

'Who says there's anything wrong?'

'How long have I known you? Usually, I can never shut you up. Tonight, the only thing you've said is, "where the hell did you get those yellow pants?" Oh – and, "excuse me, miss, there's some kind of bug in my garlic broccoli."'

I didn't know what to tell him, so in the end I told him the truth. I even told him about Pearl and the painting.

He listened intently, occasionally raising his gingery eyebrows. When I had finished, he said, 'Why worry about it?'

'I can't help worrying about it. It's all so god-damned inexplicable.'

'Sure it is. But most of life is inexplicable, isn't it? The simple truth is that we don't have the time to understand everything that happens to us, do we? We have to take some things at face value, no matter how wacky they are. Once, when I was going through Orlando Airport, I saw my grandpa standing in line for a flight to

Seattle. I hadn't seen him in about five years. I was going to go up and say hi when he put his arm around this elderly Chinese lady who was standing next to him, and gave her a kiss like they were husband and wife. The year after, he died, and I never found out who that woman was, or why he was going to Seattle with her, and I didn't dare to ask my grandma.'

'Maybe your grandpa was a bigamist.'

'Sure, maybe he was. That's pretty much the same as being in two different places at the same time, isn't it?'

When I returned to my apartment that evening, Kate was waiting for me on the landing, with Malkin in her arms. She was wearing the same gray button-through dress and she looked even more pallid than she had before.

'Where have you been?' I asked her. 'I've missed you. I've been worried.'

I bent down to kiss her but she half turned her face away and I ended up kissing the top of her ear. I opened up my front door and let her in.

'I knocked on your door a couple of times, when Victor was out.'

'You shouldn't. I'll never answer.'

'Why not? Have I done something to upset you?'

'No, of course not.'

She sat down in one of the armchairs with Malkin in her lap. It certainly appeared as if something had upset her, even if it wasn't me. She kept glancing around the room, and she wouldn't look at me directly.

'We don't have as much time as I thought,' she said.

'Excuse me? Time to do what?'

'We only have six or seven weeks or so. Maybe less.'

'You're doing it again,' I told her. 'You're speaking in riddles.'

'I've told you! I don't have any choice! I can't make accusations, even if I wanted to!'

'Accusations against who? Accusations about what?'

'You don't understand!'

'Too right I don't understand! Maybe I'm just natural-born dumb! But I can tell you one thing – I'm not deaf! I heard you and Victor the other night, yelling and screaming and throwing the furniture around! How long do you think I can put up with that?'

For the first time, she turned and stared at me. 'You *heard* us?'

'I'm surprised the whole goddamned neighborhood didn't hear you! You sounded like you were wrecking the place!'

She covered her mouth with her hand. Then she said, so quietly that I could hardly hear her, 'You heard us. My God.'

'Kate, for the umpteenth time, tell me! What is it with you and Victor? Why can't you just walk out on him? He's going to do you an injury one day. Or worse.'

Kate stood up, so that Malkin had to drop out of her lap on to the floor. 'I'm sorry, Gideon. I can't do this. I thought I could, but I don't think I have the strength.'

I took hold of her wrists. She still wouldn't look at me directly. 'Kate, listen to me. You *can* leave him. I'll take care of you. I won't let Victor do anything to you. I won't even let him *near* you. You can stay here or we can go to my parents' place, or even find ourselves a hotel.'

She shook her head. 'It's impossible.'

'Nothing is impossible if you have enough determination. You don't have to worry about money. You don't have to worry about getting a lawyer. One of my best friends is a partner in Lukas, Daniel and Roland, and, believe me, he's a *shark*.'

'No, Gideon. I'm so sorry. But if you feel like this it's not going to work.'

I tilted her chin up so that she had to look at me. Those rain-washed eyes looked darker than ever. 'What you're saying is that you don't really love me.'

'All right, if that makes it any easier for you. I don't love you. I never did.'

'You don't mean that.'

'Yes, I do. You're boring, trite, and you're full of yourself. Just because you can tinkle out some catchy little jingle about toilet freshener, you think you're some kind of modern-day Mahler.'

'You're absolutely right. I am, and I do. But I can only do it so brilliantly because of you. And you're not fooling anyone. You feel the same way about me as I feel about you. Maybe *more*, even.'

Malkin was rubbing against Kate's legs, so Kate bent down and picked her up.

'Have a nice life, Gideon,' she said, and walked toward the door.

'So that's it?' I asked her.

She turned her head and there were tears in her eyes. 'Let's just say that I misjudged you. It's my fault. I expected too much of you. Just because you have so much music in you. Just because you can see things that nobody else can see.'

'Kate—'

'I'm sorry, Gideon. I don't know why I thought it could work. It was selfish of me. I never thought about you. I never asked myself if you were strong enough to take it.'

'Kate, for Christ's sake. *Please.'*

'Goodbye, my darling.'

With that, she left my apartment and went downstairs. I stayed where I was, waiting to hear her door close, but all I heard was the muffled sound of Pearl's television, and the distant scribble of a police siren.

I went to the window and looked out. The day was still gray, and very still. I had never felt so sorry for myself in the whole of my life.

Twenty

Over three weeks went by. We had an early snowfall, and across the street, kids were running around the park, throwing snowballs and pulling plastic sledges behind them.

All I can remember about those three weeks is darkness. Every day the sky was overcast, and if the sun appeared at all, it was only as a dim crimson disk behind the Franks Building.

I had been commissioned by CBS to write the incidental music for a new courtroom-style quiz show called *Asked And Answered*, and I had signed a contract with the DDB Agency for six new Diet Pepsi commercials. But all of my inspiration seemed to have walked out of the door along with Kate. I sat at my keyboard for hours, tinkling random minor-key melodies, but they were all too discordant for TV jingles. You can't sell Diet Pepsi with music that makes you cry.

The best piece I wrote was a soft, sad song about walking through a snowstorm, trying to catch up with the woman you love. As the snow falls thicker and thicker, she disappears from sight, and you can only follow her footsteps. Gradually, however, her footsteps are obliterated, too, and you have lost her for ever. I called it *Snow Blind*.

I drank too much Zinfandel and spent hours staring out of the window, hoping to see Kate coming down the steps, or walking in James J. Walker Park, across the street. Knowing that I would never be able to kiss her and hold her in my arms again made me feel as if my stomach had been completely filled with lead, like a cold casting, and I had a dull metallic taste in my mouth.

When I was awake, I kept thinking over and over: why did she lose faith in me? Why did she think she was asking too much of me? She had told me more than once that I had vision, and sensitivity, and resonance. She had said I could make her friends come to life. So what did she think I was lacking?

It couldn't be trust. I had trusted her, hadn't I, even when she seemed to be talking in conundrums? I had stayed in Stockholm when she had asked me, even after I had seen things that would have turned my hair gray, if it hadn't been gray already. I had followed her to London, and seen horrors and pain and mysteries that seemed to have no logical connection whatsoever.

Maybe she thought I didn't have the stones to do what she was eventually going to ask me. But I had already witnessed more weirdness than most people get to experience in the whole of their lives, and even if I was baffled and confused, I was still reasonably sane, and I wasn't so frightened that I wanted to back out altogether. Why had she taken it as a sign of weakness that I had wanted to know what in God's name was actually going on?

When I slept, I had nightmare after nightmare. In one, I was running through the Westerlunds' apartment in Stockholm, trying to catch Elsa and Felicia as they fled along the corridors in their nightdresses. In another, I was hammering with my fists on our bedroom window in London, while Helena Philips stood in the yard outside, blazing from head to foot, her eyes staring and flames leaping out of her mouth, so that the skin of her lips blistered and curled.

In yet another, Kate and I were making love. As she climaxed, she threw herself backward and screamed, so that the chandelier exploded and our bedroom windows burst inward. We were deluged in glittering glass splinters, and our bed was turned into a bloodbath.

Every morning I woke up and put out my hand, even though I knew that Kate wouldn't be lying next to me. Every morning I eased myself out of bed like a man twice my age, feeling as if I hadn't slept at all.

I stopped playing music in the evening, in the hope that I could hear Kate's voice coming up through the floor. But all I ever heard was Victor, talking too loudly on his cellphone, or arguing, or singing along with Tony Bennett. Either that, or Tony Bennett himself, singing *I Wish I Were In Love Again.*

Now and again I heard the red-haired woman. Almost every time she left the house, she seemed to forget something, because she would slam the front door behind her, and then immediately unlock it again, and slam it again, and then go out a second time, with yet another slam. When

Margot was with me, and the red-haired woman left the house like that, she always said, 'slam, bam, thank you ma'am!'

Margot helped me a lot through those days. She would come around, and make me a sandwich, or one of her pasta dishes, but she didn't try to cheer me up, or take my mind off Kate. She knew that I was hurting and that only time would heal what was wrong with me, not jokes.

One day I would feel angry with Kate, for taking me for granted. The next day I would feel angry with myself, for having allowed her to do it. The day after, I would simply feel lonely, and depressed, and I would sit playing *Snow Blind* over and over, and singing the lyric in a whisper.

The snowflakes fell so thick and fast
I couldn't see where you had passed
You left me far behind
So many miles behind
Snow blind...

One evening I sat on the stairs outside the Solways' apartment for nearly three hours, hoping that Kate might come in or out. Victor arrived home shortly after 10 p.m. He gave me an odd look and said, 'Gideon! How are you doing, sport?', after which I gave up waiting and climbed wearily back upstairs.

I thought of writing to her, or recording a message on a CD. In the end, I did both, but the letter was too long and read as if it had been written by a lovesick high-school student. The CD was better, especially since I played *Snow*

Blind on it, as well as telling her how much I missed her. I addressed it to *Mrs K. Solway, Strictly Confidential* and put it into the Solways' mailbox. I was taking a risk that Victor would open it, and play it, but who gave a shit? I had lost her anyhow.

One snowy morning, a little over a week later, I looked out of the window and saw Victor leaving the house, with Kate close behind him. I called out, *'Kate!'* although she couldn't have heard me, and I knocked on the window pane. This time, though, she didn't look up at me, the way she had when I very first caught sight of her.

Victor stopped at the bottom of the steps and tugged on a pair of black leather gloves. He didn't say goodbye to Kate, or even look at her, but started to walk briskly toward Hudson Street. Kate turned left, in the direction of Seventh Avenue, and it was then that I saw that she was carrying a wrapped-up bundle inside her overcoat. It was a baby, in the same blue knitted bonnet that I had seen before, with ear flaps. I couldn't see its face.

'Kate,' I said, although no sound actually came out.

I ran downstairs in my socks and opened up the front door. I took the steps three at a time. I jogged along the sidewalk a little way, until I realized that I couldn't see her. She had vanished into the snow, just like the woman in my song. Maybe she had hailed a cab, or a friend had picked her up.

A black man overtook me. He was wearing a

huge padded coat, with a padded hood, so that he looked like a quilt on legs. He turned around and stared at me in my T-shirt and my socks, and there was such pity on his face that I almost felt sorry for myself.

I climbed the steps back into the house and it was only then that I realized that my socks were soaked.

I saw her again two days later. I was climbing out of a taxi after a meeting on Madison Avenue when I saw her walking diagonally across the park, in her overcoat and her gray woolly hat. I pushed twenty dollars into the cab driver's hand and said, 'Keep it.' Then I dodged across the street and into the park. This time I was determined not to lose her.

I glimpsed her between the trees, about eighty yards in front of me. She was walking quite quickly and I could see now that she was pushing a stroller with a baby in it. I started to run. It was growing dark in the park and I knew that it would be closing soon.

I lost sight of her for a moment, but then I saw her again, and somehow she had managed to walk as far as the south-west corner of the handball court, over a hundred yards away.

'Kate!' I shouted. 'Kate – wait up, will you!'

She kept on walking, and disappeared behind the fence. I ran after her again, but when I reached the handball court she had gone.

I walked slowly along the path toward Seventh Avenue. It was so gloomy that she could easily have hidden behind the fence someplace, or behind a tree, or the low concrete wall that surrounded the bocci ball court.

I stopped. Six or seven scraggy-looking pigeons waddled around me, expecting me to feed them.

'Kate!' I called out. 'I don't know whether you can hear me or not, but I really miss you! I don't care what I have to do, I want you back!'

My voice echoed flatly around the handball court. An old woman in a plaid coat stood watching me, only twenty yards away, with her toothless mouth turned down like a caricature of a witch.

'Kate! I need you, and I'll do anything to make you happy! I'm beginning to see what you're trying to show me! Whatever you want me to do, I'll do it, I'll help you, and I won't ask any more questions! Did you listen to my song? I meant every word of it! I love you! I miss you, and I love you with all of my heart!'

I waited for a while, but even if she had heard me, Kate didn't answer. The pigeons warbled crossly all around me, and the traffic rumbled, and after a few minutes the old woman in the plaid coat sniffed and coughed and wandered off. I don't know what kind of public drama she had been expecting, but she was obviously disappointed.

I walked slowly back to St Luke's Place, turning around every few yards to see if Kate might be following me, but the park was too shadowy now. When I climbed the front steps and opened the door, the first thing I heard was Tony Bennett, singing *The Boulevard of Broken Dreams*.

221

I trudged up to the second-floor landing. I wasn't angry anymore. I was tired, and dispirited, and just as confused by Kate's behavior as ever. She must have heard me, when I first called out to her. Why hadn't she stopped? She had nothing to be afraid of, and if she really didn't want to see me ever again, all she had to do was say so. I was a thirty-one-year-old man, after all. I couldn't pretend that it wouldn't hurt me, but I would just have to learn to get over it.

As I reached the landing, however, I saw that I had an unexpected visitor. Malkin was sitting in front of my door, her paws neatly tucked in front of her.

I hunkered down and stroked her head, so that she flattened her ears. 'Well now,' I said, 'why are *you* here, puss? Brought me a message, did you? Or did you only come up here because you were hungry?'

Malkin stretched herself up and clawed at my door. I let myself in and she followed me inside. Without hesitation, she trotted across to the window and jumped up on to the sill. I went up to her and said, 'What?'

Across the street, I saw Kate, with her stroller, although now the stroller was empty. She was looking west, toward Hudson Street, although I couldn't make out what she was looking at. All the same, I suddenly understood what she was doing; and she must have sensed how close I was to understanding it, or else she wouldn't have sent Malkin up here.

The visions that I had seen in Stockholm and London were flashbacks of traumatic events that

222

had happened in the recent past, and these visions of Kate were flashbacks, too. Once I had fitted them altogether, I would know exactly why she needed my help. She wasn't yet showing me the finished jigsaw, but she was giving me some of the most important pieces. It was not only the Westerlunds and the Philips who had suffered, it was Kate, too.

The baby in the stroller and in her arms – the baby she called Michael – he wasn't a friend's baby that she was looking after, he was *hers*. He was the baby that Victor had fathered – the baby whose loss had made Victor so angry that he never wanted them to try for another.

I walked around my apartment, switching on the table lamps, but I didn't draw the drapes. I didn't know if she was still out there, in the street, but I guess I was trying to give Kate a sign that I had seen the light.

I didn't go to bed that night until well after 2:30 a.m. I was hoping that Kate might come knocking at my door, looking for Malkin. But Malkin wolfed down a supper of liver pâté and prosciutto, which was all I had in the fridge, apart from some holey Swiss cheese, and then she curled herself up and went to sleep in one of my armchairs, as if she wasn't expecting to be disturbed.

But the next morning, around 8:30 a.m., I heard something drop through my apartment door. I rolled out of bed and found that Malkin had beaten me to it, and was sniffing at a large brown envelope. I opened the door at once, but there was nobody there. I stepped out on the landing, and called 'Hallo?' but nobody answered. As I did so, Malkin ran between my legs and fled downstairs.

I waited for a moment and then I went back inside. The envelope contained two weighty objects, nearly six inches long, and even before I tore it open I knew what they were. Two new brass keys – obviously modern copies of antique keys, with plain bows but very complicated blades.

There was also a business-class air ticket for the following morning – Alitalia 7617 from JFK to Marco Polo airport, Venice – costing $7,618. And a sheet of notepaper with a handwritten address on it: Professore Enrico Cesaretti, Apt # 1, Palazzetto Di Nerezza, Campo San Polo, San Polo, Venezia.

That was all. No note, no explanation. No invitation. Not even, *'Dear Gideon, I'm sorry for everything I said ... I really do love you after all.'* But she didn't really need to. If she had listened to the song that I had recorded for her, and heard me shouting out to her in the park, she would know that I forgave her everything.

I went into the kitchen and switched on my Nespresso coffee machine. While it was spitting and gurgling, I weighed up the two brass door-keys in the palm of my hand. I couldn't believe how much of a rush I felt. I had always wanted to visit Venice, and now I was not only going to visit Venice, but get back with Kate again, too.

I sat down at my keyboard and played *The One-Handed Clock*, deliberately out of key.

224

Whatever happened in Venice, I had no illusions that it was going to be easy; and there was every possibility that whoever the Cesarettis were, I was going to experience some very disturbing visions of them. But up until now, none of my visions had done me any physical harm, had they, no matter how terrifying they might have been. And maybe I would finally find out what had happened to all of Kate's friends, and where Victor and Kate's lost baby fitted into the picture.

I called Margot. There was a whole lot of clanking and banging going on in the background. 'Brad's here and I'm making pancakes,' she said. 'You can come on over and help us to eat them if you like. There's far too many for two.'

'Hey, I don't want to be the ghost at the breakfast. Besides, I have to pack. Believe it or not, Kate's been back in touch. I haven't spoken to her yet, but she's invited me to Venice.'

'So you two are back together again? That's good news, I hope. I just hope this trip doesn't turn out as Scooby-Doo as the last one.'

'I don't know. I think it might. But she needs me, Margot, and she's made it pretty clear that I'm the only person who can help her.'

'If she needs you, she has a funny way of showing it, walking out on you like that.'

'She was worried that she was expecting too much of me, that's all. This has something to do with the baby she lost, although I don't exactly know what.'

'Really? What does she want you to do –

father another one?'

'Hey, come on, Margot. I don't think it's anything like that. Whatever it is, though, I'm not going to push her into telling me, not until she's ready. She needs my help, and my support, and I love her, and that's why she's going to get them.'

'Well, it's all *très* bizarre, if you ask me. But if you love her, and she loves you, that's all that matters, isn't it?'

'Thanks, Margot.'

'What are you thanking me for?'

'I don't know. I can't think of anybody else who would have put up with all of my moping and all of my miserable music, the way that you did.'

'That's what friends are for, Lalo. *Brad* – stop stuffing so much into your mouth at once, will you? You look like a goddamned chipmunk.'

I was on my way out of the house to do some shopping at Sushila's when a taxi stopped at the curb, and Victor and the red-haired woman climbed out. The red-haired woman was laughing loudly, and Victor had a self-satisfied grin on his face.

'God, you're such a scream!' said the red-haired woman. "Which part did *you* get?" I'm telling you!'

'Hey, Gideon,' said Victor. 'How's our in-house musical genius?'

'Good, thanks.'

'Me and Monica, we haven't been disturbing you, have we? I haven't formally introduced you to Monica yet, have I? Monica – Gideon –

226

Gideon – Monica.'

'So nice to meet you, Gideon,' said Monica, holding out her hand as if she expected me to kiss it. She had false chisel-shaped nails, painted dark crimson. 'I've heard you playing a few times, late at night. You play so romantic.'

'I hope I haven't disturbed you.'

'There's worse ways of being disturbed, believe you me.' With that, she gave Victor a dig in the ribs with her elbow, and laughed out loud. 'Just kidding, lover.'

I was thinking of asking Victor where Kate was, just to see what his reaction would be. I would have liked to talk to her about this Venice trip before I actually flew there. I would also have liked to talk to her about her lost baby. But I wasn't at all sure that it was a good idea for me to show any interest in Kate. Victor might already be suspicious that she was seeing another man, and I didn't want to confirm his suspicions – especially since I had been warned how bad-tempered he could be. I was also beginning to think that if the baby was somehow involved in what had happened to the Westerlunds and the Philips, then maybe Victor was, too.

'You take care, Gideon,' said Victor, squeezing my arm. 'We're having a party next weekend, and you're invited. Bring a friend, why don't you? Maybe you can tinkle out some tunes for us.'

'Sure. There's nothing I like better than tinkling out tunes.'

They went into their apartment and closed the door. I heard Monica screaming with laughter, and I couldn't help wondering whether she was laughing at me.

It was sunny when I walked out of Marco Polo Airport, but the temperature wasn't much higher than 50 degrees, and there was a fresh, chilly wind blowing from the Alps.

I could have reached the city by bus, but Hazel McCall had urged me to take the water taxi, even though it was expensive. She was right. I sat in the back of the little motor launch as it made its way south-westward across the lagoon, and gradually the spires and domes of Venice rose from the horizon, like a drowned city in a fairy tale.

We puttered slowly along the Grand Canal. I felt like I was traveling through some medieval painting, with balconied palaces and colorful houses on either side, reds and yellows and greens. The waterway was teeming with gondolas and *vaporetti* crowded with tourists. We passed under the Rialto bridge, and after a few minutes we turned into a narrow canal between tall, russet-painted buildings.

We moored up against a sheer green-stained wall. The water taxi was dipping up and down, and I almost stumbled, but the driver held my elbow and helped me to balance my way on to a steep stone staircase.

'*Grazie, signore,*' he said, grinning at me with tobacco-stained teeth, and I realized that a €20 tip was probably far too much. '*Faccia attenzione. A Venezia potete non fidarsi mai di qualcuno.*'

'Sure, you too,' I told him. I climbed up to the top of the steps and found myself in a small paved garden, with a dried-up marble fountain and decorative urns that must have been filled with geraniums during the summer, but contained nothing now but trailing brown weeds.

I looked up. The palazzetto was four stories high, painted a pale tangerine, with elegantly pillared windows, although all the windows facing the canal had their shutters closed. I crossed the garden to an arched doorway, with a black-painted door. There were four bell-pushes, but none of them had name cards next to them, only Roman numerals, I, II, III and IV.

The water taxi driver was still turning his launch around, and for a moment I was tempted to call out to him, and ask him to take me back to the airport. There was something I seriously didn't like about the Palazzetto Di Nerezza, something secretive and very forbidding. But I hesitated too long, and the water-taxi burbled back toward the Grand Canal, and I was left with the black-painted door and the key to open it.

The levers in the lock opened with a series of arthritic clicks, and when I pushed open the door itself, it let out a great shuddering groan.

I stepped into a grand hallway with a marble floor, a chandelier, and an elaborate gilded mirror with candleholders on either side of it. On the right, there was a curving staircase with stone banisters and a polished marble handrail.

On my left stood a life-sized marble statue of a nude woman, holding up a headless dove. The poor bird had probably had its head knocked off centuries ago. Beyond her, there was another wide door, in natural oak. I guessed this was the Cesaretti apartment.

I knocked, and waited, and knocked again, but there was no reply. Somewhere upstairs I could faintly hear a television, with what sounded like football scores. *'Genoa, tre ... Udinese Calcio, zero...'*

I took out the second key and unlocked the door. Inside, I found myself in a long gallery, with a dark paneled ceiling, and a row of windows with pale-yellow glass in them. There were paintings hanging all the way along it, most of them landscapes, with sombre skies and shadowy forests.

On either side stood six or seven armchairs, each of them heaped with cushions in red and green tapestry, and the floor was covered in assorted Venetian rugs.

I closed the door and walked along the gallery. Through the yellow glass windows I could dimly make out a very large square, which must have been the Campo San Polo. It was crowded with hundreds of shadowy figures, as if an army of ghosts had recently arrived.

I thought that I could hear somebody walking very close behind me, but when I turned around I saw that there was nobody there, and that it must have been an echo.

At the end of the gallery I reached an enormous drawing room, with a high decorated ceiling and a pale woodblock floor. It was lavishly furnished with rococo chairs and sofas, and the drapes were patterned with flowers and leaves and songbirds. In the far corner stood a fine antique piano, with a bust of Verdi on top of it.

I looked up. Suspended high above me, from the vaulted ceiling, hung a huge multi-branched chandelier, carved and gilded, more like a giant golden spider than a light fitting.

I put down my bag. The apartment was utterly silent. It smelled of old wood and pot-pourri and faintly of cigarettes, and there was another smell, too, of damp plaster.

I was still standing there, wondering what I should do next, when I heard a sharp snoring sound, and I almost yelped out loud. I walked cautiously across the room, and found a man sleeping in one of the high-backed armchairs. He was almost completely bald, but he was only about forty-five years old, with a round face and a pointed nose and a sallow suntan. He was wearing an expensive light-gray suit, and dark-blue velvet slippers. In his right hand he was holding a pair of steel-rimmed spectacles.

I coughed, and he flinched, but he didn't wake up, so I coughed again, much louder this time.

He stirred, and opened his eyes, and stared at me, unfocused.

'*Chi sono voi?*' he snapped. *'Che cose state facendo qui?*'

'Hey – I'm sorry if I woke you. My name's Gideon Lake. Kate Solway invited me here.'

The man put on his spectacles and peered at me more closely. 'Ah yes, Gideon Lake. We have been expecting you. I apologize if I was sleeping. I had a very long night at the hospital.'

He stood up and held out his hand. He was

231

very precise in his gestures, very neat. 'Enrico Cesaretti. Welcome to Venice. Is this your first time?'

'It is, yes. I always wanted to come here but I never quite managed to make it before now. It's a pretty amazing place, isn't it?'

'Well, I would prefer it without so many tourists, but I suppose we Venetians have to make a crust of bread somehow.'

'Do you know when Kate's going to get here?' I asked him.

'Oh, she is here already. She has gone out shopping with my wife.'

'Have you known Kate long?'

Enrico pointed to my bag. 'You must be tired. I can show you to your room, then perhaps you would care for a cup of coffee?'

'Oh – great, thanks.'

He led me through a door at the far end of the drawing room and along a corridor. This side of the apartment was much less formal, with fitted carpets and framed prints on the walls.

'Here – this is the bathroom if you need it – and this is the room you will share with Kate.'

He opened up the door for me, and ushered me into a huge bedroom with an emperor-sized bed and a carved pine wardrobe that a family of five could have lived in. Outside the windows, through the fine net curtains, I could see a narrow balcony which overlooked the canal, with two cast-iron chairs on it, and a cast-iron table.

'It's real generous of you to have me here, Enrico. You don't mind if I call you Enrico?'

'Of course,' he smiled. 'I expect only my staff

and my patients to call me *"professore"*. And the generosity is yours. These days, not so many people are prepared to give up their time so unselfishly.'

I didn't really know what he meant, but I shrugged and smiled as if I did.

'Come,' he said. 'Please refresh yourself and we can have some coffee and you must tell me all about your music.'

'Oh ... Kate's told you already.'

'Of course. She considers you to be *molto speciale*. Very special.'

'Well, I think she is, too.'

'Yes,' he said. He took off his spectacles, and nodded. 'To try so hard to make amends for the unforgivable sins of others, that is almost holy.'

'I'm not too sure that I follow you.'

'Please – if there is anything you need. Anything at all, just ask.'

He left me to unpack. Quite suddenly, I felt exhausted, and I would happily have climbed into that enormous bed, pulled the quilt up over my head, and gone to sleep for the rest of the day.

After I had stowed away my sweaters and my jeans in that cavernous wardrobe, I took my toiletries bag and went into the bathroom. It was tiled from floor to ceiling in gleaming white, and fitted with a monstrous washbasin with old-fashioned faucets, an antiquated shower stall, and a massive bathtub on lion's-claw feet, surrounded by a white plastic curtain.

I splashed my face with cold water and reached for a hand towel. As I dried myself, I looked at myself in the mirror. What the hell are you doing here, dude? Pursuing some hopeless fantasy that you and Kate will ever get together as a real couple? Looking for an answer when you don't even know what the question is? Are you some kind of masochist, or just a fool?

In my bones, though, I knew I was here for a reason, even if I didn't understand what it was. This was no time for giving up. Kate had almost given up, back in New York, but she had clearly changed her mind. Otherwise she wouldn't have given me the keys to the Cesaretti's apartment, and stumped up over seven thousand dollars for me to fly here.

As I stood there, I became conscious that the bathtub faucet was dripping. It made a flat *plip, plip, plip* as if the bath were full up with water. I finished drying my face and then I went over and drew back the curtain. The tub was brimming, right up to the overflow.

But more than that, there was a distorted pink shape lying on the bottom. A naked woman, with her dark hair completely covering her face. I was so shocked that I yanked at the curtain, and pulled out some of the curtain rings.

I took hold of the chain and pulled out the bath plug. Then I plunged my hands into the water and tried to lift the woman out. The water was freezing and she was so slippery that I could hardly get a grip on her. I managed to lift her head above the surface, and pull some of her hair away from her face.

She was a young woman. Her lips were blue and she wasn't breathing. Her brown eyes were wide open and she was staring at me as if she were trying to convince me that any attempt to save her would be useless. I tried to heave her further out of the tub but she was so heavy and floppy and the sides of the bath were so high that it was difficult for me to get any leverage.

'Enrico!' I shouted. 'Enrico, help me! There's a woman drowned in here!'

By now, with a lascivious gurgle, the last of the water was draining out of the bath. I managed to maneuver the woman so that she was lying on her side, and water poured out of her nose and mouth. But she still wasn't breathing, and when I felt her neck there was no sign of any pulse.

'Enrico! I need some help in here! Enrico!'

Still no response. The walls of the palazzetto were so thick that he probably hadn't heard me, so I went out into the corridor and shouted out again.

'Enrico!'

Enrico appeared almost at once, wiping his hands on a kitchen towel. 'Gideon? Is something wrong?'

'There's a woman in the bathtub ... I think she's dead.'

'What?'

He came hurrying along the corridor, and followed me into the bathroom.

'The curtain was drawn ... I didn't see her at first.'

I looked into the bath. It was empty. Not only was it empty, it was dry. Enrico frowned at me, and said, *'Ciò è uno scherzo, si?* This is a joke?'

235

I didn't know what to say. I could only think: not again. Not more hallucinations, and people who aren't really there.

'I was sure,' I told him. 'I pulled back the curtain and there she was.'

Enrico looked down at the broken curtain rings with undisguised displeasure. 'Pah,' he said.

'Look, I realize you don't believe me, Enrico, but check my sleeves out. They're soaking.'

He didn't even bother to look. 'I expect you are tired,' he said. 'But you must understand that what you have said is in very poor taste.'

'I'm sorry,' I said. 'I was absolutely convinced that I saw what I saw. It wasn't a joke, I promise you.'

'Very well,' he said. 'Now, coffee is ready, if you are.'

Twenty-One

When I was seventeen I told Heidi Becker's mother that sauerkraut was the most vomitous vegetable on the planet, just before she served up a Reuben casserole (sauerkraut and corned beef, if you've never had the misfortune to eat one). But the discomfort I felt that day at Heidi Becker's house was nothing compared with the following hour I spent with Enrico Cesaretti.

Enrico was courteous to a fault, and told me in great detail about the transplant surgery he performed at the Ospedale SS Giovanni-e-Paolo. But he didn't leave me in any doubt at all that my 'joke' in the bathroom had deeply upset him, and he asked me nothing about myself or my music or my relationship with Kate. He half smoked a cigarette, and crushed it out in his saucer.

A little after three o'clock, I was relieved to hear the front door opening, and Kate calling out, 'Hallo there! Anybody home?'

A soon as I heard her voice, I stood up and called out, 'Kate? Kate – we're in here!' I had never felt so excited in my life. But before I said anything else, I turned back to Enrico. 'Listen, Enrico. What happened in the bathroom ... I had absolutely no intention of giving you any grief.'

He looked at me with great solemnity, as if he were a judge, or a priest, but then he nodded. 'All right, my friend, I accept your apology. I have no desire to worry Kate, and I very much appreciate your taking the trouble to come here. But, please, do not mention what you saw to my wife.'

'Of course not.'

He took off his eyeglasses. 'I had no idea that Kate had told you so much about us. We have always been a family who prefer to keep ourselves to ourselves.'

'Enrico – Kate has told me nothing at all about you. I haven't spoken to Kate for nearly a month.'

At that moment, however, Kate came into the drawing room, carrying half a dozen shopping bags.

'Hallo, musician,' she smiled. She was wearing the same putty-colored trench coat she had worn in London, and a brown beret. She was just as skinny as ever, but she had much more color in her cheeks than the day she had walked out on me, and her hair was shinier.

She set down her bags on a nearby sofa and I went up to her and took hold of her hands.

'Hallo, Kate,' I said, and kissed her, and when I inhaled her fragrance, and tasted her lipgloss, all of the misery of the past three weeks simply curled up and disappeared, like a dead chrysanthemum on a bonfire.

Kate turned around. Close behind her stood a small dark-haired woman in a red plaid poncho.

'*Ciao*,' she said. '*Benvenuto all nostra casa.*'

'Salvina, this is Gideon Lake,' said Enrico. 'Gideon, my wife Salvina.'

Salvina had a prominent nose with a bump on the bridge, huge brown eyes and pouting red lips. She took off her poncho and underneath she was wearing a black wool dress with a wide red patent-leather belt. She had a vase-like figure, with enormous bosoms, a narrow waist, and generous hips.

'I am so delighted,' she said. 'Welcome to Venice, Gideon. We are so grateful that you could come.'

'I'm extremely pleased to be here,' I told her, and kissed her on each cheek. She smelled strongly of some musky, heavy-duty perfume like Trussardi.

'I have to unpack all of this shopping,' she said. 'Enrico, why don't you ask our guests if they would care for a Punt e Mes, or maybe a glass of wine? I know I would!'

She bustled off to the kitchen, with Enrico following her, carrying the rest of the bags for her. I turned back to Kate and said, 'It's so good to see you. You're looking great.'

She turned her face away, almost shyly. I loved that very slight droop of her eyelids, as if she were feeling drowsy. 'It's good to see you, too, Gideon. I'm sorry if I hurt you.'

'You don't have to apologize. You told me right at the beginning that you couldn't explain everything, not all at once.'

I put my arms around her and kissed her again – her cheek, her hair, and the curve of her ear. She reached up and touched my face as if she couldn't believe that I was really here. 'You saw Michael,' she said.

I nodded. 'That was when I began to understand what you wanted from me.'

'Poor Michael. Do you know what I used to call him? Michael-Row-The-Boat-Ashore. I used to sing it to him, and it always sent him off to sleep.'

'How old was he?'

'Six months, seven days. He's buried in Sherman, in North Cemetery, next to his great-grandparents.'

'I'm very sorry. How did he die?'

Kate gave the slightest of shrugs. 'Heart condition. The doctors did everything they could, but—'

'I *saw* him, Kate. I saw you pushing him in his stroller, in the park. I saw you carrying him

239

along the street.'

Kate's eyes filled with tears. 'He was my little darling. I miss him so much. But that was still no excuse for Victor to be so angry.'

I held her close. It was then that Enrico came back into the room, carrying a tray with four aperitif glasses and a bottle of Punt e Mes. He spooned ice into the glasses, poured the aperitif, and added a slice of orange to each one.

Salvina came in, too, and we all raised our glasses and drank a toast.

'*Memorie felice*,' said Enrico. 'To happy memories, and happy times together.'

'*Memorie felice*,' we all echoed.

While Salvina started to prepare dinner, and Enrico went into his study to write some letters, Kate and I went for a walk outside, across the Campo San Polo. The sun was going down and the square was not so crowded now, although there were still several crocodiles of Japanese tourists winding their way from one side to the other, led by tour guides with raised umbrellas.

We sat down together on a bench, under a naked tree. The sky was still intensely blue, although the temperature had dropped like a brick, and I couldn't stop myself from shivering. Twenty or thirty pigeons came stalking up to us, to see if we were going to feed them, but when they realized that we weren't, they irritably stalked off again. I was reminded of the pigeons in James J. Walker Park.

'What changed your mind?' I asked Kate. 'All you had to do was knock at my door.'

'I know,' she said. 'But if I had done that, we would have had the same argument again, sooner or later, wouldn't we? I know that some of the things I've been showing you have been strange, and frightening. But I needed to be sure that you could accept them for what they were and gradually come to understand them, without my having to explain them to you, because I can't. But when you followed me into the park, and called out to me like that, I knew that you would understand them, eventually – and more than that, I knew that you *could*.'

Kate laid her hand on top of mine. 'Besides that, my darling, we've come too far together to stop now. And it's much too important.'

I said, 'I still don't really understand how I saw you pushing Michael through the park.'

'It's not difficult. You saw me in exactly the same way that you saw Elsa and Felicia, and the Philips boy. Life is like a flicker book. You run through the pictures, one after the other, until you get to the end. But after you've finished looking at them, all of the pictures are still there, aren't they? And some people can turn back to them, and look at them again. People like you.'

I turned toward the sinking sun, raising my hand to shield my eyes. 'I've had another vision,' I told her. 'Vision, hallucination, whatever you want to call it.'

'*Here*? Already?'

'Almost as soon as I arrived I saw a girl, drowned in the bathtub. I not only saw her, I *felt* her. I tried to lift her out. But when I called Enrico, she was gone. My sleeves were still wet

241

but the bathtub was bone dry.'

'Do you know who it was?'

I shook my head. 'She was young, with long dark hair. I tried to get her out of the tub but I couldn't.'

Kate said, 'I won't lie to you, Gideon. You'll see more visions. But I don't know everything that happened here, any more than you do. All I can tell you is that this is the last time I'll ask you to come away with me. There isn't much time left, less than a month. After that, it should all be over.'

'I sure hope so.'

She kissed me. The tip of her nose was cold. 'I'm so pleased you decided to come. I missed you so much. Heaven knows what I'm going to do without you.'

'What did you say that for? I'm not going anyplace. All I have to do is push Victor under a cross-town bus and we can live happily ever after.'

'You shouldn't joke about it.'

'Well, you're right. Nobody seems to have much of a sense of humor around here, especially Enrico.'

That evening, Salvina served us up a supper of Venetian specialties, *baccala montecato* – whipped salt cod with garlic, served on toast – and *fegato alla veneziana*, calves' liver in thyme and onions.

We ate in the kitchen, which was almost as large as the drawing room, and tiled in rich reds and greens. Enrico opened two bottles of red

Venetian wine, and poured it into decorative glasses. Then he proposed a toast.

'I drink to Kate, who has devoted herself to finding us peace. When we felt despair, she came to us, bringing hope. I thank her from the bottom of my heart.'

'To Kate,' I said, and Kate mouthed the words, *'Thank you.'*

After supper, we went back into the drawing room. Enrico poured us some sweet Venetian dessert wine and I played a few melodies on the piano, including an impromptu tribute to Venice.

'Venice is a city you surely won't forget ... especially since the avenues are all so goddamned wet...'

I was running through a medley of my best-known TV themes when I happened to glance sideways, toward the window. Abruptly, I stopped playing. My hands tingled as if I had touched a bare electric wire.

Standing in the corner, beside the drapes, was a naked girl.

She must have been about seventeen or eighteen years old, although it was hard to tell because her face was completely covered by her dark brown hair. Her skin was as white as the marble statue in the hallway, and she was wet.

I turned my head around to look at Enrico and Salvina. Enrico was sitting back in his armchair, smoking a cigarette, while Salvina was concentrating on her embroidery. They must be able to see this girl, surely? And yet both of them seemed to be completely unruffled.

I caught Kate's eye, and jerked my head

243

toward the corner.

'Don't stop,' she said. 'I was really enjoying that. What's the matter?'

I jerked my head again, and said, *'There ... in the corner.'*

She frowned directly at the drapes, but then she shook her head. 'I don't understand.'

I played a scattering of discordant notes. Then, hesitantly, like the plinky-plonky music for somebody walking a tightrope, I picked up my TV theme again. All the time, though, I couldn't take my eyes off the naked girl. I now realized that I was the only person in the room who could see her.

'What is this tune?' asked Salvina. 'It is very sad music. *Molto malinconico.*'

'What?' I said. Then, 'Oh ... yes. This is the theme I wrote for a TV series called *Doctor Paleface.*'

'Doctor Paleface?'

'Sure – it was all about a white doctor who tried to save Native American tribes from being wiped out by the diseases that the white settlers brought with them. You know – measles, cholera, syphilis – stuff like that.'

Kate said, 'I never saw it.'

'I'm not surprised. It was sanctimonious politically correct crap and they axed it after five episodes.'

The naked girl remained in the corner, totally motionless, for almost two minutes. Then slowly she began to raise her hands toward her face. I played slower and slower, and kept hitting the wrong keys, and Enrico sat up and said,

'Gideon? Is everything all right?'

'Sure, Enrico, sure. Couldn't be better.' After what had happened in the bathroom, I didn't want to upset him again.

But Kate must have sensed that something was badly wrong, because she stood up and came over to the piano, and stood close behind me.

'Do Enrico and Salvina have any kids?' I asked her, out of the corner of my mouth.

She leaned close to my ear. 'A boy and two girls, yes. The boy's name is Massimo and the girls' names are Amalea and Raffaella.'

'How old?'

'Massimo's only seven but the girls are both in their teens. Why do you want to know?'

'Because I can see a girl standing in the corner. She has no clothes on, and she's dripping wet.'

'What does she look like?'

'Hard to say. She has her hair hanging all over her face.'

Even as I said that, though, the girl took hold of her hair, as if she were grasping two dark curtains, and parted it. I stopped playing again, and said, 'Shit, Kate. Tell me you can see her. You *must* be able to see her.'

The girl appeared to be staring in my direction, but where her eyes should have been she had only two black holes. I felt as if my skin were growing tighter and tighter.

She stayed motionless for a while, with both hands still clasping her hair. Then she opened her mouth and let out a falsetto scream. She went on and on, screaming and screaming, and I stumbled up off the piano stool and knocked it over backward.

'Gideon?' said Kate. 'Gideon, what's wrong?'

I pressed my hands over my ears, but the naked girl only screamed louder and shriller. It was then that my wine glass shattered, spilling wine all over the top of the piano. Immediately, the girl stopped.

Enrico stood up. He came over to the piano and picked up the broken stem. He stared at it, as if it could be miraculously mended by staring alone. 'These glasses ... they are Murano.' It was obvious that he was very angry.

'I'm sorry, Enrico. I didn't touch it.'

'This set ... they are eighteenth century, irreplaceable. They used to belong to my grandparents.'

'I swear to God, Enrico, I was nowhere near it.'

Salvina stood up, too. 'They are very fragile, these glasses,' she said, trying to be conciliatory. 'Perhaps it was not wise to use them. Careful, *caro*, don't cut yourself. I will bring a dustpan and clear it up.'

Kate was standing very close to me. 'Is the girl still there?' she murmured.

'Yes,' I said. 'She *screamed*, for Christ's sake, and that's what broke the wine glass.'

'What's she doing now?'

'Nothing. She's not moving. But she's parted her hair, so that I can see her face. She looks like the girl I saw in the bathtub, except that she doesn't appear to have any eyes.'

'*Che cosa?*' asked Enrico. '*Che cosa avete detto?*'

'Nothing,' said Kate, quickly. 'He was only saying that the glass was very beautiful and he's sorry it broke.'

'Well, for my part I apologize. I did not intend to lose my temper.'

The naked girl stayed silent, and she had stayed totally still for over a minute. But then she began to turn around, so that I could see her back. She was extremely thin: her shoulder blades were as prominent as triangular plowshares, and I could see the knobbles of her vertebrae. It was her skin, though, which horrified me. I wanted to tell Kate what I could see, but now Enrico was standing close to me, too.

All the way up the back of the girl's arms and legs, and across her shoulders, there were two continuous rows of small holes. The holes were swollen but they weren't bleeding, although some of them were torn open so that they joined up with the next one, especially the holes in the back of her forearms.

At first I couldn't understand what they could be. But then I suddenly remembered visiting my dad in hospital, when he was recovering from his gall-bladder operation. The nurse had been changing his dressing when I was there, and I had seen the six-inch incision in his stomach. On either side of the incision, there had been suture holes exactly like the holes that this girl was showing me.

For some reason, somebody had taken a needle and thread, and stitched something to her back. I couldn't imagine what.

Enrico said, 'Maybe it is time we all went to

bed. You will want to see the city tomorrow, Gideon, and I always recommend an early start. By the middle of the morning, everywhere is so crowded with tourists. You even have to stand in line to cross the bridges.'

I nodded. I still couldn't take my eyes away from the naked girl. Enrico laid his hand on my shoulder and said, 'I know that you will do your best for us. It is all a question of time, and understanding. As for the wine—'

I turned to him. His expression was infinitely regretful, as if he had suffered a loss from which he would never recover.

'I'll do my best,' I told him.

'Yes. We have a saying in Venice, you know. *"Oggi in figura, domani in sepultura."* It means today we are present in person, talking to each other, eating, laughing, sharing a bottle of wine. Tomorrow we will all be in the grave.'

'Thanks,' I said. 'I needed cheering up.'

Kate laughed and took hold of my hand. 'Come on,' she said, 'why don't we have one last drink before we go to bed? And one last tune. Why don't you play *The Pointing Tree*?'

I turned back toward the window. The naked girl had disappeared.

'OK,' I agreed, even though I remembered what Axel had said, in Stockholm. *'There is no such tree. Once you are lost, there is no way back.'*

When we climbed into bed that night, Kate handed me a black silk scarf.

'What's this for?'

248

'We're going to make love, aren't we?'

'It had crossed my mind, yes.'

'Well, I want you to gag me. We don't want any more broken glasses, do we? And these water glasses are Murano, too. They must be worth at least a hundred and fifty dollars each.'

'You want me to *gag* you?'

She smiled. 'I think it will be quite erotic, don't you? You can blindfold me, too, if you like.'

'No way. I like to see your eyes.'

'Not as much as I like to see yours.'

I propped myself up on my elbow. 'That girl I saw—'

'I can't tell you anything, Gideon, I'm sorry.'

'But why would anybody want to stitch anything to her skin like that? And what do you think it was?'

'Try not to think about it. Not tonight, anyhow. Just make love to me. I've missed you so much.'

'Was she one of Enrico and Salvina's daughters?'

Kate gently touched my face with her fingertips, even my eyelids so that I had to close my eyes.

'I didn't see her, my darling. Only you did.'

I lay my head back down on the pillow. 'OK ... I promised not to ask questions. But just answer me this. Why are Enrico and Salvina so pleased that we're here?'

'They think that we can give them justice, that's why.'

'Justice?'

'Most people never get it. But justice is more

important than anything – even revenge. When you've been given justice, you can sleep at night.'

'Well, sleep isn't exactly what I had in mind.'

I picked up the black silk scarf. I twisted it, and then I put it between her teeth, and knotted it tightly behind the back of her head. I have to admit that I felt more than a little kinky. I had never been into any kind of bondage before – you know, handcuffs or anything like that – but it was unexpectedly arousing, seeing Kate with a gag in her mouth.

That night, she didn't scream. She couldn't. But she shuddered from head to toe, and uttered a low, muffled groan that I can still remember, even today.

At about 2:30 a.m., I was woken up by the sound of a woman sobbing.

I lay on my back for a while, trying to make out where it was coming from. Enrico and Salvina's bedroom was more than fifty feet away from ours, and the doors were so heavy that, once they were closed, you couldn't hear anything at all.

I sat up. The sobbing went on and on, growing even more wretched with every sob. I thought I could hear the woman calling out, too. I got out of bed and walked over to the window. When I drew back the net curtains, I could see the narrow canal at the back of the house, and the paved garden with the dried-up fountain in it.

There was no moon that night, but a single bare bulb shone over the top of the door, throwing a raw electric light across most of the garden. A woman was standing by the stone balustrade overlooking the canal, close to the steps. Her head was covered by a black loosely woven shawl, but I was pretty sure from her figure that it was Salvina. She had both hands clasped in front of her, and she was clutching a rosary.

I didn't know any Italian, but I could tell by the tone of her voice how distressed she was, and it sounded as if she was crying out to somebody.

I opened the windows and stepped out on to the balcony. The night was damp and foggy and bone-penetratingly cold, and I was wearing only my T-shirt and my shorts. I stood by the cast-iron railing and I wondered if I ought to call out to her, and ask her what was wrong. After all, she was only about fifteen feet away from me. But before I could say anything, I saw movement, down in the shadows, and heard a hollow knocking sound. I leaned over the railing and saw that a launch was moored at the bottom of the steps, and that there were two men on it, both of them wearing dark coats and caps.

'Please! Please! No!' Salvina cried out, in English. 'Not my Amalea! Please!'

'Salvina?' I said. 'Salvina, what's wrong?'

She didn't seem to hear me. The two men on the launch didn't appear to hear me either, because neither of them looked up at me. Instead, one of them climbed up the steps and held out his hand.

'Are you coming? Do you want to see her

251

maiden voyage? Maybe we can crack a bottle of champagne on her head, to send her on her way.'

'My husband, he will do anything you want! I promise you!'

'I'm sure he will, ma'am.' What the man said next was indistinct, because he turned his back on me, but then he said, 'We need to protect ourselves, that's all. We need a sure-fire guarantee.'

He helped Salvina to negotiate the steps, and climb on to the launch. It dipped and swayed in the narrow canal, and there was a gurgling and slapping of water up against the wall.

'That's it, lady, you're doing just fine,' said the second man, and I was sure that I recognized his voice. They were both Americans, but the second man was definitely familiar.

'Oh, Amalea!' Salvina wept. *'Come hanno potuto fare questa cosa terribile a voi?* You men, you are not men at all! You are demons!'

'Well, we'll see about that,' said the second man. 'It depends on how ready the good *dottore* is, to give us what we're asking him for.'

With that, he started up the launch's engine, and the first man loosened the ropes with which it was fastened up against the steps. The launch slowly moved away, and as it did so, the light from the top of the door fell across it, and I saw for the first time why Salvina was so distressed.

Across the rear seat at the stern of the launch, there was a single-bed-size mattress. Lying on the mattress, face up, naked, was the same young girl I had seen in the drawing room while I was playing the piano that evening. She was gagged, in the same way that Kate had been

252

gagged, but she didn't appear to be tied up with any other cords or bindings. Yet she was twisting and struggling as if she were trying to free herself.

The launch burbled off toward the Grand Canal, with the girl still struggling on top of the mattress. It was only then that I remembered the suture holes that I had seen in her skin, in the drawing room, and realized why she couldn't get free. She must have been *sewn* to the mattress – her back and her arms and her legs – and she was unable to break away from it without tearing the stitches open.

I stood on the balcony, watching in horror as the launch was swallowed by the darkness between the buildings, and then veered left into the Grand Canal, and completely out of sight.

I stepped back into the bedroom and closed the balcony doors, and fastened them. I didn't know for sure if I had witnessed a real abduction, in real time, or if I had seen something that had happened before. Or maybe I had seen an event that hadn't even happened yet, and the reason that Kate had wanted me to come here was to prevent it, before it did.

I said, 'Kate – *Kate*,' and shook her shoulder, but she was sleeping like she was dead. I switched on my bedside lamp and it was then that I saw the packet of Dormomyl next to her wristwatch. My mother always took Dormomyl because my father snored so much, so I knew that it was one of the strongest non-prescription sleeping tablets you can buy.

I went to the bathroom and took down the

dark-blue toweling robe that Salvina had left for me. Then I opened the bedroom door and went out into the corridor.

The apartment was silent, except for the measured ticking of the central heating system, with its big old-fashioned radiators. I walked along the corridor until I reached Enrico and Salvina's bedroom. From my experiences in Stockholm and London, I knew better than to knock, and disturb them. Instead, I took hold of the decorative door handle, and very quietly opened it.

Enrico and Salvina's bed was even grander than ours, with drapes hanging from the ceiling, and drawn back on either side of the bed with velvet cords and tassels. Enrico was facing me, but he was fast asleep, although his spectacles were shining on his nightstand as if they were watching me. I couldn't see Salvina, so I stepped cautiously toward the bed, only two or three paces, to make sure that she was there.

She was buried deep in the bedcovers, but yes, she was there, and not out on a launch on the Grand Canal. Her wiry dark hair was untied, and spread out over the pillow.

Enrico stirred in his sleep, and murmured something in Italian which I couldn't understand, like, '...*saffron darer ... saffron darer...*' and then he shouted, *'Voi bastardi!'* which I *could* understand. But even though he shouted quite loud, he didn't wake himself up. He didn't wake Salvina, either.

I closed their bedroom door behind me. It made the softest of clicks, and I held my breath for a moment and waited, in case Enrico had heard it. There can be a hundred-decibel electric storm right over my apartment, but I can carry on sleeping like a hibernating groundhog, but if somebody were to tread on a squeaky floorboard somewhere inside my bedroom, it would wake me up instantly.

Eventually I tiptoed my way along the corridor to the next bedroom door. At one time, this must have belonged to one of Enrico and Salvina's three kids. Again, I opened it very quietly and peered inside.

It was a boy's room, with a carved oak bedstead, and a matching toy chest at the foot of it. The lid of the toy chest was tilted open, and the floor was strewn with toys. A plastic ball, a tinplate tank, a scattering of metal soldiers. There was also a tinplate Bugatti racing car, and a Venetian doll: a scary-looking figure in a dark cape, with a bird-like mask for a face.

On the left-hand wall hung a large framed print which showed a winding procession of grotesque figures, all in medieval costumes, dancing across a city square. They were waving sticks and pigs' bladders and swords, and all of them wore expressionless masks. Kate had already told me enough about Venice for me to know that these were the characters from the *commedia dell'arte*, the traditional street theater of Venice, which told ribald stories about rich men and rogues, beautiful sluts and unscrupulous twisters.

I was just about to leave the room when I saw something move, on the opposite side of the bed.

255

To begin with, I couldn't make out what it was. Then, out of the darkness, a figure materialized. It was about four feet tall, like a dwarf, but instead of a head it had a crudely-shaped ball on top of it, made of sacking. I couldn't help thinking of the terrifying midget in *Don't Look Now*, with her shiny scarlet raincoat.

The figure swayed from side to side for almost a minute, without uttering a sound, but then it suddenly whimpered.

I circled around the toy chest, being careful not to tread on any of the toys. As I reached the other side of the bed, I saw that the figure was a young boy, in a thick gray sweater, dark-blue knee-length shorts, and sandals. His head was covered by a rough sacking bag, tied around his neck with string.

I realized with some surprise and even elation that I wasn't afraid. In fact, I was beginning to understand that none of these strange events would be happening if I weren't here to see them.

I hesitated for a moment and I sat down on the bed. The boy must have heard me, or sensed me, because he took a wary step back.

'What's your name, son?' I asked him. 'Who did this to you?'

He whimpered again. He sounded like a beaten puppy.

'It wasn't your dad, was it?' I knew that parents in different countries had some pretty unusual ways to discipline their kids, so I didn't want to tread on anybody's toes here. But to my mind, tying a bag over a young boy's head amounted to cruel and unusual punishment.

'*Non li capisco,*' he said, in a thin, breathy voice. He sounded as if he had a head cold.

'You don't understand? I'll try to say it slower. Who did this to you? Who put this bag over your head? This *saccho*? Was it your dad? Your *padre*?'

The small boy shook his head, and then he said something very soft and hurried, which I couldn't possibly follow.

'OK, listen,' I said, 'let's get this furshlugginer bag off, and then you can maybe talk some sense.'

'*Non tolga la mia mascherina!*' he screamed out, and his voice was high with hysteria.

'What?'

'*Non tolga prego la mia mascherina!*'

'You don't want me to take it off? Kid, believe me, you're going to spifflicate in there, unless I take it off.'

He tried to pull away, but I caught hold of his skinny right wrist, and held it tight. Meanwhile I used my right hand to loosen the twine around his neck.

'*Please,*' he begged me.

'Listen to me,' I told him, 'I'm just here to help you, that's all. No demands, no consequences.'

'*Oh, please,*' he moaned, as I managed to untie the first of the knots. He began to shiver and his little legs sagged underneath him. '*Oh please no, please do not take it off, sir, please.*'

I stopped, and said, 'Why not? Is there something wrong with your face? You don't want me to see your face, is that it?' I had suddenly

257

thought of the Elephant Man, hiding his lumpy features under a cotton mask, with a single eye-hole cut into it.

I managed to unfasten the last of the knots, and all I had to do now was drag the twine out of the holes in the sacking. The boy gripped the bottom of the hood with both hands and held on to it tight.

'Please, sir,' he whispered, but how could I possibly leave a kid of that age with a sack over his head?

He still wouldn't let go, so I took hold of the sides of the hood, where his ears were, and said, *'Uno – due – tre—!'* and yanked it upward.

The hood came off and to my horror the boy's head came with it. I tumbled back on to the bed, still clutching the hood, and jarred my shoulder against the headboard.

His body remained standing for a split second, headless, both of his hands still raised, his fingers still curled where he had tried to keep hold of the sacking. Then he pitched sideways, on to the rug, on top of a higgledy-piggledy jumble of plastic soldiers and farm animals, one arm swinging up as if he were waving to one of his friends.

With the boy's detached head inside it, the hood was as heavy as a bowling bag. I lowered it on to the pillow. I didn't have the nerve to open it and take a look. There was no blood. I would have expected *fountains* of blood, if I had pulled somebody's head off, but there was nothing at all.

There's no need to panic, I told myself. *This*

isn't real. This is just another hallucination. All the same, my heart was beating like the long-case clock in the drawing room, ga-*thump*, ga-*thump*, ga-*thump*, and I could hear my blood rushing through my ears.

Maybe I should open the hood, I thought. Maybe this was nothing but a trick, or an optical illusion, and the boy's head was made out of nothing but papier-mâché. But supposing he was real. He had pleaded with me so desperately not to take off his hood, and I didn't think I could face his dead eyes staring at me, accusing me of killing him.

I stood up, almost losing my balance. I stepped over his body and all of his toys, and quietly left the room, closing the door behind me. I listened, but the apartment was still silent.

When I got back to our bedroom, I went around to Kate's side of the bed and this time I switched on her bedside lamp, too, and shook her hard.

'Kate – wake up! Kate, for Christ's sake – it's happening again!'

Kate stirred and murmured and opened her eyes. She blinked at me as if she had never seen me before in her life. 'What – what is it?'

'It's happening again. The visions. The nightmares. Whatever you want to call them.'

She sat up, and took hold of my hands. 'What did you see?'

'It's not what I saw – it's what I *did.*'

I told her about the young boy in the hood and she listened to me seriously, but she didn't seem to be surprised. 'That would have been

Massimo,' she said.

'But I pulled his goddamned head off!'

'No, you didn't. Do you want to see for yourself?'

She climbed out of bed and led me back toward the young boy's bedroom, still holding my hand. She opened the door, and led me toward the bed. The toy chest was closed, and there were no toys lying on the floor. In the middle of the bed a young dark-haired boy was sleeping, his cheeks flushed. His mouth was open and his breathing was sticky, as if he had a slight cold.

'This is Massimo,' said Kate. 'You'll meet him at breakfast. He's such a sweet boy.'

'I'll meet him at breakfast? How come I didn't see him this evening?'

Kate kissed my cheek. 'Because people come and people go. Doors open and doors close, and people go through.'

'Pearl said something like that. Pearl upstairs. I don't really understand what she meant.'

'Oh, I think you do. Or you're beginning to. Anyhow, you'll see young Massimo in the morning. And the girls, too, Raffaella and Amalea.'

We left Massimo's bedroom and went back to bed. 'So long as I didn't really hurt him,' I said. 'He was begging with me not to take his hood off, so you can imagine what I felt like when his head came with it.'

'You didn't hurt him. You won't ever hurt him. You won't hurt any of this family. Somebody else will hurt them, yes. Somebody else *has* hurt them. But not you.'

Twenty-Two

As soon as we opened our bedroom door the next morning we could hear the family chatting and laughing in the kitchen. I looked at Kate but all she said was, 'Go on. They're lovely kids. You'll like them.'

We went into the kitchen and the three Cesaretti children were sitting around the table, eating zucchini fritters. Salvina was standing by the stove, frying a whole lot more. Apart from the smell of zucchinis and hot butter, the kitchen was filled with a rich aroma of freshly brewed coffee and baking bread.

As soon as we came in, Enrico stood up, one hand pressed flat against his necktie, and drained the last of his coffee.

'*Buon giorno*, Kate! *Buon giorno*, Gideon! I hope you slept peacefully. I am sorry that I have to rush. I have a very complex operation to undertake this morning.'

He turned to his children and said, 'Amalea – Raffaella – Massimo – this is Kate's friend Gideon. Say *buon giorno*, and *benvenuto alla nostra casa.*'

'Good morning,' said Amalea. 'You are very welcome to our house.'

I nodded, but I couldn't think what to say to

her. It was hair-raising, meeting her here in the kitchen, when I had seen her white and naked in the drawing room yesterday evening, and stitched on to a mattress on the back of a launch.

And here was young Massimo, too, whose head I had pulled off his shoulders, chatting away as if nothing had happened to him. In a way, I was even more disturbed by seeing him here, because he was so young, and so cheerful, and when he looked up at me he gave me such a conspiratorial grin, as if we had shared some huge joke together.

'Please, sit,' said Amalea, pulling out a chair for me. She was pretty in a thin, dark, almond-eyed way, with a curtain of shiny black hair that fell straight to her shoulders. She could almost have been Egyptian, rather than Italian. She was wearing a skinny-rib sweater, in black, and Essenza designer jeans.

I couldn't take my eyes off her, but I couldn't detect the slightest trace of what might have happened to her, or what was *about* to happen to her. All she did was smile back at me shyly, embarrassed that I was staring at her so intently.

'Papa,' she said, 'on your way home tonight, can you buy me some of those Ducale *biscotti*? Pretty please?'

'You're so *greedy*,' Raffaella protested. 'You're always eating but you never get fat. It isn't fair!'

Raffaella was plumper than Amalea, with fraying blonde hair and blue eyes and rosy-red cheeks. She was just as pretty, though, and she had her mother's generous breasts, which she

262

showed off with a V-necked sweater dress, in ultramarine.

Young Massimo was big-eyed and pale-skinned, with a dark bowl-shaped haircut, and when he grew up, I could see that he would look like his father. Except that he would never grow up.

Kate and I sat down opposite them, and Salvina laid knives and forks for us. 'You like *zucchini frittata*?' she asked me. 'And maybe some pomegranate juice, and coffee?'

'Sounds great,' I told her.

Kate said, 'How's art college, Amalea?'

'Oh, it's *wonderful*,' smiled Amalea. 'We are making lace now, in the style of Anita Belleschi Grifoni, it's so beautiful. I passed my second-level exam last month, with a commendation for my tulle.'

'Amalea is brilliant with all kinds of needle-work,' put in Salvina. 'She has been taught the classic techniques, yes? But her designs are very young, *molto moderno*.'

I thought of the suture holes that I had seen in Amalea's back. Maybe it had just been a grisly coincidence that somebody had sewn her to a mattress, or maybe they had known how skilled she was with a needle and thread, and had been playing a deeply sick joke.

'How about you, Raffaella?' I asked her. 'Are you at college, too?'

'I study to be a nurse,' said Raffaella. 'I want to care for young children.'

'And how about you, Massimo? What do you want to be when you grow up?'

'Football,' said Massimo, promptly.

'You're good at football?'

Raffaella said, 'He would be much better if he did not keep kicking his footballs into the canals. He lost so many that papa stopped buying them for him. In one week he lost five!'

'But I make a new one, myself!' Massimo told me.

'That was pretty smart,' I told him. 'What did you make it out of?'

Salvina served me a plateful of *frittata*. 'There – for a very special musician!'

'Salvina, that's enough to feed the New York Symphony Orchestra!'

'You need your strength, Gideon.'

'I make my new football from a sack,' said Massimo. 'Inside it I put my *maglione*.'

'He used a canvas bag that used to have soap in it,' Amalea explained. 'He stuffed it with one of his old sweaters.'

'It was good!' declared Massimo. 'It was a good football!'

'Of course it was, until you kicked it into the canal, just like you did all the others!'

I was beginning not to like the way this conversation was going. It seemed like both Amalea and Massimo were about to be tortured or even killed by somebody who knew what they liked the most. Because what had Massimo's head most resembled, when I walked into his bedroom last night? An improvised football, made out of a sack.

'So, what will you two do today?' Salvina asked us, sitting down at last.

264

'I'm going to take Gideon for a walk,' said Kate. 'From here, to San Sebastiano, and then to the Piazza San Marco, and then lunch at Harry's Bar.'

'Lunch? After a breakfast like this? Are you kidding me?'

'You only have to have the *carpaccio*, and a Bellini cocktail. But you can't visit Venice without going to Harry's Bar and trying those.'

'You will love it,' said Salvina. 'Your credit card will scream out loud. But you will love it.'

The morning was damp and foggy, and we walked through the streets of Venice with our coat collars turned up and scarves wrapped around our chins. It felt as if the city were detached from the rest of the world, a forgotten archipelago populated only by memories.

Kate took me down the narrow alleys that led from the south-western corner of the Campo San Polo to the Campo San Tomà. In the square itself, we went to look at the church, with its bas-relief of St Thomas the Shoemaker over the doors.

'Can I save them?' I asked Kate, as we walked beside the Rio di Santa Margherita Canal.

'The children, you mean?'

The water was very dark, and the buildings that were reflected in it were distorted by the constant gliding past of gondolas. Everybody I saw sitting in a gondola looked decidedly glum, as if they would rather be doing anything else than sitting in a narrow boat on a freezing-cold morning, being punted around a maze of canals and diseased-looking houses.

'Yes, you can save them,' said Kate. 'But not in the way that you think.'

I told her what I had thought at breakfast, about Amalea's stitches and Massimo's football.

'You're probably right,' she nodded.

'Well, if I *am* right, then we're dealing with some seriously sick sadistic bastard, wouldn't you say?'

She didn't answer. We kept on walking until we reached the church of San Sebastiano, which looked like an ordinary little Italian church on the outside, with a flat gray facade, but its interior had been lavishly painted and gilded by the sixteenth-century painter Veronese. It was chilly inside, and hushed, because it was still too early for the usual crowds of tourists, and our footsteps echoed on the shiny stone floor. Kate took me to the south wall, to look at a vast painting of a half-naked guy lying on the ground, being pummeled by an angry mob.

'The martyrdom of San Sebastian,' she told me.

'I thought Saint Sebastian was the dude who had all those arrows shot into him, like a pincushion.'

'He survived that. Some peasant woman found him and nursed him back to health. But later the Romans caught him and tried him again, and this time they beat him to death.'

'Second time unlucky, huh?'

Outside the church, Kate took hold of my hands and stood very close to me, although she wouldn't look me directly in the eye. 'I want you to know this, Gideon. I love you.'

I didn't say anything. What could I say, except 'I love you, too, sweetheart'? and for some reason I felt that would have sounded trite, especially on that foggy, spectral day, with the black gondolas passing us like funeral boats.

'I didn't expect to fall in love with you,' she said. 'Not like this. I thought that it was nothing more than a way to get myself free.'

'I thought you said that you couldn't leave Victor, no matter what.'

'You still don't understand, my darling. But you've never let me down, not once, even when you must have thought that you were going crazy. I promise you that you will soon see everything clearly.'

We continued our walk, hand-in-hand, not saying much, but taking deep pleasure in each other's closeness. We crossed the Grand Canal over the high steel arch of the Ponte del Accademia, with *vaporetti* and motor launches passing underneath us. Then we made our way through a warren of alleyways where we passed every high-end jeweler's and fashion boutique I could think of. Chanel, Bulgari, Dolce e Gabbana, you name it.

'I'd like to buy you something,' I said. 'A ring, maybe.'

'No,' said Kate. 'It's too late for that.'

'Too late or too early?'

'Both.'

We shuffled our way through more and more tourists until we eventually arrived at the Piazza San Marco, the wide square that you always see in travel pictures of Venice. It was thick with scabby gray pigeons and crowded with even more tourists, and there was already a long line to climb up the Campanile, the tallest tower in Venice.

It should have been romantic and heartbreakingly beautiful – the Basilica of San Marco and the Ducal Palace, and the two granite columns that stand in front of the palace, by the waterfront, one topped by the lion of St Mark, and the other by St Theodore and some mysterious beast of unknown origin. But it was impossible to ignore the hordes of sightseers, pushing and jostling and posing for photographs.

'Don't walk between these two pillars,' Kate warned me. 'They used to execute people here, and it's supposed to be bad luck.'

I gave one last look around. 'My dogs are barking,' I said. 'Why don't we find this Harry's Bar and treat ourselves to one of these famous Bellinis? Eleven o'clock isn't too early, is it?'

She smiled. 'I know how you feel. That's the trouble with Venice. You feel like somebody has trodden on your dream. Well, about a thousand people have trodden on your dream, in sneakers.'

We walked back across the piazza. We had just reached the colonnades in the north-west corner when I caught sight of two men in the crowds up ahead of us – two men with a young boy in between them. One of the men was wearing a black cap and a black topcoat, the other had a squarish head and iron-gray hair. The boy was wearing a dark-blue duffel coat with the hood pulled up.

'Kate,' I said. 'Who do those guys remind you of?'

I lost sight of them for a moment, but as we left the piazza and entered the pedestrian street beyond it, I saw them again, pushing their way through a milling crowd of Danish tourists and turning left. I elbowed my way after them. Kate kept up with me, but she said, anxiously, 'Gideon – maybe you shouldn't.'

'It's the same guys we saw in London, I'm sure of it.'

'But even if they are, what can you do about it?'

'I don't know. I don't care. They're all part of the puzzle, aren't they? You said so yourself.'

The two men were heading west, past crowded cafes and glassware stores and Nigerians selling fake designer purses. Considering they had a young boy with them, they were moving with surprising speed, and they seemed to be able to melt their way through the crowds as if they were no more substantial than shadows.

They hurried up a flight of shallow stone steps, and over a bridge. As they crossed it, I saw the boy trip and stumble and almost fall over, but the two men seized his elbows and lifted him up, so that his feet didn't even touch the ground.

I started to run, pushing people out of the way.

Kate called, 'Gideon! This is not the same as London! Be *careful*!'

I glanced back briefly and she was still standing on the bridge. I raised my hand to acknowledge that I had heard her, and then I continued

269

running – dodging and jinking and shoving as if I were still in my high-school football team, and heading for a touchdown.

'*Pazzo!*' one old woman shouted, as I knocked over a row of chairs outside her cafe.

But now I was less than twenty yards behind the two men and the boy, and I was determined to catch them and confront them, no matter how crazy or embarrassing it turned out to be.

Without warning, they took a right turn into an even narrower passageway, and promptly disappeared from sight. I ran to the corner, but as I did so, six or seven German tourists came down the passageway toward me, with bags and cameras, and for several precious seconds I danced from one side of the passageway to the other, trying to get past them.

They all thought this was highly amusing, and one of them bowed from the waist, and cried out, '*Vielen Dank für den Walzer, mein Herr!*'

By the time I reached the end of the passageway, the two men and the boy had vanished. I didn't know whether to turn left or right. There were signs on the wall, pointing in opposite directions, but both of them said *S. Marco Rialto*. A Venetian idea of a joke, I supposed.

I took a guess and went to the left, because that was the general direction in which they had been heading before. On either side of the alley there was one dead end after another, most of them giving access to tenement doors, with bicycles and plant pots in the, but no men and no boy. *Shit.* I had lost them. But when I reached the sixth or the seventh dead end, and looked into it, something hit me hard across the bridge of my nose – so hard that I staggered back against the opposite side of the alley, and collided with a souvenir store window. If it hadn't been covered by wrought-iron security bars, I probably would have crashed straight through it, and into a display of colorful glass necklaces and carnival masks.

The man in the black cap had hit me with a thick wooden walking stick. I lifted my left arm to protect myself, but he took two steps toward me and struck me on the knuckles, and then on the side of my head. I slid down the wall into a sitting position, with my left ear singing.

Behind the man in the black cap, in the dead-end alleyway, I saw the man with the iron-gray hair, and he was holding the boy in front of him, gripping his shoulders so that there was no chance of him running away. The boy had the hood of his coat still raised, but I could see his face. He was pasty and thin, with two crimson bruises around his eyes. He looked terrified. But he wasn't Massimo. I didn't recognize him at all.

The man in the black cap, though – *him* I recognized, even though his collar was turned up and he was wearing dark glasses.

'Jack!' I said. 'It's Gideon, for Christ's sake! What the hell did you hit me for, man? What are you doing to that kid?'

Jack took off his dark glasses and prodded me with the end of his stick. He had grown two or three days' worth of black stubble, and his eyes were pouchy. He looked even more Satanic than he had in New York.

'What did I hit you for? What did I hit you for? What the fuck do you *think* I fucking hit you for? You were *following* me, you asshole.'

'I just wanted to talk to you, man,' I protested. 'I recognized you and I wanted to know what you were doing here, that's all. Come on ... I meet you in New York and here you are in Venice, of all places.' I didn't mention that I had seen him, twice, in London.

Jack prodded me again. Two middle-aged women tourists stopped and stared at us, but he bared his teeth at them and snarled, 'Get lost, you nosy old witches! *Vada via!*' and they bustled away.

I climbed to my feet. My left hand felt as if it had swollen to twice its normal size, and my nose felt enormous, too.

'You're a maniac, you know that?' I told him.

He came up close to me, with his stick still raised. I could smell garlic on his breath, and both of his eyes were bloodshot.

'You listen to me. You didn't see me today and if you ever happen to see me again, you didn't see me then, neither. You got it?'

'OK. But supposing I call the police?'

He blinked, in slow motion. 'You're not serious, right?'

'Come on, Jack, I don't know what you and your friend are doing here, with this kid, but it sure doesn't look kosher.'

'Kosher?' At first Jack stared at me with a wide-eyed look that was close to insane. But his lips gradually started to twitch at the corners, and curl up, and he gave me the oiliest of smiles.

272

'Kosher, yes, sure, see what you mean. Two guys, hauling off a nine-year-old boy between them. But rest assured. This kid belongs to the Grimani family, and he's been cutting school and mixing with all kinds of undesirables, and my friend here and me, we've been commissioned by his parents to bring him home. So you could say that what we're doing here is performing a valuable social service.'

'Why should I believe you?' I asked him.

'How many reasons do you want?'

'One is fine. So long as it makes some kind of sense.'

'OK. Let's see if this makes sense. If you fucking follow me again, slick, I'll chop off your fucking fingers.'

There was a long, long stretch of silence, during which Jack continued to stare at me as if he were daring me to challenge him, so that he could hit me again. Eventually I raised both hands, and said, 'Fine. I don't care one way or another, to tell you the truth. I'm leaving now, OK? I won't follow you anymore. Whatever you have to do – well, you just go ahead and do it.'

Without another word, Jack beckoned to the man with the iron-gray hair, and he brought the boy out of the dead end and into the street. The boy looked up at me as if he badly wanted to say something, but Jack laid an arm around his shoulders and hurried him away, so fast that he could barely keep up. As they reached the next turning, the boy turned his head to see if I was still there, and he looked seriously frightened, but I didn't know what I could do about it.

I was still standing outside the souvenir store when Kate caught up with me.

'My God, Gideon, are you all right? Your nose is bleeding.'

I patted my upper lip. When I took my fingers away they were sticky with congealing blood.

'It was Jack,' I said. 'Your husband's pal Jack. He whacked me right on the beezer with a goddamned walking stick.'

Kate pulled two or three sheets of Kleenex out of her purse and dabbed my face. 'I told you to be careful. You know what Victor's like, and his friends are the same. Worse, some of them.'

'I don't give a shit. I'm going to report him to the cops.'

Kate shook her head. 'Hold still ... there, that's better. But no. Don't report him.'

'Kate – that was out-and-out assault and battery! And who knows *what* they're going to do to that kid.'

'Did you ask him?'

'Sure. He gave me some cock-and-bull story about the kid playing hooky, and that he and that other mook had been hired by his parents to find him. But, come on. Do you believe that? So maybe the kid's cut a couple of Play-doh classes, but who hires a thug like Jack to bring him back home? I'm calling the cops.'

Kate dabbed the bridge of my nose, and I winced.

'It's not too bad,' she told me. 'Only a bruise. Let's go to Harry's Bar and get you a drink and then we can decide what to do next.'

* * *

Harry's Bar is small and gloomy and very formal, and also seriously expensive. It's historic, I'll grant it that, and it has plenty of 1930s atmosphere, with its wood paneling and its marble-topped cocktail bar and its white-jacketed waiters. Orson Welles used to come here, as well as Truman Capote and the Aga Khan, and Ernest Hemingway was a regular.

Kate and I sat down at one of the small circular tables by the window, and a snooty waiter took our order. Kate wanted a Bellini, peach purée and champagne, which is the signature drink at Harry's Bar, but I badly needed a double brandy.

'Whatever the Italian is for "police station", I'm going to have this drink and then I'm going to find one and Jack Friendly is going to be toast.' I couldn't stop squeezing the bridge of my nose, which felt as if it had swollen to five times its normal size, and had started to throb. When I picked up my glass of Vecchia Romagna, my hands were trembling.

'Gideon, I don't think that going to the police is a very good idea.' Kate was sitting with her back to the tinted glass window, so that it was difficult for me to see her face.

'Oh, no? And specifically why not? He had a nine-year-old boy with him, Kate, and the kid was obviously terrified. Don't tell me we're going to do nothing.'

She reached across and held my hand. 'You feel cold,' she said. 'You're still shaking.'

I looked at her narrowly. 'You know what Jack is going to do to that kid, don't you?'

'Yes,' she admitted.

'He's not going to hurt him, is he?'

'I don't know. I hope not. It depends.'

'And you still don't think we should call the police? I mean, it looked very much like abduction to me. And I'm talking about forcible abduction.'

'I know. But if we call the police, worse will happen, very much worse, and very much more quickly.'

'Like what?'

Kate leaned forward and tenderly stroked my cheek. 'You're so nearly there, my darling. You nearly understand. I think it's time you went back to New York and asked for some answers.'

She finished her Bellini. 'Do you want another one?' I asked her.

'No.'

'Well, I'm going to have another brandy.' I beckoned to the waiter, and said, *'Un altro brandy, per favore.'*

'You didn't like this one, *signore?'* he asked me, with the smoothest sarcasm.

'Molto divertente,' Kate snapped at him. *'Un nuovo brandy, per favore.'* The waiter gave her a smile like a spoonful of virgin olive oil and went off to get it. I said, 'You keep telling me to look for answers. But I'm not sure I know what the question is.'

'Follow your heart,' Kate told me. 'If I could tell you any more, I would. You know that. But your heart will open your eyes, Gideon, I promise you, and your eyes will show you everything you need to know.'

The waiter brought the check. With tip, three

drinks and a bowl of pistachio nuts had cost us the equivalent of $96. Ernest Hemingway must have been earning damn good royalties.

As we walked back along the Calle dei Fabbri toward the Grand Canal, a very fine rain began to fall, and the street was suddenly crowded with umbrellas. It was raining even harder by the time we reached the Rialto bridge, and we had to jostle our way through scores of tourists who were trying to shelter beneath its covered archway.

Halfway across, we were brought to a temporary standstill by a crowd of Japanese girl scouts. The warmth of the brandy had all drained out of me now. My head was thumping and I was shivering like a mongrel that had been rescued from a ditch.

As we shuffled impatiently behind the scout troupe, I looked out over the Grand Canal, which was gray and freckled with rain. A gondola passed underneath us, with a black couple huddled together on its red heart-shaped seat, both of them wearing bright yellow waterproof ponchos. They looked spectacularly miserable. Venice is not a city for the confused, or the sad. If you want romance, you should bring it with you.

'Come on,' said Kate, 'let's push our way through.' She took hold of my hand and tried to pull me along, but at that moment I glimpsed something floating in the water, six or seven inches beneath the surface, so that it was barely visible. It was following in the wake of the

277

gondola, almost as if the gondola were drawing it along, but it must have been carried by the current.

I said, 'Wait,' and went closer to the parapet. I glimpsed it only for a few seconds, but a few seconds was enough. It was the white figure of a naked girl, lying face upward on a sodden mattress. It was Amalea, drowned.

'What is it?' asked Kate, and I pointed, but at that moment an anemic sun came out, and shone on the herringbone ripples that the gondola had left behind it, and Amalea disappeared from sight.

'I saw Amalea. They must have set her adrift, so that the mattress gradually got more and more waterlogged, and she began to sink.'

We stayed where we were for a minute or two, trying to see below the surface of the water, but the sun grew brighter and brighter, and the Grand Canal began to glitter, and we gave it up.

'I saw her,' I insisted. 'Just like I saw her last night.'

'I know you did,' said Kate, clinging to my arm.

'So what should I do? Let her float away, out to sea?'

'Maybe she already has.'

'But what if she hasn't?'

'Let's go back to the Cesarettis',' said Kate. 'You look like you could do with a couple of hours' rest.'

'I still think I ought to report Jack Friendly to the *polizia*. And Amalea's body to the coast-guard, whatever they're called.'

'*Guardia Costiera*. But they'll never find her.'

I didn't know what to say to that, so together we walked back to the Campo San Polo in silence. The sun grew even warmer, and steam rose from the paving stones, until the streets were filled with a shining fog.

When we got back to the Palazzetto Di Nerezza, Salvina was already there, as were Amalea and Raffaella and Massimo. Salvina was in the kitchen, stirring a large saucepan of spaghetti sauce, while Amalea and Raffaella were both doing their homework at an antique desk in the corner of the drawing room, and Massimo was connecting a long model railroad track along the corridor.

'Oh! *Il vostro naso!*' Salvina exclaimed, when I walked into the kitchen. 'Your poor nose! What is happened?'

'Little accident,' I told her.

'It looks like *un pomodoro grande!* A big tomato! You must be careful in case I use it for my bolognese!'

Kate and I went to our bedroom, kicked off our shoes, and stretched ourselves out on the bed. Kate looked into my eyes from only four or five inches away, so that I could hardly focus on her.

We lay together for a while, and then I said, 'I'll head for home first thing tomorrow morning. Are you going to fly with me, for a change?'

She shook her head.

'Can you explain to me exactly why not?'

'You'll see, my darling.'

'OK,' I said. 'I promised not to ask too many

279

questions, and I won't. But I will ask you one thing.'

'Go on.'

'Do you and Victor still sleep together? It's none of my goddamn business, I know that. But I can't help thinking about it.'

Kate gave me a smile that was almost coy, and kissed me. 'You don't have to worry, Gideon. Victor won't touch me, not the way that you do, because he can't.'

Twenty-Three

When I woke up the following morning I felt as if I had been drugged. My eyes were swollen and there was a sweetish metallic taste in my mouth. I said, 'Kate?' and reached across the rumpled sheets but Kate wasn't there. I picked up my wristwatch and tried to focus on the time. It was only six minutes after seven. Surely she couldn't have left already.

I climbed out of bed, went to the window and drew back the drapes. Outside, it had only just started to grow light, and the air was thick with a greenish-gray fog. I could just make out the wallowing surface of the water below the balcony, and the lights along the Grand Canal. The bedroom felt chilly, as if the heating had been turned off.

I wrapped myself in my toweling robe, opened the bedroom door and walked along to the kitchen. There was nobody there, so I went across to the fridge to help myself to a swig of orange juice. But the fridge door had been wedged half-an-inch ajar with a piece of folded cardboard, and it was switched off, and completely empty.

Shit. This was Stockholm all over again. I opened up all of the kitchen cupboards, one after the other, and every one of them was empty, except for some glass pickling jars. There was no cutlery in the kitchen drawers, and no saucepans or mixing bowls anywhere. The whole apartment was numbingly cold.

I went back to our bedroom, and through to the en-suite bathroom. Kate's toothbrush and toiletry bag had gone, and when I opened up the bedroom closet, I found that she had taken her clothes, too. On the bed I found her black silk scarf, thin and twisted in the middle where she had gripped it between her teeth to prevent herself from screaming, but that was all that she had left behind.

I went across the corridor to Enrico and Salvina's bedroom, and knocked.

'Enrico? Are you there? It's Gideon.'

There was no answer. I waited for a moment and then I opened the door. The bedroom was empty. The bed itself had been stripped right down to the mattress.

I went to the girls' rooms, and it was the same story. Nobody there, and the beds both stripped. In Massimo's room, the bed had even been dismantled, and stacked against the wall. There was no sign of Massimo's toy box, or his train set, and the picture of the dancing mummers had been taken down.

I tried calling Kate on my cell, but there was no reply. All I could do was get dressed, and pack my suitcase. I was jonesing for a strong cup of coffee, but I was sure that plenty of cafes would be open by now.

I carried my case along the corridor, softly whistling my Purina music. *'I met a girl called Kate ... too early or too goddamned late...'* When I opened the drawing room door, however, I stopped whistling, dead. I think I said, *'Oh, Christ,'* but I might have just thought it, rather than saying it out loud.

Hanging by their necks from the giant chandelier, six feet above my head, were Enrico and Salvina. They were both wearing their night-clothes – Enrico a pair of maroon silk pajamas, and Salvina a cream silk nightdress. Their eyes were bulging and Salvinatongue was sticking out.

They were rotating, very slowly, in opposite directions, as if they had been caught by the spider-like chandelier, and entwined in its web.

I stood there and watched them for over a minute, overwhelmed with dread, and with a terrible sense of pity, too, and helplessness. What had they done to deserve to die like this, hung from the ceiling of their own apartment, so that they gradually strangled?

I couldn't think what the hell to do now. Call

the *polizia*, as I had wanted to do when Jack Friendly had assaulted me? But supposing the *polizia* arrived and Enrico and Salvina weren't here any more, or if they *were*, and *I* was arrested for stringing them up?

I decided that I couldn't leave them hanging there, and leave Venice without telling anybody what had happened. Apart from the sheer inhumanity of it, my fingerprints were all over their apartment, and the police would inevitably come looking for me.

But I needed some time to get over the shock of finding them, and also to make absolutely sure that this wasn't another one of those weird distortions in time and space. There was no doubt in my mind that Enrico and Salvina had been hanged, but the question was, *when*? Had it really been this morning, or weeks ago? Maybe it hadn't even happened yet. Apart from that, where had Amalea and Raffaella and Massimo disappeared to? And when had Kate packed her clothes and left me?

I left my suitcase in the hallway and went outside, into the Campo San Polo. It was almost deserted, although the cafes and trattorias were beginning to open up, and a few spectral figures were taking their dogs for a walk through the fog. I found a small cafe called Al Assassini, and went inside. It was warm, and it was bright, and it smelled of fresh coffee and freshly baked panini.

I sat down in the corner next to the window and ordered an espresso.

'Maybe you want something maybe to eat?'

asked the waiter. He had only one eye, and his black hair was varnished with gel. 'Pastry, maybe? Sandwich?'

'No, *grazie*.'

'You know what day it is today, *signore*?'

'Thursday, isn't it?'

'This is San Baltazar's Day, the day of lies.'

'Oh, yes?' All I wanted was a large espresso, not a guide to Venetian saints' days – especially the way that I was feeling.

'This is the day that you must confess all of the lies that you have told during the year to your friends and your business partners and your loved ones, or else evil things will happen to you.'

'Well, that's very interesting. No, actually, I'm telling you a lie. It's not at all interesting.'

The waiter lifted one finger, as if to admonish me, and gave me an enigmatic smile. *I know your game*, signore. *I can see right through you.* Then he went off to get my coffee.

I tried calling Kate again but she still wasn't answering. I was attempting to get through to Margot when I noticed a white cat sitting under one of the tables on the opposite side of the cafe, staring at me. *A white memory is watching you, so keep your door locked.* I stared back at it, and eventually it stood up and haughtily walked away. Maybe it was Malkin. It certainly *looked* like Malkin, even though there was no sane or logical way to explain how Malkin could be sitting under a table in a cafe in Venice. But I was beginning to think that Malkin *was* a memory, rather than a real animal. She was a constant

284

reminder of what Kate wanted me to do for her, whatever that was.

I finished my espresso and paid the check. The waiter said, 'You want some good advice, *signore*?'

'Not particularly.'

'Remember that your eyes can tell lies, as well as your tongue.'

'Well, I'll try to. Whose cat is that?'

'Which cat, *signore*?'

'The cat I just saw, sitting under the table over there.'

The waiter shook his head. 'There is no cat here, *signore*. For health regulations, you understand?'

I looked into the back of the cafe, but there was no white cat. 'Maybe my eyes are telling me lies.'

The waiter smiled again, and turned away. But I saw his face reflected in one of the wall mirrors, and the only way that I can describe his expression was *sly* – like Gollum.

I walked slowly back toward the Palazzetto Di Nerezza. I stood outside the front door, holding the key in my hand, for over a minute. A small boy with a green balloon in his hand stopped a few yards away and stared at me solemnly, as if he wanted to see what I was going to do next.

'Ciao,' I told him.

He gripped his balloon-string tighter and said, *'Ciò è il aerostato mio.'*

I opened the front door of the palazzetto and went inside. It was still very cold in there, and silent. I walked along the corridor toward the drawing room. Through the yellow-tinted windows I could see the sightseers on the Campo San Polo flickering like ghosts.

I reached the drawing room and immediately looked up toward the chandelier. Enrico and Salvina's bodies had gone.

I made a quick search of the entire apartment. The bedrooms, the bathrooms, the study, the linen closet. I opened up the wooden chests that stood at the foot of each bed. There was nobody here now: no Cesarettis, either dead or alive.

After I had completed my search, I went back to the drawing room. I opened up the lid of the piano, and picked out the theme music from *Doctor Paleface*. I didn't expect Amalea to reappear, in any form, but I guess it was a kind of a requiem for the Cesaretti family, wherever they were, and whatever had happened to them.

I was still playing when I heard the front door being unlocked, and opened. Footsteps came along the corridor toward the drawing room, and a thirty-ish woman in a smart black-and-white houndstooth suit appeared, carrying a briefcase.

'Signore Morandi?' she said. *'Era il portello aperto?'*

I lifted both of my hands. 'I'm sorry. No – I'm not Signore Morandi.'

'I have an appointment with Signore Morandi,' she snapped, looking around the drawing room as if she expected to see him playing hide-and-go-seek behind one of the sofas. 'So who are you? What are you doing in here?'

'I'm a guest of the Cesarettis. They invited me here.'

She stalked up to me and frowned at me fiercely. Her lipstick was orange and she smelled of
some very strong perfume. 'The *Cesarettis?*'

I took my door key out of my pocket and
showed it to her. 'That's right. Doctor and Mrs
Cesaretti. They even lent me a key.'

'Impossible,' she retorted. 'The Cesarettis,
they have not lived here now for more than two
years. Doctor Cesaretti, he took up a new appointment in Africa – Dar-es-Salaam, I think, to
a children's hospital.'

'Maybe he did. But he's back. Well, he must be
back. I had dinner with the Cesarettis here last
night.'

The woman looked at me very seriously, and
then she said, *'Signore* – I think you must leave.
I do not want to cause any trouble.'

'All right, fine. I was leaving anyhow. But
believe me, the Cesarettis were here. We had
calves' liver. We had *baccala montecato*. We
played music.'

'Please, to leave,' said the woman. 'My client
will be here soon.'

'Your client?'

'For rental. Please.'

I was beginning to realize that she thought I
was mad. In fact, she was terrified of me. She
thought I was some loony who had somehow
managed to break into the palazzetto, and was
wandering around playing the piano and pretending that the Cesarettis still lived here, even
though they didn't.

But now I knew that they didn't. In fact, everything was rapidly falling into place.

'Who owns these apartments?' I asked her.

'The owners, they are my clients, of course. I cannot discuss this with you. You must go.'

'If you answer me that one question, I'll leave immediately – *prontissimo*. I promise you.'

The woman hesitated, and then she opened her purse and took out a business card. 'Here,' she said. 'Speak to my manager, Ettore Gavazzi. He will tell you.'

I found the offices of Agenzia Gavazzi on the third floor of an elegant pale-green building overlooking the Rio di San Polo. Although the building was probably fifteenth century, the interior of the offices was stark and modern, with white walls and bronze statues of twisted-looking nudes and glass-topped desks.

A tall receptionist in a strident red suit led me into Sig. Gavazzi's office, wobbling ahead of me on high stiletto heels.

Ettore Gavazzi was short and swarthy, with black curly hair through which his scalp shone like a polished copper bowl. He wore a striped blue shirt with red suspenders, and very expensive brown shoes.

'Mr Lake? My assistant Signorina Cappadona called me. She told me that somehow you had found entry into the Palazzetto Di Nerezza.'

'That's right. But I didn't break in. I was a guest of the Cesarettis and I was given a key.'

'The Cesarettis ... yes, she told me that, too. But the Cesarettis have not lived in the Palazzatto Di Nerezza for more than two years. Dottore Cesaretti made over the title of the

288

property to a holding company and then as far as we know he emigrated to Africa.'

'This holding company,' I asked him. 'Can you tell me who owns it?'

He stared at me with protuberant eyes. He reminded me of a cartoon frog. 'Who *are* you, *signore*?' he said. 'What is it exactly that you want?'

'I'm a friend of the Cesarettis, that's all. I want to find out exactly what happened to them.'

'You are not from SEC?'

'The Securities and Exchange Commission? Of course not. I'm a musician. I'm not trying to cause any trouble here.'

Ettore Gavazzi said nothing for a while, but kept on blowing out his cheeks, which made him look even more like a frog. There were no flies buzzing around the office, but I had the feeling that if there had been one, his tongue would have whipped out and caught it.

'You told Signorina Cappadona that you had dinner with the Cesarettis last night.'

'I guess she must have misunderstood me. I said that it was the Cesaretti's wedding anniversary yesterday, and that, on their wedding anniversary, we always used to have dinner together.'

Even as I told him that, I thought of the waiter at Al Assassini, telling me that today was Saint Baltazar's Day, the day of lies.

'If you were such a good friend of the Cesarettis, why did they not tell you that they had sold their apartment and gone to Africa?'

'I don't know. We haven't been in contact for

289

a while. Sometimes, friends become estranged, don't they? I guess Enrico was too busy being a surgeon and I was too busy writing music. You know how it is.'

Again, Ettore Gavazzi stayed silent, and blew his cheeks in and out. Eventually, though, he opened his desk drawer, took out a plain white card, and a blue enameled pen, and scribbled down a name for me.

'There ... these are the owners of the Palazzetto Di Nerezza. If you have any questions about the Cesarettis, you should ask them.'

He waved the card backward and forward to dry the ink, and then he passed it across to me, without looking up.

'Is there something you're not telling me?' I asked him.

He still didn't raise his eyes. 'I can give you no more information than that. But it was not usual, the way in which the property was transferred.'

'Not usual? What do you mean?'

'The Cesarettis' lawyers were concerned because he wanted to sell the property so quick. What was the hurry? The palazzetto had been owned by the Cesaretti family for generations. They did not even have to sell it. My agency could have rented it for them, while they were away, and they could have returned to it when they came back from Africa. His lawyers advised Dottore Cesaretti to consider that option most seriously.'

'But?'

'But he said absolutely no. He wanted to give it up completely. And by Venetian standards the transfer of deeds was very quick. Usually, it takes the notary at least six weeks to go through all the *preliminare*, the searches and so forth, especially with such an historical building. But Dottore Cesaretti's lawyers told me that from the first *proposta* to the final *rogito notarile*, the sale took less than a month.'

'I see.' I looked down at the card which he had given me. It read, *Penumbra International Property, New York.*

Ettore Gavazzi said, 'Maybe ... if you discover more about your friends, you would be kind enough to contact me again. I had the sensation from the very beginning that something was not quite right about the way in which they sold out so fast.'

I thanked him and shook his hand. Outside, heavy gray clouds were moving across the city from the north-west, and rain began to sprinkle the windows.

By the time I was sitting in a water taxi, making my way back across the lagoon to Marco Polo Airport, it was raining heavily. I had to sit inside, with my suitcase pressing hard against my knees.

At the Alitalia desk, I changed my flight so that I could catch the 14:40 Swiss International flight to Stockholm, changing planes at Zurich. Then I went to the airport's shiny new wine bar, bought myself a large Pinot Grigio, and perched on a high stool to drink it.

I called Margot.

'Lalo – do you know what time it is?' she

protested.

'Sure. It's six-twenty a.m. Time you were up and at 'em.'

'I didn't go to bed till *three*, you sadistic bastard. I was at Megafly, having a party with all of my friends from high school. Plus a few gorgeous men. Well, they looked gorgeous, after five tequilas. What do you want?'

'This whole Kate thing is beginning to make sense. I'm flying to Stockholm and then I'm going on to London. I should be back sometime Sunday, but I need you to do something for me.'

'Go on,' she said, suspiciously.

'I need you to check out a real estate company called Penumbra International Properties, based in New York. You got that? Penumbra. But don't contact the company directly and don't give them any indication that you're checking up on them.'

'What?'

'Please, Margot. Do this one thing for me.'

'You know I will. I love you, Lalo.'

'Sure,' I said. 'I love you, too.'

And the strange thing was, as I switched off my cell, I knew that I *did* love her. Not in the same way that I loved Kate. There was no danger in it, no edge-of-the-seat stuff. But when I had finished talking to Margot, I always felt warmer about the world, and the people who can do that are very few and far between.

My flight was due for boarding so I finished my glass of wine and went to the men's room. I was standing in front of the mirror trying to work out how to turn on the high-tech Italian-style faucet when the door opened and Jack Friendly walked in.

He was wearing his black overcoat and his black sunglasses, but as he came up behind me he took off his sunglasses and tucked them into his inside pocket.

'Well, well,' he said. 'Fancy meeting you here.' He looked more like a predatory hawk than ever.

'What are you going to do, Jack?' I asked him, trying to keep my voice steady. 'Give me another whack on the beezer?'

'Just wanted to give you a tip, Gideon. That's all.'

'Oh, yes?' I suddenly managed to turn on the faucet, and cold water sprayed all over the front of my pants.

Jack managed a sloping, superior smile. 'Kind of accident-prone, aren't you, Gideon? So if I was you, I'd keep my nose out of other people's business.'

'Oh, really? And what particular business is that?'

'You know what business I'm talking about. I know people who know people, and those people tell me everything that's going on. You know why? Because they like what I give them if they do and they don't like what I give them if they don't. You went to see Ettore Gavazzi this morning, didn't you?'

'What's it to you?'

'You were asking questions about a certain property, that's what. And that property and who

293

owns it is none of your concern.'

'Supposing I was interested in renting it?'

'It's taken.'

I turned to face him. 'Supposing I wanted to know why the Cesarettis sold it so quickly? You know – just out of academic interest.'

Without warning, Jack took hold of my throat. At the same time, he grabbed me between the legs, and squeezed me hard. I yelped like a puppy whose tail has been accidentally slammed in an automobile door, but he didn't let go. Instead, he kept on gripping me until my eyes began to water.

'You have no fucking interest in that property, academic or any other kind. *Capisca*?'

I could hardly breathe. 'OK, OK, I have no fucking interest in that property.'

'Not now, not ever. Got it?'

'Got it. Now let me go, will you, for Christ's sake! That hurts!'

He gave me one more vicious squeeze, and let me go, but he still didn't relax his grip on my throat. He reached into his coat pocket and took out a craft knife. He held it up in front of my face and used his thumb to slide out the blade. It was narrow, and triangular, with a sharp tapered point.

Very slowly and deliberately, he moved the blade toward my right eye, until the point was less than a half-inch away from my eyeball. I was blinking furiously, even though I didn't want to.

'That Beethoven – he was deaf, right? – but he wrote music, didn't he? I wonder how difficult *you'd* find it, if you were blind?'

I didn't know what to say to him. I was whining for breath, and I felt as if my knees were going to give way under me.

'You understand what I'm saying to you, Gideon?' said Jack. The blade didn't waver, and I was sure that he was going to stick it straight into my eyeball. 'You carry on your life like a good little jingle-writer, and you don't look right and you don't look left, and in particular you don't go looking into dark corners, because some dark corners have some real nasty surprises hiding inside of them.'

I didn't even dare to nod, in case that blade went into my eye. Jack held it there for a few seconds longer, and I could smell the garlic on his breath. Then the men's room door opened, and two Japanese came in, and he immediately released me.

'Remember what I told you,' he said, and clapped me on the back, as if we were the best of buddies. Then he put on his sunglasses and walked out.

I stayed where I was for a while, holding on to the washbasin and staring at myself in the mirror. I looked pale and very washed out, and the bump on my nose had turned an odd mixture of yellow and purple. Jack hadn't blinded me, thank God, but I didn't have the slightest doubt that he was capable of doing it.

I left the men's room. Swiss International Airways were announcing the last call for flight LX 1663 for Zurich. I had a choice now. I could change my flight again, and return to New York, and forget about the Cesarettis and the Philips and the Westerlunds, and what Kate had been trying to show me. Or I could fly to Stockholm and see what I could find out about number 44 Skeppsbron – at the very real risk of Jack Friendly coming after me. I mean – how had he found me in the men's room at Marco Polo Airport, if he hadn't been following me?

I covered my eyes with my hand, so that all I could see was blackness, as if I were blind. But when I took my hand away, a white Persian cat was sitting close to my stool in the wine bar. It stayed there for a few seconds, staring at me, and then it disappeared in the direction of the departure gates.

'God help me,' I breathed, and followed it.

Twenty-Four

I had sworn black and blue that I would never come back to Stockholm, but here I was, standing outside the Westerlunds' apartment on Skeppsbron, at 7:30 in the evening, with thick snow whirling down all around me.

The snow clung to my hair and the shoulders of my coat and it even clung to my eyebrows. I had booked myself a room at the Sheraton, but I had decided to walk here because it was only ten minutes away, across Kornhamnstorget, and

296

after four hours' flying and another hour in an overheated taxi, I was gasping for some fresh air, no matter how bitter it was.

I had kept the keys to the Westerlunds' apartment that Kate had given me, but I had left them back in New York. In any case, I didn't think it would exactly be polite to let myself in, uninvited and unexpected, even if the Westerlunds *were* still here.

I rang the doorbell and waited, while the snow fell faster and thicker. My shoes and socks were soaked and my toes were numb, and I wished that I had called a taxi to bring me here.

I rang again. No answer. Maybe I would have to come back later, or early tomorrow morning. I was looking around for a taxi to take me back to the Sheraton when I heard a complicated rattling of bolts and keys, and the front door opened.

A handsome middle-aged woman with silvery-blonde hair and rimless spectacles was peering out at me. 'Ah!' she said. 'Herr Andersson?' I could feel the warmth flowing out of the interior of the house behind her.

I scuffled the snow off my hair. 'No, ma'am. I hope I'm not disturbing you. Do you speak English?'

'Of course, yes. I'm sorry. I was expecting an acquaintance of my husband's.'

'My name is Gideon Lake and I'm a friend of Axel and Tilda Westerlund.'

'The *Westerlunds*? Oh. They do not live here now, I'm afraid. They used to own our apartment – I don't know, maybe three years ago. But they left Stockholm. I don't know where they went. You are not the first friend who has come here looking for them.'

'They left no forwarding address? Nothing like that?'

She shook her head. 'We still receive mail for them, even now. Not so much as we used to. But we don't know where to send it on, so we just have to return it.'

'I'm sorry. This is kind of intrusive, I know – but do you *own* the apartment? Or rent it?'

'It is rented on our behalf by the Royal Institute of Technology. My husband is a professor.'

'I see. Thanks. You don't happen to know who actually owns it? They might have some idea where the Westerlunds went to.'

'Why don't you come in, out of the snow?' she asked me. 'My husband will be home very soon and I'm sure he knows who the owners are. Our heating broke down last winter, and the agents had to contact the owners to pay for a new boiler. Come on – come inside.'

'You're sure?' I asked her.

She opened the door wider, and smiled. 'If you were a rapist I don't think that you would be standing in the street with a little mountain of snow on top of your head, flapping your arms like a *pingvin.*'

I stepped into the hallway. The glass lantern that Tilda Westerlund had shattered with her screaming had been repaired, but the murky mirror was still hanging there.

The woman held out her hand. It was small

and very warm. 'My name is Anna-Carin Olofsson and my husband is Professor Berthil Olofsson. Berthil is quite famous for his research into global warming.'

I brushed the melting snow from my shoulders. 'Global warming? I could sure use some of that right now!'

'Come upstairs. I have a good fire going.'

Now that I was standing next to her, I realized how small she was. She hardly reached up to my shoulder. But she had a very trim figure, for her age, and a faded tan, and I guessed that she spent all summer swimming and all winter skiing and she probably ate two bowlfuls of muesli every morning. She made me feel seriously unhealthy.

Upstairs, the apartment had changed very little since the last time I had visited it. The same statuette of Freya in the corridor. The same gilded sofas in the living room. The same Malmsjö piano on which I had played *The Pointing Tree* for Elsa and Felicia.

Anna-Carin Olofsson took my overcoat and hung it up for me. 'Sit down by the fire,' she said. 'Would you care for some coffee?'

'That's kind of you. Thanks. Just black, please.'

She went into the kitchen and I followed her. 'We love this apartment,' she said, as she spooned coffee into the percolator. 'We lived in a brand-new apartment before, in Uppsala, and it had no character. But this place – sometimes my husband thinks that he can still hear the voices of the people who lived in it before us.'

'Really? What do they say?'

Anna-Carin Olofsson flapped her hand dismissively. 'Of course it is just his imagination. For a scientist, he can be very superstitious. If he spills any salt on the table, he always throws a pinch of it over his left shoulder to protect himself from bad luck. Two pinches, in fact.'

'Have *you* heard any voices?'

'Me? No. Not voices as such. One evening, though, when Berthil was away at one of his conferences, I thought I heard a woman crying. I went from room to room, but there was nobody here. I think it must have come from the alley, at the back, or maybe another apartment.'

She paused, and then she took two cups down from the cupboard. 'It sounded so sad. How can I say it? It sounded like a woman who is in complete despair.'

She poured us each a cup of coffee, and we took them through to the living room. As we sat down, the front door opened and Professor Olofsson arrived home, stamping his feet on the mat.

'Berthil!' called Anna-Carin. 'We are in here, my darling!'

A stocky, gray-bearded man appeared, wearing a brown overcoat and a long brown-and-white scarf. He was balding, with shiny spectacles, and cold-reddened cheeks. He almost looked like a professor out of a child's comic book.

'My darling, this gentleman is a friend of the Westerlunds. He came here to look for them.'

'Gideon Lake,' I said. 'Sorry for intruding, but your wife has made me very welcome.'

Professor Olofsson tugged off his woolen

glove and shook my hand.

'*God afton,*' he said. 'If you have come here looking for the Westerlunds, I regret that you have had a wasted journey. I hope you haven't come too far.'

'New York, originally. But it hasn't been a total bust. I believe that I'm a whole lot nearer to finding out what happened to the Westerlunds than I ever was before.'

Professor Olofsson took off his overcoat, and Anna-Carin took it into the hallway to hang it up. He said, 'Nobody seems to know where the Westerlunds went. After we moved in here, we had letters and phone calls for them for months, and people calling here to ask if we knew where they had gone. Even their relatives.'

He sat down, and unlaced his shoes. 'I think Dr Westerlund's sister went to the police, and reported them as missing, but as far as I know nothing ever came out of that.'

Anna-Carin came in with a mug of frothy coffee, with chocolate sprinkles, and set it down on the table.

Professor Oloffson took two or three noisy sips, so that chocolate sprinkles clung to his beard. Then he said, 'You think you might have found out where they moved to, Mr Lake?'

'No. It would surprise me if anybody ever sees them again. Not alive, anyhow. But I'm beginning to understand what happened to them, and why.'

'You believe that they are *dead*?'

'I think that it's a very strong possibility, yes.'

'All of them? The whole family?'

301

I nodded. 'I don't have any proof yet. But it seems very likely. And I don't think it was accidental, either.'

'But Dr Westerlund was a surgeon, wasn't he? Why would anybody want to kill him?'

'I think I know what the motive was. I also think I know who did it. As I say, though, I don't have any proof. None that makes any sense.'

'Well, I wish you luck. If the Westerlunds really have been murdered, then they deserve justice.'

I put down my coffee cup. 'Your wife tells me that you know who owns this apartment.'

'How would this help?'

'I'm not sure. But whoever bought it from the Westerlunds, maybe the Westerlunds gave them some clue about where they were going.'

Professor Oloffson dragged out a handkerchief and blew his nose. 'Of course our lease was all arranged by my university, and so I never saw the original contract. But when the heating went wrong I got in touch with the letting agents, and when I visited their office, the paperwork was all there, lying on the agent's desk. *Penumbra.* Not a name you would forget.'

'I've heard of Penumbra. They're based in New York.'

'In that case, it will not be so difficult for you to talk to them, yes?' He blew his nose again. *'Murdered.* That would be terrible. What a world this is turning into!'

We sat in silence for a short while, punctuated only by the lurching of logs in the fireplace, and the clink of coffee cups. Then I said, 'I under-

302

stand you've been hearing voices, professor.'

Professor Olofsson looked across at Anna-Carin and wagged his finger at her. 'My wife shouldn't tell you such stories! I don't want it getting out that I'm going a bit funny in the head.'

'You have, though?'

'Well – I don't think they can really be voices. More likely, it's just a draft, blowing under the door. You know how the wind can sound as if it is talking to you, especially at night, when you're very tired.'

'Can you make out anything of what they're saying?'

Professor Olofsson looked at me sharply. 'It's the wind, Mr Lake. I'm almost sure of it. I just like to think that in an old apartment like this, the spirits of the people who used to live here are still keeping us company.'

'Did you ever hear them saying the word *drunkna*?'

'Drowning? Who told you that?'

'So you *did* hear them say it?'

Professor Olofsson shook his head. 'No, of course not. I heard nothing except whispering.'

'Have you ever heard any unusual noises – like children, running along the corridor, in the middle of the night?'

'Sometimes the plumbing makes a banging sound. But that is simple physics. Expansion and contraction. Not children.'

'And you've never seen anybody? Or felt anybody touching you?'

'You sound like one of those mediums, Mr

Lake. I don't believe this apartment is haunted. I hear whispering sometimes and it sounds like voices, but that is all.'

He looked at his watch and I could tell that he didn't want to discuss this any more. Anna-Carin gave me a sympathetic shrug.

'OK,' I said. 'I think I've probably taken up too much of your time already. Thank you for your hospitality, sir, and thank you for your coffee, Mrs Olofsson. Is it OK if I use your bathroom before I go?'

'By all means,' said Anna-Carin. 'I will show you where it is.'

I knew, of course, but she led me along the corridor anyhow. Outside the bathroom door, she stopped and said, 'Berthil does not want you to think that he believes in such things. But he has told me that he can sometimes catch what the voices are saying. One of them said, *vilja de drunkna oss?* Will they drown us?'

'OK,' I said. 'Thank you. You don't know how helpful you've been.'

Professor Olofsson called, 'Anna! Anna! *Kanna Jag har något mer kaffe?*' and she called back, 'Coming, my darling!' and left me alone in the corridor.

I was pushing open the bathroom door when I thought I heard singing, coming from one of the bedrooms. I stopped, with my hand still holding the doorknob, straining my ears. It was very high, and very faint, but it was definitely singing.

I walked further along the corridor until I came to what had once been Elsa and Felicia's bedroom. I pressed my ear against the door panel, and I could still hear it. Two girls' voices, clear and infinitely sad, and singing in English.

'The forest may be tangled ... but every time you stray ... you can always find a Pointing Tree ... to help you find your way...'

I opened the bedroom door, and as soon as I did so I had that skin-shrinking feeling. Elsa and Felicia were sitting together on the end of the bed, facing each other and holding hands. But they were *transparent*, as if they were nothing more than holograms. I could see the closet and the dressing table right through them.

'Elsa?' I said. 'Felicia?'

I stepped into the room and they both turned their heads and smiled at me, although their eyes were so dark and shadowy that it was impossible for me to tell if they could see me or not.

'Elsa, Felicia, it's me – Gideon. The guy who wrote you that song.'

Neither of them spoke, although they both kept smiling. As I came nearer, I could see that they were both wearing white nightdresses, but that both of their nightdresses were soaked, and clinging to their skin.

'The men who did this to you – I'm going to find them, and I'm going to make sure they get punished for it. Do you understand me?'

Elsa reached out for me. I tried to hold her hand, but there was nothing there, only the faintest of chills, as if she had breathed on me.

'We knew that you could save us,' she said.

'Yes,' said Felicia. 'We told each other that Gideon would never forget us.'

They faded away right in front of my eyes. Within seconds, I was standing in the bedroom on my own – panting, as if I had run all the way along Skeppsbron and up the stairs and along the corridor, to catch them before they disappeared.

Self-consciously, I laid my hand on the cream woven bedspread, to feel if it was damp – but it was completely dry. Wherever Elsa and Felicia had been soaked in water, it hadn't been here.

I left the bedroom and closed the door quietly behind me. Then I went back to the bathroom.

It was dark inside, so I reached for the light cord, and tugged it. The ceiling light clicked on, and I almost shouted out loud.

Standing on the tiled floor right in front of me, her dress plastered in blood, was Tilda. Her hair was as wild as a cockatoo. Her eyes were bulging and her mouth was stretched wide open in a silent scream.

She took one lurching step toward me, almost falling over – and then another. Her face had been cut all over – her forehead, her cheeks, her nose, her lips. There were gaping cuts on her shoulders and blood was running in thin streams from her elbows. *'Behaga döda jag,'* she mumbled, and bubbles of blood burst out of her nostrils. 'Please kill me.'

I could have called out for Anna-Carin. I could have taken Tilda in my arms, and tried to give her first aid. But I knew that Anna-Carin would not be able to see Tilda, and I knew that Tilda was just as insubstantial as Elsa and Felicia. None of them were really here, not any more. They were nothing more than a terrible echo.

I did the only thing that I could think of. I switched off the light and slammed the bathroom door behind me. I stood in the corridor for a moment, breathing hard. I thought of taking another look in the bathroom, just to make sure that Tilda wasn't really there, but I decided against it, in case she was. Stiff-legged, I walked back to the living room. Anna-Carin smiled at me and I tried to smile back.

'Are you all right, Mr Lake?' she asked me. 'You look a little – I don't know. *Off balance.*'

'I'm just pooped, I guess. Venice, Zurich, Stockholm, all in one day. I think my bed's calling me, back at the Sheraton.'

Professor Olofsson shook my hand, very firmly. 'I wish you well. I hope that you find the answers that you are looking for, and that the conclusion of your quest is not too tragic.'

'Well, me too, professor. But between you and me, I'm not holding out too much hope of a happy ending.'

Margot called me at 2:35 in the morning.

'This is my revenge for you waking *me* up,' she said.

I rolled over in bed and pulled down the toggle of the bedside lamp. 'Sorry to disappoint you, sweetheart, but I wasn't asleep yet.'

'What's the matter? Insomnia?'

'If you'd seen what I saw, *you'd* have insomnia, too. For weeks.'

'Not *more* weirdness?'

'You'd better believe it. The same weirdness, only worse. I'll tell you all about when I get back to New York.'

'You're OK, though?'

'Sure, I'm OK. Did you find out anything about Penumbra?'

'Not a whole lot. They have a website but all it gives you is a few photographs of ritzy apartments, and a blurb about "prestige apartments worldwide ... rare and distinguished rental properties in some of the most historic cities of Europe and Scandinavia ... homes for international players of taste and influence." '

'Underneath that it says "Rome – London – Stockholm – Venice – Prague." '

'Any contact information?'

'There's an email address, and a line which says "a wholly-owned division of Sunpath Holdings." But that's all. I called my friend Gavin who works for Manhattan Realty Group. He knows everybody in property but he's never heard of Penumbra, or Sunpath.'

'Have you tried Googling Sunpath?'

'Yes ... but there's nothing listed ... except for some elementary school in Minnesota and a housing development in Arizona. It's a word used by realtors to describe the position of a house in relation to the sun, but that's about it.'

'OK, Margot. Thanks.'

'Listen – you're stopping off in London, right?'

'I'm catching the eleven o'clock flight tomorrow morning. Well – in eight and a half hours' time.'

'Will you have time to buy me some British rock candy? You know, that pink stuff with

308

LONDON written all the way through it?'

'You're a kid, Margot. Did you know that?'

I put down the phone. Sunpath Holdings. I wrote it down on the Sheraton notepad beside the bed.

I ordered breakfast on room service the next morning, hard-cooked eggs and cheese and thin slices of salami. It was 8:00 a.m., but outside it was still dark and snow was falling into Lake Mälaren.

I watched CNN News while I dressed and drank my coffee, black with three brown sugar cubes in it. I didn't usually take sugar but this morning I felt like I needed the energy.

Every now and then the television picture crackled and jumped. At the end of his 8:15 a.m. bulletin, weatherman Carl Parker said, '...apologies for all of the interference, folks ... this is being caused by unusual solar flare activity ... so blame the sun, not your set...'

I was standing in the bathroom, washing my teeth, before the words came together in my head. I looked at myself in the mirror, and I felt as if I was in one of those reverse zooms they do in the movies, when the background dwindles rapidly away but the character seems to be coming toward you.

Blame the sun. Solar flare activity. Sun equals sol. Path equals way.

Solway. Penumbra was owned by Victor Solway. In his arrogance, in his supreme self-confidence, he had hardly even tried to disguise it.

309

* * *

The sun was shining sharply when I arrived at 37 Wetherby Gardens. When you see London in the sunshine, you realize how grimy it is, and how gray, and how decrepit. I think it was Samuel Johnson who said that when you're tired of London you're tired of life, but London itself looks tired these days, a city of exhausted dreams.

I paid off the taxi and managed to work out a reasonable tip – or maybe it was too much, because the cabbie called out, 'Cheers, mate! Cheers! Thanks a lot!' before he drove away.

The first thing I noticed as I climbed the front steps was that there were no drapes hanging in the living room windows of the Philips' apartment. When I reached the porch I shaded my eyes so that I could look inside. There was no furniture in the living room, either – and no paintings hanging on the walls. All I could see were bare floorboards and a half-open door leading to the hallway.

I rang the doorbell but there obviously wasn't much point. The Philips were gone. All I could do was find myself another taxi and fly back to New York.

Halfway down the steps, however, I stopped and turned around, just to take a last look. And there she was – sitting on the right-hand window sill, watching me. The white Persian cat who may or may not have been Malkin.

Slowly, I climbed up the steps again, and confronted her.

'What are you?' I mouthed, even though I

knew that she couldn't hear me through the glass – and even if she could, she wouldn't be able to answer me. *'What are you doing here? What are you trying to tell me, for Christ's sake?'*

She stared at me for a few seconds longer. Then she jumped down from the window and ran out of the living room, into the hallway, toward the kitchen.

I glanced around. There were three or four passers-by on the opposite side of the street, but none of them was taking any notice of me. Why should they – a scruffy-looking guy in a rain-coat? I went back down the steps, and around to the side of the house. There was a white-painted wooden gate, but it was unlocked, and I was able to make my way along the narrow alley where the garbage bins were stored.

At the end of the alley, on the right-hand side, I came across a second gate, but this was un-locked, too. I climbed three shallow concrete steps and found myself on the Philips' patio. I could see into their kitchen, and into the master bedroom, too. There was a double bed in the bedroom, although it had been stripped down to the mattress, and the kitchen was empty. But the white cat was sitting at the window, as if she had been expecting me.

I approached the window and hunkered down in front of her. She touched the glass with her nose, and licked her lips.

'What are you trying to tell me, puss?' I demanded, much louder this time. 'Come on, Malkin – show me!'

She looked up, and so I looked up, too. In the

311

window, I saw the reflection of a young boy, standing right behind me. I twisted around, losing my balance, so that I had to grab hold of the window frame to steady myself.

I stood up. The boy was about twelve or thirteen years old, with a short brown haircut. He was wearing a gray sweater with a school badge on it, and baggy gray pants. His face had been badly beaten. His lips were split and his cheeks were swollen, and it looked as if his jaw might have been dislocated.

But it was his eyes that shocked me the most. They were wide open, as if he were staring at me, but the irises and the pupils were milky-white, while the eyeballs around them were deeply bloodshot. His eyelids were encrusted with a transparent crystalline substance, some of which had dripped halfway down his cheeks like tears, but then solidified.

'Daddy?' he said, reaching out in front of him. 'Is that you, Daddy?'

'It's Gideon,' I told him. 'Listen – I can get you some help.'

'Is that you, Daddy?' he repeated. 'It hurts so much. Please tell them to stop. Please tell them not to hurt me any more.'

I gently took hold of his hands. He flinched, and tried to tug them free, but I wouldn't let him go.

'Listen,' I said, 'my name's Gideon. I'm not going to hurt you. Can you tell me your name?'

'My eyes,' he said, twisting his head around and around as if that might help to clear his vision. 'They hurt my eyes. They're burning and they won't stop burning and I can't *see* any more.'

'Tell me your name,' I repeated. 'I can help you, I promise. But I need to know your name.'

He suddenly stopped twisting his head and stared in my direction, although he was blinded.

'Giles Nicholas Philips,' he said. 'Thirty-seven Wetherby Gardens, London SW5. Please give them what they want. Please, Daddy. *Please.* Don't let them hurt me any more. *Please!'*

I knew that it was far too late for me to help him, and that nobody else could help him, either. I could call for an ambulance, but they wouldn't find anybody here.

I squeezed his fingers tight, and then I gripped his shoulder, to try and show him that I understood what he was going through, although he was plainly going through hell and how the hell could I understand that?

I left him there, on the patio, still calling for his father, and I went down the steps and closed the gate behind me. Sometimes other people's agony is too much for us to listen to. Shit, listen to me, philosophizing. I left him because I simply couldn't bear it any more.

As I crossed the paved front yard, the door opened and a young man in a dark business suit came out, carrying a briefcase.

'Excuse me!' he called out. 'Can I help you?'

'I – ah – not really.'

He came briskly down the steps, on very shiny black shoes. He had one of those smooth fresh faces that you see in high school photographs, still unmarked by life's disappointments.

313

'Were you looking for somebody?' he asked me. 'Perhaps I can help.'

'Well, uh – I was wondering if this apartment was for rent. I've been looking for a base in London for quite a while, and I just happened to be walking past.'

'It *is* available, as a matter of fact.' The young man opened his briefcase and took out a business card. Keller & Watson, Letting Agents, 161 Brompton Road, Knightsbridge. 'If you'd like to take a quick look around, I have the keys with me.'

I glanced up and I could see Malkin back on the window, watching me. 'No, thanks. Maybe I can make an appointment. You know – bring my wife along with me. She doesn't come over from New York until next week, but I daren't make any kind of major decision without consulting *her* – if you get my drift.'

The young man smiled sympathetically. 'Of course, Mr—'

'Schifrin. Lalo Schifrin.'

'Very well, Mr Schifrin. Any time you like. Just for your information, the rent is three thousand, two hundred and fifty pounds a week. Council tax on top of that, of course.'

I wasn't very good at working out the exchange rates of small amounts of British currency, but I knew that the pound was worth about twice what the dollar was – which meant that the Philips' apartment would have cost me nearly twenty-five and a half thousand bucks a month.

'Sounds very reasonable,' I nodded. 'By the

314

way, who owns it?'

'Funny thing, they're a New York company. Perhaps you know them. Penumbra.'

'Oh, Penumbra! Sure, I've heard of them. Very upscale. Run by that – what's-his-name feller.' I paused, and waited for the young man to give me the answer. When he didn't, I said, 'You know. What's-his-name? Always escapes me. Galway? Solway?'

The young man shook his head. 'I'm afraid I don't know, sir. Mr Watson usually deals with Penumbra.'

'Oh, well, not to worry. But thanks for your time. I'll call you just as soon as the wife arrives in town.'

The young man shook hands, and walked off. I waited outside the house for a while, but the white cat had disappeared and I had no intention of going back to the patio to see if Giles Philips was still there, blinded or not.

I hailed a taxi. On the way back to my hotel, I sat watching London go past, sunlit and shabby, a city well past its prime. I felt exhausted. I also felt guilty – more guilty than I had ever felt before – because I had turned my back on Tilda, and Giles Philips, too. But now I had a pretty good idea of what Kate had asked me to do, and I was more determined than ever not to let her down.

Twenty-Five

When I arrived home, New York was in the grip of a bitter spell of weather from Canada. It wasn't snowing, but those north-west winds made your nose drip whenever you ventured outside, and all the city's fountains were frozen into lumpy shapes, like ice-trolls.

I put the heating on full blast, and poured myself a large glass of *krupnik*, the honey vodka which had been given to me two Christmases ago by my Polish friend Piotr Kús. He could play the drums like a demented marionette, Piotr, but only after two joints and half a bottle of Wodka Wyborowa.

I had only been home about an hour when there was a knock at my door. I opened it, and it was Kate, wearing a silver fox hat and a long silver fox coat. She was carrying Malkin in her arms.

'Hallo, stranger,' I greeted her. 'Come on in.'

She stepped into my apartment on very high-heeled black boots. I closed the door behind her and then I took her into my arms and kissed her. Her lips were very cold, but the inside of her mouth was very warm. Her cold eyelashes brushed my cheek.

I untied her coat, and put my arms around her,

and held her very close, and kissed her again. 'You don't know how much I've missed you,' I told her.

She took off her hat, and shook her hair. 'You could have come back from Venice non-stop.'

'No, I couldn't. I had to find out for myself what happened to the Cesarettis and the Westerlunds and the Philips. You couldn't tell me, could you? You could only *show* me. I still don't completely understand why, to tell you the truth. Something to do with a wife not being able to give evidence in court against her husband? But it doesn't really matter. All of those apartments are owned by Penumbra International Property and Penumbra International Property is owned by Sunpath Holdings and Sunpath Holdings is owned by Victor. Do I have that right?'

'Yes,' she said. Her chin was uptilted as if she were challenging me. 'So what are you going to do now?'

'First off? First off I'm going to take off your coat. Then I'm going to take off your dress, and your underwear, if you're wearing any, and I'm going to carry you into the bedroom and make love to you.'

'What about my boots?'

'Your boots? No – you have to leave your boots on.'

'What about Malkin?'

'Malkin will have to look the other way.'

So she made love with her boots on – black leather and white skin. She seemed to be even thinner than ever, with prominent ribs and hips,

317

and hollows above her collarbone.

We both knew that we had something dreadful to share, but we needed each other more, and somehow the impending horror of it made our love all the more perverse and erotic.

Kate rode me dreamily up and down, clasping my thighs between her boots. She arched her back, and I could see myself sliding in and out of her, like a Chinese conjuring trick. Now you see it, now you don't. Then she leaned forward and kissed me, and bit me, and began to ride me harder. I panted, she panted. She rode faster and faster. Then I could feel my climax rising and then I could feel her shuddering and then she screamed.

I knew that she had screamed because my closet mirror cracked from one corner to the other, with a sharp *snap!* – even though her actual scream was so high that I couldn't hear it. She shook, and she shook, and then eventually she toppled sideways on to the bed.

'You did it,' she whispered, holding me very close, and repeatedly kissing my cheek, and my chin, and my forehead, and my eyes. I was still trying to catch my breath. 'You've seen, at *last*, what I've been showing you.'

'Well, I do see it, yes. And then again I don't. Like – I understand that Jack Friendly abducted and tortured all of these families' kids, and that he probably did it on Victor's instigation. But why? For their apartments? For their money? For their possessions?'

'For all of those, yes. But it was more than that.'

318

'Then *what*? Because they didn't just kill the kids, did they? They wiped out the whole god-damned family. Mother, father, brothers and sisters – everybody. And they got rid of their bodies, without any trace at all. None. Even their relatives don't know where they've disappeared to.'

'They don't want anybody to find out what they've done. No living witnesses, that's what Victor said.'

'But *you* know what they've done, don't you? I don't know how you can go on living with Victor, when you know that he's responsible for torturing and murdering all of those innocent people. How can you even bear to be in the same *room* as him, let alone allow him to touch you? Jesus Christ, Kate, why haven't you gone to the police?'

'There's no *proof*, Gideon. There are no living witnesses.'

'Surely the police can find some evidence, once you tell them what Victor's done.'

Kate didn't answer that. I sat up and looked at her, expecting her to tell me more, but she simply turned away, so that she could see her broken reflection in the cracked closet mirror.

'So what *is* his motive?' I asked her, at last. 'You don't massacre entire families, not like that, no matter how much wealth it's going to bring you.'

'You don't know Victor. You don't know the people who work for him. They don't have any conscience whatsoever.'

'I'm glad I don't know them. But tell me

something else. Why did he pick on the Westerlunds, and the Philips, and the Cesarettis? All of
them were very wealthy, for sure. They all had
money, and multi-million-dollar properties. But
there are just as many rich families in New York,
aren't there? Why not kidnap *their* kids? Why
take the trouble to go all the way to Stockholm
and Venice and London, for Christ's sake?'

'That's the answer,' she told me.

'What? I thought that was the question.'

'Once you know the answer to that, Gideon,
then you'll know the answer to everything.'

'Jesus, Kate. Let's forget about the riddles.
You have to go to the police. I'll come with you.
I'll tell you what he's been doing, him and that
Jack Friendly bastard.'

She turned back to me. 'Do you think for one
moment they'll believe you? You saw two girls
running down a corridor when they were fast
asleep in bed, and they weren't even fast asleep
in bed, either. They were missing, without trace.
You saw a girl drowned in Stockholm harbor
when she was still at school, but then again,
maybe she wasn't at school at all. You saw a
woman burning in a London garden, although
she wasn't really there.'

'OK – but you actually live with Victor. You
must be able to find some kind of proof. Credit
card receipts, or bank statements. There must be
some incriminating evidence in his cellphone, or
his laptop.'

'I *can't*, Gideon.'

I thought about it, and then I said, 'No, I guess
not. Too risky. If Victor finds out you've been

going through his things—'

'*You* can find proof,' Kate encouraged me. 'Victor's been very clever, when it comes to setting up his holding companies. But he's complacent, too. It never occurred to him that anybody would ever find out what he's been doing. And he certainly never imagined that anybody would come after him.'

I kissed her forehead. Her skin was very cool and smooth.

'Does Penumbra have an office in New York?' I asked her.

'As far as I know they have a postal address – 200 Madison Avenue – but it's probably nothing more than a mailbox.'

'There must be some way of connecting Victor to Penumbra. But we also have to connect Jack Friendly to Penumbra, and prove that he was working for Penumbra when he tortured and killed all of those people. And that Victor instigated it. It's not going to be easy.'

'You can do it. You have to do it.'

'I can try. But I write jingles, remember? I'm not Mike Hammer.'

She kissed me again, and trailed her fingers slowly down my stomach, and squeezed me, but not in the way that Jack Friendly had, in the men's room at Marco Polo Airport.

'You need to know something,' she said. 'We only have three days left.'

'What do you mean? Why only three days?'

'I can't tell you. Not yet. Not till this is over.'

I sat up. 'Kate – I have gone along with you every step of the way. I've trusted you, I've supported you, I've never asked you to explain yourself – even when children have drowned and women have burst into flames and husbands and wives have been hanging from the ceiling. But now I'm asking you straight. Why do we have only three days?'

She kissed me again. 'Can't you wait? It won't be very long, and then you'll know everything.'

'Kate—'

'I can't tell you, Gideon. That's all.'

What was I going to do? Storm out in a temper? I had gone along with her so far, hadn't I? And I sensed even more strongly that if this all worked out, and we managed to get Victor and Jack Friendly put away, then she and I could be together.

'OK,' I said. 'I don't know why, but I give in. But I'll ask you again in three days' time.'

I climbed astride her, and pinned her down to the bed, and kissed her, but then Malkin mewed, from the living room.

'She's hungry,' said Kate.

'Jesus Christ. Can't she wait?'

'She'll go on mewing like that until we feed her. And, besides, I could *really* use a drink.'

Just after nine o'clock that evening, we heard Victor letting himself into the house. He was talking loudly, as if he were using his cell. He slammed his front door but we could still hear him talking.

'I'd better leave,' said Kate, buttoning up the front of her dress.

'Why? You don't have to. He's a murderer,

Kate. He's a total sadist. Maybe he didn't personally torture and kill all of those people, but he might just as well.'

'Gideon, I'm not frightened of him. I'm not frightened of Jack Friendly, either, but I don't want to make them more suspicious than we have already. I'd better go, anyhow. You need your rest.'

I showed her to the door. 'Tomorrow I'm going to start looking for evidence,' I told her. 'The sooner we can get Victor and Jack in the slammer, the better.'

She picked up Malkin, and held her close. She kissed my left ear, and murmured, 'Take care of yourself, won't you?'

'When will I see you again?' I asked her.

She looked at me with those rainy gray eyes and gave me an oddly enigmatic smile. The Mona Lisa wasn't in it. Then she disappeared down the stairs, leaving me standing on the landing.

'Kate?' I called her, but she didn't answer.

I listened for her to open her apartment door, but Victor suddenly switched on his stereo player, at top volume, so all I heard was a howl of feedback and then a booming surge of Tony Bennett singing *You'd Be So Nice To Come Home To*. Go on, I thought, rub it in. You just wait until you're sitting in a 10 by 8 cell upstate, you sadistic murdering bastard, and Kate is coming home to *me*.

I had over thirty answerphone messages to deal with, most of them from Hazel McCall, my

323

agent, wanting to know if I had finished scoring the next *Billy Wagner Show*. 'Where the hell *are* you, Gideon? Freddie Sansom is going apeshit.'

After I had called Hazel and reassured her that I was almost done, and dealt with most of my other messages, I got down to playing detective. I spent the next four and a half hours calling realtors and lawyers all across Manhattan, trying to find anybody who had done business with Penumbra International Property.

My first break came from Mimi Liebowitz, a high-end rental agent in Murray Hill. Her secretary told me that she had seen a display advertisement for Penumbra properties in last month's issue of *Prestige Homes* magazine. I promised to buy her lunch and so she faxed it to me. One apartment was in Geneva; another was in Rome. But here, too, was the Palazzetto Di Nerezza in Venice.

I called *Prestige Homes* and their advertising executive was snooty and camp but very co-operative. He told me that the advertisement had been placed and paid for by an intermediary agency called Nussbaum Media, but when I called Nussbaum Media, they could only tell me that they had been instructed by a woman calling herself Edie Johnson and that she had paid them on a personal checking account.

Finally, I called the number on the Penumbra advertisement. A young woman's voice answered me almost immediately.

'Penumbra International Properties, how can I assist you?'

'Oh – I saw your advertisement in *Prestige*

Homes. I'm planning on moving to Venice, Italy, and I was wondering if that Palazzetto Di Nerezza was still available.'

'May I take your name, sir?'

'Coleman – Franklin Coleman,' I lied, using my mother's maiden names. 'Maybe you've heard of Coleman's Fine Art Auctioneers? An apartment like that Palazzetto Di Nerezza would suit me down to the ground. Or – hey – down to the water, being Venice.'

The young woman was unamused. 'If you can give me a moment, sir, I'll check the status of that particular rental.'

I waited for a few seconds, listening to some glutinous string music. Then the girl came back and said, 'I'm so sorry, Mr Coleman. The Palazzetto was taken only about a week ago. But we do have an equally fine rental property coming on to our books within the next few days, the Palazzetto Grimani. I can send you the particulars as soon as we receive them from our agents in Venice.'

'Well, I have to tell you that I'm very disappointed,' I said. 'I saw those pictures and I said to my wife, "that is exactly the kind of apartment I've set my heart on." It has class. It has substance. Is there any way I can persuade the new tenants to find themselves someplace else? Maybe you could interest *them* in this Palazzetto Grimani.'

'I'm sorry, Mr Coleman, that wouldn't be possible.'

'Can I talk to your boss?'

'I'm really sorry, Mr Coleman, that wouldn't

make any difference. The new tenants are already in occupancy.'

'All the same, I'd like to talk to your boss. Victor Solway, isn't it?'

'Excuse me?'

'Victor Solway. I'd like to talk to Victor Solway.'

It sounded like the girl had stopped breathing for a moment. Then she said, 'Can you bear with me for a moment, sir?'

I had to listen to more glutinous strings, and then the girl came back and said, 'Hallo, sir? I'm afraid that nobody of that name is in any way associated with Penumbra International Property. The manager is Mr Lowenstein, but Mr Lowenstein is away from his desk right now.'

'Oh, come on. Victor Solway is not only associated with Penumbra International Property, he *owns* Penumbra International Property.'

'Nobody of that name is in any way associated with Penumbra International Property, sir. But if you let me have your contact number, I can have Mr Lowenstein call you back.'

'I don't want Mr Lowenstein to call me back. I want to talk to the engineer, not the oily rag. Put me on to Victor Solway. Tell him I know all about his international property business, and how he runs it. And tell him that if he doesn't talk to me, he's going to regret it, big time.'

The young woman immediately hung up, without saying anything more. That was the surest sign that she could have given me that Victor Solway *did* own Penumbra. If she had genuinely never heard of him before, why would she have cut the connection? I would have bet money that Victor was standing right next to her, drawing his finger across his throat.

It was nearly midnight. I was hunched over my keyboard, finishing off my score for the next *Billy Wagner Show*. I wanted to add a 'hurry', which is that excitable burst of music they play when a music-hall entertainer comes running out on to the stage.

Twelve o'clock was just beginning to strike when I heard a devastating crash from downstairs, as if a bookcase full of books had fallen over. This was immediately followed by shouting and banging and hysterical screaming.

The voices were muffled by the floorboards, but I could recognize Victor. He must have been right below me, because I could hear him roaring, '*—you whore! You goddamned whore! Did you think that I wouldn't find out? Do you think I'm goddamned stupid or something?*'

Then I heard a woman. I couldn't tell if it was Kate or not, but she was obviously sobbing.

Victor shouted some more, and then there was another crash, and a series of bumping noises. The woman screamed.

I listened hard. Last time this had happened, I had made a fool of myself. But this time, I was sure. The bumping noises were definitely coming from downstairs, and that was definitely Victor's voice. That's it, I thought. I don't care if Kate doesn't want me to face down Victor or not, I'm her lover now, and I'm going to protect her.

I was wearing only a T-shirt and shorts, so I dragged on my discarded jeans, almost falling sideways as I did so, and pulled on the mustard-colored sweater that my mother had given me for my last birthday. Then I opened my door, left it on the latch, and bounded barefoot down to the hallway, three stairs at a time. The screaming and shouting and bumping was still going on, and I heard something smash.

I beat on the door with my fist. 'Victor! This is Gideon! What's going on, Victor? *Victor!*'

There was no answer, but there was plenty more shouting and bumping. I heard Victor shouting, 'If this was one of those Muslim countries, do you know what they'd do to you? They'd stone you, that's what they do! They'd fricking stone you!'

I hammered on the door even louder, with both fists. 'Victor! This is Gideon! Open the god-damned door, will you?'

Everything went silent. I waited, and waited, wondering if I ought to knock again. But after a while the door opened and Victor appeared, in a rumpled yellow shirt and purple pants. His hair was all mussed up and his eyes were unfocused, as if he had been drinking.

'Gideon,' he said. 'What a surprise. Was I making too much noise?'

'You could say that.' I was aware that my nostrils were flaring. 'I want to see Kate.'

He blinked at me. 'You want to do *what*?'

'I want to see Kate. I want to make sure that you haven't hurt her.'

He swayed, and held on to the door to steady

himself. 'You want to fricking *what*?'

'I told you, Victor. I want to see Kate. If you've hurt her, I'm going to call the cops.'

Victor said, 'I know all about you, Gideon.' He swayed, and then he wagged his finger at me. 'I know your fricking game.'

'Whatever you know about me, I know a whole lot more about you. Now I want to see Kate.'

'You want to see Kate? You really want to see Kate? Well ... you can't.'

'You want to bet? If you don't call her to the door right now, I'm going to force my way in there, I promise you.'

Victor shook his head, and gave me a stupid drunken grin. 'She's not here, Gideon. That's why you can't see her.'

'I heard her.'

'No, you didn't, because she isn't here. Monica – come here and tell this clown that Kate isn't here. *Monica!*'

Monica appeared, looking as disheveled as Victor. She was wearing a tight red satin dress with a broken shoulder strap.

'Tell him,' said Victor. 'Is Kate here, or not?'

'Not,' said Monica, making a grab for the nearest armchair to steady herself.

'So where is she?' I demanded. 'If she's left you, I can't say that I blame her.'

Victor shook his head again, and carried on shaking it, as if he was deeply amused. 'You want to see Kate. What a *putz.*'

'OK, if she isn't here now, when is she coming back?'

'When is she coming *back*?'

'That's what I asked you.'

Victor said nothing, but hesitated for a moment and then closed the door in my face. I stood in the hallway for a while, wondering if I ought to try knocking again, but if he was telling me the truth, and Kate really wasn't there, what was the point? I would only antagonize him even more than I had already, and I knew what he and Jack Friendly were capable of doing to people who rubbed them up the wrong way. Or even people who didn't.

I went back up to my apartment. As I opened the door, I saw the old guy in the pale gray smock standing deep in the shadows at the bottom of the stairs. I said, 'Hi,' and lifted my hand to him in greeting, but I wasn't sure that he saw me, because he didn't acknowledge me at all, and immediately started to climb the stairs up toward Pearl's apartment.

I went back to my keyboard. I sat down and played the hurry a couple more times, but I couldn't make it snappy enough, and I decided to finish it in the morning. The past few weeks traveling around Europe with Kate had exhausted me. My mind was scattered all over the place, like a jigsaw that somebody has dropped on the floor, because everything that I had ever believed in had been proved to be false. I had believed that time was sequential, that one day followed another. I had believed that when people die, they're dead, and they can never reappear.

I went to bed and punched my pillow into

shape, pretending it was Victor Solway's face. The moon was shining through my bedroom window again, a cold reminder that time was passing by. Kate had said that there were only three days left, and now there were only two. But two days until *what*? And where was Kate? If she hadn't gone back to Victor, where had she gone? And with whom? I was not only baffled, I was jealous, too. Maybe she had another lover, apart from me. Maybe she had dozens of lovers. Maybe she was stringing us all along, with hallucinations and tricks and optical illusions. I felt as I everybody I met was wearing a mask, like the carnival masks of Venice, and that I was taking part in some mysterious dance whose steps and eventual purpose I couldn't even begin to understand.

The following morning was darker and colder than ever. Victor left the house at 9:15 a.m., followed about fifteen minutes later by Monica. As soon as I saw Monica climb into a taxi, I went cautiously downstairs and knocked. Maybe Kate *had* been there last night, but had been too intimidated by Victor to come out.

I knocked again, and called, 'Kate? Are you in there? *Kate*?' but there was no reply.

I was about to go back upstairs when Malkin appeared at the end of the hallway, by the door which led to the yard in the back. She mewed at me, and stood up on her hind legs, clawing at the door panels.

'Hey, kitty-cat, do you want to go outside? You will freeze your furry little ass off, I warn you.'

But Malkin mewed again, more impatiently this time, and I unbolted the door for her and turned the key. Outside, it was absolutely bitter, with a north-west wind blowing, and the sky was that weird orange color which warns of impending snow.

I expected Malkin to go running off to do her business, but she stopped and turned around and mewed again.

'What's the matter, puss? Go and do what you have to do, for Christ's sake, and then come back. It's too damned cold to hang around.'

But Malkin stayed where she was, mewing at me.

'What do you want? You no speak-a da English, you dumb moggie? I know you can when you feel like it.'

She trotted off a little way, and then stopped again, as if she were waiting for me.

'Oh, I get it! You want me to follow you! Why the hell didn't you say so?'

I followed her round the back of the house, across the brick-paved yard. A crowd of sparrows were perched in the branches of a leafless apple tree, but when I came around the corner they all burst into the air.

Malkin went to Victor's window, the one with the window box outside, and jumped up on to the ledge. She scratched at the glass, and mewed at me again.

'What? You want me to open the window for you? It's probably locked, and alarmed. Victor's going to think that I was trying to break in and steal his reproduction furniture. As if.'

But Malkin wouldn't let up. She kept on scratching and scrabbling at the window, her claws squeaking on the glass, and mewing at the same time.

I went closer to the window and when I looked inside I could see that the catch wasn't properly fastened. If I rattled the window frame a few times, I could probably work it loose. I looked at Malkin and said, 'You don't want me to open this window for you, do you? You want me to open this window for *me*.'

I thought: Maybe Kate *is* inside, after all. Maybe she's tied up, and gagged, but she sent Malkin to find me, so that I could rescue her. But almost immediately, I thought: that's insane. Why should Victor tie her up? And no cat is intelligent enough to find somebody and lead them anyplace, even Malkin.

All the same, I gripped the bottom edge of the window frame, and I shook it. I kept on shaking it and shaking it, and with every shake I could see the brass fastener edging its way out of its stay. After twenty or thirty shakes, the fastener popped out, and I was able to slide the window upward and open. I could see an alarm contact, but no alarm went off, so I guessed that Monica had forgotten to set it.

I wondered if Malkin had *known* that. And if she had, how?

I looked around the yard, and up at the windows of the houses on either side, to make sure that nobody was watching me. Then I climbed up on to the window box, and maneuvered myself inside. Once I was over the window ledge, I lost my balance and fell heavily on to the carpet, twisting my ankle, but I quickly picked myself up. Malkin jumped in after me.

I closed the window and locked it. It was very warm inside the apartment, and silent, except for the murmur of the traffic outside and the ticking of Victor's reproduction long-case clock.

'OK, Malkin,' I told her. 'Where's your mistress? Come on, kitty-cat – show me.'

I went from room to room, opening every closet and looking behind every curtain. I knelt down and checked under Victor's bed, and under the guest beds, too. I looked in the bathroom. I opened the shower stall. But – nothing. Kate wasn't here. *Nobody* was here.

I went to Victor's mock-antique desk, and opened all the drawers. In the right-hand bottom drawer I found a box of writing paper, with the letter heading *Penumbra International Properties, 200 Madison Avenue*. But Victor's name wasn't on it, and so it wasn't really *prima facie* evidence that he was Penumbra's owner. Upstairs, I had a whole stack of writing paper from the Sunset Marquis Hotel in Hollywood, but that didn't prove that I owned it.

I gave up. I couldn't work out why Malkin had encouraged me to break in here. There was nothing here to show that Kate was being battered or mistreated, and there was nothing to establish that Victor had anything to do with Penumbra.

Taking a last look around, though, I noticed again that there were dozens of photographs of Victor on the walls, but no photographs of Kate anywhere. And the usual touches that a woman would add to her apartment were remarkable by their absence. No fresh flowers, no fragrant bowls of pot-pourri, no lace tablecloths on any of the side tables. There were only a few ornaments – one of them an ugly bronze statuette of a pit bull terrier – and none of those had been positioned with any sense of scale.

Maybe – just maybe – Victor had been telling me the truth. Maybe Kate *wasn't* here.

I went back to the master bedroom, with Malkin following close behind me. I opened up all of the closets again. Shirts, suits, pants, men's sweaters, pajamas. No women's clothes at all. I opened the drawers in the bureau. All Calvin Klein undershorts, and socks. No panties, and no bras.

I was mystified. It was obvious that Kate didn't live here any more – and for that matter, neither did Victor's girlfriend Monica. Yet Kate had said that she couldn't leave Victor, even if she wanted to. He had a hold on her, and she couldn't break free – how many times had she told me that? Yet for some reason she must have been lying to me.

I left the apartment by the front door, giving it a sharp slam, just like Monica did, to make sure that it was properly closed. Just as I was slamming it, however, I heard footsteps outside, on the stoop, and the house door was suddenly unlocked. Jack Friendly walked in, wearing his dark glasses and his long black coat.

He looked at me, and then he looked at Victor's front door. He took off his sunglasses.

335

'Victor in?' he asked me. His eyes kept flicking from Victor's front door, and back to me.

'No – no, he isn't. I don't think so, anyhow. I just knocked, and there was no reply.'

'No hard feelings about Venice?' he said. He really looked conciliatory, not. His eyes were like two ball bearings.

I gingerly touched the bridge of my nose. 'I kind of think you overreacted, Jack, to tell you the truth.'

Jack didn't blink. 'I'm paid to overreact. That's my job.'

'OK, if you say so. But next time I'd prefer it if you didn't overreact on my nose.'

He glanced toward Victor's front door again. 'You haven't been *in* there, have you?' he asked me.

'*In* there? How would I get in there?'

'I don't know. But when I was coming up the steps, I could of sworn I heard this door shut.'

I shook my head. 'Nah ... I came down to see Victor, to say I was sorry for last night. He was making a noise and I complained about it. But – you know – everybody has a right to party, don't they?'

Jack took out a key and pushed it into Victor's door, although he didn't take his eyes off me once.

'Come on, puss,' I told Malkin. 'Let's see if we can find you a can of anchovies.'

Jack froze, as if I had insulted him to his face.

'I was talking to the *cat*,' I explained, but when I looked down there was no sign of Malkin anywhere. I saw a muscle working, in Jack's left cheek. 'She must have, like – run off,' I ended, lamely.

Jack let himself in, and slammed the door behind him.

Twenty-Six

The afternoon passed, and it began to snow – very lightly at first, but then thicker and thicker. I finished off my score for *The Billy Wagner Show* and worked on a few ideas for Diet Pepsi. It grew so dark that I could barely see my keyboard.

I tinkled away at what I hoped would be a light, bubbly melody, which would make everybody who heard it feel like drinking low-calorie cola. But somehow my fingers strayed into playing *Snow Blind*. I played it, and sang it under my breath, and I felt a terrible sadness for Elsa and Felicia and all of those other families who Victor and Jack had destroyed. One way or another, I had to give them justice. If I didn't give justice, they would never be at peace.

'The snowflakes fell so thick and fast ... I couldn't see where you had passed ... you left me far behind ... so many miles behind...'

I still hadn't heard from Kate. I missed her, like an ache, and quite apart from that, I needed to ask her why there were none of her clothes in

Victor's apartment. It was obvious that she didn't live there any more, and I needed to know why she had been deceiving me. If she wasn't living downstairs, then where was she living, and who with? I didn't want to get myself tangled up with people like Victor and Jack unless I was absolutely sure that I wasn't being used as a patsy. This whole situation was looking darker and more complicated and infinitely more dangerous by the minute.

Around 6:15 p.m., Margot called me.

'Why aren't you here?' she demanded.

'Why aren't I where?'

'Here – at Down The Hatch. I've been waiting for you for twenty-five minutes.'

'I didn't know I was supposed to meet you at Down The Hatch. When did we arrange that?'

'About two o'clock this afternoon. You texted me.'

'I texted you? I don't think so. I've been working all day.'

'Well, somebody did. Somebody who signed themselves Lalo.'

'Not me, sweetheart. But I can meet you there if you want me to. I could sure use a drink. *And* a plateful of atomic wings.'

'OK ... I'll give you ten more minutes. But then I'm going. I've already been approached by five different guys who think I'm a hooker.'

'Come on, Margot ... you'd make a *great* hooker.'

I put on my Timberland boots and my overcoat and wound my scarf around my neck. Through the living room window, I could see that it was

338

snowing furiously now. I was just pulling my gloves on when there was a brisk, staccato knock. *Kate*, I thought. Thank God.

I opened the door, but it wasn't Kate. It was Victor. His hair was slicked back and he was wearing a brown chalk-striped suit and a bronze necktie with zigzag patterns on it. He smelled strongly of Aqua di Selva.

'Victor!' I said. 'To what do I owe this honor?'

'Mind if I come in?' he asked me. Somehow he gave me the feeling that it wasn't a request.

'Well – I was just about to go out, but sure.'

He walked into the middle of my living room on shiny brown leather shoes and his heels clicked like death-watch beetles. He looked around, and sniffed.

'You've done the place nice,' he said. 'Kind of minimalist for my taste, but nice. Better than old Mr Benjamin had it. Doesn't smell of geriatric any more, either. I hate the smell of geriatrics. Elderly smells worse than dead, in my opinion.'

He picked up the statuette of Pan and then put it down again. 'Did you want something?' I asked him.

He looked at me sideways and gave me a wolfish grin. 'I could ask you the same question, Gideon. For instance, why pretend that you're Franklin Coleman, and ask about the Palazzetto Di Nerezza? Why follow Jack, in Venice? And why go poking around my apartment?'

'I, ah—'

'You're going to *deny* it? You broke into my apartment today and you spent over ten minutes going through my stuff. I have closed-circuit

339

television, Gideon, triggered by movement. Mostly, I use it for personal amusement. But now and then it records something even more exciting than some dumb cocktail waitress polishing my pecker. Like you, for example, rummaging through my desk.'

I shrugged. I didn't know what to say. I couldn't even think of a plausible lie.

Victor came up to me and looked me directly in the eye. I realized now that he was trembling with rage, even though his voice was completely controlled. 'If you're going to stick your nose into other people's private business, Gideon, you need to be wilier than they are, if you get my meaning. Like you don't make calls from your own personal phone that they can trace you back to. And you don't have face-to-face confrontations with people who are perfectly capable of ripping your face off. And you certainly don't break into my apartment and go through my fricking desk.'

'Well, I'm sorry about that,' I told him. 'I didn't take anything, I swear it.'

'Oh, you didn't *take* anything? That's good. But I'll tell you what I think, Gideon. I think that you overheard something about me and Jack Friendly that didn't concern you. I don't even pretend to know what, or how. Maybe you just got extra-sensitive ears. But you decided to find out more, didn't you? And that was your big mistake.'

I said nothing. I wasn't going to tell him about Kate, and how she had arranged for me to fly to Stockholm and London and Venice – especially since she didn't seem to be living with him any more, and I had absolutely no idea where she was, or how to get in touch with her.

Victor prodded my chest with his index finger. I really hate it when people do that, but I could hardly pretend that I hadn't searched his apartment, or phoned his office, or challenged Jack Friendly when I met him in Venice.

'Whatever you think you know, Gideon, you don't know it no more. You get my meaning?'

'Listen – I've forgotten it already.'

'And you think I trust you? I don't fricking trust you one inch. You're up to something and I don't know what it is, but whatever it is, it's going to stop.'

I raised both hands, as if his index finger was a gun. 'It's stopped. I promise you. Period.'

Victor smiled. 'And I'm supposed to take your word? I don't think so. So let me tell you this: a – you're going to keep your nose out of my business, and b – you're going to give me your apartment.'

I frowned at him. 'Excuse me?'

'You heard me. You are going to make this apartment over to me, for a nominal fee, i.e. one hundred dollars. I am going to allow you to live in this apartment for as long as you keep your lip zippered up, but the second I hear that you've tried to take this matter any further, you are out on your extra-sensitive ear.'

'You're crazy,' I said. 'I'm not going to give you my apartment – especially not for a hundred dollars! Do you know how much this place *cost*?'

341

'Of course I know how much it cost. Which is why I think I'm getting myself a bargain.'

'There is absolutely no way, Victor. No way whatsoever. I'm going to the cops.'

'No, Gideon, you're not.'

'Try and stop me. What are you going to do, tell Jack Friendly to throw me in the East River, tied to a mattress? Or set fire to me, in my own back yard?'

Victor covered his eyes with his hand for a moment, as if he were suffering from eye strain. Then he covered his mouth, as if he didn't know what to say. Eventually, though, he took out his cellphone, and punched in a number with his thumb. The phone rang, and he listened for a moment.

'It's me,' he said. 'Put her on, will you?'

With that, he handed the phone over to me. 'Go on,' he coaxed me. 'Ask her how she is.'

Oh my God, I thought, *it's Kate*. But then I heard a man's voice blurting, 'Talk to him, will you? Tell him we ain't pulled your fingernails out. Not yet, anyhow!'

'Kate?' I said.

I heard a gasping, panicky voice. 'Lalo – Lalo – it's me! They just grabbed me, when I went to the restroom!'

'Margot?'

'I was waiting for you and I went to the restroom and there were two of them there and they grabbed me! Please, Lalo – help me! I don't know where they're taking me!'

'Where are you now?'

'I'm in a car! They're taking me someplace but

I don't know where! Please, Lalo!'

The phone was abruptly cut off. Victor smiled and said, 'There – you didn't think that I wasn't going to take out some kind of insurance policy, did you? What did I say to you, Gideon? If you're going to stick your nose into other people's business, you need to be wilier than they are. And I'm pretty wily. I'm surprised my beloved momma didn't christen me "Coyote", God rest her soul.'

I was so angry that I could have hit him, very hard. I could have put him over my upraised knee and broken his back, so that he never could have walked again. I don't know how I managed to control myself, but I guess there was something in the back of my mind that warned me what would happen to Margot, if I beat up on Victor, or called the police. I didn't know where she was, or who had abducted her, and they could easily kill her before anybody could find her. That's if they could ever find her at all.

'OK,' I heard myself saying, almost as if somebody else was talking for me. 'What do you want me to do?'

Victor laid his hand on my shoulder. 'You don't have to do nothing, Gideon. Nothing at all. I'll have all of the paperwork drawn up, and all you have to do is sign.'

'I'm not signing unless you let Margot go free.'

'Oh ... we won't keep her for longer than we have to. But you don't go to the cops, Gideon. Not now, not tomorrow, not ever. This is one of those secrets that you carry to the grave, you got me?'

I looked at him. I felt utterly defeated. I had never been in the presence of pure evil before, and it was like that moment when you've been climbing a very steep hill and you realize that you simply don't have the strength to climb any further. Your legs just won't work.

'What would your beloved momma think of you, Victor?' I asked him, in disgust. 'What would your beloved momma think of you, if she could see you now?'

'My beloved momma was a fat stupid cow,' he replied. 'If there's one thing she taught me, it was greed. Take what you want, and as much as you want, and never *ever* feel guilty about it.

'But I think my beloved poppa taught me an even better lesson than that. My beloved poppa taught me that if anybody ever does you harm, you should never let them get away with it, ever. Never forgive nobody for nothing, that was my poppa's motto. And make sure you do a hundred times worse to them as they ever did to you. If they take something away from you, you make sure you take everything away from them.'

I took a deep breath. 'If you hurt Margot, I will kill you. I don't care what happens to me. I don't care if they give me the death sentence. But I swear to God that I will kill you.'

Victor let out a sharp bark of laughter, and squeezed my shoulder again. 'No, you won't, Gideon. It takes a very special sort of selfishness to kill people, and you just don't have it.'

What else could I do but take off my coat and

my scarf and my gloves and pour myself a very large glass of wine? Victor had said that he would arrange for the property transfer as soon as possible, but it would still take several days, and he wasn't going to let Margot go free until I had signed it.

Several times during the evening I picked up the phone and thought about dialing 911. I knew that it was the right thing to do. But I kept thinking of Margot, broken and covered in blood, or drowned, or cremated, and I simply couldn't risk her getting hurt. I had seen what Jack Friendly had done to the Westerlunds and the Philips and the Cesarettis. I was sure that he wouldn't have the slightest compunction about doing the same to Margot.

The nightmarish visions that I had seen in Stockholm and London and Venice had been frightening enough, but at least they had seemed detached from reality, and Kate had been there to reassure me that they had some kind of a purpose. This was real, and I had nobody that I could turn to for help.

I refilled my glass and switched on my laptop. For at least the twentieth time, I Googled the Westerlunds and the Philips and the Cesarettis, searching through their backgrounds for any fragment of information that might connect them with Victor Solway or Penumbra Property.

I came across a BBC website story about the disappearance of the Philips family, and how their relatives had made a broken-hearted appeal for anybody who had seen them to get in touch.

But the Westerlunds and the Cesarettis had disappeared so completely that it was just like they had evaporated, like patterns of steam on a window.

For the first time, I looked for the families on Google Image, too, to see if there were any photographs of them. I found six or seven pictures of Axel Westerlund on a tour of hospitals in Angola; and a blurry black-and-white image of David Philips to accompany some *Financial Times* article about international investment. But I almost missed the most important photograph.

It was a group picture of thirty-five delegates at a conference in Geneva in June, 1997, hosted by Worldwide Surgical Solutions, Inc. I enlarged it, and there was David Philips standing on the right-hand side of the picture, looking younger and trimmer and smiling broadly. But right next to him, in a smart gray suit, was Enrico Cesaretti; and on the other side of the same group – wearing a neatly trimmed beard but still instantly recognizable – was Axel Westerlund. I peered at the picture even more closely, and then I printed it out. This was no coincidence, it couldn't be. These three men knew each other.

Next I surfed the net for any mention of Worldwide Surgical Solutions, Inc. It turned out that they were a high-tech medical research company based in Philadelphia that had gone bankrupt early in 1999. Their business plan had been to set up a worldwide database for organ donors, and at the same time to develop new ways of harvesting donor organs more quickly and transporting them more efficiently. If a patient in San Francisco suffered from catastrophic renal failure, he could be supplied within hours with a replacement kidney which came from as far away as Addis Ababa, or Rio de Janeiro, or Vladivostok.

But here was the crunch: Worldwide Surgical Solutions had gone bust after accusations had been made that several of their donors had been slightly less than dead when their hearts and their livers were taken out.

There was surprisingly little background information about it. One French newspaper had suggested that government ministers in at least three African countries had accepted substantial kickbacks in return for supplying organ donors. In one case, in Ethiopia, it was claimed that an entire village had been massacred to supply livers and lungs for private patients in the US. But it seemed obvious that the story had been heavily censored.

I switched off my laptop and walked to the window. I could see my own reflection suspended out there, like a ghost.

Everything was clicking into place. Axel Westerlund and Enrico Cesaretti and David Philips had all attended the same conference to set up an international transplant business. All three of them were wealthy men, with exceptionally fine apartments and very comfortable lifestyles. All three of them had had their children kidnapped and tortured, and all three of them had been killed in the grisliest way that anybody could imagine.

Victor Solway had arranged for their killings,

347

and Victor Solway had taken everything away from them: their families, their apartments, their money, their very existence.

'You make sure you do a hundred times worse to them as they ever did to you.'

I didn't yet have the final piece of evidence – the reason why Victor had taken so devastating a revenge on them. But the only connection between them that I had been able to find was Worldwide Surgical Solutions, Inc.; and the only connection that I had been able to find between Victor and the medical profession was Michael, his baby son.

What had Kate said about Victor? *He was angry with God. Angry with the doctors. Just angry.*

Shortly after 10:00 p.m. there was a hesitant rapping at my door. I opened it, and there was Pearl, in her old pink bathrobe. It looked as if she had tried to pin up her hair, but it was even more chaotic than usual.

'I do live here, don't I?' she asked me.

'Yes, Pearl, you do. Do you want me to take you back to your apartment?'

She peered at me closely. 'You're that Gideon Lake, aren't you? I remember you. I shall always remember you. You're a good man. *Resonant.*'

'That's right, Pearl. Hold on. Just let me get my keys.'

I closed the door behind me and took hold of her elbow. I guided her to the bottom of the stairs, but she had only taken two steps up before she turned and said, 'You're worried, aren't

348

you? I can tell.'

'I have a couple of things of my mind, Pearl, yes.'

'No ... you can't fool me, Gideon Lake. You're *very* worried. Come upstairs, I have something to show you. I think the time has come.'

'OK, Pearl. Whatever you say.'

We climbed the stairs. She had left her apartment door open, and I followed her inside. It smelled even more strongly of oil paints than it had before. The artist in the pale-gray smock had obviously been here, adding some more touches to his figure study.

'Would you like a drink?' Pearl asked me. 'I think I have some whisky someplace, I think. Or is it rum? There was this black fellow, he was always bringing me rum. He used to sing Paul Robeson songs to me, in the bath. *Old Man River*.'

'No – I don't need a drink, thanks. What do you want me to see?'

'My painting, of course! It's almost done.'

I circled around the easel so that I could take a look at it. I was prepared for some changes, but when I actually saw it, I felt a crawling sensation all the way down my back. There was Pearl, as before, naked and insouciant, smoking her cigarette, and there were the Westerlunds, and the Philips, and the baby boy that Kate had been pushing in the park. But now the Cesarettis had joined them, with Enrico and Salvina standing at the very back, and their three children standing next to the ottoman, on the right-hand side.

The painting was nearly finished, because

everybody's face was now rendered in perfect detail. Nobody was smiling, however. They all looked desperate, as if they were trapped inside this picture, and would never be able to escape.

I stared at the canvas for a long time, and then I turned to Pearl and said, 'What?'

Pearl was lighting a cigarette. She blew out a long stream of smoke, and then she said, 'Don't tell me you *still* don't get it? You know who murdered all of these people, don't you, Gideon? You and you alone. But if only *one* living person knows who did it, that's enough.'

I looked back at the painting. 'I still don't understand. I know who murdered them all, yes. But what am I supposed to do about it? I can't go to the police because I don't have any evidence. Besides, they're holding my friend Margot, and if I go the police they say that they'll hurt her, or worse.'

Pearl said, very gently, 'I can see these people, too, Gideon. I used to be a singer, when I was young. I have resonance, too. I doubt if I can see them as clearly as you do, but I *can* see them, coming and going, opening doors and closing them again.'

She paused, and smoked. 'The problem is that once they've passed over, the dead can't accuse the living of any crime or misdemeanor, even if it's torture or murder. The dead can't name the people who killed them. Heaven is not a place for people to seek revenge. Heaven is a place for forgiveness – for new beginnings.'

'I'm sorry, Pearl. I don't actually believe in heaven.'

350

Pearl shrugged. 'That doesn't matter. You can call it whatever you like. But it's the world beyond, where all of us go when we die.'

'You say that dead people can't name their killers?'

'If they could, think how many living people would be wrongly accused, by dead people who were bitter and resentful. Death is a time to move on, no matter what happened in your previous life. Death is not just the end ... it's a brand-new beginning.'

'But all of these dead people, I *saw* them. I talked to them, I touched them.'

Pearl smiled, and nodded 'That's because you're so *receptive*. When you stand close to them, they reappear, they take on flesh, and substance, just like they did when they were alive. You can feel them, you can kiss them, and while they're close to them, other people can see them, too. It's a very great gift.'

'But I saw what happened to them,' I told her. 'I saw how they were tortured, and how they were killed.'

'Of course. Because they wanted you to know how they died, and who murdered them. Like I say, they can't make any accusations. They're dead. But they did the next best thing, and they *showed* you. Those horrible things you witnessed, they're always there, waiting for anybody who has the sensitivity to pick them up. It's no different than listening to an Elvis record. He's dead, but we can still hear him singing. Or watching a Buster Keaton movie. He's dead, too, but he can still make us laugh.'

351

'What about this baby? This is Kate's baby, right? The baby she had with Victor?'

'Little Michael, that's right. Michael-Row-The-Boat-Ashore.'

'How did he die? Do you know that?'

Pearl laid a hand on her left breast. 'It was his heart. I can't remember exactly what they call it, but it's something to do with the blood pumping all the wrong way.'

'Did he have a heart transplant? Is that it?'

Pearl nodded. 'Kate was against it, for some reason. I remember that. There was a lot of shouting. A lot of crying. A lot of slamming doors.'

'But Michael did have the transplant?'

Pearl blew out smoke. 'Columbia University Hospital. The very best. But he died, anyhow.'

'And Victor?'

'Hmmh,' she said, almost in amusement. 'I never saw a man in such a rage. It was the rage from hell.'

I said, 'You knew all about this, right from the beginning, didn't you? You're not half as bananas as you pretend to be, if you'll forgive my saying so.'

'You had to find out for yourself, my dear. You couldn't be told.'

'You knew what Kate was doing, didn't you? You knew that she was going to fly me to Stockholm and London and Venice, to see these people? And not only that – you knew *why*.'

'I did try to warn you, my dear. I didn't let you go into it with your eyes closed. What did I say to you? She's only using you, for her own

352

purposes. She's only using you to do something that *she* can't do. But what did you say? It's only about pleasure, you said. It's only about affection, and friendship. But it was always much more than that. And now it's time for you to do what she wanted you to do, and you have no choice, not if you're going to save your Margot. In her own way, your Kate is holding her hostage just as much as Victor.'

'I don't get this,' I protested. 'I really don't get this.'

Pearl came up to me and gently touched my cheek, as if I were a child, and she were my mother. 'You don't have any choice, my dear. She's painted you into a corner.'

'But what am I supposed to do now?'

She went across to the bureau, which was crowded with ashtrays and pots of moisturizer and paintbrushes and books, and brought back a photograph in a tarnished silver frame. 'Here,' she said. 'This will point you in the right direction.'

It was a faded color picture of a family – a father, with glasses, and a suit with flappy lapels – a mother, in a flowery-printed frock – and a young girl in a T-shirt with braces in her teeth. They were standing in front of a handsome colonial house, with cherry trees in blossom all around it.

'That's Kate,' I said. 'This must have been taken at her parents' house, in Connecticut. She must be about fourteen years old.'

Pearl nodded. 'She gave me this photograph, to show to you, when the time came.'

353

'So what are you trying to tell me – that she's gone back to stay at her parents' house?'

'In a manner of speaking.'

'Her parents are dead. That's what she told me, anyhow.'

'What difference does that make?'

'For Christ's sake, Pearl! Now you're talking in riddles, just like she always does!'

Pearl said, 'No, Gideon. Not riddles. *Clues.* Anybody who gives you a straight answer, they're not telling you the truth – or not the whole truth, anyhow. But people who give you clues ... they're allowing you to make up your own mind, wouldn't you say?'

I turned over the photograph frame and looked at the back. Somebody had written on it, *Old Post House, Brinsmade Lane, Sherman, May '92.*

'You're telling me that I should go there?' I said.

'Up to you,' she replied, looking the other way.

Shit. I really didn't know what to do. For all I knew, Pearl was completely senile, and she was telling me nothing but gibberish. Yet here on the canvas was the evidence that what she was saying must make some kind of sense. The Westerlunds, and the Philips, and the Cesarettis – all of them staring at me as if they were pleading with me to help them.

'Tell me about Kate,' I asked Pearl.

'What's to tell? You know her much better than I ever will.'

She was right, of course, and that was just the answer I was afraid of. But if I could hold her,

354

and feel her – if we could be lovers, what difference did it make?

'There's one thing,' I said. 'Two days ago, Kate said that there were only three days left, but she wouldn't tell me what she meant.'

Pearl pulled a face. 'I guess she meant that time was running out. I mean, time does have an exasperating habit of doing that, doesn't it? It runs and it runs and you can turn that hourglass over as many times as you like, it just keeps on running.'

I took a taxi to Starlite Records and interrupted my friend Henry Brickman in the middle of an A&R meeting with a country-rock band who looked like the crows from *Dumbo*.

'I need to borrow your car, man. I wouldn't ask but it's seriously urgent.'

He blinked at me unhappily through his blue-tinted glasses. 'It's new, Gideon. I only took delivery last week.'

'I'll treat it like my own, I promise.'

'That's what I'm worried about. I remember that GTO you used to drive around in. It was one big dent.'

All the same, he gave me the keys, and I drove his brand-new metallic gray Malibu out of the parking structure and up Park Avenue. The sky was the same metallic gray and it was starting to snow again, and I wasn't at all sure that it was either wise or practical for me to drive all the way to Sherman, but I simply couldn't think what else I could do.

If Pearl was right, and Kate had been giving

me clues instead of riddles, maybe that photograph of her with her parents was the answer to everything I needed to know.

I switched on the radio, right in the middle of a commercial break. Almost unbelievably, they were playing the music for Mother Kretchmer's Frozen Scrapple, which I had adapted as the melody for *The Pointing Tree*. It was a truly weird coincidence, but in a way it reassured me that I had made the right decision.

'The Pointing Tree will guide you ... along the forest track ... your loved ones soon will weep with joy ... so pleased to have you back.'

It began to snow thicker and faster, and even with the windshield wipers flapping at full speed, it was growing increasingly difficult to see the highway up ahead. For the first time in a long time, I asked God to take care of me.

'God,' I said, quite loudly. 'Please take care of me.'

Twenty-Seven

By the time I had driven up to the northern end of Candlewood Lake it was dark, and all that I could see was whirling snow. But I managed to find Sherman, with its little snow-covered bandstand, and an elderly woman in a bright yellow parka pointed me in the direction of Brinsmade Lane, while her dog yapped impatiently around

356

her rubbers.

I drove up and down for almost twenty minutes, trying to find Kate's parents' house. Most of the property along Brinsmade Lane was hidden behind the trees, and almost every driveway had a gate, so that it was impossible to drive in close enough to see what the houses looked like.

I was close to giving up when God answered my prayer. A white Cadillac CTS came along the highway in the opposite direction, and turned into an entrance about twenty yards ahead of me. As it turned, my headlights caught the driver's face, and it was unmistakably Victor.

My heart started beating inside my chest like a drum pedal. I drove about a half-mile further on, and then I turned around. I switched off my lights and drove very slowly back toward the entrance, and parked deep underneath the branches of an overhanging laurel bush. I just hoped that Henry's paintwork wasn't too badly scratched.

I climbed out of the car and walked down the driveway. The shingle was frozen so my feet crunched loudly as I walked. As soon as the house came into view I recognized it from the photograph that Pearl had shown me, even though it was hooded with snow. It reminded me of the house in those Amityville movies: a rambling colonial with tall chimney stacks, and dormer windows like clown's eyes. I recognized the cherry trees, too, although their branches were clogged with snow, instead of blossom. Two vehicles were parked by the garage block –

Victor's Cadillac and a black Ford Explorer.

What Victor was doing here, I couldn't even begin to guess. Kate had told me that her parents were dead, but she had never told me that she had inherited their house. Was *she* here, too? She hadn't been in touch with me for two days, after all. Maybe she lived here in Sherman most of the time, and only visited Victor occasionally, which is why she didn't keep any of her clothes at St Luke's Place. But no clothes at all? Not even a spare sweater or a change of underwear?

I could see lights shining in the hallway, and the living room. I crossed the lawn where Kate had been photographed with her parents, all those years ago, and I stood in the snow-covered flowerbed so that I could look inside the living room window.

The room was furnished and decorated in colonial style, with dark oak chairs and tables, and chintzy drapes. A large stone fireplace dominated the left-hand wall, but it was blackened and dark and heaped with dead ashes. Above the fireplace hung a nineteenth-century portrait of a Puritan woman in a bonnet, her lips pursed as if she disapproved of everything, especially being painted.

I listened. I was sure that I could hear very faint music coming from someplace inside the house. Tony Bennett, singing *The Boulevard of Broken Dreams*. I dodged around the side of the house, keeping my head down and staying close to the wall, until I reached the kitchen window at the back. There were no lights in the kitchen, but the door was half open, so that I could see into

358

the hallway. A mirror was hanging on the wall, just beside the front door, and for a second I glimpsed Victor in it, as he crossed from one room into another. I had the chilling feeling that he had caught sight of me, but that was only an optical illusion.

I climbed the steps to the kitchen door, and tried the handle. Unsurprisingly, it was locked. Maybe there was a cellar door, or a window I could pry open. I circled around the house as quietly as I could, although I managed to kick over a stack of flowerpots, filled up with snow. I stayed perfectly still, listening, in case Victor had heard me, but Tony Bennett continued crooning, and nobody came out of the house to take a look.

At the side of the house, I found a small high window which probably illuminated the cloak-room, or the stairs. Not far away, underneath a fir tree, there was an old wooden chair with a broken arm. I dragged the chair close to the house, right underneath the window. Then I picked up a rusty old trowel that somebody had left embedded in the soil, and climbed up on to the seat.

I was trying to force the point of the trowel into the side of the window when I heard a crackling noise close behind me. I turned around and almost lost my balance. It was Jack Friendly, in his long black coat, his breath smoking like Satan himself.

'Well, well. If it ain't my nosy friend from Venice. What brings you here, slick, as if I didn't know?'

I climbed awkwardly down from the chair, and held up the trowel in front of me.

'Where's Margot?' I challenged him.

Jack took a step closer. 'Margot's safe and sound for now, always providing that you play along. So what are you going to do with that? *Plant* me to death?'

'Just take me to her. I want to make sure that you haven't hurt her.'

'Hurt her? Now why should we hurt her?'

'For the same reason you hurt the Westerlunds, and the Philips and the Cesarettis, and God alone knows how many more families.'

'Life is just a horse race, Gideon. You have your winners, and you have your losers. Can't be helped, no matter how hard you try.'

'You're a total bastard, Jack.'

He grinned at me, and his eyes glittered. 'I certainly like to think so.'

He led me around the side of the house, toward the front door. Halfway there, I tossed the trowel into the snow.

He opened the door for me and we stepped into the brightly lit hallway. It was freezing cold, but I could hear a furnace rumbling in the basement, and smell the dusty tang of radiators heating up.

Jack closed the door and called out, 'Victor! Hey, Victor! Found your friend outside!'

I looked around. The pink floral wallpaper was scuffed, and most of the pictures were all hanging crooked, as if somebody had been fighting in here. On the right-hand side there was a curving staircase, with a galleried landing, but upstairs was in darkness. I had the impression of an elegant family home which had been visited by tragedy, and hadn't been lived in ever since.

Victor suddenly appeared from the living room, still wearing his overcoat and black leather gloves. Under his bright orange tan, he looked tired and pale, and he had bags under his eyes. He didn't seem at all surprised to see me.

'Gideon,' he said. He sniffed, and wiped his nose with his finger. 'Crappy night for driving out to the sticks. You thought about my proposition?'

'I'm more worried about Margot. Is she here? You haven't hurt her, have you?'

'She's here, yes. And, no, my friend, we haven't hurt her. In fact we don't have any intention of hurting her, nor you neither, if you're cooperative.'

'I want to see her.'

'Sure. No problemo. Follow me.'

Victor beckoned me along the hallway. We entered the kitchen, which was huge, and chilly, with a brown-and-white tiled floor, and a massive butcher-block table. A motley collection of antique copper saucepans was suspended from the ceiling, although they were tarnished almost black. Two red-and-green sacks of IGA groceries were standing on the hutch, waiting to be unpacked.

'Takes a hell of a time for this dump to warm up,' said Victor. 'By the time it's livable-in, it's usually time to drive back to the city.'

'Does this house belong to you, too?' I asked him. 'Or should I say Penumbra?'

'I told you, Gideon. I'm a man of substance.'

'So what happened to Kate's parents? They sell you the place, for a nominal price?'

'I got it very reasonable, let's put it that way.'

'In other words you put the squeeze on them, just like you put the squeeze on the Westerlunds, and the Philips, and the Cesarettis, and just like you're putting the squeeze on me?'

Victor crossed the kitchen to a large green-painted door, took a key out of his coat pocket, and unlocked it. 'I don't like the word "squeeze", Gideon. "Negotiation", that's what I prefer.'

'Oh, really?' I challenged him, although I can't say that I wasn't frightened of what he was going to do next. 'How about "extortion"?'

Victor grinned, and for the first time I saw a gold tooth shining. 'I like you, Gideon. You got class. You got character. And I have to say it took some nerve for you to drive out here. I like nerve.'

'I want to see Margot,' I insisted. I was still shaking with cold.

He lifted one finger and said, 'Follow me. But mind the steps, OK? There's one or two of them loose.'

He opened the green door and went down the steps into the cellar. I hesitated, but Jack said, 'Go ahead, go on,' and I followed him.

Victor was right: two steps wobbled when I trod on them, and one of them was missing.

When I reached the bottom of the steps, I could see how vast the cellar was. It had a very low ceiling, but it stretched the whole length of the house, so that its further recesses were

362

hidden in darkness. On the left-hand side there were rows and rows of wine racks, more than half filled with dusty bottles of wine, but the rest of the cellar was crowded with tea chests filled with books, and ornaments, and lampshades. I saw an old Zenith television, and a hula-hoop, and a wooden ironing board, and a child's bicycle with its front wheel missing.

In a recess on the right-hand side stood a large old-fashioned gas-fired furnace, which was roaring stentoriously as it tried to heat up the house. In front of it, Margot was lying on a lumpy red couch, blindfolded with a red woolen scarf and her wrists and her ankles fastened with silver duct tape.

As we approached, Margot swung her legs around and sat up. 'Let me go, you skunks!' she screamed. 'You can't keep me here! Let me go!'

'Hey, easy,' said Victor. 'I brung your friend to see you're OK.'

'What? Let me go! You're going to go to prison for this! Let me go!'

I went over and knelt down beside her, and took hold of her hands. 'Margot, it's OK, it's me.'

'Gideon? Oh, thank God! Get me out of here! I'm going crazy!'

'It's OK, sweetheart. They want me to promise that I'll keep my mouth shut about Penumbra, and I've said that I will.'

'Please get me out of here, Gideon! Please!'

I turned to Jack. He was smiling, and popping his knuckles. 'Just untie her,' I said. 'I've given you my word. I won't say anything to anybody, ever, about what you did, even if that means I deserve to rot in hell the same as you do.'

'No need to be hostile, Gideon,' said Victor.

'Hostile? You should both get the death penalty for what you've done.'

Victor shrugged. 'They don't have the death penalty in Sweden. Nor in Britain. Nor in Italy, neither. Sorry to disappoint you.'

'I should kill you myself.'

'Well, there's no need to go to extremes. All I'm asking is that you keep quiet about something which you don't have any proof of anyhow. And that you make over the title to your apartment.'

Margot said, 'What? What does he want you to do?'

'He wants me to hand over my apartment, the same way he made the Westerlunds and the Philips and the Cesarettis give him *their* apartments.'

'But you can't, Lalo! That's *your* apartment! That's your *home*!'

'I don't think I have a whole lot of choice. It's either that, or you and I disappear and nobody ever sees us again.'

Margot took a deep breath and screamed out, 'Help! Somebody help us! Help! Somebody let us out of here! Call the police! Help!'

Victor waited until she had finished, and then he said, 'Nobody can hear you, doll-face. You're down in a cellar, more than a half-mile from the nearest highway, and the same distance from the nearest neighbor, so you might as well save your breath.'

I stood up. 'Come on, Victor. I've agreed to keep my mouth shut, and you can have my apartment just as soon as you've drawn up all the paperwork. Let her go, why don't you?'

Victor shook his head. 'I'm not stupid, Gideon. But I promise you this. As soon as your signature dries on that deed, she'll go free.'

'Do you really think I trust you?' I retorted. I was trying very hard not to rile him, but I was so angry and frightened that my voice was shaking. 'You're a cold-blooded murderer, Victor. Maybe Jack did all of your torturings and killings for you, but there's just as much blood on your hands as there is on Jack's.'

'Hey,' said Victor, in a conciliatory tone. 'There's no need to get all gnarly about it.'

But at that instant, there was a loud slamming sound, and all of the lights in the cellar went out. We were plunged into darkness...

Victor said, 'Goddamned circuit-breaker! Jack – you got a lighter?'

I thought of grabbing Margot and trying to head for the stairs, but it was so dark that I was completely disoriented, and I doubt if we would have made it even halfway there before Jack or Victor caught up with us.

'Don't you move, Gideon!' Victor warned me. He must have read my mind. 'You try anything cute, and so help me you'll regret it!'

Jack flicked his lighter, and it scratched, and it scratched, but it wouldn't light.

'For Christ's sake, Jack!' Victor barked at him. 'Find the goddamned circuit-breaker!'

The flames inside the gas furnace were throwing a dim, wavering light across the floor, and as my eyes grew accustomed to the darkness, it was enough for me to make out Margot, and Victor, and then Jack.

But then I realized that the four of us had company. There was a fifth person standing in back of the couch, a woman, pale-faced, and very still.

'*Margot*,' I said.

'What is it, Lalo?' She must have been able to hear the warning in my voice.

Jack was stumbling around, close to the bottom of the steps, trying to find the fuse box. He collided with a tea chest that must have been filled with old china, because I heard a muffled crashing noise, and then Jack shouting, 'Fuck! Fuck, my knee!'

But I couldn't take my eyes off the woman behind the couch. Her head was covered in a black scarf, and she was holding a black-wrapped bundle close to her face. Protectively, but also defiantly. And I knew who she was, even though her appearance here was impossible, and unbelievable, and scared me so much that I could barely speak.

'Who is that?' Victor demanded. 'Who's there? Jack will you fix those fricking lights for Christ's sake!'

He didn't need to. Gradually, the lights came back on by themselves. The filaments burned brighter and brighter, although they still shone unsteadily, as if the wires were shorting out.

'No,' said Victor. Then he raised one hand, as if to shield his eyes. 'No, no. This is not happening. No.'

'Victor?' called Jack, treading on broken china.

'This is not happening!' Victor shouted. 'Jack! What the hell are you doing? Tell me this is not happening!'

But the woman behind the couch came forward, and stood staring at him. It was Kate, all dressed in black; and in her arms, in a black wool blanket, she was carrying her baby.

'What's going on?' Margot asked me. 'Tell me, Lalo – what's going on?'

Victor sank to his knees on the concrete floor. He kept covering his face with his hands and then opening them up again, like a hymn book, as if the next time he looked, Kate would have disappeared. Jack stayed where he was, looking tetchy and confused and off balance. Jack only knew how to solve problems by hitting people, or hurting them, or killing them, but it was obvious even to him that this wasn't one of those problems.

'*Kate*,' I said, and cautiously approached her, holding out my hand.

But she didn't look at me. She continued to stare down at Victor.

'Victor,' she said. Her voice sounded very distant and breathy, as if it were the wind talking.

Victor kept his hands closed over his face.

'You're not here,' he told her, in a muffled voice.

'I'm here, Victor. You can hear me, can't you?'

'You're not here! You're not here! You can't be here!'

Kate waited for a moment. Then she said,

367

'Aren't you ashamed, Victor, of what you've done?'

'I've just told you! You're not here!'

But Kate persisted. 'Aren't you ashamed of all the pain you've inflicted, all the people you've murdered, all the property you've stolen?'

Victor lowered his hands and looked up at her. To my surprise, his face was glistening with tears. 'They took our son, Kate.'

'Yes,' she said. 'But he would have died anyhow.'

'I gave them everything. I gave them nearly three million dollars! Three million dollars, Kate! They bankrupted me! And for what? How did you expect me to feel, when Michael died? They promised me that he would live but he died!'

'That's no excuse, for what you did.'

Victor climbed to his feet. He almost lost his balance, but Jack stepped forward to steady him. 'What was *their* excuse, for what *they* did? What was *their* excuse, for killing all of those innocent children, so that they could sell their hearts for millions of dollars?'

'None,' said Kate. 'There was no excuse. It was wholesale murder. Why do you think I tried to stop you from doing it?'

Victor was so angry now that he had almost forgotten his fear. He stalked up to Kate and shouted, 'Michael deserved a chance! He was our son, Kate! He was going to carry on the Solway name, for ever! Not just substance, Kate! *Reverence!* One generation of Solways, after another!'

Kate pulled back the black scarf that was covering her head. 'What was the price of that chance, Victor? You paid for the killing of another child, so that our child could have a new heart. But he died, regardless, as God had probably meant him to.'

Victor said, 'They promised me. "The best chance he'll ever have, Mr Solway" – that's what they told me. They were quick enough to take my money, weren't they? But what am I left with? Nothing. No son. No heir. Not even a fricking refund.'

'We could have tried again.'

Victor shook his head. 'With *you*? After you told me that you wouldn't take some other kid's heart, to save Michael's life? That other kid probably came from some slum someplace, Rio, or Darfur, or Christ knows where. He probably had a life expectancy of seven years old, and for all of those seven years he would have been miserable, and hungry, and sick. Tell me – go on, tell me – what was the best possible use of that other kid's heart?'

'We could have tried again, Victor.'

'And the odds were, the same thing would have happened all over again, you know that. What was the point of trying again? My family carries Ebstein's Anomaly, once every other generation, and that's all there is to it. There never can be a Solway dynasty.'

Jack laid his hand on Victor's shoulder. 'Come on, boss. This isn't real. This is some kind of scam. I'll deal with this broad.'

'Oh!' Kate retorted. 'You don't think this is

369

real? What do you think happened to the baby, who was murdered for Michael's new heart?'

'They said it was going to be painless!' Victor shouted at her. 'They said it was an orphan, with no quality of life whatsoever!'

But Kate unraveled the black woolen blanket she had been carrying in her arms. Inside was a dark-skinned baby of about six months old.

'Here,' she said. 'This is what happened to it, because of you, and all the people like you.'

She turned the baby around, so that it was facing them. He looked like a grotesque caricature of a ventriloquist's dummy. His eye sockets were empty, and he had been split open from its chest downwards.

'They harvested his corneas. They harvested his kidneys, his liver, his lungs and his gall bladder. And of course, they took his heart.'

'I don't believe this,' said Victor. 'I'm having some kind of nightmare.'

'You're not the one who's having a nightmare. This baby was healthy when they took him into the operating theater. Healthy, and alive. He came from Benin, in Nigeria. Under normal circumstances, he would have expected to live to the age of forty-seven, at least.'

'They promised me that Michael would survive!' Victor screamed at her. 'They promised me, those bastards!'

With infinite gentleness, Kate rewrapped the gutted baby in its blanket. 'Kate—' I began, but she touched her finger to her lips, to indicate that she wasn't finished yet. And I trusted her now, because I knew from what Pearl had told me that she couldn't do this – not unless I was here to give her substance. There was only one person who could help her to bring Victor and Jack to justice, and that was me.

'Come on, Victor,' said Jack. 'Let me sort this out for you, OK?'

I don't know what Jack had in mind, and I never found out, because at that moment there was a sharp shuffling noise from the darkest corners of the cellar. It sounded like people shuffling into church for a funeral service.

'Holy shit,' said Victor, and he was so frightened that his face had turned a dirty orange color.

Toward us, through the cellar, came the Westerlund family – Axel and Tilda and Elsa and Felicia – as well as the Philips – David and Helena and their son Giles – and the Cesarettis – Enrico and Salvina, as well as Amalea and Raffaella and little Massimo.

But there wasn't just one Axel, or one Tilda, or one Elsa and Felicia – or only one appearance of any one of them.

Jostling close to each other, I saw four different Axels: one bearded, one with his face badly bruised, one with dark-brown runnels of blood congealing on his forehead, like a crown, and yet another who was so green and swollen and puffy that he was barely recognizable. Next to him, there was a pretty rosy-cheeked Elsa, with her hair beautifully braided, but there was also a pale straggly-haired Elsa like the girl who had been lifted out of the harbor at the Wasa Museum.

It was the same with the Cesarettis and the Philips. They advanced slowly toward us out of the darkness, and there were so many different manifestations of each of them. When they were alive, when they were being tortured and beaten, and after they were dead. There must have been nearly fifty of them, maybe more.

I turned to Kate again, although she still wouldn't look at me. I wanted to tell her that I realized what was happening. Here were dozens of pages from these families' lives, just the way that Kate had described them, like pages from a flicker book.

Young Giles Philips stood near the front, in his British school uniform; but next to him stood the same apparition that I had seen in his parents' back garden, with his eyelids glued together. There was little Massimo, too, unmarked but serious; but close behind him stood another Massimo, his face beaten like a smashed melon.

The most horrifying of all was Helena Philips. She stood next to Kate's right shoulder, with a sad but gentle expression, in a flowery summer frock. But she had a terrible twin who was almost hidden from sight, right behind her. A terrible twin whose scalp was raw and whose face was burned black, and whose nightgown was still smouldering.

'What's this, Gideon?' said Victor, his voice shrill with panic. 'Did *you* do this? These are holograms, right? They're holograms!'

He took two nervous steps toward little Massimo, who was standing closest to him, and he reached out and quickly touched his shoulder.

'*Shit!*' he said. 'They're real! They're fricking *real*! Jesus, Gideon, what the hell have you done here?'

Jack looked even more confused. He kept looking behind him, as if he expected more apparitions to come down the steps. He was rapidly whispering something under his breath, although I couldn't hear what it was. Knowing him, it was probably some kind of blasphemy.

Victor turned to me. 'Make them go away!' he demanded. 'You hear me, Gideon? Make them go away!'

'He can't,' said Kate.

'I'm dreaming this,' said Victor. 'This isn't true, none of it. I'm having a nightmare. Make them go away, Gideon! *Make them go away!*'

Kate said, 'Didn't you hear me, Victor? He can't.'

Victor whirled around, off balance. His eyes were staring and he looked as if he were just about to have an epileptic fit. Jack meanwhile was slowly backing toward the steps, sinking to his knees, still praying. I caught the mumbled words, '*...forgive me my fucking trespasses, forgive me my fucking trespasses ... give me a goddamned sign, God ... forgive me my fucking trespasses!*'

'Kate!' I called her.

Now she looked across at me and smiled, although her smile looked weary.

'Hallo, Gideon. You did it. And here we are. The moment of truth.'

I reached out and took hold of her free hand, and she felt real, and warm, and that was all

373

I needed.

'How did you get here?' I asked her.

'This was my parents' house. Well, you know that. I never really left.'

Victor stalked across to me and screamed at me, so close that I could feel his spit flying in my face. *'Make her go away! Make her go away! Make all of them go away!'*

Kate shook her head. 'The people you murdered couldn't accuse you, Victor. After they had died, they had to stay silent. But Gideon can accuse you. He knows what you and Jack did. He's seen it for himself.'

'This is a nightmare! This is nothing but a nightmare!'

'Yes, Victor, this *is* a nightmare. For you, anyhow.'

Kate paused. She was breathing very hard, but she seemed to be elated, as if she had been running, and knew that she was going to win.

'These families couldn't speak out against you. Neither could I. But Gideon can. You're finished, Victor. You and Jack. You're both finished.'

'Gideon doesn't have any proof!' Victor shouted at her. 'What did he see? When? It's his word against ours!'

'Oh, you think so?' Kate asked him. 'Where are my parents?'

'You think I'm going to tell you that? You're crazy!'

'What did you do with them, Victor? *Where are my parents?*'

'Wouldn't you like to know? They signed it

374

over to me, and then they left for parts un-known!'

'You had them murdered, Victor! Where are they?'

Victor staggered around again, and then he stabbed his finger at her. 'Screw you, Kate! Screw all of you!'

Kate didn't answer, but looked down at the baby that she was carrying in her arms, and drew down the blanket that was covering his head. Then she turned him around and held him up in both hands, so that Victor could see him clearly.

I felt a crawling sensation all down my back that was partly dread and partly elation. The baby was white, with blond hair, and he was staring at Victor with dark-blue eyes.

'You bitch,' said Victor. 'You just wanted him to die. He was *my* son, and you just wanted him to die! And I was totally cleaned out! And he *still* died! And you have the nerve to bring him here, whatever you are, and *taunt* me!

He lunged toward her, with both hands raised, trying to grab the baby. But Kate flung the blanket over the baby's head, and turned away.

'Michael!' shouted Victor. And in spite of all the terrible things that he had done, or maybe because of them, his voice was filled with pain and desperation.

But Kate lifted the blanket, and shook it, and like a parlor trick, it was empty.

'You bitch,' said Victor. The tears were stream-ing down his face. Jack came up to him and laid his hand on his shoulder.

'Let's get the fuck out of here.'

'She killed my son! She killed my Michael!'

But the murdered families were beginning to crowd forward now, and Jack's eyes were darting apprehensively from one apparition to another.

'Victor, I'm telling you. Whatever the fuck's going on, we need to get out of here.'

At that moment, however, the scream started.

It wasn't a scream of anger, or of fear. It was an intensely high-pitched sound, right on the furthest horizon of my hearing. It grew louder and louder, and as it did so, I realized that it was coming from Kate, and all of the other dead people in the cellar. Their mouths were slightly open, and they were letting out the same ear-splitting scream that Kate had screamed, whenever she made love, and that Tilda Westerlund had screamed, in her panic and frustration, when she shattered the lantern.

I looked from one to the other – to Axel and Tilda, to Elsa and Felicia – to David and Helena and Giles – and to Enrico and Salvina, and Amalea, and Raffaella, and Massimo. They were standing here, in the cellar, but there was no living expression in their eyes. They were dead, and they had come here to get their revenge, that was all. The sound rose higher and higher, like fingernails scraping on a chalkboard, until I couldn't hear it any more. But Victor and Jack both clamped their hands over their ears, and Victor started to roar with pain.

'*Stop it!*' he begged. '*Stop it! You're killing me!*'

Kate stopped screaming, and approached him, although everybody else carried on.

'Victor? Where are my parents? Tell me where they are! Where are my parents?'

Victor dropped to his knees, next to Jack. *'Make it stop!'* he wailed, thrashing his head from side to side. *'You're killing me, you witch!'*

'Where are my parents?' Kate demanded.

Victor jabbed his finger at the cellar floor. 'They're here, goddammit! They're right here! *They're under the goddam floor!'*

Kate stepped back a little. 'There!' she said. 'Now Gideon has his proof! You're finished!'

She raised her hands again and closed her eyes. She had the same beatific expression on her face as she did when we made love. She uttered a note that began with piercing clarity, and then grew louder and louder until it sounded like a thousand church choirs. She wasn't directing it at me, but even so my head rang and my vision blurred and my insides felt as if I was being shaken apart, as if I were riding a bicycle down an endless flight of steps.

A whole boxful of china vases suddenly shattered, and two light bulbs popped. Victor screamed even louder and bent over double, hitting his forehead against the floor. *'I can't see! I can't see! I've gone blind!'* But Jack had kept his hands clamped tightly over his ears, and he managed to raise himself up on one knee, and then, very unsteadily, to stand.

He turned toward me and I had never seen anybody stare at me with such hatred. He took one lurching step toward me, like a zombie, and

377

then another.

'You *fuck*,' he hissed at me. 'I'm going to tear your fucking head off.'

He swung at me, but I stepped back and he missed me by a clear six inches. He almost lost his balance, but then he lurched forward again, and took another swing. I backed off again, but now I was right up against the cellar wall.

'You thought you could mess with me?' he said. 'You thought you could mess with Jack Friendly?'

He jabbed at me, but I parried him away with my elbow, and he stumbled so close to me that we were almost embracing each other. I could *smell* him, smell his aftershave and the garlic on his breath. And all the time Kate and all of the others continued to scream that intense, piercing note, so that my eardrums started to ache, too, and my vision started to blur.

I punched Jack in the stomach, just below the sternum, as hard as I could. If anybody had punched *me* like that, I would have gone down like a knackered horse. But Jack's abdomen felt like a sack of cement, and he didn't even flinch.

Jack hit me back, on my collarbone. I bent forward, winded, and he hit me again, right on the cheek. I thought I heard Kate cry out, *'Gideon!'* but then Jack hit me in the mouth, and I toppled backward and struck my head against the wall. For a count of five, everything went black-and-white, like a photographic negative.

When I managed to pull myself up again, I saw Jack heaving Victor up the cellar steps, with one of Victor's arms around his shoulders. They

378

climbed upward as if they were drunk, missing every second or third step and clinging to the handrail to stop themselves falling back down.

Nobody from any of the families tried to stop them, but all of them slowly walked after them, toward the bottom of the steps, where they gathered in a semicircle, still singing. Victor dropped on to his knees, sobbing, but Jack managed to pull him up again.

Kate came up to me and gently touched my cheek with her fingertips. 'Gideon – are you all right?'

'Don't know. My head's ringing like a goddamned bell.'

'Hey – you're my hero. But you didn't have to fight him. He's not going to get away, my darling, I promise you. And neither will Victor.'

I shook my head, trying to clear it, but with all that singing going on, I couldn't think straight. Victor and Jack had pushed open the door at the top of the steps and crashed their way through it.

'It sure *looks* like they're getting away.'

'No, they won't,' said Kate, and firmly took hold of my hand. 'This is where Victor and Jack get what they deserve. You'll have your evidence against them. They'll both get life sentences, if they're lucky.'

Together, we climbed up the cellar steps. When we reached the hallway, I saw that Jack and Victor had left the front door wide open. An icy wind was blowing, and snow was whirling into the living room.

'There – they've escaped, Goddamn it.'

'Have a little faith,' said Kate. She hurried

toward the open door and I followed her, cupping my hand over my swollen mouth to shield it from the wind.

Red tail lights flared, and I heard the *whoomph* of the Explorer's engine starting up. Jack was driving. Victor was lolling in the passenger seat, his face against the window. I thought at first that he was staring at me but then I realized that he was blindly staring at nothing at all.

The Explorer backed up, and then turned, heading for the highway.

'All right, I have faith,' I said. 'But how are we going to stop them now?'

But Kate laid one hand on my shoulder and said, *'Look.'*

I blinked through the thickly billowing snow. As the Explorer sped toward the entrance gates, a host of figures appeared in its headlights, blocking its way. More than fifty of them now, maybe seventy or eighty, and more of them approaching out of the gloom. Above the bellowing of the Explorer's engine, that high, eerie screaming was even more penetrating than ever.

The Explorer skidded to a halt, with its exhaust fuming red. The figures started slowly to encircle it. The Westerlunds, and the Philips, and the Cesarettis, in different moments from their lives – when they were happy, when they were suffering, when they were close to death. I thought: *why doesn't Jack simply run them down*? But then I saw him twisting around in the driver's seat, trying to back up, and I realized that he was terrified of them. If he tried to run them down, he would have to admit to himself that they were here, that they were real, and that they wanted revenge for what he and Victor had done to them. Either that, or he knew that they were dead already, and he couldn't kill them a second time.

The Explorer's tires slithered and whinnied but the driveway was too icy, and he succeeded only in sliding diagonally toward the ditch.

He slammed the Explorer into drive, and then reverse, and then drive, and then reverse, and at last the SUV began to creep backward. He had only traveled a few yards, however, when I heard a sharp, crackling noise, and saw a shower of yellow sparks. A power line crossed over the driveway, and its glass insulators had shattered, so that the cable had dropped down on to the snow. It was spitting and writhing like an angry anaconda.

The Explorer's rear wheels ran right over the power line, but as it passed under the front wheels, it became entangled with the driveshaft. There was a loud thump, and the Explorer was brought to a halt, with sparks gushing out from under its wheel arches.

The ghostly figures remained where they were, but now I realized that they had stopped screaming. All I could hear now was the venomous fizzing of the power line, and the revving of the Explorer's engine, as Jack tried desperately to drag it free.

Kate gripped my hand. Her own fingers were very cold. 'They can't escape, Gideon, whatever they do.'

I glanced at her. For some reason, the movement of her lips didn't quite match what she was saying, as if her words had been dubbed. I felt as if she were two or three seconds ahead of me; or maybe two or three seconds behind.

The Explorer's engine screamed again, but the power line was far too securely wound around the driveshaft, and Jack was only pulling it tighter.

Nearly a minute passed, with the Explorer just ticking over. By the light that was coming from the open door of the house behind me, I could see Victor and Jack, sitting side by side behind the snow-blurred windshield like two accused men sitting in the dock. In a way, this garden was now a courtroom, where they were being judged for the crimes that they had committed.

Off to my right, about fifty yards away, I saw two figures struggling. I shielded my eyes with my hand, and realized that they were Jack and Felicia, and that Jack was dragging Felicia away, just as I had seen him dragging her away at the Wasa Museum in Stockholm. Both figures moved in a jerky, fitful fashion, as if they were characters in a home movie, or a flicker book. But I clearly recognized both of them. Jack was wearing his black coat and Felicia was wearing her yellow windbreaker.

I looked back at the Explorer. The real Jack was still sitting behind the wheel, but I could see that he was staring at the image of himself that was pulling Felicia through the snow. He looked ghastly. His face was enamel-white, like a Venetian plague doctor's mask.

Felicia let out a blurry scream, and the image

382

of Jack twisted her around and threw her face first on to the ground. He knelt on her back, pinning her down, and then he grasped her neck with both hands and started to throttle her.

I shouted, *'Hey!'* and made a move toward them, but Kate quickly snatched at my sleeve.

'Just watch,' she said. 'Now that you're here, they can show you their stories. But they're only stories. There's nothing you can do to change them.'

Out of the corner of my eye, I saw a light dancing, and when I turned around, there was Helena Philips, blazing from the waist upward. She was *howling* rather than screaming, while a tall flame flapped from the top of her head, and her ears shriveled up. Another image of Jack was standing close beside her, with his hand raised to protect his face from the heat.

All around us, the ghosts of the Westerlunds and the Cesarettis and the Philips were playing out their different scenarios of pain and desperation. The snow-filled garden had become a theater of agonizing memories. There was Jack, again and again, strangling and mutilating and burning. There was Victor, too, pacing impatiently and vengefully around every act of torture, almost as if he were angry that he couldn't make his victims suffer more.

Off to my left, I saw David Philips with his hands clasped over his eyes, and Amalea, sewn to her mattress, circling through the snow as if she were actually floating on the Grand Canal. I saw Elsa, drowned; and eerily, high in the air, hanging from nothing at all, I saw Enrico and

Salvina, slowly rotating from a chandelier that wasn't there. Below them, though, stood Jack, with a coiled rope over his shoulder, his head raised, and a smile on his face that was almost beatific; and not far away, Victor, although Victor wasn't looking up at them. Victor was looking at something else that wasn't there: one of the Cesarettis' antique vases, perhaps, or the view out on to the Campo San Polo. He had the creepiest look of satisfaction on his face.

The ghosts weren't screaming any longer, but the garden was filled with intermittent cries and shouts and sobbing, and the awful shuffling of people fighting for their lives.

I put my arm around Kate and watched all these scenes with a growing feeling of helplessness and rage. There was nothing I could do to save these families now. Their fathers had damned them all, and Victor Solway had made sure they had all gone to hell. But I was sure of one thing: I was going to see Victor and Jack convicted for what they had done, and pay the price for it.

After a few minutes, one after another, the jerky images faded. The last thing I saw was the yellow of Felicia's windbreaker, like a sunflower seen through a misted-up window. Eventually, only the figures remained, wordless and watchful.

There was a long, long pause, while the Explorer's engine continued to tick over. Then I saw the driver's door open. I thought: *Jesus – he's not going to try to climb out? If he does, he'd better jump way clear. Those feeder lines carry more than four thousand volts.*

It was then that I saw his arm waving, as if he were groping to find his way. The singing must have blinded him, too. That's why the families had stopped. Now, patient and unmoving, they were waiting for him to bring himself his own retribution.

'You scum!' he screamed. 'Couldn't even beat me face to face, could you? Didn't have the balls! Didn't have the fucking *cojones*!'

Maybe he did it on purpose. You can never tell what a man like that might be thinking. *Pain. Death. I've given them to plenty of other people, maybe it's time I found out for myself what an agonizing death really feels like.*

He stepped down on to the driveway while he was still holding the door handle, and he exploded, blown into tattered black shreds. Electricity jumped and spat like firecrackers all around the outline of the Explorer, and for a split second the interior was all lit up. I saw Victor Solway, his blind eyes bulging, his lips stretched back as if he were laughing at some monstrous joke.

Then, with a deafening bang, the Explorer's fuel tank blew up. The vehicle was thrown into the air and crashed on to its side, where it lay furiously blazing.

'Jesus,' I said. I felt utter shock. But the crowd of figures stood quite still and watched the inferno in silence, as if they were doing nothing more than burning last year's leaves. One of the apparitions of Tilda Westerlund turned toward us – the one whose cheeks were bruised, and whose lips had been split apart.

'What are they going to do now?' I asked Kate.

'They're leaving now. They came here to get justice, no more than that.'

One by one, the assembled company turned away from us, into the falling snow, and as they turned away, they vanished, as if they had been images in mirrors, turned sideways. Within a few seconds, they were all gone.

I turned to Kate and said, 'Will they be at peace now? I know they don't have proper resting-places.'

'At peace? I don't think anybody who ever lived is ever at peace.'

'First things first, though,' I told her. 'Let's go rescue Margot.'

It was dark in the house, because the power was out, but we went through to the kitchen and found half a dozen large white candles in a drawer. We lit one each and went back down to the cellar. 'Margot,' I said, as I came down the steps, 'your knight in shining armor has arrived.'

'What was that *terrible* noise?'

'Victor and Jack had a little car trouble. A power line came down, got itself wrapped around their wheels.'

I tugged off her blindfold and loosened the cords around her wrists.

'Oh God, Lalo,' she said. 'I thought they were going to kill me.'

'You don't have to worry about them now. They were both electrocuted. They're dead. Both of them.'

'You're not serious. *Dead*?'

I knelt down to untie Margot's ankles. Kate said, 'It was no more than they deserved, believe me.'

'Are you OK, Margot?' I asked her.

'Stiff. Sore. Dying to go to the bathroom. But thank you for saving me. Thank you so, so much! You're a superhero.'

I stood up, and turned to Kate. 'I guess I'd better call the police. And the fire department. And the power company, too.'

Kate said, 'Not yet. There's something else I want you to do first. I want you to find the proof that Victor and Jack were murderers. I want to show them up for what they were. Think of all the relatives and friends who never found out what happened to the families they killed. There should be a pick in the garden shed.'

'You want *me* to do it? We're talking about your parents here.'

She nodded. 'They disappeared, and everybody presumed they were dead, but nobody ever knew where they went. Now we know.'

I hunkered down again. Now that I knew what I was looking for, I could see that there was a rough rectangle of different colored cement in the center of the floor.

I didn't have to ask Kate if she was sure that she really wanted me to do this. If the remains of *my* parents had been lying under this floor, I would have wanted to dig them up, too, and give them the kind of funeral they deserved.

I found a rusty pick in the garden shed, and carried it back into the house, and after tying my handkerchief around my nose and mouth, attacked the cellar floor with it.

Lucky for me, the cement had been mixed very dry, and most of it broke up into crumbly lumps. All the same, it took me over four hours of hacking at it before I eventually struck the top of a large wooden box, and I was sweaty and gritty and exhausted.

I wearily trudged up the cellar steps and found Kate and Margot in the living room. Margot was asleep on one of the couches, covered in an overcoat, while Kate was standing by the window, watching the sky gradually grow lighter. The gardens were still covered in snow, but it was going to be a sharp, sunny day.

I came up to her and put my arms around her. 'I think I've found them,' I said. 'There's a big wooden box under the floor, but I haven't opened it up yet.'

She nodded. 'At least they can have a decent burial. Not like all of those other poor people.'

The sun was shining through one of the beech hedges along the driveway, so that it looked as if it were on fire.

'We made it, anyhow,' said Kate. She looked at her watch. 'Look – eight o'clock. Less than an hour to spare.'

'Less than an hour to spare before *what*?'

She turned around and kissed me. 'You won't be sad, will you?'

'Sad? Why should I be sad?'

'The air tickets ... Pearl bought them for me. And the keys ... she took them out of Victor's desk. She used to invite herself in to his apartment for a drink, and borrowed them when he wasn't looking.'

'Wily old bird, that Pearl, isn't she?'

Kate smiled. 'There were certain things I couldn't do. I didn't have a credit card anymore. And I couldn't take anything from Victor's apartment.'

'Well, I thought you lived there, but when I took a look around, it was pretty obvious that you didn't.'

'I haven't lived there in three years, Gideon. Three years exactly, to the day.'

'But you told me you couldn't leave.'

'It wasn't the apartment I couldn't leave. It was Victor. You can be tied to somebody by hatred, just as much as you can be tied to them by love. I was determined that he wasn't going to get away with what he'd done to Michael, or the child who was murdered for Michael's new heart. Or what he'd done to my parents. Or to *me*.'

Kate looked at me with those rainy gray eyes, and suddenly they were shining with tears. 'We all have three years to make amends. Three turnings of the seasons to make things right. Don't ask me why.'

'Amends? Amends for what?'

'Anything you like. Some people don't bother to make amends at all. Some people only do very small things, like help their loved ones to find a lost piece of jewelry, or a photograph, or a diary. Some people simply make their presence felt, so that they can bring comfort to those they've left behind.

'But I wanted to make sure that Victor was punished. That was the hold he had over me. I couldn't accuse him myself, as you know. I couldn't find any evidence, and I couldn't find anybody to help me. Not until I saw you looking out of your window, and realized that you could see me.'

'Of course I could see you,' I told her. 'I can still see you. I can *feel* you, too, goddammit. You're real. Other people can see you, too.'

'When I'm with *you*, yes – because you have the gift. But otherwise, no. And you know it, don't you? You've known it for a long time.'

'Yes,' I admitted. 'I didn't want to believe it. But, yes. But if I can see you, and feel you, and talk to you, what difference does it make?'

'Gideon, I'm the same as them. I'm the same as the Westerlunds and the Philips and the Cesarettis.'

'But we're lovers, Kate. How can we be lovers, if you don't exist? How can we possibly be lovers if you're—?' I couldn't bring myself to say the word *'dead'* without tipping myself right over the edge of human reason.

Kate led me over to the window seat. I sat down and grasped both of her hands so that I could feel how real her fingers were, and so that she couldn't pull away from me. If I let her walk out of that door, who knows if I would ever see her again?

'Gideon – I can't stay here any longer. No matter how much I want to.'

'Who says? God?'

Outside, the whole garden sparkled. 'You still

have your gift, Gideon. You can help scores of other people, too. So many murders go unpunished. You can help the victims to get justice – just like you did for the Westerlunds and the Cesarettis and the Philips – and the Kilners, too.'

'The Kilners?'

'My parents. Henry and Joyce Kilner. Victor killed them because they refused to pay for a second heart transplant for poor little Michael. And he killed *me*, too, because I persuaded them not to. I couldn't get any answer from them, on the phone, so I came up here looking for them. Jack Friendly was waiting for me, with a hammer.'

'All right,' I said. I was trembling with stress, and with exhaustion. 'Supposing I accept that you're some kind of spirit? Is that what you are, some kind of spirit? You say that you were given three years to put things right, which is what you've managed to do. But what happens after that? Who's to say you can't stay around?'

'Gideon, I *died*!'

'I don't care! So long as I can see you and feel you, so long as we can go on being lovers, what difference does it make? I have a gift, and I can use it to help other people. But who says I can't use it to get what *I* want, too? And what I want, Kate, is *you*!'

She looked at me for a very long time without saying anything. Then she turned and looked out at the snow. The Explorer had burned out now, until it was nothing more than a blackened skeleton, although brown smoke was still drifting across the driveway.

'I don't know, darling,' she said. 'I just don't know what happens now. I'm no more of an expert on the world beyond than you are.'

'Then stay,' I told her.

The sunshine in the garden was dazzling now. I kissed Kate's hair and I kept my arms tightly around her waist, so that I could feel her breathing. As long as I kept her close like this, there was no way that she could leave me.

I don't know how long it took me to fall asleep. They say that the average when you're really tired is seven minutes. But I slept, and I dreamed that Kate and I were walking through the gardens of Drottningholm, in Sweden, and that the air was filled with shining snow, like thistledown.

Somebody was shaking my arm. At first I thought it was one of the palace guides, trying to tell me that we were walking the wrong way, but then I opened my eyes and it was Margot.

'Margot? What's wrong?'

'You were talking in your sleep. I just wanted to make sure that you were OK.'

I blinked, and looked around the living room. 'I'm fine. Jesus, it's cold in here. Where's Kate?'

'Kate? I haven't seen Kate.'

I sat up. 'What do you mean? She was here only a couple of minutes ago. She was sitting right here.'

Margot said, 'If she was, she's not here now. I didn't see her.'

I stood up, and went to the front door, and

opened it. The garden was deserted, and there were no footprints in the freshly fallen snow.

'She's gone,' I said.

'Maybe she went to get some supplies,' Margot suggested.

'Maybe.'

I went back into the house and closed the door.

It took me another forty minutes to clear the cement from the lid of the wooden box. When I managed to lever it open, there was a soft exhalation of gasses, like somebody with very bad morning breath. Inside, closely packed together, there were human thigh bones and arm bones and ribs and pelvises, as well as mummified flesh the color of smoked bacon rind.

So this is what Victor and Jack had done with Kate's parents. Terrorized them, tortured them, and forced them to sign over their house. Then he had killed them, and cemented them under their own cellar floor.

There were two skulls, one at each end of the box, and both of them still had skin and hair on them, although their eyes had been reduced to the size and color of pickled walnuts. They were both grinning at me, as if they were pleased to see me.

I didn't want to disturb the remains, because the state police would want to see them exactly as I had found them. But as I lifted away the lid, one of the skulls rolled sideways, and I realized that there was a third skull underneath it. A skull with straight, ash-blonde hair, still clogged at the back with black dried blood.

'Kate,' I said. My voice sounded like some-body else altogether.

We got back to the city around 5:00 p.m., in the middle of the rush hour. I dropped Margot home, and then I took Henry's Malibu back. He was deeply relieved to see that it was undented, although he had been forced to take the commuter train back to New Rochelle.

'You look like shit,' he told me. 'Also, I hate to tell you this, but you *smell* like shit, too. Don't you musicians use a deodorant?'

'I just exhumed three bodies,' I told him.

'Sure you did. You owe me a steak dinner at Angelo & Maxie's.'

I paid a visit to Pearl, upstairs. She was sitting in her pink bathrobe playing solitaire.

'How did it go?' she asked me. Cigarette smoke trailed across the room, and shuddered when it reached the open window, like a ghost.

'Good. I guess things worked out the way they were supposed to.'

Pearl nodded toward the painting on the easel. 'I thought they had.'

I walked around and took a look. The painting was finished, but the only person in it was Pearl. Everybody else had gone, as they had in the snow. Turned around, like mirrors turned sideways, and vanished.

'Where do you think people go, when they die?' I asked her. 'I mean, what do you think it's *like*?'

Pearl took a long drag at her cigarette, with

one eye closed against the smoke. 'It's just like being in the movies, that's what they tell me, except that you're in the movie instead of the audience. Don't you worry, you'll find out for yourself one day. We all do.'

She paused, and then she said, 'You miss her, don't you?'

I nodded. I suddenly found myself very close to tears.

Pearl said, 'Very strange thing, love. When you don't have it, it hurts. And when you do, it hurts like hell.'

I went back downstairs. Sitting outside my door, waiting patiently, was Malkin. She mewed when she saw me, and she followed me inside.

'You hungry?' I asked her, as she wound herself persuasively around my ankles. 'Of course you're hungry. Stupid question.'

But it's so goddamned difficult to open a can of anchovies when you're crying.

Twenty-Eight

Late the following afternoon, as it was beginning to grow dark outside, I sat down at my keyboard and I started to compose *Spirit Song*.

Spirit Song is so familiar now, and so well known, that I sometimes find it difficult to believe that there was a time when it didn't exist. But as I was scoring it, there was no doubt in my mind that it was one of the best melodies that I had ever written, or might ever write. It was all of my love for Kate, and everything that she had showed me about the real world and the world beyond, in music.

By 9:00 p.m. that evening, I had almost finished it. I played it over, very slowly, while Malkin sat on one of the couches, watching me with slitted eyes.

'What do you think, puss?' I asked him.

'*I* think it's beautiful,' replied a very quiet voice, close behind me.

Before I could turn around, two cool hands covered my eyes.

'Guess who?' she said.